EY_ __

'PREPARE TO ENGAGE!'

The lieutenant was ignoring the bulking, blazing battle-ship, the flashes of battle visible over a range of thousands of miles. He was pointing down towards the World Eater planetoid.

Brother-Sergeant Magron switched to visor magnification and directed his gaze likewise. Combat assault craft, small, lumpy images even at maxmag, were rising from the surface of the planetoid. World Eater Space Marines, ready to take on even a battleship in close order combat!

Magron bellowed into his helmet microphone, aware that the whole company had heard the lieutenant's order, and had also seen what their sergeant had seen.

'Embark and attack!'

The response was an eager roar from fifty throats: *'IT SHALL BE DONE, BROTHER!'*

A WARHAMMER 40,000 NOVEL

EYE OF TERROR

By Barrington J. Bayley

A BLACK LIBRARY PUBLICATION

First published in Great Britain in 1999 by
Games Workshop Publishing
Willow Road, Lenton,
Nottingham, NG7 2WS, UK

10 9 8 7 6 5 4 3 2 1

Cover illustration by Kenson Low

A CIP record for this book
is available from the British Library.

ISBN 1 84154 105 2

Set in ITC Giovanni

Printed and bound in Great Britain by
Caledonian International Book Manufacturing Ltd., Glasgow.

See the Black Library on the Internet at
http://www.blacklibrary.co.uk

Find out more about Games Workshop
and the world of Warhammer 40,000 at
http://www.games-workshop.com

ONE

SHRIEK OF THE PSYKER

'IS THAT HIM?' the Space Marine librarian said.

'That is him, lexicanium,' the technomat guard answered in a flat, amiable tone. 'He was brought in thirty days ago. Despatched by the Schola Psykana.'

The librarian mentally forgave the guard for answering questions it had not been asked. A technomat had only a rudimentary personality. Its mind wiped clean for some misdemeanour, or possibly grown in a vat to serve the purposes of the Administratum, it served only one function and knew only that function. It certainly did not understand the finer points of protocol when speaking to a person of rank.

On a flickering screen by the door, the librarian could see into the cell. The pale young man within was huddled on a bench. He was clad in a single simple garment of tanned animal skin, fringed at the skirt and sleeves – the apparel of the primitive world from which he had been taken, most likely.

Even from here, the librarian could pick up his almost uncontrollable fear.

'Bring him out.'

The guard's hooded eyes dimmed, switching to the infra-red it used when escorting prisoners. The rough cast iron door

5

clanged open. The burly technomat lumbered inside, hauled
the young man to his feet and manhandled him into the corridor.

Black-clad librarian and leather-clad primitive regarded one
another, one with an aloof curiosity, the other with apprehen-
sion. The librarian knew that the young man could psyke him,
too, and that this frightened him all the more. He did not
know why he had been brought here. He did not know who or
what the librarian was. He did not know what was intended for
him. There was no point in trying to reassure him. If he were to
know, his terror would likely cause his heart to stop.

'Come.' The librarian turned and led the way down the long
corridor, followed by the guard occasionally assisting the prisoner, whose knees were wont to buckle every few steps.

It was a feature of Mars, home of the Adeptus Mechanicus,
that there was no standard level of technology. The most developed, that is to say the most prehistoric, arts stood side by side
with the crudest of modern improvisations. The visual scanners
for viewing the interiors of the holding cells had been made by
young pre-initiates as a trial exercise, and utilised spinning
charged discs instead of powered scanning screens. At the end
of the long corridor, whose iron walls ran with moisture and
grew green mould, and behind whose ranks of cast iron doors
languished many a silent captive of the Adeptus, lay an elevator cage with folding bronze gates. With a clashing sound, the
gates were thrown open. The three men, of such widely differ-
ing origins, stepped inside. The technomat flung the gates shut
and threw a heavy lever. There was a clunk, a thud, and then a
loud, strained whining as the lifting cables took hold. The cage
went up.

Up, up, and up. Endlessly aloft.

ATOP THE HIGHEST tower in this part of Mars, thick weather-worn
windows gave a panoramic view for hundreds of miles over the
landscape of what was still called the Red Planet. In the main
its reddish hue was not, as it had been in past ages, due to its
ochre deserts. It was due to rust. What lay below the tower
resembled nothing so much as a riotous, decaying jungle,
spreading and spreading without end. But that jungle was not
natural. It consisted of gigantic machinery, both new and abandoned; of hive cities both new and abandoned; of colossal

engineering constructions, some of it twisted and sagging and covered with an oily fog of pollution. It was, in fact, the result of nearly forty centuries of the Cult Mechanicus, the worship of the Machine. For here it was, and here alone, that the scientific arts had been preserved for mankind during the long dark ages of anarchy when Earth itself had fallen into barbarism. During that time the adepts of Mars had rarely bothered to clean up the spoils and derelict production areas. Ever busy with the sacred task of new fabrication, the tech-priests of the Machine God regarded the work of bygone ages as holy relics. And so the machinery of Mars had proliferated like a cancer, piling over the surface of the planet.

Here and there patches of the original desert were still visible. When the wind rose the ancient sand came howling over the works of man, pitting and eroding the rusting surfaces, laying down a patina of red Martian dust over the metal environment. But at the moment the weather was calm. The wan sun shone serenely through a pink sky. In that sky, long, glinting objects could be seen moving in leisurely fashion from horizon to horizon, following one another in a continuous train. They were the orbiting docks and factories that were also part of the Martian industrial monolith, turning out the ships of the Warfleet Solar and other specialised constructions requiring zero gravity.

Leaving the top of the lift shaft, the three men were ushered by a lexomat secretary into the office of Magos Technicus Ipsissimus.

The technomagos was himself of venerable years. Just how many centuries he had lived was known to few, chiefly to his personal tech-priests and the Magos Biologis who attended to his body modifications. His lined, aged face bore an expression of pained anxiety as, clad in his scarlet robe and seated at a desk of electrum inlaid with sapphires, he conducted a conference with a visiting emissary of the Inquisitorial Representative, who was one of the High Lords of Terra. He barely seemed to notice the entrance of the prisoner.

The emissary, wearing a rich blue tabard and matching cap, was listening carefully to the technomagos's words. 'It is a hundred and seventy-eight years,' Ipsissimus was saying, 'since the Inquisition sent a nullship into the Eye of Terror. The reason is simple. Of the previous twenty such spy ships despatched, none have returned, or succeeded in sending back any useful information.'

'The Eye is an extremely dangerous place,' the Inquisitorial Representative pointed out smoothly. 'Best left alone, in some people's view.'

'Hah!' Ipsissimus waved his hands in exasperation. 'Left alone! To wreak whatever havoc it can? Yes, I know, people have different opinions as to the dangers it represents... not everything is made known. But you of the Inquisition surely know better than anyone else that it is in fact the greatest peril to face mankind. Come, now, do not frown. I mean no disrespect to the Inquisition... There is no point in sending out men and ships to sure destruction, without purpose. Still, the problem rankles. It has annoyed me. So I have put my mind to it over the past few years. I have engaged myself on a new type of nullship. It has ten times the screening of the old model. It could cross the Eye from end to end without being detected! It is better armed, and larger, so it can carry more fighting men if it is detected. And it is fortunate that I have so exerted myself!'

The emissary politely ignored the technomagos's boastfulness. Age had its privileges. 'Is such a ship practicable?' he asked thoughtfully. 'Is it even possible? I recall the difficulties with the old nullships. They were more an act of desperation than anything else, and were believed to be the best that could be built.'

'You may safely leave that to the ingenuity of the Adeptus, and of myself in particular. We do not like to be defeated by any problem. It calls into question our devotion to the Machine God.'

The leather-clad prisoner whimpered. He had been silent until now, standing by the side of the room with one arm expertly gripped by the guard, gawping through the thick glassite windows, deaf to the conversation taking place nearby. To be transported from the depths of a dismal dungeon to the height of this tower, three Imperial miles above the surface of the planet, standing in real sunlight and open to the view of the panorama below, left him even more stunned than had his previous experiences. He shrank as faces now turned towards him, and words in an unfamiliar, intimidating Gothic dialect began to wash around him.

'This young man was about to be burned as a witch on some Emperor-forsaken planet or other,' Technomagos Ipsissimus was saying, 'when he was picked up by agents of the Adeptus Telepathica. He is a very strong psyker, very strong indeed, one of the strongest ever found in a number of respects. It was judged he would burn out too quickly to be worth training as an astropath, so he was sent to serve the Astronomican. Even there, he was rejected on account of his instability – even the Astronomican has its requirements, it seems. He was handed back to the Schola Psykana for review, and would have been sacrificed to the Emperor like any other uncontrollable psyker, were it not for certain visions he recounted. As these bore a relation to my nullship project, I had him transferred here.'

'For one born with such a disability, he seems to have had an unusual degree of luck, to escape death so regularly,' the emissary said with a wry smile.

'Hmm. That may not necessarily be the case,' the technomagos murmured. 'What do you make of him, lexicanium?'

The librarian regarded the primitive psyker again. 'He seems not to have fallen foul of daemonic possession in any form, which is unusual in one of his advanced talent... his 'luck' again, perhaps. He is tormented, and very unstable, mainly due to the fact that he lives in constant terror.'

'Terror, yes, terror. Get him to tell us about the Eye of Terror.'

At the mention of this phrase, which the psyker had failed to hear earlier while his mind was on the landscape below, he now let out a great howl: 'The Door! The Door! Flee! The Door is opening!'

'"The Door" is what he calls the Eye of Terror,' Ipsissimus said gravely to the emissary. 'A poetic phrase. A cosmic door into the warp. His visions are fragmentary, but the Schola Psykana are convinced he has seen that something significant is happening there. Something we need to know about. Therefore I propose we send the new nullship into the Eye. Perhaps it can find out.'

He made a gesture. 'Allow me to introduce Epistolary Librarian Merschturmer, of the Purple Stars Chapter of the Adeptus Astartes. Conditional on your approval, he will accompany the mission and act as astropath – should it become necessary to try to despatch a message out of the Eye.'

The technomagos's wheezy voice paused. The emissary turned his gaze to the librarian for the first time, nodding in cool, but genuine, respect. Any Space Marine, because of the ancient though indirect link with the Emperor, was regarded with a measure of awe, quite apart from his almost superhuman qualities.

At that moment the wild psyker, in one convulsive movement, broke free of the guard's grip. He threw himself to his knees before the aged technomagos and spoke with a strangled, desperate voice, in the vowel-twisting accent of his home planet.

'Noble sirs, I beg you, do not kill me!'

'Kill you?' the magos echoed, raising his bushy eyebrows. 'We weren't thinking of killing you.'

With a supercilious curl of his lip, the emissary of the Inquisitorial Representative looked down at the fawning captive.

'What would you like us to do with you, young man?'

'Make me unconscious, like a vegetable, and keep me alive forever! Do not let me live, but do not let me die! If I die, my soul goes to the other side of the Door!'

'He means the warp, my lords,' the librarian offered. 'He has seen into the warp, and fears what he has seen.'

Tottering forward, the venerable technomagos took the psyker's arm and brought him gently to his feet. 'Take heart. You are to be of great service to the Imperium. You will have brave companions. You are to go into the Eye of Terror, the place you call the Door. Your talents will be of use there. With others like yourself, Emperor willing, you will find out what is really going on.'

When he heard this, the terrified psyker's body went rigid. His eyes bulged.

With a strangled yelp, Epistolary Librarian Merschturmer staggered back and raised his hands to his head as if he had been struck a physical blow. The emissary of the Inquisitorial Representative and the technomagos both flinched as well. For although he had not made a sound, the psyker had uttered a mind-shriek: a psychic scream that tore through every living consciousness around him. A ragged, rending mental howl of utter, absolute horror, terror and despair.

TWO
DREAD MISSION

TO THE ORDINARY VIEW, the great swirl of close-packed stars designated by the Imperium the Eye of Terror resembled just what the name implied: a baleful glowing eye glaring in space, set like an evil jewel in the north-west of the galaxy. To many, that was all it was. Among the Imperium's teeming trillions, few knew much by way of history. Even less had ever had explained to them the true nature of that other realm, the alternate, insubstantial universe that was called the Immaterium, or simply the warp, by the tech-priests whose great engines drove their vast interstellar ships from star to star.

It was not that such knowledge was hidden, though officially its existence would be denied. It was simply not generally disseminated. And so to many of the more educated, the idea that the warp was a realm of Chaos inhabited by spirits, monsters and daemons, was either ignorance, the stuff of myth and legend, or else rank superstition. True, the Eye of Terror – which also went by many other names in the regions surrounding it – was held to be a dangerous place. The navigators of the Navis Nobilite avoided it. It was a warp-storm, the greatest in the galaxy, and to enter it was to throw one's life away.

To the academically minded on some planets even the Cult of the Emperor, the official religion of the Imperium, was not always to be taken literally. If there were no such things as spirits, some argued, then it was obvious that the Emperor could not be what it was claimed he was, and which in truth he really was – namely, the greatest of the gods.

True, there could be a reason for such lack of knowledge. Perhaps it was the case that ignorance suited the Administratum. Already too many human beings were psychically sensitive to the warp. Some, often unwittingly, opened a path for warp-creatures to enter the material world. The consequences were dire, both for themselves and for those around them, and not infrequently for entire planets.

So it was that even people living in the crescent of worlds skirting the Eye of Terror did not know that even the wildest of rumours fell far short of the reality. For in the heart of the Eye was what some called the Byssos, a hole in the stuff of space through which poured the raw energy of the warp, mutating and corrupting all it touched.

Moreover, all around that gaping rent in reality, right up to the fringes of the terrible storm, which had existed for thousands of years and showed no sign of ever abating, were innumerable worlds under the corrupt sway of Chaos, of daemons, and of Chaos-possessed warriors who were every one mortal enemies of the Imperium.

One set of people under no illusions as to its nature were the occupants of the unnamed, secretly built Imperium null-ship. Transported by starship from the planet Mars to an airless moon jointly under the control of the Adeptus and the Inquisition, it underwent its final trials. Then, psychic screening set at maximum, it nosed through the Cadian Gate, the only properly navigable path into the Eye. Once within the starry whirlpool, it was beyond the Imperium. It was among the hell-worlds, swimming through the heady sea of shimmering supernal energy, where the warp and realspace overlapped.

The exterior of the nullship was a forest of baffles, turrets and antennae. It was the boast of the Adeptus Mechanicus that the vessel was invisible to any psychic or material probes which the Chaos worlds could throw at it. Within the narrow hull, the only illumination was the dim green glow of the instruments and phosphorescent runes, the only sound the muttering of voices against a background of whining engines. Aboard were the tech-priests who had helped build the nullship, two navigators, three inquisitors, one of whom captained the vessel, half a squad of Purple Stars Space Marines, including Epistolary Librarian Merschturmer, and the specially trained team of psykers whose task it would be to spy on the hidden realms within the Eye.

And also, bound into a bucket chair, half insane, mouth frothing with terror as he felt the loosened power of the warp surging all around him, was the benighted young man whose uncontrolled psychic power had made his life a misery, who had somehow cast his mental vision into the Eye to see something taking place there, something dangerous to the Imperium, and who was now to be the expedition's guide.

The Space Marine librarian knelt beside the young man, injecting him with a calming drug. The psyker's jaw was already slack. Now his head lolled as Merschturmer spoke quietly to him.

'Which way?'

There was no need for the prisoner to speak. The entire team of psykers was tuning into his mind. No two saw quite the same, as their own nervous systems interpreted what the shivering young man perceived, but they also shivered with him. None of them had ever before had the experience of sensing psychic energy that reached for light years in every direction, permeating the very space they occupied, mixing with the air they breathed. For the psykers it was like drowning in electrified foam. Not all of them would have been able to describe what they sensed. But for most it was like seeing a vast multicoloured expanse in which were abstract shapes, blocks, cubes, swirling spheres, building and dissolving.

The wild psyker closed his eyes. 'The Door…' he mumbled. 'They are going to open the Door.'

They saw where his mind tended. They relayed instructions.

The two navigators conferred, hunching together in the cramped cockpit in the nose of the nullship. One of them turned to the inquisitor-captain.

'The Astronomican is barely perceptible as it is, lord. In that direction we shall lose it altogether.'

'Then lose it. We didn't come here to play safe.'

They both nodded, wondering why they had even bothered to inform the ship's commander of their concern. Partly, it was simple reflex. Without the Astronomican, the immense psychic navigation beacon provided by the Emperor and drawing on the power of ten thousand young psykers, the Imperium could not be maintained. Warp travel over more than a few light years was impossible without it. To a navigator, it was a constant presence, of which he had been conscious since birth. When assigned to this mission, the two had known that for the first time in their lives they might lose sight of it. They might, for the first time ever, have to guess which way was out.

They turned the ship, plunging through the warp.

The Astronomican faded, and was gone.

They were directionless.

Still, it might come back. The roiling warp-storm that was the Eye of Terror only differed from other such cosmic tempests in that it was bigger, much bigger. The Astronomican could still shine through, but patchily, as the currents of the Immaterium raged and swirled. The navigators fought down their panic, steering the ship guided only by the extravagant shapes forming and dissolving within the Eye.

Worlds were swaying past them. Not normal worlds such as would have been found in calmer regions of the galaxy. Weird worlds, nightmare worlds, worlds which made no sense either in terms of astrophysics or of mental perception. It was as if the darkened, cramped interior of the nullship was an iron bullet of rationality in an insane universe. As if it had no right to be here.

In truth, it did not have any right to be here. Despite its adamantine strength, the hull of the ship creaked as it sank further into the Eye, like a submarine diving too deep and coming under intolerable pressure. But the pressure was not physical; it was psychic. The screens were groaning as they strained to keep out the worst of the storm.

Here. Here was the place I saw.

The thought came from the wild psyker in a blaring warning, like a baby crying for its mother. Now came the moment of maximum danger. For the spy team to probe clearly, the screens would have to come down for a brief interval, leaving the null-ship visible should any daemon or renegade psyker be looking this way.

The ship's present position was too dangerous. Should they unscreen in the middle of a particularly violent warp torrent, the minds of all aboard could be ripped to pieces. The nullship drifted, allowing the current to carry it into a calmer backwater. There it emerged from the warp, insofar as that was possible in this mixed realm of warp-realspace overlap.

The screens came down.

For the psykers, it was like having a glass window wiped clean of obscuring mud and grease. They were given a clear view over a distance of fifty light years. Minds of the strangest, most perverted sort revealed themselves to their gaze, on planet after glowing planet. But that was not all. The works of those minds were revealed, too. The works of minds and hands, and manic, distorted machines.

A shocking panorama opened to the psykers' view. They saw construction yards for interstellar warships, on continent after continent, on planet after planet, and, for those warships too massive to be lifted off a planet except by magic, construction docks in orbit, or in what seemed to be a miasma, floating in some strange region which was nowhere at all.

Battleships! Battleships by the hundred, too many to be counted, a panoply of military power for which there could be only one reason – to challenge the Imperial Fleet!

An armada, a great invasion battlefleet, was being prepared.

'It's impossible!'

The inquisitor-captain snarled in protest as the terrible news was relayed to him. His incredulity was understandable. The Chaos worlds had never been able to organise on a large scale – the one great weakness of the Chaos realm was that is was chaotic. War within the Eye was constant. Much as they hated the human Imperium, neither the Chaos gods nor their worshippers were capable of co-operating with one another for any practical purpose. Few new warships were ever built. In the main, the Traitor Legions still used the same ships aboard which they had fled into the Eye so many thousand years before.

The psychic screens had been down for only moments. But towards the end of that time, the psykers felt the awful gaze of some malevolent intelligence. An amused, booming voice echoed through their consciousness. It seemed to make the very adamantium of the nullship's hull ring.

'GREETINGS, MY LITTLE ONES!'

'Get us out of here!' roared the inquisitor-captain. Even he had felt the daemonic owner of the dread voice insinuating into his mind.

The navigators needed no prompting. They dropped the ship back into the warp. The nullship was under way, moving in the immaterial currents like a fish carried by the tide.

'We cannot see the Astronomican, captain.'

'Just get away from here, as far away as you can, until you find it.'

'Yes, lord.'

Not knowing which way was out... It was a suffocating feeling, a panicky feeling. Ignoring the flimmering horrors all around them, the navigators plunged the spy ship into the endless depths.

No! Surely this could not be right! They were sinking. The warp was getting denser, harder to peer through. Many navigators had learned the trick of seeing in more than three dimensions, of being able to understand shapes and labyrinths in four, five, even six dimensions, but this was different. A writhing maze stretched all around them, but it was a maze in a hundred dimensions at least. It was impossible for any human mind to unravel it.

Which way? Which way?

'Gag that idiot, somebody!' the inquisitor-captain barked. He gestured at the wild psyker, whose last shreds of sanity seemed to have gone now. The young man sagged in the chair to which he was bound, drooling, eyes closed, a continuous bleating sound coming from his open mouth. The navigators conferred briefly. They agreed that there was no wise choice to be made. Everything depended on pure chance.

They spun the nullship, selected a direction at random, and continued on.

Librarian Merschturmer stuffed a cloth into the wild psyker's mouth and taped it over. The sound of the man's straining breathing was the loudest noise to be heard. The presence of the daemon had faded. How far away had the Chaos being been when it had called to them? Light years away, in realspace, probably. Perhaps no distance at all in the warp. Time and distance did not have the same meaning, here in the Eye of Terror.

At length, the multi-dimensional swirl flattened out. The mad extra dimensions dropped away, folding up like a cosmic house of cards. Then, as one, the navigators breathed a fervent sigh of relief. From far off, in their warp vision, came a faint pearly glow, the pure light of a holy beacon. The light of the Emperor! Shining, even here! Mentally intoning heartfelt prayers of thanks, the navigators again turned the nose of ship, seeking the way back towards the Cadian Gate.

Then, without warning, the nullship spontaneously dropped out of the warp.

It was in realspace, or what passed for realspace in this infernal region of the galaxy. The twin warp engines were gunned again, without result. The ship stubbornly refused to make the transition to the realm of the Immaterium.

After inspecting the instruments the crewmen looked at one another questioningly. Was this some unrecorded feature of the warp? Could it be what had happened to the other nullships? Had they simply become stranded?

Or was it enemy action?

A tremulous voice rang out in the near-darkness: 'Unknown vessel approaching.'

Pale phosphorescence lit up their faces as they leaned towards the scanner screens. The vessel on course for them was a Chaos ship, no doubt of that, and it was close. From this distance it was possible to estimate its size. Though not large – not much bigger than the nullship itself – it evoked fascinated awe in the watchers.

A tech-priest spoke up. 'Strange… Despite all the, em, embellishments, shall we say, I recognise the design. It was built in the Martian orbital yards, perhaps ten millennia ago. The design was discontinued after the Horus Heresy. And yet it looks brand new. Except, of course, for the embellishments…'

The embellishments, as he called them, were quite grotesque. It was as if the small space cruiser had contracted a cancer or had mutated, putting forth flesh-like protuberances. In places it seemed squashed, in others bloated. A pair of gigantic coral-coloured claws sprouted from its front end. Fronds, whorls and fins, brilliantly hued in green, lavender and scarlet, gave the main hull the appearance of an exotic fish.

The pilot-navigator fed power to the realspace motor. It was no use. The Chaos cruiser easily matched their velocity and continued to close in. The nullship had no external armament, but on the other hand the approaching ship gave no sign that it intended to use its own. It came directly on, its great claws extending and reaching out.

'Prepare to repel boarders!' the inquisitor-captain ordered.

He had already guessed what was about to happen, despite its seeming impossibility. The Chaos ship expanded and filled the viewscreen as if seen through a magnifying glass. There was an ear-shattering crunching noise, accompanied by brittle snapping sounds, and followed by the hiss of escaping air as the curved wall of the long narrow cabin caved in.

The enemy cruiser's claws were chewing through the pure adamantium of the hull!

All except the Astartes reached hastily for breathing masks. The Space Marines didn't need any – they could survive unprotected in the hard vacuum of the void. In the event, none were needed anyway. As the Chaos cruiser nestled in close to the nullship, gripping it in its great claws and tearing open a gap in its hull, it also sealed the edges of the hole and prevented any further escape of air.

Lumbering and pushing its way through the rent came a hulking figure in crimson power armour. Like the ship from which it came, the armour seemed to have mutated in some way, growing grotesque excrescences in glowing colours The stranger made an odd contrast with the Space Marines, whose own power armour, though almost equally bulky, was clean of line and gleaming.

The boarder seemed to have foreseen what he would find. A hand flamer hissed point-blank straight into the chest of the leading Space Marine, burning instantly through both his mesh armour and the black carapace which augmented his rib cage, charring his heart and lungs. Even as he fell, one of the Marine's comrades avenged him, chainsword in one hand slicing through the attacker's luridly decorated armour, power axe in the other following up and striking deep into the wearer's body, tearing him apart.

The Purple Stars did not draw their bolt guns. To discharge them would have sent exploding bolts ricocheting off the adamantium walls, slaughtering friend and foe alike. Their weapons were chainswords and power axes, and with savage cries they rushed to the boarding point, where already other bestial invaders were forcing themselves through the rent. Beyond it, a red glow could be seen, from which, as if emerging from the heat of a furnace, came more Chaos warriors, similarly armoured. Merschturmer found he could not immediately identify from the intricate designs which of the Ruinous Powers they served, if any – not all Chaos renegades had pledged their allegiance to any particular disgusting deity. But scurrying after them were creatures that might once have been human and were completely naked, They waved long pincers in place of arms, had hooves instead of feet, the legs of goats and the faces of horned beasts. They carried no weapons. Their pincers were razor-sharp. A kick from their hooves could smash a limb or break a back, as they quickly proved.

The intruders did not in the least mind firing flamers and bolters in the pipe-like cavity. They brought pandemonium with them. The team of psykers cowered as the Marines fought hand to hand with almost twice their number of armoured warriors, in a display of wanton ferocity. Bravely the tech-priests rallied to join the fray, attempting to take on the beastmen with axe and sword and so give the Purple Stars a free hand. They were no match for the Chaos monsters. Arms and legs were snipped off in an orgy of butchery, the beast-things yowling their delight as the priests fell screeching and gouting blood.

The armoured Chaos boarders were howling too while they fought, howling with joy and abandonment as bolt gun flared, power axe fell, chainsword ripped and scythed, and hissing gouts of condensed flame washed through the nullship without mercy. Combat to the death seemed but a game to them. The confined space within the nullship filled with a mist of spattered blood.

Then a different kind of creature bounded from the other ship, a creature whose shape could not properly be made out, but which sizzled and snapped with a blue energy as it leaped shrieking about the cabin, bringing death to all it touched.

Librarian Merschturmer knew that this foul thing was a materialised warp creature. Pushing the now twitching form of a pincer-armed beastman off himself, he concentrated his mind and fired its full charge of spiritual power in a bolt of pure psychic energy. The warp-thing exploded like ball lightning, and was gone.

Suddenly all was quiet, except for the puking groans of the dying. All the Space Marines save he were dead. Nine or ten Chaos renegades were also dead, as were a dozen naked pincer-armed monstrosities. The tech-priests had all died. Merschturmer himself was badly wounded, having taken the backlash of a hand flamer shot in the abdomen.

The Chaos ship was disengaging, pulling away, its claws releasing them. There was a bang as the cabin partly depressurised, air whipping into the void before the nullship's emergency sealant surged into place, blocking up the ragged hole as if with a smear of mud. Oxygen hissed softly, bringing the pressure back to normal.

It was strange to see friends and enemies piled together in so narrow a space, blood mixing in the scrum and congealing as one. The stench of spilled blood and burned flesh was choking. Merschturmer fought to stay conscious and cast his gaze around the cabin, looking for anyone else who might still be alive and also capable of action. Forward, in the nose of the ship, he saw one of the two navigators, his head smashed to a pulp. Then, beside him, the second navigator, one arm a bloody mangled mass, raised his head, his face twisted in pain, and looked at the librarian in despair.

Glancing at the external viewscreen, Librarian Merschturmer saw the Chaos raider retreating. 'Try the warp engine,' he gasped.

The navigator obeyed, pulling himself into the pilot's seat. With his good arm, he pulled down a control lever, intoning a prayer, though the words came through gritted teeth.

The ship dropped into the warp.

'Get us out of here,' Merschturmer ordered in a faint gravelly voice. 'Get us back to Cadia.'

He did not know if the navigator could stay conscious for long enough to carry out that duty, or indeed would live that long. The few groans to be heard were dying now, as life slipped away from those who could still feel pain.

Among them was the wild psyker, the poor young wretch who had escaped being burned as a witch on his primitive home planet, who had escaped death at the hands of the Adeptus Telepathica, who had escaped being sacrificed to the Emperor as a morsel of psychic food, of whom no one had ever even bothered to ask his name, and who now was to suffer the fate he dreaded most, as the lifeblood drained away from his smashed chest cavity, and who uttered a faint, final whinnying cry of despair as he felt his soul being sucked into hell.

'A BLACK CRUSADE is coming!'

'Impossible! There hasn't been one for a millennium and a half.'

'There has never been one such as this is going to be.'

The private office of the Lord Militant Commander of the Imperial Fleet's Segmentum Obscurus was a place given to calm and quiet. The wood panels lining the walls were carved with scenes from the fleet's glorious past – battles fought, worlds subdued, planets destroyed, relief ships got through in apparently impossible conditions. Carved there, too, were the bleak figures of commanders of the past, in full dress uniform, breasts covered with medallions, staring out from the grained wood as if grimly reminding the present incumbent of the gravity of his duty.

Seated with the commander around a table of mahogany inlaid with platinum, were all his admirals in high-collared dress jackets. He had just finished giving them as much information as had been brought back by the stricken nullship sent into the Eye of Terror by the Inquisition, aided by the Adeptus Mechanicus. Only one man had returned alive aboard the damaged spy ship, the inside of which had resembled a charnel house. That had been the one surviving navigator, who had guided it back to Cadia. Luckily the librarian who had accompanied the Purple Stars detachment, Merschturmer, had recorded a full report before he, too, died of his injuries. In a final act of heroism he had even managed to remove the progenoid glands from the mangled bodies of his fallen comrades for re-seeding.

The librarian's report was still being exhaustively studied and evaluated, but it was the overall commander of Segmentum Obscurus, Lord Militant Commander Drang, who would have to make a decision. The Eye of Terror lay within Obscurus, one of six segments into which the Imperium was divided. And here, at Cypra Mundi, was based Battlefleet Obscurus, the force which would have to be committed if any action was to be taken.

Judging by the report before them, there definitely would have to be action, and soon.

No one knew how many human-inhabited worlds lay within the Eye of Terror. Conceivably there were as many as there were in the human Imperium itself. And conceivably those worlds were just as densely populated. Sometimes the Eye was called the Imperium of Chaos, though that was a fancy misnomer, because it was not an Imperium at all, but a disorganised melange. If the Chaos powers had finally learned to organise themselves, then the prospect was terrible indeed. The Imperium itself would be under threat of being overrun. The ten-thousand-year ordeal of torture the Emperor had imposed on himself, to preserve humanity from the horrors of Chaos, would have been in vain.

'Gentlemen,' Commander Drang said in a soft voice, 'it is not hard to guess the enemy's intention. This is not the first time he has come out of the Eye in a crusade to conquer surrounding star systems. Such crusades have always been contained and defeated in the past. But what has now been revealed is on a different scale. The enemy is building a battle-fleet large enough to overwhelm Cadia, guardian of the Cadian Gate, from where he will be able to invade all the worlds fringing the Eye to the galactic south. These worlds will give him a base from which to launch a major war in Segmentum Obscurus and beyond.

'He will lose that war, of course. Indeed I do not believe he will break out of the segmentum. But it is our duty to see that such a war does not take place. Gentlemen, we must define a strategy.'

Drang paused, raised his chalice and breathed deeply of the fumes given off by the mixture of sweet herbs smouldering in it. The others, following his example, breathed from the cups before them.

The youngest of his admirals, who perhaps had not yet learned to refrain from questioning anything the commander said, took the opportunity to speak.

'My lord, can we trust the reliability of this observation? No Black Crusade has held together before. And all we have is the reports of psykers, not hard evidence.'

'Since that report, a second nullship of the old design has also been sent into the Eye, though without Space Marines aboard,' Drang said. 'It failed to return. However the Imperium's most powerful psykers have directed their powers into the Eye. They confirm that there is something afoot there, something unprecedented and very dangerous'

Letting the herbal smoke drift leisurely from his nostrils, Drang surveyed the gathered admirals with his one normal eye and the implanted monocle which jutted out a good two inches from his right eye-socket. The admirals stared back stoically, meeting the stony regard. None dared flinch or allow his gaze to waver. The sporting of visually enhancing monocles was something of a tradition in the Obscurus fleet, but the one worn by the Imperial commander was different: it was a replacement, not an aid. Everyone knew the story of how he had lost his right eye when a young fleet captain, in an engagement with ork raiders. He could easily have had the eye replaced with another natural one. Instead he had chosen to have the present prosthetic fitted. It was said to be unique and irreplaceable. There were even some dark rumours concerning that monocle. Some said it had been made by a tech-priest of genius, whom Drang had had murdered after the fitting to preserve its uniqueness. Another version of the story gave the monocle an alien origin, Drang then having ordered the Exterminatus of the entire alien planet, again to satisfy his craving to own something unique.

Whatever the real story, it was a matter of record that Drang had boasted that, standing on the upper deck of a battleship in hard vacuum, he could spot an enemy warship up to half a light-year distant.

'Here is my proposal, gentlemen,' Lord Drang said. 'We shall serve the Emperor by removing the threat at the outset. This will be a manoeuvre which has never been carried out before. An incursion by massed naval forces into the Eye, the object being to annihilate the invasion fleet while it lies in the construction yards. We shall go in through the Cadian Gate and hit them before they know what is happening, then withdraw just as quickly.' He shrugged. 'A pity we cannot land ground forces and fortify a few planets, too, but such an action is ruled out at a very high level. The Eye of Terror is the strangest of places, as you are all aware. The Adeptus Terra believes the risk of mental contamination is too great to allow Imperium forces to spend any length of time there.'

When Drang uttered a proposal, everyone present knew that he was issuing an order. Here was a plan daring to the point of madness, but one did not argue with the Lord Militant Commander. Discussion would be limited to ways and means of effecting the aim Drang had outlined.

'Gothic-class battleships, supported in the main by Styx and Hades-class heavy cruisers, will make up the bulk of the task-force,' he continued. 'All those in Battlefleet Obscurus, except those that must be held in reserve, will be committed to the attack. And after I have consulted with my good friend, Lord Militant Commander Invisticone, I am sure we can confidently expect substantial elements of Battlefleet Pacificus to join us also.' Drang gave a mirthless smile. 'Invisticone will not want to leave all the glory to me.'

Servitors brought more dried herbs to refill the golden chalices. An invigorating mood of grim determination took over the admirals' conference. The planning talk went on, far into the night and beyond the next dawn.

THREE
WARP TERROR

INTERSTELLAR TRADER Maynard Rugolo was wishing he had never set foot in the miserable city of Gendova. Indeed he was wishing he had never turned the prow of his ship towards the pesky planet calling itself Apex V, being the fifth world from the dim, smouldering star labelled Apex on the star charts for no clear reason. Sun, planet and city alike were all afflicted with the same grim dullness. It made Rugolo want to pull his head into his coat like a tortoise retreating into its shell. Even the reddened rays of the dismal sun, when they actually managed to filter through the smoky sky, had the appearance of prison bars.

Which was quite untypical of the sweep of worlds out here among the fringe worlds close to the great warp-storm some called the Eye of Terror. The Imperium's hold was not strong here, since the Eye presented a danger to shipping, and generally a frontier atmosphere prevailed. Rugolo had heard stories of dark raiders sallying out of the Eye to pillage and destroy, carrying back slaves to their fiendish dens. Not that Rugolo had ever been able to find anyone who had witnessed or even had personal knowledge of such a raid.

Whether the stories were true or not, the ruler of Apex V came from distant Terra itself and was rigidly orthodox. He had imposed his own unbending version of the Imperial Cult across the planet. Public proctors were everywhere, seeing to it that the citizenry observed strict uniformity of dress and conduct. One could probably find oneself in prison, Rugolo thought glumly, just for breaking wind.

He was sitting in a coffee house, almost the only form of meeting place in Gendova. It dispensed red Folian coffee, a sweet, sticky, rather nauseating hot drink which was the nearest thing to a stimulating beverage allowed in the city, though all it accomplished was to keep one awake when one wished to go to sleep. On a raised dais in the corner sat the house's proctor, able through his battery of softspeakers to hear everything said throughout the room.

Rugolo was pleading with his starship's navigator, Dean Abrutu. The two made an odd pair. Rugolo had the over-ruddy face of a man who had stood under many suns, easily identifying him as a free trader or wandering adventurer – types all-too-common in the fringe worlds and not particularly welcomed on Apex V. His black goatee beard and dark, ever-shifting eyes gave him a slightly piratical look, while his maroon jerkin with scarlet braid and lime-green knee-breeches with silver buckles stood out like a blazing beacon amid the drab black-and-brown clothing the Gendovans all wore.

Abrutu, on the other hand, shunned sunlight of whatever intensity or colour – though in any case nothing could have taken away his navigator's pallor – and like most of his kind wore subdued colours. His gaze was downcast as he listened to Rugolo's words, the red bandanna across his forehead concealing his warp eye.

'Things will get better, I promise.'

A regretful frown on his broad face, Abrutu politely but firmly shook his head. 'I'm sorry, captain. You've said that too many times before. Everything you touch turns to dust. You haven't paid me for nearly a year now.'

'I'll pay you everything you're due! The very next contract I get! Even if it leaves me with nothing!'

'You've said that too many times as well. Sometimes I think you deliberately don't pay me just to hang on to me. But now I'm cutting my losses. The job I've been offered suits me perfectly.'

'On a piffling regular line. With a hereditary charter? Under a captain who can't trade anywhere else even if he wants to? Where's your sense of adventure?'

'I haven't got one,' Abrutu stated calmly. '*You're* the one with the sense of adventure. And if I may say so, it's about the only kind of sense you have got.'

Rugolo groaned softly to himself. Everything was slipping away. He couldn't operate at all without a navigator! All he had left now was his ship, the *Wandering Star*, for which he had a deep affection, perhaps because of its advanced age more than in spite of it. That and the trader's charter, of course, the Letter of Marque…

He twitched his head as if brushing away flies. It didn't do to think about that too much.

It looked as if he wouldn't have the *Wandering Star* much longer either. Thanks to Abrutu's defection it was now stranded. At the same time, a Gendovan merchant had filed a claim on it, in recompense for a ruined shipment of apple-peaches, an exotic, very expensive fruit which rotted within minutes unless stored at a precise temperature of eighteen and a half degrees. How was Rugolo to know his hold's temperature regulator was faulty? Damn Apex V's ruler, and damn his meticulous legalities!

Rugolo glanced up guiltily. The proctor had risen to his feet. He strode haughtily across the room to Rugolo's table. In his skullcap and stiff black uniform he made a sinister figure as he leaned towards the pair with an angry expression on his face.

'You two have been talking together in this coffee house for the past twenty minutes,' he thundered, 'and in that time *I have not once heard you praise the Emperor!*'

'Ah! Er, He is always so much in our minds, sir, that every word we speak is in thanks to Him.' Rugolo smiled ingratiatingly. 'He is indeed the source of all that is good and worthy in our lives.'

'Do not take me for a fool, outworlder. Watch your speech in future, both of you.'

Abrutu stood up with a slow, ponderous motion and turned to address the proctor. 'May I express my thanks, sir, for your correction of our manners. Since I intend to make Gendova my home, I for one will heed it.'

Smiling slightly, he made a gesture of farewell to Rugolo, then walked out of the coffee shop. With a final backward scowl, the proctor returned to his duty station.

Rugolo was alone. Pensively he surveyed the shop's customers. They were a dull lot, as befitted this dull city. Their depressingly drab clothing covered everything except their faces – in some cases, they even wore gloves, as if it was indecent to show one's hands. What a place to be stuck in!

Then his slowly sweeping gaze abruptly stopped. A spindly, pale young man was sitting at the other end of the room, playing nervously with his coffee cup. There was a certain soulful look about him. A look which Rugolo knew well.

The look of a navigator!

True, there was no sign of a warp eye. The young man wore no bandanna and the skin of his high forehead was smooth. But Rugolo was not fooled by that. It would not be the first time he had known a navigator to cover his third eye with synthetic skin in an attempt to disguise himself and hide what he truly was.

Surreptitiously Rugolo studied the stranger. His unassuming apparel fitted in well with the local custom, but then navigators never were flashy dressers. The only point at odds was the shabbiness of what he wore. The local people were hard-working and wore clothing of quality, if not style. This young man clearly had little money to spend. That alone set him apart from the locals.

After a shifty glance at the proctor, Rugolo stood up and sidled to his table.

'Praise be to the Emperor!' he said in a voice loud enough for the proctor to hear even without his eavesdropping microphones. Then, more quietly, 'May I sit with you?'

'Praise be to Him.'

Rugolo seated himself quickly, giving the other no chance to express his obvious wish to be left alone. The young man avoided his eye, shifting uncomfortably and ignoring Rugolo's strained smile.

'Something tells me you are not a native of Apex V...'

The young stranger gulped. 'Why not?'

'Oh, I'm good at reading people.' Rugolo's smile became more relaxed. He was on the right lines. 'My name is Maynard Rugolo. I'm a trader. May I know yours?'

'Um, Calliden. Pelor Calliden.'

Rugolo wondered if that really was his name. He leaned forward so that he could get a closer look at the young man in the subdued light. He fancied he saw a slight bump in the middle of his forehead. That would be his warp eye.

'I have a proposal to put to you. Shall we talk here, or outside?'

'Proposal?'

'Yes. Of a *professional* nature.'

The look of genuine fright this remark evoked told Rugolo for certain that his judgement was correct. He had found a navigator. One who, for some reason, did not want it known that he was a navigator.

Calliden's voice almost trembled as he replied. 'The Emperor is the source of all my blessings. I have nothing to hide. And I don't see how I can be of service to you.'

'As He is of mine.' Rugolo leaned closer and spoke in a low, conspiratorial voice. If Calliden didn't care what the proctor heard, then neither did he. 'I am a trader. I have a ship out at the spaceport – the *Wandering Star*, my pride and joy. I am in need of a navigator. I can pay you well.'

Again the young man gulped. He seemed to be in a panic. He looked this way and that as if seeking a way of escape. 'I don't know how I can help you. I don't know any navigators. Go to the naval office.'

If Rugolo could have acquired a navigator through official channels he would not be sitting here now. 'I prefer more informal arrangements. Come, now, let us not prevaricate. It is perfectly obvious to me what you are.'

'You're mistaken. I don't know anything about space-flight, except as a passenger.'

Glancing over at the proctor, Rugolo saw that he was sitting on his dais with eyes downcast. It seemed to him that he was listening to their conversation with interest. 'The Emperor is the source of all truth and wisdom,' he said emphatically. 'Where would we be but for His guidance and protection? Likewise we should all strive for truthfulness, should we not?'

He paused, then added hopefully, 'Would you be interested in just one trip? Whatever your present circumstances might be, that wouldn't take up too much of your time.' He let his eyes wander pointedly over the other's worn garments. 'I'm sure the fee will come in useful.'

Calliden's agitation did not go away. His fragile voice rose almost to a shout, causing other customers to look around in curiosity. 'I am not a navigator, as the Emperor is my witness! Leave me alone!'

Almost knocking the table over in his hurry, he rushed from the coffee house. Rugolo smiled grimly as he in turn rose to his feet.

'You just need persuading, my friend,' he murmured to himself, then left in pursuit.

DUSK HAD COME to Gendova, giving the drab buildings a sooty look. It would not be safe to be out much longer. The city arbitrators required all those without special dispensation to be in their homes one hour after the onset of darkness, and in their beds half an hour after that.

Earlier that afternoon Rugolo had chanced to walk through Gendova's central park, where a preacher of the Adeptus Ministorum, or Ecclesiarchy to give the Adeptus its other title, had been haranguing a crowd. Given that the planetary ruler was a Ministorum fanatic, requiring everyone to believe with absolute faith that the Emperor was lord and saviour of all humankind, no passing Gendovan would have dared to do otherwise than to stop and listen. Just the same, Rugolo had been struck by how quiet and well-behaved the crowd was, doing no more than clap politely as the preacher made point after vociferous point. He could well understand why the parish clergy did not include in its ranks a confessor, one of those masters of crowd emotion whose sermons nearly always ended in hysterical lynchings on the slightest suspicion of heresy. Such wild behaviour just did not accord with the orderly conduct of Gendovans.

As he stood listening to the preacher's nonsense, Rugolo had also realised for the first time how much his garments stood out here, restrained though they were by his own standards. He was receiving stuffy, suspicious stares. But with the proctors filtering among the crowd he had thought it unwise to follow his impulse to scurry away, and had lingered for nearly an hour!

Now the street was full of people hurrying home. He looked up and down, and saw a dark-clad figure hurrying around a corner. It had to be the disguised navigator, who was nowhere else in sight. As fast as he could stride without actually running, Rugolo followed. He found himself in an empty cul de sac. There was no sign of Calliden.

He ran to the end of the narrow side street, and discovered an alley running at right angles, parallel to the main road. His quarry must have hoped to use it as an escape route – which meant that he had been afraid Rugolo would come after him. As he jogged up the alley, Rugolo asked himself the reason for the young man's odd behaviour. Could it be that he was an outcast, expelled from the Navis Nobilite for some crime or misdemeanour? Even forbidden to practise his profession, perhaps? Oh joy! A solitary, abandoned navigator, cast out of his House! With no means to earn a living! Just what Rugolo needed!

With a suddenness he had now come to expect after the two or three days he had spent on the planet, darkness closed in, the last few gloomy rays of Apex's light failing to penetrate the cloud-polluted sky. The dimmest of dim street lights took their place, but did not even prove equal to the previous murk. In an hour, even they would be switched off.

Rugolo reached the end of the alley, and saw that it divided in two directions. He cursed. He had lost the navigator.

Then, from somewhere up the right fork, he heard a strangled cry. He hesitated, torn between need and self-preservation. Pulling a tiny plastic handgun from a slim holster next to the skin of his abdomen – the carrying of any kind of weapon was illegal in Gendova – he loped forward, keeping close to one wall.

Under the feeble amber glow of a street lamp, four figures were struggling. One of them was the young man calling himself Pelor Calliden. The synthskin had been torn from his forehead. His third eye, the warp eye, stared blankly out.

His three attackers, to Rugolo's mild surprise, appeared to be Gendovans. Like Calliden, they were all young men. They probably thought their apparel wildly daring, even subversive: Their sombre, conventional black garb bore one or two tiny patches of muted colour, reddish brown or dark blue. No wonder such rebels kept to dark alleys.

Two held Calliden by the arms while the third yelled in his face. 'See! You are one! We thought so – we've been watching you!'

'No–' Calliden groaned.

'Yeah! And you're taking us into the Eye!'

'Come on, let's get him out of here.'

As far as Rugolo could tell, the hoodlums were unarmed. He emerged nonchalantly into the gleam of the lamplight, the tiny gun concealed in his palm.

'Such manners! And I thought everyone on Apex V was a perfect gentleman. Wait till I tell the proctors.'

Calliden slumped, while his captors stared at Rugolo with disbelief. He gave them no further chance to deploy any weapons they might have hidden about them. He extended his right arm and discharged the plastic gun twice with a double popping sound. The first bullet hit the young man who had been haranguing Calliden in the chest. The other thudded into the abdomen of one of the two holding him prisoner. Eyes bulging with shock, both were hurled back by the impact and collapsed.

Rugolo side-stepped, seeking a clear line of fire so as to deal with the third assailant in the same way, but there was no need. He fled.

Initially dragged off-balance as the stricken Gendovan fell, Calliden recovered himself. He was shaking.

'Thank… you!' he gasped.

With interest Rugolo looked at the young navigator's warp eye, set amid his forehead. The pupil was quite large and dark, almost purple, with a soft lustre. But it displayed his youth, and the fact that it had not been used much. The older and more experienced a navigator, the more the pupil became enlarged. In his years in space Rugolo had seen some where the white was gone altogether. Such navigators were reputedly dangerous to be around, liable to strike a man dead with a glance.

Just the same, Calliden's third eye gave Rugolo the same impression that all navigators' warp eyes did: an alien, unblinking stare. It did not seem like a natural organ at all, more like something artificial that had been set in place.

He spoke in an amused drawl. 'Not a navigator, eh?'

Guiltily the young man put a hand to his third eye, feeling the torn synthskin. Then he reached into his pocket for a kerchief, which he tied hastily in place to cover his forehead.

'I was telling the truth!' Calliden insisted in a quavering voice. 'I'm not!'

'Why continue to lie when you're caught red-handed?'

'I'm not a navigator!'

Rugolo grinned cynically. 'Of course not. You've only disguised yourself as one. And then disguised the disguise. Come on, we'd better get moving. It'll soon be curfew time.'

Calliden stared appalled at the two sprawled bodies. 'What about those?'

'What about them?'

'You've killed them! Did they deserve that?'

'Oh, they deserved it all right. But they're not dead.' Rugolo opened his right hand and displayed the little gun nestling neatly in his palm. 'This fires low-velocity slugs, broad-nosed. They only kill you if you're unlucky. They don't break the skin, instead they squirt a knock-out drug through it. These goons will wake up in about twenty hours, with a lot of internal bruising. They might even be able to stand up again after a couple of weeks.'

'I can't stand violence!'

'You've met some, navigator.'

'I'm not–'

'I know, you're not a navigator.'

Calliden was still staring at the tiny gun. 'What are you doing with that anyway? Weapons are forbidden here. You can't even get out of the spaceport with one.'

Rugolo marvelled at the young man's naivety. 'It's made of a soft plastic. The spaceport detectors can't see it.'

He put the gun back in its holster and beckoned, leading the way back to the main thoroughfare. The streets were emptying and already had a deserted appearance in the dimming light.

He turned to Calliden. 'What did those fellows want of you?'

'Like you, they think I'm a navigator. You know the great warp-storm? The one they call the Eye of Terror? There are stories in this region that the worlds inside it contain fabulous treasures. Some insane people get the idea of going to look for those treasures. They wanted me to guide them into the Eye.'

Thoughtfully Rugolo gazed up at the sky. In this part of the galaxy the Eye of Terror, or *Ocularis Terribus* (it had other names: Hell's Whirlpool, the Cyclone of Chaos, and so forth) was actually visible to the naked eye as a great swirl of stars, like a miniature galaxy. He wasn't sure if this hemisphere of Apex V faced that way at this time of day, and anyway the night sky was obscured by cloud, but the idea of a cosmic treasure-house suspended overhead was appealing.

'I thought it wasn't possible to navigate into the Eye. Because of the warp-storm.'

'It's always possible to enter. Getting out again is another matter. Though that, too, can be done.' Calliden's voice fell to a mumble. 'I must thank you for coming to my aid. Now I'd better be going to my lodgings. I don't want to be caught outside.'

Rugolo noted with satisfaction that Calliden was speaking with a navigator's knowledge. 'It's not the proctors you have to worry about,' he said. 'Your hopeful travelling companions who have just tried to kidnap you will doubtless have friends who know where you are staying. You can't go back to your lodgings.'

In point of fact Rugolo thought it unlikely that the young man was in any further danger. The Gendovans had been disposed of too easily. They were amateurs, well out of their depth. His main motive was to get Calliden back to the *Wandering Star*, where he could again try to persuade him to accept employment.

Seeing Calliden hesitate, a frightened frown on his features, he added, 'You'd better come with me.'

'Well, just till tomorrow. Then I'll see if I can get a ship out of here.'

I wonder if he has the fare, Rugolo asked himself, hoping otherwise. The forlorn navigator seemed as though in a trance as he walked alongside him to the spaceport.

The streets of Gendova, almost completely empty now, were narrow, the buildings huddled, with steeply slanted roofs for draining off the frequent rain. The city was like its inhabitants, insular, without light or colour. The proctors had disappeared, their place taken at night by the regular police force, the arbitrators. Already a patrol car was prowling. It slowed down as it passed by, a helmeted figure within scrutinising the pair. Despite the hour's grace after dark, the arbitrators did not like to see anybody about when they came on duty.

Perhaps it was their foreign apparel which saved the two from being challenged. They passed through a spacious arch which marked the limits of the town and led to the wrought iron gates of the spaceport. These swung open after Rugolo showed his permit to the guard. Before they could enter the spaceport proper, they had to pass through the scanning machine which looked for contraband. Rugolo passed a wink to Calliden as, once again, it failed to detect his plastic weapon.

None of the spaceport staff bothered to ask for Calliden's credentials. With his bandanna and his pale, exhausted appearance, it was plainly taken for granted that he was Rugolo's navigator.

Outlined in the garish light of tower lamps, Gendova's spaceport lay before them. It was like some bizarre, gigantic junkyard, littered with hulking, crenellated forms having the appearance of crumbling metal castles. These were cargo ships of various kinds. Such ornate, convoluted shapes made no sense in terms of aerodynamics – though that hardly mattered, spacecraft pushed themselves beyond the atmosphere by brute force – but the intricate turrets, the baroque decoration and leering gargoyles were an essential part of the arcane tech-wizardry of the Imperium.

The largest of these ships was only modestly sized as spacecraft went; the really big bulk carriers, which in any case were unable to land and ferried their cargoes to and from parking orbit, would not bother coming to an out-of-the-way planet like Apex V at all. Interspersed among them were even taller travelling cranes – the only way of getting merchandise into the ships' holds – while further off, almost out of sight in the gloom, were the repair yards.

Steam and acrid-smelling vapour billowed around the two as they crossed the concrete-clad field. With a mixture of pride and embarrassment, Rugolo eventually pointed out his own ship, the *Wandering Star*.

'There she is!' he declared, forcing cheerfulness into his voice. 'Home at last!'

Calliden looked up at Rugolo's cargo carrier with a critical frown. It was a squat, tattered lump, dwarfed by nearly all the surrounding ships and definitely showing its age, the hull scored and pitted as though rotted with rust, the fluted columns covering the engine vents battered and dented. Its lines were cleaner and more aerodynamic than anything else on the field. Such simplicity was a sign of how cheaply it had been built. The gargoyle faces on its four sides were worn away and barely visible. They were supposed to help ward off daemons while in the warp, but Rugolo was sceptical of their efficacy and had never bothered to have them reshaped or even cleaned.

The *Wandering Star* stood no more than ninety feet high. To a citizen of Gendova that would have seemed enormous – larger than almost any building in the city. To Rugolo and any other spacefarer it was small. He had seen armed scout-ships almost as big. Had he a bigger ship, he might have found life less difficult. As it was, he was forced to carry small-volume, high-value goods, which brought two problems with them. Either he had to buy such goods himself, for which he did not always have the money, or failing that he had to find a merchant who would trust him to carry them, which wasn't always easy. Often he found himself transporting cargoes which barely covered his running costs.

Like those damnable apple-peaches, he reminded himself ruefully.

At his urging they climbed an access ladder, went through the port and into the small hold which took up most of the bulk of the ship, then up a companionway to the crew quarters in the nose of the vessel. These consisted of the pilot's cabin and a slightly larger area for living space.

Calliden hesitated and trembled at his first sight of the claustrophobically cramped control cabin. He seemed about to panic, until Rugolo gently ushered him inside. Of three electrolumens which were supposed to give light, only one was working, and the brass fittings, tarnished from years of neglect, gave off only the dullest gleam. The ceiling was concave, striated with supporting arches, drooping with ribbed conduit hoses, and was so low that it barely gave headroom. There was a musty, suffocating smell to the air. The runes and sigils surrounding the two pilots' seats, supposed to give comfort, had the opposite effect on Calliden. He felt completely cut off from the world, as though they were already in the warp, or – although that would not be nearly as bad – as though they were in one of those peculiar vessels he had heard of but never seen, which dived miles beneath the ocean or tunnelled far beneath the crust of a planet. There was not even the comforting aroma of Ministorum incense, which most space captains burned to bring the blessings of the Emperor.

Rugolo had long ago given over the living quarters to his navigator, Abrutu, and shifted himself into the control cabin permanently. It was therefore cluttered; even the flight controls were littered with domestic objects such as a boot brush and nail clippers. A pallet on the floor was where he slept. And he had managed to find room for a small table and two straight-backed chairs.

He gestured Calliden to one of these now. Rummaging in a cupboard, he brought out a cut-glass decanter and two crystal glasses – items he had kept back from a cargo of such glassware – and placed them on the table.

'Let's hope no stuffy Emperor-worshipping spoilsport is able to spy on us here!' he said jovially, and poured a pale green, locally illegal liqueur into the glasses, handing one to Calliden. The young man sipped at it cautiously, while Rugolo swallowed his glassful in one gulp and then filled it up again.

'Now,' he said, in the tone of an interrogator, 'tell me why you pretend not to be a navigator.'

'Because I'm not one!' Calliden retorted angrily.

'Don't be stupid, of course you are. And come, now, what's the use of being a navigator if you don't ply your trade? There has to be a reason. Are you in trouble with your House, perhaps? You can tell me. I'm an understanding man.'

The plainly miserable Pelor Calliden sighed and relaxed a little, huddling in his chair.

'I'm not a navigator,' he said slowly, 'for the very simple reason that I can't navigate.'

'Can't navigate?' Rugolo stared at him nonplussed. '*Can't navigate?*'

He pursed his lips. Could the navigator gene have failed in this young man? Was he a reverse mutation? A throwback? Born of navigators but unable to see into the warp?

If so it was no wonder he had been thrown out of his Family – but no, that couldn't be it. They were more likely to have had him quietly put down, rather than throw him out to fend for himself. A non-navigating son of a Navigator House would be bad publicity for the entire Navis Nobilite, an arm of the Imperium which jealously guarded its reputation.

'Are you... warp-blind?' he asked gently.

'No, no, not at all. That's the trouble. I can see only too well!'

That was all Rugolo could get out of him for now. Calliden turned the tables, asking in a rather impudent tone why the trader was in need of a navigator – and how he had lost his last one.

Rugolo shrugged evasively. 'Oh, he was a dull fellow who didn't like travelling from place to place. He took another position. With a hereditary charter!'

He spoke scathingly. Looking around at the poorly appointed, musty-smelling cabin, Calliden curled his lip and clearly was not convinced.

It was not until much later, when Rugolo had succeeded in plying him with more of the green liqueur, that Calliden told his tale.

'It's true that I am a trained navigator,' he admitted for the first time. 'But I am a disgrace to my House! I am de-registered, not allowed to practise. Neither could I, even if I were allowed.'

He took his head in his hands and did not speak for some time. Then, in a burdened voice, he went on. 'The training of a navigator is long. It is not simply a matter of being able to see warp currents. Knowing how to find a way through them, and how to use them to reach a far destination, is both a science and an art. Eventually, in my thirtieth year – which is young for a navigator, by the way; we live longer than you who are without the navigators' gene – I was to make my first full flight, with my trainer present only as an observer.

'This was just three days after... after my mother died. I was very close to her, and her death affected me strongly. After marrying my father she had ceased working as a pilot, so she didn't have a very great experience of the warp. Anyway, shortly after we made the warp drop–'

Again Calliden buried his face in his hands. His tone was anguished. 'I saw her! I saw her! Outside the ship, in the warp! She was clawing at the hull trying to get in, pleading with me to help her!

'I went crazy,' he went on in a mutter. 'I actually abandoned the pilot's seat and tried to get to the external hatch so I could open it and let her in. They had to drag me back. My trainer took over the ship immediately, of course, and took me back to the House under restraint. I was in complete shock. There I was examined and pronounced unfit for pilot or navigation duties. Eventually, my father let me leave the House. I've been wandering from place to place ever since. Most of the time I scarcely know where I am. But I've never used my warp eye since. The very thought of it–'

He broke off for a moment. 'So you see, you will never be able to hire me as your navigator. It's impossible, quite apart from being against the laws of the Imperium.'

Rugolo now understood what a lost soul he had chanced upon. The poor fellow lived in a state of pathological terror. As well as horror, of course, at wondering what torments his mother's soul was enduring.

'Has it crossed your mind that grief for your mother's death might be responsible for what you *thought* you saw?' he asked in as kindly a tone as he could muster. 'You don't really believe it was your mother out there, do you?'

'That's what the apothecaries all tried to tell me,' Calliden retorted. 'But they were lying, or else fools. It *was* her. Her soul, of course, not her body. Anybody who knows the first thing about the Immaterium can tell you that such things are possible.'

Obviously nothing he could say would free Calliden from his delusion, Rugolo thought. If it was a delusion...

'But every time you travel from world to world you have to go through the warp, unless, that is, you stay within the same planetary system,' he pointed out. 'Doesn't warp flight frighten you, as a passenger?'

'No,' Calliden answered after a weary pause. 'The ship's screens are sufficient protection, or warp flight wouldn't be possible at all. I don't think about it, any more than a passenger on an ocean ship thinks about the depths he's floating on.' Calliden's face glazed over thoughtfully. 'In the training college it was described as a paradox: a material object moving through the Immaterium... all by the grace of His Divinity, the Emperor!' he added with sudden passion.

Curious, Rugolo asked, 'You really believe the Emperor is a god?'

Calliden seemed to have regained his self-control now. He was his usual miserable self. 'Of course. Don't you?'

Rugolo uttered a short barking laugh. 'Only when there's a preacher near at hand! It's not something I worry my head about. He could be a god, for all I know, but if I'm seriously to believe that, then I'd have to start believing all those stories

about the enemy's gods, too. And all that stuff about daemons.
I don't believe in daemons. At least, I don't think I do.'

'Yes,' Calliden said stiffly, 'I can see you don't, just by looking
at the state of your ship's outer hull. If you take my advice
you'll clean up the warding images and have them reconse-
crated. They're not there for nothing, whatever you might
think.

'As for the Emperor,' he went on, 'He most definitely is a god.
Any navigator can tell you that, even a de-registered one like
myself.'

Rugolo decided it was time to change the subject.
Thoughtfully he tugged his goatee beard, remembering what
Calliden had said about the Eye of Terror. No one had ever told
him that money could be made by going there. Mostly its reputation was as a dwelling place of daemons. Rugolo didn't
believe in daemons, as he had said. By the same token he was-
n't ready to take tales of fabulous trading opportunities too
seriously either. No doubt there were inhabited worlds inside
the Eye, out of reach of the Imperium because of the storm, but
probably they were primitive and poverty-stricken.

But on the other hand–

'Those young scum I rescued you from,' he remarked casually, 'I'm surprised to find cheap criminals like that in a place
as rigidly controlled as Gendova.'

'Apex V wasn't always like that. It has only received the ben-
efits of regulation since the present High Commander took
over. There are still some renegade types lurking about, though
they mostly keep their heads down.'

'What you said about the Eye of Terror – is there any truth in
that?'

Calliden looked at him guardedly. 'You don't seem to know
much about this region,' he commented. 'Have you been in the
Obscura Segmentum very long? For that matter, how long have
you been a free trader?'

By now Maynard Rugolo was in his cups. The night was well
advanced, and he was halfway into a second bottle of
Masteuse, the thick green liqueur he plainly liked. He hic-
cuped, drew himself up, and spoke with all the dignity he
could summon.

'I am not a free trader. I am a *Rogue* Trader.'

Calliden blinked, then threw back his head and laughed.

'You're a Rogue Trader?' he spluttered. 'It seems I am not the only one travelling in disguise. Where is your fleet of ships? Your private army? Your specialists and technicians? If you are in need of a navigator, why do you not go straight to this planet's commander with your charter, your Letter of Marque, and demand he supply you with one?'

There was good reason for Calliden's scepticism. A Rogue Trader was a person of rank, someone who had risen high in the Adeptus Terra and to whom considerable resources had been entrusted. He was outside the reach of the priesthood. He acted on or beyond the edges of the Imperium, exploring, trading, fighting, coming into contact with unknown alien races. He was a law unto himself. In short, he was utterly unlike the bluff but quite obviously unsuccessful common merchant who sat here.

'I wonder if you are even a *free* trader,' Calliden went on, twisting the knife in the wound. 'If my guess is correct you're an unlicensed privateer, scratching a living like ten thousand others, by buying and selling whatever and wherever you can.'

'Oh, you think so, eh?'

Enraged at having his word doubted, Rugolo jumped to his feet and strode unsteadily to a timber chest bolted to the floor of the cabin. Flinging open the lid, he began rummaging inside. Odd items – items of clothing, trinkets, various small instruments – flew across the cabin as he burrowed furiously for what he sought, until he produced a vellum scroll tied with silk cords, which he flung at his accuser.

'*There* is my Letter of Marque!'

Calliden picked up the scroll from where it fell to the floor, pulled open the silk knots and unrolled it. He studied it carefully. It was indeed an impressive document, hand-scribed in ink of three colours, gold, silver and purple. The lettering was of an ancient, elegant style. And, supposing it was not a forgery, it did appear to be the licensing document of a Rogue Trader, replete with dozens of empowering clauses.

There was only one thing wrong. Calliden glanced up at Rugolo, then back at the scroll.

'This isn't made out to you. It's to someone called *Hansard* Rugolo. You told me your name is Maynard. Furthermore, it's dated fifty years ago, when I would guess you hadn't been born.'

Rugolo sighed deeply and nodded, his eyes downcast. 'Well, it works sometimes.'

'So who is Hansard Rugolo?'

'My father,' Rugolo said wearily. 'He was a Rogue Trader. A most impressive man. As a boy I accompanied him on his expeditions. It was a wonderful life! I was a young man when he was killed on one of those expeditions, and by then I had grown used to such a life and I didn't want to lose it. So… I tried to take his place. I became an impostor, impersonating him every time we communicated with the Administratum. It worked for a while. My father's former staff co-operated out of loyalty to him. But I didn't have his flair. Things started to go wrong, and after a few years my people had all slipped away, taking most of the ships with them to become freebooters. In the end I had only one left, with just four crewmen, and they wanted to quit as well. It was too big for me to handle alone. So I traded it for the *Wandering Star*.'

Defiantly, Rugolo grinned. 'So you see, I *was* a Rogue Trader, in a way, or rather my father was. Some captaincies are hereditary, aren't they? Why shouldn't this one be? As far as I know the charter had never been revoked – my father's death was never reported – so as far as I am concerned I still *am* a Rogue Trader.'

'Then it's as I thought,' Calliden said softly. 'You are operating without a licence at all.'

Rugolo blew out his cheeks. 'Well, that depends on your point of view.'

Calliden wondered why Rugolo didn't carry out the imposture in earnest, assuming his father's name and perhaps making himself look older. Then he realised that he was too slippery an individual to allow himself to be boxed in like that. He didn't look like a Rogue Trader. There would be too much risk of exposure, in which case he would have no way out.

'We're both a couple of frauds, it seems,' Rugolo said. He swallowed the last of the Masteuse. 'Let's get some sleep.'

The ex-navigator had to steady him on his feet at one point as Rugolo showed him to the rear chamber and pointed to a bed. Then Rugolo reeled back into the pilot's cabin and collapsed on his pallet.

* * *

WHEN HE AWOKE he raised his head and stared blearily at the external view-screen, which he had left switched on. The lights of the spaceport were being diluted by a faint lightening of the dark, starless sky. Then, quite suddenly, streaks of light showed through the sooty cloud covering. It was dawn.

Rugolo forced himself to his feet. His head throbbed as a result. He staggered to a drawer, opened it and took out a tattered liber bound in the mottled skin of some unnamed animal. It was a book of prayers and charms. Hurriedly he riffled the pages until he came to the much-used ritual for curing hangovers, muttering the ancient words to himself, though he almost knew them by heart.

He nearly forgot the footnote. *Use in conjunction with Saturn snake oil.* Tossing the grimoire back into its drawer, he stumbled to the cupboard and groped until finding a phial. Pulling a face, he forced down a single swallow of the nauseous-tasting syrup. Whether it was the spell or the snake oil or both, he did begin to feel better. He splashed water on his face and ran his fingers through his hair.

What was he going to do about Calliden? There had to be some way of pulling him together!

He was about to look for something to eat when he noticed a movement out on the spaceport, which was in full visibility now – daylight on Apex V came with the same rapidity with which it departed. It was the same on all the Apex worlds, due to the smallness of the Apex sun.

The wrought iron spaceport gate had opened and a party of black-clad, black-hatted men was walking purposefully through it, making for the *Wandering Star*. Turning up the magnification, Rugolo recognised one of them immediately. The merchant Fustog must have got up very early indeed and hurried through the streets the very second it was legal to do so. And so must the bailiffs he had brought with him, one of whom was carrying a bundle of documents under his arm.

They had come to seize his ship!

'By the Emperor!' Rugolo looked about wildly. Then he flung himself into the pilot's seat and began the pre-launch check procedure, clicking switches and darting his eyes from rune to rune in near-panic.

By the billion hells, there wasn't time for that! He had to get away now! Rugolo stopped checking. It was lucky he had spent the last of his money on reaction mass. He booted up the power. Before it was even safe to do so, he opened up the conduits, keeping his eye on the external screen. What looked like steam billowed up from the vents at the base of the ship, quickly taking on a luminescent quality as it became white-hot. Fustog's party flung up their arms in alarm and ran for cover.

With a rumbling sound the *Wandering Star* lifted off, swaying in the air thanks to Rugolo's unsteady hand on the controls, and accelerated away.

In minutes the ship was outside the atmosphere. Apex, small, white and bright, shone in blackness, surrounded by stars. If he looked in a certain direction Rugolo could make out a diffuse nebula, a large, indistinct patch of brightness: the Eye of Terror.

Briefly he stared at it, remembering the various legends he had heard about it. Then he started wondering what to do next. He had yet to establish an orbit about Apex V, though he thought there was little chance he would be pursued – surely the planet's defence forces wouldn't be mobilised just to execute Fustog's warrant! He was on a parabolic course which, if uncorrected, would bring him crashing back down on the surface.

He could never make a landing on Apex V again. He would be arrested immediately. And it was the only inhabited planet in the whole Apex system. A system which he could not leave because he did not have a warp navigator. Or did he?

He let the *Wandering Star* coast, reaching the apogee of its trajectory. Slowly, but surely, he came to a decision.

In his time Rugolo had worked without a navigator before. Then, he had been trading between the three inhabited planets of the same system. Navigators weren't necessary if you didn't want to go from one star to another. In fact one couldn't drop into the warp at all until one was outside a star's 'warp island', a distance of some tens of millions of miles, depending on the size of the star. So he had got used to piloting for himself in real-space. It was easy, really. The ship's machinery did all the calculating. All one had to do was enter the co-ordinates of the destination and make some adjustments towards the end of the flight.

Plus land and take off, of course. In this case it was simplicity itself. He only had to get a certain distance from Apex. And no great distance, either. Apex was a small star.

Rugolo got to work, choosing a direction at random as long as it was away from the sun, and kicked in the real-space engine. The *Wandering Star* surged away from Apex V. He rose, gingerly opened the cabin door, and peeped into the living quarters. Calliden was still asleep. He hadn't even been awoken by take-off.

Thanks, no doubt, to good old Mr Masteuse, Rugolo thought with satisfaction.

He himself was still tired. He lay down and dozed off. When he awoke it was three hours later. The real-space engine had switched itself off. The ship had put itself in a parking orbit around Apex.

The cabin door opened gingerly. Calliden crept through, peering around him, his face even paler than before. His eyes fell on the external view-screen, which showed a background of stars. He looked puzzled, then alarmed.

'Where are we?'

'About twenty million miles from Apex. Why?'

Calliden screeched. '*What do you think you're doing?*'

While speaking Rugolo had moved from his pallet bed to the control panel. He smiled confidently at Calliden.

Then, reaching over the pilot's seat, he grabbed a slide lever on the right hand side of the panel and pulled it down.

They both felt a lurch in the pit of the stomach. On the view-screen, the stars vanished. There was only a swirling greyness. The external scanners found nothing to focus on, now.

The *Wandering Star* had slipped into the warp. There came a whining sound as the warp engine began moving the cargo ship through the Immaterium.

Invitingly, Rugolo gestured Calliden towards the pilot's seat and released the navigator's cocoon. It bulged weirdly, waiting to engulf its occupant. Calliden seemed paralysed. He stared wildly.

'*Stop it! Take us out of the warp!*'

'It's too late now,' Rugolo pointed out. 'We're underway. The gods alone know where we'll come out. Light-years from any-where. Maybe right in the middle of the Eye. We're hopelessly lost without a navigator.'

'*Take us out!*'

Calliden flung himself at the controls, reaching for the warp lever. Rugolo intercepted him. The two men struggled briefly, but the slim young navigator was no match for the burly trader. Soon Rugolo was sitting on his chest.

'It's up to you!' he shouted. 'We're dead unless you do your job!'

Slowly he got off Calliden, allowing the younger man to come to his feet. The two stared at one another.

Then Calliden looked again at the swirling view-screen. He began shrieking in a high, hysterical voice, closing his eyes and stopping up his ears with his hands while Rugolo continued to berate him.

Rugolo's patience snapped. He seized hold of Calliden, tore off his bandanna and pushed him towards the pilot's seat with its gaping cocoon.

'Navigate! Look into the warp, else we are dead!'

Calliden ceased shrieking and began to sob.

'Look into the warp,' Rugolo repeated, this time in a firm, insistent voice. He felt the young man's body stiffen under his fingers.

As if in a trance, Pelor Calliden summoned his psychic energy, directed it into his third eye – and looked.

He was not looking at the external view-screen. That would have shown him nothing. To his warp gaze, matter did not exist. He looked straight through the hull of the ship, right into the sea of non-existence through which the *Wandering Star* swept like a ghost. Just *what* he saw, Rugolo did not know. Every navigator saw the warp differently, as his brain constructed sense out of what was, essentially, senseless.

'We're lost,' he muttered. 'We've been drifting without guidance.'

'Very well. This is what I'm paying you for. Take over.'

'I can't,' Calliden protested again.

Nevertheless he stumbled towards the navigator's chair. He reached out and collapsed the cocoon. 'I don't want that,' he muttered. 'It makes me feel trapped.' Rugolo said nothing. The cocoon was a restraint. Navigators sometimes started thrashing about because of what they saw in the warp, but if Calliden wanted to dispense with it, that was up to him.

Calliden's hands trembled as he reached for the warp controls. Rugolo hoped he really did know what he was doing. He had no assurance that Calliden's ejection from his Navigator House was not for mental instability only, but for navigational incompetence as well. He stood by, leaning over the shivering young man. There was a flat plate on the control board on which symbols flickered as the ship moved through the warp. Only navigators knew how to read such a plate. Calliden, however, hardly glanced at it. Navigators rarely did. They relied on their warp vision.

Calliden was glancing all around, not just forward but to the sides, overhead and below. Suddenly he uttered an ear-piercing shriek and leaped to his feet, pointing at the cabin wall, his face distorted.

'MOTHER!'

Rugolo looked. He could see nothing.

'She's there! Mother! Mother! We must help her!'

'There's nothing there, Pelor. Whatever you're seeing, it's not your mother.'

'Yes, yes, it is! She's trying to get in. She's calling to us. Quickly, we must help her!'

Calliden had the strength of a madman as he fought with Rugolo in his attempt to get to the hatch. Rugolo did not know what would happen if a ship broke its air seals while in the warp. It was such a crazy notion that he had literally never thought about it before. But he had no intention of finding out. Momentarily Calliden broke free of his grip. Instead of going after him, the trader lurched to the control board and shoved on the warp-jump lever. With a descending groan from the dying warp engine, the ship dropped out of the Immaterium.

Maybe it was the stomach-churning sensation accompanying such a transition that did it, but Calliden was stopped in his tracks. He turned around.

'She's gone.'

'She was never there.'

'She *was*. I saw her.'

'Your mother's dead. You're just having delusions.'

'Am I? No, you don't understand...' Calliden looked bewildered. 'Where are we?'

'You're the navigator,' Rugolo said. 'You tell me.'

As if sleep-walking Calliden moved to the control board and studied the screens, comparing the charts with the stars in view. He shook his head dolefully.

'We're stranded in open space. Light-years from anywhere.'

'Of course. We've jumped blind. We're lucky we didn't smash into one of those asteroids that drift between the stars. You'll have to get us out of here.'

'But I can't.'

'Okay, we'll just sit here until the air runs out.'

Calliden buried his face in his hands. Neither spoke for a long time.

'It *was* her, you know,' he said accusingly.

'How do you know that? You're in no condition to judge. Most likely it was a mental delusion. Or perhaps it was something real, but not your mother at all. Perhaps it was one of those daemons you talk about, making you think it's her.'

Rugolo didn't believe what he was saying for a moment – daemons did not exist, in the warp or anywhere else – but he was willing to say anything if it would bring Calliden out of his mood. The navigator did seem to be taking his words seriously. He was frowning.

'A daemon… I hadn't thought of that.'

'Yes, and the more you think it's your mother, the more you can be sure it is a daemon. It's getting into your mind and manipulating your emotions.' He let that sink in, then added, 'Come on, let's get a planet under us.'

Calliden clenched his fists. The look on his face was pure misery. Slowly he seated himself at the control board, carefully removed Rugolo's boot brush, nail clippers and one or two rumpled, grubby small garments from it, and then sat studying it, his hands shifting uncertainly.

Rugolo moved to the rear of the cabin, out of Calliden's way. It was up to him to overcome his sickness now.

Calliden took hold of himself. His hands reached for the controls. His warp vision opened. Again there was a lurching in the stomach, like dropping in a high-speed elevator. The ship phased back into the warp.

Every navigator saw the warp in a different way. To one, it might resemble an endless green landscape, marked out in meadows and woods, dotted with lakes, and here and there, towering palaces. Another might see a jumble of steel girders, like an endless three-dimensional city. Still others saw hierarchies of heavens and hells, bursting with twisted inhabitants. For many, though, the warp appeared as a nightmare of mad colours and abstract shapes, not always in three dimensions – sometimes in only two, sometimes in four, five or six. But always, there were two constant features. One was that everything was continually moving, surging, swirling, in response to the passage of the warp currents. And the second was the Astronomican, a pure white light that shone from a distant beacon and penetrated everything.

For Pelor Calliden, the warp was a lush tropical jungle. It had no bottom, no top, and no boundary. As he guided it, the ship was pushing aside lush foliage, easing itself between enormous boles and tangling creepers. This jungle had inhabitants, too. Leering faces, animal, human and what might have been dae-monic, poked between the fleshy petals of luscious orchids, flitting by as the *Wandering Star* made its majestic progress.

None of this occluded the Astronomican. It was like a uni-versal luminescence that filtered through everything, revealing its source, the god-like light that was the source of every navi-gator's deep-rooted faith.

Maynard Rugolo, of course, was aware of none of this. He only knew that Pelor Calliden was staring as if in a trance, and that his hands were applying themselves artistically to the steering controls. Suddenly Calliden spoke, but this time he stayed in his pilot's seat.

'She's there.'

'It's not her, Pelor.'

'She's there. She wants to come in.'

'Ignore it. It's not really her.'

'She's pleading with me. She says I can save her if I really want to.'

'It's a daemon, wanting you to breach the screens so it can drag us into the warp.'

Knowing the deadly danger they were in should Calliden again lose his composure, Rugolo almost found it possible to give credence to his own invention. He saw the navigator's body stiffen as he struggled with himself. Calliden spoke again, his voice breaking into a sob.

'She's been swept off the hull. She's falling away behind, holding her arms out, imploring me–'

'Keep going.'

This time Calliden obeyed, though tears were streaming down his face. He was looking for a patch of darkness. In the warp, that always meant proximity to a star.

Time went by. It was rarely possible to predict how long a warp journey would take. That depended on how swift were the warp currents available, and the skill and experience of the navigator who utilised them. Calliden, Rugolo granted, was not experienced. He sat in his straight-backed chair and said nothing.

At last, Calliden spoke. 'All right, we're somewhere. Do you want to come out?'

'Might as well.'

Calliden pushed the jump slide lever. There was a sickening, skipping lurch. The warp engine fell silent. Stars appeared on the main viewscreen. They were different from before. And the vague nebulosity, the misty swirl of light which had been visible from above the atmosphere of Apex V, seemed much bigger and brighter.

Swivelling the pilot's seat, Calliden turned to confront his abductor. 'All right, I've done the job for you.'

'I've done the job for *you*,' Rugolo countered. 'I've cured you of your phobia. Aren't you going to thank me?'

'Thank you for what? For forcing me to abandon my mother?'

Rugolo waved his hand dismissively. 'Are you still clinging to that?' he retorted. 'I've explained to you! It wasn't your mother. It was a warp daemon, or else something in your mind. You've got to forget it.'

Calliden's face looked haunted. 'Perhaps. But I still believe it was my mother, even if she's gone for good, now that I've forsaken her. Do you realise what that means? When we die we all go into the warp.' He shuddered, and his next words were agonised. 'What's the good of being alive, if that's what's in store for us?'

'You'll get over it,' Rugolo told him impatiently. 'You'll see it my way. Where are we, by the way?'

'By the nearest star I could find.' Calliden glanced at the instruments behind him. 'We're closer to the Eye than before. Right on the edge of it, in fact. This system has fifteen planets, one inhabited, though with only a small population. Nominally in the Imperium, though not appointed a planetary commander. It's called Caligula. A frontier world.'

'Sounds interesting. Take us there.'

Obediently Calliden turned back to the board. Privately Rugolo was smiling to himself. He had found a navigator.

Calliden set a course. With a cough and a roar, the realspace motor burst into life. They sped towards the planet Caligula.

FOUR
STRANGE GOODS

THEIR LANDING on Caligula, fifth planet of a star bearing only a number on the Imperial charts, was unusual for anyone versed in the ways of the Imperium. No planetary defences were in evidence. No voice came through the communicator demanding identification, or challenging their right to visit, or warning that a laser cannon was already trained on the ship. There was not even the personal clarion call of the local Imperial Commander – a strange omission indeed. It was as though the world below, with its shining white clouds basking in the light of its brilliant sun, was virgin and untouched by man.

Which was not quite the case, though the planet was far from being densely populated. Only when Pelor Calliden took the *Wandering Star* down into the atmosphere and went soaring over the landscape did a number of medium-sized settlements reveal themselves.

'Find the biggest one,' Rugolo said. They landed outside a straggling township on the shore of a storm-tossed ocean. It did not even boast a spaceport, only a large rolling expanse of bare earth which was scorched and blasted by the propulsion motors of vessels which had landed and taken off there previously. A few of these littered the field at present, battered and scored, pressing their landing legs into the earth. There were also some which would plainly never take off again – turned on their sides, half-crushed, dragged to the side of the field and left to rot. Calliden grinned when he saw these.

'Pilots are used to setting down on adamantium, or at least hardened concrete,' he said. 'This field isn't even levelled. It's like landing on a hillside. Looks like some people forgot what they were doing.'

'Probably too drunk,' Rugolo muttered. Ruefully he recalled times when he too had been obliged to land his ship on an uneven surface and had nearly come to grief.

There was no customs shed, indeed no administration buildings of any kind, only a dirt track that led into the town. Calliden sighed and shook his head. 'Don't they care at all who comes here?'

'Obviously not. Just the sort of place I like! Let's go outside and have a look.'

They clambered down to the main hatch, which Rugolo slammed shut. He took some care over the way he engaged the locks. There were no guards here, and therefore no protection against thieves – or worse, shipjackers. Then he climbed down the ladderway and joined Calliden on the ground.

The navigator looked on with horror as the trader turned away. 'No, no, by all that's holy! You've got to do more than that!'

He almost pushed his companion aside in his hurry to reach the rune-plate at the foot of the ship and place his right palm on the inlaid protective sigil. Closing his eyes, he intoned a prayer, while Rugolo stood by with a cynical smile. Finishing the rite, the navigator turned to him with a sigh.

'No wonder you're such a failure! You don't do anything at all to bring yourself good fortune!'

Rugolo shrugged.

The two looked around them. The sky was light blue, streaked with white cloud at a great height. The air was warm and balmy, and had a resinous smell to it. A light wind was blowing.

For once the *Wandering Star* did not look out of place. More than a few of the ships on the ground had an improvised look, as though they had been bolted together from pieces of other ships – which was probably the case. What there was of the traditional ornate decoration was crushed and distorted, the warding gargoyles, in some cases, absent altogether. The whole impression was definitely edge-of-the-Imperium. A frontier. And yet it was deep inside Segmentum Obscurus, one of the five Segmentae Majoris into which the Imperium was divided. The Eye of Terror was a frontier all of its own.

Then Rugolo's gaze chanced on a ship near the outer limit of the field that was like no other he had ever seen. The first astonishment was its colour – not the dull scored and pitted grey-and-black of any other craft that travelled in space, but a pearly white, iridescent with shimmering hues. It was as though the ship had passed through a rainbow and become smeared with its colours. It was hard to understand how such a display could withstand the rigours of space.

The second novelty was its shape – not the heavy and crenellated bolts-and-rivets of any other spaceship. This was sleek, as if cast in a mould, and elongated. It looked like some elegant flying animal about to leap into the air.

Following his gaze, Calliden became tense. He spoke in a hushed tone.

'That can't be an Imperium ship! It must be… alien. There are aliens here! Maynard, perhaps we should leave.'

Rugolo smiled again. Having just overcome his very worst fear, Calliden was now willing to go into the warp again rather than face an alien life-form. True, for the average person the prospect was frightening in the extreme. Aliens – all aliens – were mankind's mortal enemies.

'Take courage, friend. I've talked with aliens and survived.'

They set their faces towards the settlement. Ahead of them lay a sprawl of hastily erected metal structures and large tents whose coverings flapped in the breeze.

It was a shanty town, which they approached along a single dirt road. Calliden paused and had to be urged on at the first sight of the inhabitants who passed to and fro, rough, hard-looking men who cast feral glances, clad in a motley variety of costumes, weapons not holstered but carried in the hand or thrust casually into clothing, as if ready to use at the slightest provocation. There was no sign of law here, no arbitrators or police. If there was an Imperial Commander at all, he was probably resident on another planet, taking little interest in the lawless world he nominally ruled. Instead it was left to adventurers, hunters, freelance miners – and possibly, pirates.

Rugolo had a good feeling about this place. He felt a premonition that he would find business here. Not that he had much to trade with.

Calliden had once more put synthskin over his warp eye. He still did not like to be recognised as a navigator. He shrank nervously as they strode up the dusty track. This was not the orderly, fairly safe Gendova he had grown accustomed to.

Rugolo glanced at the ribbed or corrugated sheet metal which had been used to throw the shacks together. Some of it, he saw, came from the industrialised worlds of the Imperium; that was easy to spot, for Imperium metal-forgers could rarely resist stamping a piece of bare metal with some image or other – baroque designs, banners, flags, reliefs of cowled adepts or hideous beasts, or helpful runes. Whoever had built the shacks had little regard for any of this. Sometimes the decorations were sideways or upside down, which drew displeased frowns from Calliden.

Rugolo made an attempt to cheer him. 'Well, I don't see any aliens yet!'

They came to where an awning cast a shade. Over it was a banner with a legend: *DRINKS-SMOKES-STUFF.*

It was the entrance to a drab red marquee. A hubbub of conversation came from within. Peering inside, Rugolo saw a large space about the size of some minor cathedral of the Cult of Emperor. Parts of the overreaching canvas roof had been opened to admit air and sunlight. Tables and chairs had been laid out. On the further side a long bar had been set up, composed of empty crates.

The marquee was filled with men and women drinking, smoking herbs of various kinds, or simply talking. As in the dirt street outside, the people were dressed in ways which would have made some of them subject to arrest in many parts of the Imperium. Rugged-looking men in heavy, durable clothing, frequently torn or muddy, were probably prospectors or miners. Others, mostly women, wore flamboyant, even indecent garments, while others again wore almost nothing, dressed in rags.

Rugolo touched his companion on the arm. 'This looks like the place to find out what's going on.'

They went inside. At the bar, it was something of a relief to find that almost any kind of money was accepted. He had been in places where the local Imperial ruler, quite illegally, decreed all trade to be in his own local money, making a profit on the currency exchange. Rugolo bought two mugs of a watery, evil-smelling brew which he brought to the table. From its gingery taste, he guessed it was made from some vegetable root. Calliden sipped his with distaste and played nervously with his mug. It was plain he felt intimidated by the company around them.

Rugolo had left his plastic gun behind and instead had a lethal needle gun and a small laspistol hidden on his person. He had found it an advantage to show no visible weapons. It made people wary of him once they knew he was a trader. It was always assumed that a merchant would be armed.

'Why are we here?' Calliden asked plaintively.

'That business on Apex V left me low in both trade goods and money. I need to build up my business, without interference – informally, so to speak – before I have the wherewithal to enter a more regular trade. Sometimes one can pick up valuable items quite cheaply in a place like this.'

While speaking Calliden had been casting his bland, sun-reddened face about the drinking hall. Suddenly he stopped, his jaw dropping.

'What by His Mightiness is *that?*'

He was staring at a figure leaning nonchalantly against the bar, surveying the general scene with glittering eyes. Taller than most men and slender, the figure had a head that was partly ovoid, partly angular, as if moulded by a whimsical sculptor, and it wore a fixed, supercilious expression. The figure was humanoid, but not human. It was not even organic. It was a machine, but not one made by the hand of man. An electric-blue cloak covered it. Beneath that could be seen a pearl-grey sheen.

'A robot,' Calliden said, staring openly.

Rugolo let out his breath slowly. 'Not one made by human hand.'

Calliden realised that he was right. The mechanical creatures of the sacred Adeptus Mechanicus were clumsy, clanking beasts of burden with little intelligence, most often used as bomb-carrying cannon fodder. This machine-creature was a thing of grace and beauty, and it had an air of self-assurance about it.

'So there are aliens here,' he said in a tremulous voice.

But Rugolo had already left the table. He strode to the bar to confront the robot. He could see at once that its body-shell was neither metal nor plastic, but some other glistening material. A shiver of excitement went through him. What might this robot be worth on more civilised worlds!

He had to look up at the mysterious construct to speak to it. 'Who owns you?' he said in a quiet but demanding voice.

After a pause, the answer came, in a distant, ghostly voice, as if from someone talking in his sleep.

'Whoever can overcome me will own me. No one else.'

It was a more intelligent answer than a human-made robot could ever have given. In the human world an artificial brain would never have been able to manage such enigmatic phrasing.

He returned to the table. 'It's alien, all right,' he muttered to Calliden.

'What sort of aliens?'

'I don't know, but...' Rugolo swallowed hard, looking around him again as if searching for them, whatever they were. 'Have you ever heard of 'eldar'?'

'Are they anything to do with orks?'

Rugolo shook his head. To most people, an alien was just an alien. Ask the average person for the name of any particular alien race, and 'orks' was the answer one got, if any.

He began to explain in a low, hurried voice, glancing up at the robot every so often. 'I'm not sure myself if they are real or mythical, but the eldar are said to be an ancient non-human race adept at making robots. The way I heard it, every eldar wears a special gemstone on his breast. It's a spirit stone, which absorbs the wearer's experiences. When the eldar dies, the stone contains his spirit. It can be put in a machine or robot and is able to animate it. In that way the eldar comes back to life again, usually in order to fight in a battle or something.'

He stopped, searching his mind. 'There's a word for these spirit-animated fighting robots: *wraithguards*.' He nodded his head towards the figure at the bar. 'I think that might be a wraithguard.'

Calliden stared at the humanoid machine, revulsion contorting his pale features. 'Alien arts – disgusting! It even *looks* evil, just like that ship at the spaceground! You see how different it is from the holy work of our tech-priests, imbued as that is by the sacred light of the Emperor. Why, I'll bet those aliens have to invoke daemons to make anything function at all!'

'Yes, I expect so,' Rugolo responded absently. He had to admit that both the robot and the coloured spaceship looked very strange, even sinister, but he had been exposed to alien tech-arts several times before, and was less inclined to be religious about the subject.

Just the same he was far from sure of his own explanation. The wraithguard, if that was what it really was, was neither armoured nor armed. Also it bore no markings, and he had heard that eldar society was elaborately colourful. In any case, what was it doing on a human world? He remembered something else he had heard: the spirit in a wraithguard lived a dreamlike, almost somnambulistic existence. Perhaps it had somehow wandered away from where it belonged, got lost or had been abandoned.

He didn't believe the robot's claim to have no owner. How it had ended up in Caligula was a mystery in itself, but it could not possibly have survived among humans without becoming enslaved. Someone must have control over it.

At that moment someone sidled up to the wraithguard, muttered to it briefly, and stood close by with a proprietorial air, giving Rugolo a single questioning glance. He was a small, middle-aged human with a mild round face, lined as if with habitual anxiety, his eyes an affable blue. His apparel was simple: a cerise singlet, blue doublet, and a pale green beret peaked at the front.

Rugolo rose once more to approach the stranger, and spoke politely, but with the tone of one accustomed to being given an answer. 'Are you the owner of this machine?'

Smiling, the other shook his head and pointed to the further end of the long bar. There, invisible until a knot of people moved out of the way, was another extraordinary figure, lounging against the counter in exactly the same way as the wayward wraithguard. This alone drew Rugolo's attention to him. Robots were nothing if not imitative, and the eldar machine would most likely ape its master.

Attentively Rugolo fixed his gaze on him. He was about the same height as the robot, but there the resemblance ended. The man was of stick-like thinness. Stiff black hair stuck up like fire-blasted wheat from his narrow skull. His clothing was also

black, but tatty and crumpled, and it stuck to his skinny frame
as if it had not been removed for years. As for his face, it was
wild – the eyes staring, the bony nose jutting from between sal-
low cheeks, ears jutting out from either side of his head as
though they had been glued there as an afterthought.

More extraordinary than his appearance was his behaviour.
He appeared to be haranguing the people around him, though
they took absolutely no notice: gesticulating jerkily, bending
his angular body this way and that as if demented, which possibly he was. Rugolo rose and made towards him through the
throng. As he came nearer he heard the man's words through
the hubbub, spoken in a strident tone as if he addressed not
those around him but instead was conducting an inner mono-
logue.

'Have I not discovered the roots of my desire? You who hear
me, do you not see that all is but a plain dish and a nothingness? No, because you have not been where I have been. You
have not seen the roots of my desire! You have not seen... You
have not seen.'

He paused to drink deeply from a tankard he had been waving in his right hand. The brew seemed to disappear with
extraordinary rapidity into his narrow mouth and down into
his stomach without the necessity of his swallowing. He
belched, then continued his nonsensical tirade.

'None can know the roots of my desire. None who has not
been there! Is that not so, my dearest one? Tell him of the
roots!'

As he spoke, he flung out an arm to indicate a young woman
sitting by herself nearby, her arms resting on a table. She smiled
up at Rugolo and licked her lips.

As soon as he set eyes on her, Rugolo received an impression
of seductive wildness that was almost vampiric. She had a
round, smooth face which for all its prettiness reminded him
of some cat-like beast. Her hair was jet black and slicked down.
Her eyes were green and oval, and rarely blinked, giving her a
hypnotic staring quality. Her costume consisted of a brief
basque of dark blue, revealing her full figure and smooth,
plump limbs. As she leaned on the table he could see how full
her rump was, pressing down on the seat.

He started back, startled. The girl rose and stepped to him.
Her movements were lithe. Still smiling, she raised a hand and

drew her fingernail down the side of his neck. The sensation sent a jolt of pleasure through him. He found himself unable to meet her steady, gaze, and shuffled away from her touch.

In a thrilling contralto, she spoke. 'My name is Aegelica. What is yours?'

'Maynard Rugolo,' he responded gruffly. Then he turned to the tall black-clad man, whose face, seen close up, was flaky and whorled, as though he suffered from an affliction of the skin.

'I'm told you own that robot I see standing down the bar.'

The tall stranger turned to give Rugolo an unnerving stare.

'Ah, the wraithguard! My friend and colleague, Kwyler, gave out the information, no doubt, and without even charging for it! Always too generous, always too loose with his tongue!'

So it was a wraithguard. Rugolo was disappointed that the man knew the origin of the machine. He had been hoping to acquire it for a trifling fraction of its real value. Not that he was giving up yet.

'I have seen its like a few times before,' he said offhandedly. 'Generally they are not worth much. As servants they are useless. Also they are apt to break down a good deal, and no one in the Imperium knows how to repair them. They are Eldar-made. Still, I know where I can dispose of it as a curiosity, and would be willing to take it off your hands.'

'Aha! You hope to cheat an honest trader! By the roots of my desire! I should squeeze your giblets and make wine of your gall! Is he not a man of deceit and treachery, my darling Aegelica, my slaking of deepest desires?'

Aegelica's green eyes were on Rugolo, seeming to pierce him with their emerald stare. 'He is indeed nothing but lies and plots and manipulations, my dearest Gundrum. I see them laid out in his mind like an evil map. He thinks that we are but simpletons, being far from the great cities and worlds where men swarm like ants. He thinks that for a few coins, for a few baubles, for a few pleasant words, he can take from us the wraithguard and all the rest of our hard-won treasures. In truth he could not raise the wraithguard's value even if he were to sell all that he possesses and then sell his soul into the bargain too. But then a soul is a little thing, worth less than a pebble on a beach.'

All the while that she spoke in her enchanting voice, Aegelica continued smiling at Rugolo, as if she loved him and wanted only to please him. At first Rugolo was entranced. Then he shook himself and laughed.

'I can see that I have met my match!' he congratulated, and turned back to Gundrum. 'So you are a trader, too?' he said.

'We would not sell you the wraithguard even if you had its price,' Gundrum told him, in a more friendly tone. 'It is destined for the palace of the Imperial Commander, to become one of his pets. It is his hobby to have exotic and beautiful animals roaming freely about his spacious halls. The wraithguard will look well among them.'

'I see. I confess I am curious to know where you got it.'

'I am sure you are.'

Gundrum was looking over Rugolo's shoulder. Turning, Rugolo saw what had attracted his attention. Three men had advanced on Pelor Calliden and surrounded his table, leaning over him, mouthing something at him. One was bull-necked and burly, a heavy pistol of some sort thrust into his belt, his hairy chest bared. His two companions were smaller and raffish-looking, the sort Rugolo had seen on countless planets, usually making a living as thieves or hired murderers. Calliden looked terrified, especially when one of the latter pulled his head up by his hair and placed the edge of a knife at his throat.

Gundrum suddenly raised his voice and shouted in a language unknown to Rugolo.

'*H'k cuwhaiole! Aeilreowth shuwele-ha!*'

Swift as a snake-creature on some death-world, the eldar wraithguard moved into action. Its electric-blue cloak swept behind its shoulders like the wings of an eagle as it leaped to the table, revealing in full the glittering beauty that was its naked form. First of all it seized in one hand the wrist holding the blade which threatened Calliden. There was an audible snap as the bones of the forearm, both ulna and radius, broke, and a cry of pain as the ruffian fell back, hand dangling, knife clattering to the floor.

The bare-chested leader of the trio was not slow. He yanked his weapon, a slug gun, from his belt and managed to get in a shot. The heavy metal bullet ricocheted off the robot's pearly casing without leaving a dent. By then the pistol was in the wraithguard's grasp. It closed its fist. Fragments and shards, all that remained of the gun, tinkled to the tabletop. Moving like a dancer, the eldar machine seized the weapon's owner, turned him upside down, and brought his head down with force on the stone floor.

The third assailant had already fled, along with his injured friend. Calmly the wraithguard returned to the bar and lounged against it as before, surveying the scene. The man Gundrum had called Kwyler had disappeared.

Rugolo had been pushing his way through the crowd. Now he reached the shaking Calliden, looking down on the unconscious form slumped on the floor.

'What did they want?'

Calliden shrugged. 'They'd run out of money for drink, that's all.'

Gundrum strolled up and watched as the body was dragged through the door and dumped in the dirt of the street. No one bothered to check whether the bare-breasted man was still breathing.

Rugolo now noticed distinct circular lines round the wraithguard's wrists. He realised that its hands were detachable, probably so they could be replaced with weapons.

He turned to Gundrum. 'You must be getting a very good price for your property. Not only is it unusual to look at, you'll be losing an excellent bodyguard.'

'Rarity always commands a good price. Is that not the supreme dictum of we who buy and sell?' Gundrum challenged. 'Though, my friend, in this region the *rare*, the *special*, are not always as rare and special as you might think, for I would say you come from more orderly parts, or you would not have left your companion defenceless.'

'Yes, well... Where did you get the wraithguard?'

He had not expected any answer to his question, but Gundrum gestured him to a canvas flap near the end of the bar.

'You wish to trade? There is a more private place...'

With a nod to the barman he led them through the flap and into a small compartment made of a fabric so thick that no sunlight penetrated it, so that it had to be lit by a lamp on a hook. Ushering Calliden in ahead of him, Rugolo glanced round to see the cat-faced girl following them.

He held the door open for her. Her bosom pressed against him as she squeezed through.

As soon as they were seated, the strange trader became direct. 'You have a ship?'

Rugolo nodded.

'You wish to buy?'

'It depends what you have.'

'Oh, you will want what we have. But what will you buy it with?'

Rugolo thought of the small hoard of trade goods in his hold. A few weapons, some ornaments, some odds and ends. And of his limited amount of currency. It had been some time since he had possessed any real amount of working capital. That was why he had been working, in effect, as a lowly merchantman, transporting other people's goods for a modest payment – a humiliating come-down, which had ended in his landing at Gendova with a cargo of rotting peach-apples. Just the same, he sensed a tantalising opportunity here.

So Gundrum's next words were music to his ears. 'We may be able to help one another. You think of me as a rough, uncouth frontiersman, do you not? But no, it is you who is ignorant and untutored. It is you who is from the wilderness, from deep in the Imperium where everything is stultified by laws, laws and more laws! From here on, one becomes free! From here, one travels off the Imperial charts, to far, strange, distant places. There, I found the roots of my desire. There, I became changed. *Everything* is changed there!' He leaned closer to Rugolo. His voice dropped to a low, conspiratorial tone. 'Even space is different.'

Rugolo frowned his puzzlement. 'Space can't be different,' he said. 'It's the same everywhere.' His frown cleared. 'Do you mean the big warp-storm? The Eye of Terror? It's not space that's different. It's the Immaterium. It forms a big vortex.'

Gundrum was half-crazed, he reminded himself. He didn't know the difference between realspace and the warp. He had probably misunderstood remarks made by his navigator.

Navigator. Where did someone as mentally deranged as Gundrum seemed to be acquire one of those?

He put the thought out of his mind. Aegelica had not joined them at the table. Instead she stood behind Rugolo. Now she placed her hands on his shoulders and began to massage them gently. A feeling of pure pleasure suffused through him, sending him into a trance. For a moment he seemed to go spinning through a dark tunnel and was robbed of his will. Then, with a gasp, he broke away from her, his chair scraping on the floor.

He looked up at her, then at Gundrum. Calliden, he noticed, was looking on with a blank expression on his face.

'Is *she* from the Eye, too?' Rugolo asked.

'Aegelica? She is my own, very dear sister, who accompanies me on all my journeys. It is she who pilots my spacecraft. She is changed, too, my dear sister Aegelica.'

'She is your pilot?' Calliden broke in, sounding mystified. 'But she isn't a navigator.'

An awkward silence was all the answer he got, until, after a long pause, Aegelica broke into sudden trilling laughter.

'Why do you wish to do business with a stranger you have only just met?' Rugolo asked suspiciously.

Gundrum laughed. 'A man without resources who tries to buy a wraithguard must be a good trader! Besides, you look like a man who is willing to take chances. Now here is what is at stake. My Aegelica knows a route into the Eye. But there is not much profit to be made bringing out goods from there and selling them in the fringe worlds. They will command a higher price elsewhere. Now I myself do not wish to trade deeper into the Imperium. It is unfamiliar to me. There are too many rules. I have no charter. Besides–' He twisted his peculiar form into a travesty of a shrug. 'There are too many priests, preachers and arbitrators. Anyone who looks the least bit odd receives their attentions, so I am told. You, however…'

Rugolo was feeling excited. What a piece of luck! His natural optimism began to soar like a bird. *I knew things would start looking up again*, he told himself. 'That's all very well,' he said calmly, hiding his feelings, 'but what sort of goods are we talking about?'

'You come directly to the point. By the roots of my desire, that is good. By the Byssos, by the Great Gods, by the greatest whirl of wonders this galaxy has seen, you must pass through reefs, through storms, you must twist and turn, and then you come to the universe of marvels which the gods have prepared, and there is our treasure-house. Within the Eye are more worlds than can be named. Upon those worlds are artisans, craftsmen, distillers of liqueurs: consummate, intricate, miraculous! What would the cognoscenti of the rich worlds of the Imperium not pay for them? I am tired of supplying our Imperial Commander with his toys. An Imperial Commander is only as wealthy as the planets he rules, and ours is therefore impoverished, having for subjects rogues and vagabonds.'

Aegelica moved aside, giving Rugolo a passing caress which sent shivers running through him. 'Let me show you one or two trinkets to reveal to you what I mean,' Gundrum said.

He shrugged something off his shoulder. Rugolo wondered why he had not noticed before that he carried a shoulder bag, as black as the ragged garments he wore. Then again, it clung so tightly to his form as to be almost invisible. Then, as he placed it on the table, it seemed to Rugolo that it expanded to several times its former size.

The trader from the Eye of Terror dipped his hand in the bag and brought out a box about the size of a large book. It was made of a reddish wood which gave off a faint perfume. As it was laid on the table Rugolo saw that it was decorated with relief carvings of what he presumed were imaginary beasts, or if not that then the denizens of some fabulous planet unknown to him. The carvings were very faint, however. They seemed to disappear and reappear as the box was moved.

With an air of deliberation, Gundrum lifted open the box's hinged lid. It seemed to exude a rosy glow, from which ascended a large moth-like creature, coloured red and orange. The moth began flitting about the room, and as it flew, it left a trail of golden light behind it in the air. Steadily the space of the room was filling with the criss-crossing luminous lines. At the same time, like the lighting of a candle, a feeling of contentment began to grow in Rugolo's chest. He felt that he could watch the fluttering moth forever, could wait until the whole room was one mass of glowing lines in which he was trapped. What then?

He saw a glaze in Calliden's eyes, and knew that he was experiencing the same. Not Aegelica, however. She was fidgeting and writhing, licking her lips, her face enraptured. She was feeling some different, more stimulating pleasure.

The expression of Gundrum's face revealed nothing. It was utterly impassive. With a snap he suddenly shut the box. The moth-like creature, together with the golden mesh it was creating, vanished at once.

'A pretty thing, is it not?' said Gundrum enticingly. 'An ideal after-dinner entertainment to offer some high-born lady. If one could mass-produce such a trinket, one would make a fortune.

The artisans of the Eye, unfortunately, work by hand, and tire of producing the same item over and over. Hence, rarity is the norm! Now take a look at this.'

He returned the box to the bag, then felt about in it before withdrawing another object, which he also placed on the table. It had the form of an ornate pagoda, tinselled and trimmed with multicoloured metal which flashed in the lamplight. It was considerably larger than the box with the moth in it. Rugolo wondered how he had managed to hide both in the black bag.

Discerning a movement within the pagoda, Rugolo and Calliden both leaned closer. There was indeed something going on inside it, a confused roiling and struggling, but the body of the pagoda was of frosted glass and it was not possible to see within it clearly. Rugolo then noticed that among the intricate decoration was a chute winding round the outside of the tower from top to bottom. It ended in a door in the shape of a gaping fanged mouth.

The thing was a toy helter-skelter. As he watched, a tiny doll-figure emerged on to the platform which surrounded the crown of the tower like the brim of a hat. It looked for all the world like a real miniature human being, a man dressed in motley red and green clothing. Rugolo marvelled at the craftsmanship which had gone into the manikin, if it was not a holographic projection, which it did not seem to be. Almost immediately it went sliding down the chute, arms and legs waving, face staring up, its features distorted in utter panic. It seemed to be yelling something.

As soon as it reached the bottom it was swallowed up by the fanged mouth. Its place was taken by a female figure which also went sliding down the helter-skelter, yellow gown billowing, legs kicking, arms raised imploringly, shouting and grimacing like the first. More manikins followed: men, women, children, struggling, writhing, screaming as they followed one another down the chute in a seemingly endless procession.

'A story accompanies the toy,' Gundrum explained. 'A gruesome tale to tell one's children.'

'Maybe another time,' Rugolo mumbled, horrified.

Reluctantly Gundrum replaced the pagoda. Mystifyingly it made barely a hump under the folds of black cloth. 'Would you care for a taste of this liqueur? Men would sell their daughters for a bottle of this.'

This time the bag produced a small cask-shaped container of ribbed glass, and four tiny cups, hardly bigger than acorns. Placing these on the table, Gundrum unstopped the bottle, and very, very carefully poured measured amounts into the cups. The fluid which oozed into them was thick and syrupy, and seemed reluctant to leave the bottle. It almost seemed alive, or electric, sparkling and effervescing as it flowed, first amber, then scarlet, going on to an ever-changing succession of colours. Even when it had settled in the little glasses it continued to seethe and change colour.

Gundrum lifted his glass to his thin lips, took a quick swallow, then set it down again. Aegelica did the same. Neither of them showed any reaction. Rugolo and, a little more reluctantly, Calliden followed their example.

Rugolo had intended to take no more than a sip at first, but somehow the slug of liqueur spilled as one big drop into his mouth. It felt as though a flavour bomb was slowly exploding on his tongue. Fleetingly everything he had ever tasted he experienced over again, bringing a delirious rush of past memories. First of all the taste of every liqueur he had ever drunk, then other beverages, then delicious cold drinks, iced confectioneries, delicacies, expensive foods.

It was all over in a moment. He did not remember swallowing. The liqueur seemed to pour itself down his throat of its own volition, as if eager to get to his stomach. Then a savage jolt like an electric shock went through him, releasing a surge of exhilaration which blew through him like a roaring wind. He went quite rigid.

Then it was over. Rugolo relaxed, letting out an ecstatic sigh. 'It's wonderful!' he breathed.

Calliden was looking even paler than before.

At that moment the door-flap was shoved open. A burly man strode into the room, taking in the scene at a glance. He seemed angry, and had an air of pent-up energy. Like many on Caligula, his clothing was torn and dirty, as if getting dressed was an afterthought. His blond hair was shorn close to his skull, the skin showing through the bristles.

He looked down at the cask-shaped bottle, at the tiny glasses, at the black bag. He opened his mouth, revealing large ragged teeth.

'What are you doing, Gundrum? Why was I not told of this?'

Hunched over the table, Gundrum looked up at the intruder, his body bending in apparently impossible places. 'Making contacts, Foafoa! Making contacts! Why do you fret?'

The big man bent, rudely looking straight into Rugolo's face, then into Calliden's. Rugolo got the same uncomfortable feeling he had from Aegelica, of having his character inspected in a way no normal person could.

Then a big beefy fist was shaken in front of his nose. 'You are after our secrets! You want to get into the Eye! You want to take our trade!'

Aegelica chuckled. 'And what would that avail him, Foafoa? How many merchant adventurers has the Eye swallowed up? Many have gone in. How many have come out? Only Gundrum and myself.

'Of course,' she added in a teasing tone, 'I could always decide to offer him my services. Where would you and Gundrum be then?'

Foafoa growled. He rounded on Rugolo again. 'Stay out of the Eye, do you hear me? That's our business.'

'I've no intention at all of going there,' Rugolo said, trying to sound as though he meant it. 'It's not possible to navigate there, is it?'

As soon as the words were out of his mouth he regretted them. He had unthinkingly revealed his true thoughts. Gundrum and Aegelica had succeeded in going in and coming out again. Therefore it was possible. And what one person had done, another could do. And look what delightful trade goods could be obtained there! Probably quite cheaply, though Gundrum had not explained what he used to pay for them. It would be much better to obtain these goods at source, if at all possible. If he simply acted as Gundrum's go-between he would realise only a small fraction of their value.

Frantically he tried to suppress this line of reasoning. This Gundrum was not a fool. Any trader worth his salt was adept at guessing what another was thinking. He could only hope that he and his sister were so confident of their secret route that they did not believe anyone else could find or use it.

'I should kill you now,' Foafoa said in an aggrieved tone, though he sounded a little mollified by what Aegelica had said. He turned to go.

And then it happened. Rugolo saw the back of his head smooth out, the cropped hair disappearing. The skin puckered, and then formed itself into a second face, an ugly, dwarfish face with protruding lips and a snub nose, glaring out from the back of Foafoa's skull and grimacing at Rugolo as if trying to attract his attention. A high, squeaky, chattering voice came from it, a shrill voice of panic: 'No, no, no! Don't go! Don't go! No, no, no, don't go!'

It was still screeching at him as Foafoa went through the door, closing it behind him. No one else gave any sign of having seen the apparition or of hearing the voice. Rugolo shook his head, trying to clear it. He couldn't believe what he had seen. It was a hallucination, he decided, brought on by the liqueur. A powerful potion, indeed.

Gundrum scooped up both bottle and cups and returned them to the bag.

Rugolo could not contain himself. 'I need hardly point out,' he said slowly, 'that the bag you carry is hardly large enough to contain everything you have taken out of it. Or put back into it'

'This?' Gundrum picked the bag up. Its silky material contracted as he did so, folding in on itself, until it was no more than a slip of cloth smaller than a handkerchief, which he tucked into a side pocket.

'The Eye of Terror has clever weavers, too,' he said, his small mouth pursing in the suggestion of a smile. 'Now, here is something else for you.'

Dipping into the same pocket, he displayed in the palm of his hand a number of small crystals or gemstones. They were pale blue in colour, translucent but otherwise unremarkable. Rugolo picked one up, inspecting it. It was not an amethyst or anything he recognised.

'Are they valuable?'

'Not as gems. They are dream jewels. Put this under your pillow at night, and what you dream of can become real.'

Rugolo was disappointed. 'That's all it is? A good luck charm?'

'No, no, you misunderstand. It really does make material objects out of dreams. A wonderful device to give a child. It might dream of some marvellous toy, game, or whatever it desires – and there it will be at the bottom of the bed in the morning. Is that not miraculous?'

'Certainly, if true,' Rugolo said doubtfully. He was trying to imagine what kind of technical art could make such a thing possible.

'Try it. Take that one with you.'

Gundrum motioned to his sister. Silently, the two left the canvas room.

Holding the gem up to the lamplight, Rugolo tried to examine it more closely. But it still seemed unremarkable. The light filtered through it as it might any uncut precious stone or lump of crystal. Perhaps there were two or three shadowy patches in it, which normally he would have thought of as flaws. He put it away in the purse he carried inside his jerkin.

The pair emerged back into the drinking hall. Gundrum and Aegelica were gone, along with the eldar wraithguard. Foafoa was skulking along the other end of the bar, talking with Kwyler.

Rugolo sent Calliden to the bar for two more tankards of the evil-tasting brew. Before the navigator had had time to return, he became aware of someone else sidling into the seat beside him.

He looked sidewise. It was an elderly man whose face was half hidden by a swathe of cloth which went over his head like a burnoose, such as he had seen worn by those living in very hot deserts. Rugolo could see why. Close up, it was possible to glimpse behind the burnoose. The left half of the man's face seemed to have melted, the flesh to have run like molten lead. Otherwise he wore a plain tabard and leggings.

Making no apology for his presence, the man spoke directly. 'Do not travel off the charts. You will regret it, most seriously.'

'What makes you think I intend to do that?'

'I have lived here a long time. I am used to seeing men like you, looking for profit. I have seen them fall to temptation. If you travel into the galactic whirlpool, you will lose your souls. The worlds of the Eye are infested with daemons. Do not go there.'

Rugolo said, 'Have you been there?'

He received no answer. The man stood up quickly, as though the question frightened him, and strode off.

Calliden returned with the tankards. Thoughtfully, Rugolo drank.

FIVE
THE DREAM GEM

'So what do you think, Pelor?'

They were back in the *Wandering Star*. Rugolo was rolling the blue gemstone around his palm and grinning. 'I'm going to dream of a slave girl!'

Calliden was shocked. 'You're not going to try it!'

'Of course. We have to test our merchandise, don't we?' He held the jewel up to the light and squinted through it thoughtfully. 'This gem is not unique. Gundrum had several of them. Perhaps we could acquire a bulk load. We're in luck, Pelor! I sense riches!'

'Don't meddle in arcane powers!'

'Oh, don't worry,' Calliden assured him. 'If it works at all I expect it just makes your dreams more vivid, or something, like making you have the same dream twice but stronger the second time. That would be like having a dream come true, wouldn't it?'

'You should be more careful,' Calliden warned him glumly. 'I sense magic. As for riches, somehow I don't imagine that peculiar character Gundrum will leave us much of a profit margin. His sister unnerves me too. Didn't you notice her interest in you?'

Rugolo had to admit that Aegelica's attentions had made him uneasy. She had been playing with him, no doubt of that. It gave him the sense of being a hapless prey hypnotised by a predator. He wasn't sure he would be able to resist her advances for any length of time, in spite of how strange they made him feel. Still, he didn't intend to let matters reach that stage.

'We'll make our own profit margins.' he said confidently. 'Can you follow a ship through the warp, Pelor?'

'You're not thinking of trailing Gundrum?'

'Why not? There's a trade route to be discovered.'

'The Astronomican is weak out here. We could get lost. Or more probably get blown out of space for our pains. That trade route, as you call it, is those people's secret. You've seen how much they want to guard it.'

'That's a chance we'll have to take.'

'I don't like it. And I don't think you should use that jewel.'

Rugolo tossed the gem in the air and caught it again. 'Well, I'll tell you in the morning if anything happened.'

It seemed there was nothing Calliden could do. He left the cabin, retiring to his quarters.

Rugolo prepared to settle down. He pulled off his outer garments, lay down on the pallet on the floor and pulled a padded blanket over him for cover. The uncut gem he placed under his pillow.

He didn't expect anything particularly remarkable. However, he fell asleep with unusual swiftness. And sometime during the night, he began to dream.

Usually Rugolo's dreams were confused and dim, and he remembered little on waking. Now, for once, they were vivid and full of wish-fulfilment. He was on the bridge of what had been his father's flagship, and was now his flagship. In echelon around the flagship were all the other vessels in the retinue, fully manned and equipped. He was a successful Rogue Trader, fully accredited in his own right, with more than thirty years' experience. Currently, as so often in the past, he had gone far beyond the range of the Astronomican, like the adventurers of those wild and heady days of millennia before, when there was no Astronomican, fearless and daring anything, pitting his wits as a man of the Imperium against all comers.

A planet swelled below them, mottled and coloured like a rotting fruit, glowing in the light of its sun. His outfit had discovered – not for the first time – an unknown alien civilisation that was beginning to develop space travel. Nuclear-tipped missiles arced up from the planet's surface. Rugolo's little fleet was about to engage in a war with an entire world, indeed with an entire alien species. Rugolo would win that war, of course, and would make off with his ships' holds filled with alien treasures, as well as data on the defeated world for which the Administratum would pay well…

The dream dissolved in a jumble of images, as dreams will. Rugolo was a boy again. He was visiting the house of his friend, the son of a wealthy noble family. In his bedroom he opened his toy chest and took out a casket, lavishly filigreed with rich workmanship. Words were carved on its sides: *KILL THE MUTANT! DESTROY THE ALIEN!*

Setting it on a table, he lifted the lid to reveal four model figures lying inside. Two were of Space Marines in full power armour, one crimson, one purple, blazoned with their chapter emblems. Of the other two, one was a grossly mutated human, head three times normal size, eyes, mouth, nose and ears all misplaced, as were the arms and legs. The other was a monstrous, black-tentacled creature with gleaming scythe-claws at the end of each limb. Both mutant and alien were ugly, vicious and wicked.

There were also two control units for animating the mechanised models as they were pitted against one another. How Rugolo had envied the spoiled rich boy his expensive toy! And of course, his friend always made him play either alien or mutant, and the game was cleverly engineered so that, with two players of equal skill, the Space Marines nearly always won; any other arrangement would have been bad for a child's education.

Now here he was playing with this fantastic toy again, only this time it belonged to him. It was he who was holding the Space Marine control in the palm of his hand, and the crimson-armoured Adeptus Astartes warrior's chainsword was disposing of the mutant, limbs detaching and flying everywhere. It was at that moment that he realised, with a sudden lucidity, that he was dreaming.

Sadness overcame him, a great feeling of loss. When he woke up he would lose his marvellous possession.

How to keep it?

Inspiration came to him. He placed the figures back in their casket. Then he willed himself to dream that he was lying in bed. He placed the casket at the foot of the bed.

Then he went to sleep.

MAYNARD RUGOLO opened his eyes to see that the chronopanel was signalling early morning at the settlement's Caligula longitude. The dream of being a boy was fresh in his mind. This was unusual for him. He rarely remembered his dreams.

He threw off the cover and sat up stretching himself, thinking of the day ahead. The Eye trader, Gundrum, was an oddball. He wasn't sure quite how to deal with him.

He was about to come to his feet when something at the end of the pallet caught his attention. It was a casket, richly filigreed. On the sides, in carved relief and painted silver, were words: *KILL THE MUTANT! DESTROY THE ALIEN!*

'Pelor!' he shouted urgently. 'Pelor. Come here, quick!'

Calliden appeared in seconds, alarm on his face. 'What's the matter?'

'Tell me in all seriousness: am I still dreaming?'

Perplexed, the navigator stared at him. 'Not unless I am too.'

'Look at this!' Rugolo lifted the lid of the casket, showing the exotic models within. 'I dreamed of this in the night. Now it's here, real!'

'You used the jewel?'

'Yes, I used it. It works!'

Calliden stepped forward and gingerly took one of the Space Marines from the casket, almost as if afraid it would burn him. Experimentally he moved the model's arms and legs.

'A child's toy,' he remarked blankly. 'Are you really sure it wasn't here before? Part of your cargo?'

'I'm certain. I haven't seen one of these since I was a boy.'

Calliden replaced the figure, then wiped his hand on his clothing as if it had become tainted.

'It's impossible,' he announced. 'It must be sorcery. The gem is making us see and touch things that aren't there. Get rid of it!'

Rugolo considered this. 'Well, let's put it to the test.'

He went to his pallet and retrieved the dream gem from beneath his pillow. 'I'll take this out of the ship, walk away with it and bury it. If what you say is right, the toy should disappear. A sorcerous delusion couldn't work at a very long range, I imagine.'

Swiftly he dressed, left the cabin, climbed out of the port and descending to the ground with the gem in his pocket. It was no more than an hour after dawn. Steam rose from the mossy plain surrounding the spaceground, a daily morning effect caused by the strong sunlight on damp plant-life.

He looked around him, allowing his gaze to rest on the painted spaceship parked some distance away. He knew now that it was Gundrum's ship. He had seen him and his party entering it the night before.

Walking away from the *Wandering Star* until he had reached what he judged to be a safe distance, he looked around to make sure he was unobserved before digging his heel into a soft patch of earth. He dropped the gem into the shallow depression, covered it with a large stone and walked back to the ship.

He entered the control cabin to find that Calliden had cleared a space on the table, and was manipulating the crimson-armoured Space Marine from the control unit, swinging the chainsword, making it step forward and back. The navigator started guiltily as Rugolo came in, hurriedly putting down the unit.

'I hid the gem almost a mile away,' Rugolo said with quiet satisfaction. 'And the toy is still here.'

Calliden gave a worried shake of his head. 'Materialising dream objects – how could it be possible? Not even the technomagi of Mars can do that.'

'Who cares?' Rugolo said feverishly. 'Perhaps the Mars magi *can* do it. People high up in the Adeptus Terra keep a lot of things to themselves. Or maybe it's a secret known to alien tech-priests. Gundrum found the wraithguard in the Eye, too, and that's alien. There's all sorts of stuff in there. It's a treasure-house, all unknown to the Imperium, and just because the navy hasn't the nerve to go in there! By the Emperor! What a find!'

'I don't believe any tech-priest could do it, human or alien,' Calliden said, his voice burdened. 'Daemons. Daemons might be able to do it. That's the only thing I can think of. Leave that gem where it is, Maynard.'

'Pelor, Pelor! There are no daemons! It's a story to frighten the ignorant with!'

Calliden's lips curled sardonically. 'That's a foolish attitude to take, if I may say so. The Navy commanders seem to be wiser. Not only is the Eye a warp-storm, the biggest in the known galaxy where navigation is impossible, it's also a place of mystery and evil if everything one hears is true.' He glanced at the casket and Space Marine. 'I think there might be dae-mons there.'

'People here on Caligula are trading with the Eye. Maybe the storm has quietened down or something. Gundrum and his sister know a way in and out, for a start.'

'Don't believe everything that Gundrum says. Neither he nor his sister are navigators, unless there's a new breed outside the Houses, which I don't believe for a moment. I suppose they could be doing four-light-year jumps without using a naviga-tor, but I don't believe that either. You can't get anywhere that way.'

'Four-light-year jumps.' Rugolo nodded thoughtfully. Navigators were taken so much for granted that one tended to forget that the navigator gene didn't occur among alien races, as far as he knew. They had no individuals who could see into the warp, without which only short warp-jumps were possible. Hence there was nothing to match the vast, glorious Imperium of mankind.

He dismissed the matter with an impatient wave of his hand. 'Negative thinking! That's no way to get rich!'

AFTER HIS EXPERIENCE the day before, Calliden was reluctant to visit the settlement again. Rugolo elected to go alone.

He retrieved the dream-gem and left the spaceground. Carts were passing down the dirt street of the settlement, hauled by beasts of burden with long matted fur and an ambling gait. The carts were filled with farm produce, traded, Rugolo guessed, for money or for goods brought in from elsewhere. From the Eye, perhaps?

He entered the same drinking hall as before and cast about for Gundrum. There was no sign of him or his sister, the rav-ishing Aegelica. There was no wraithguard, either. Neither, he was glad to note, was there any sign of the three who had molested Calliden the day before.

He strode to the bar and spoke to the barman. 'Where's Gundrum?'

The barman answered in an unfamiliar accent, offhandedly wiping his hands on a cloth 'Think you that I know the whereabouts of all? I serve drinks. I serve smokes. Have you money?'

Reluctantly Rugolo parted with a few coins for a tankard of evil-tasting brew. Gundrum was probably in his ship, he reflected, but knowing the ways of traders, there was no point in trying to visit him there. It was regarded as ill-mannered.

For the first time he spotted, seated at an empty table, the small man in the green beret and cerise singlet who had pointed out Gundrum to him the day before. After a moment he recalled his name: *Kwyler*.

He sauntered over and casually joined him.

'Remember me? I'm looking for Gundrum. I gather you know him.'

'Sure.' The man gave a lopsided smiled. 'I'm his partner.'

Rugolo raised his eyebrows. 'I didn't know he had a partner, except for his sister Aegelica. What's the nature of your partnership, exactly?'

He knew this was an impudent question. The stranger, however, did not seem offended.

'I go with him on his trips.'

'Indeed? Tell me, do they have a navigator? Gundrum said his sister does it, but that's hardly possible.'

The man laughed. 'Possible or not, Aegelica does it.'

'She doesn't have a warp eye…'

Rugolo fell silent, realising he had been making an assumption. Because Aegelica did not have the air of a navigator he had presumed she wasn't one. But she could be hiding a warp eye, as Calliden did.

'So… where's Gundrum now?'

'Delivering the eldar robot to the Imperial Commander's men, somewhere along the coast.'

'How did he come by that alien-built ship of his, the coloured one?'

'It isn't alien,' Kwyler grinned. 'He had it painted out in the Eye. For some reason its shape changed, too. Almost anything can change out there. It's a place of wonders, or perhaps I should say 'places'. It's huge. Bigger than the whole rest of the universe, some people say. Of course, that's an exaggeration.'

Rugolo was surprised at how ready Kwyler was to talk. Hadn't Gundrum criticised him for that? But despite his glowing description Kwyler's chirpy attitude seemed to be fading. He looked weary, and his words were forced. He glanced shiftily at the bar, then stealthily produced a coloured bottle from the shoulder bag he carried, and poured from it into a tiny goblet. He knocked the drink back with one toss of his head.

Ecstasy transformed his face. Rugolo recognised the liqueur Gundrum had given him the day before. He waited until the man seemed recovered before speaking again.

'Do you know what dream-gems are? I'm interested in getting some. A bulk load. Can you and Gundrum get them?'

'Gundrum can get them by the barrel-load, I expect, but what do you want to do with them? They're not as easy to sell in the Imperium as you might think. Stuff like that can bring the Inquisition down on your head.'

Rugolo smiled to himself. What Kwyler had said was certainly true in principle, but not in practice. There was a big demand for alien contraband in the Imperium, especially among the wealthier members of the Administratum, who hungered for the exotic.

And how much would the Adeptus Mechanicus pay for something that could produce matter out of nothing? Neither Gundrum nor the man he was talking to appeared to understand what the gems implied. To them, they were just curios.

'Will Gundrum be back today?'

'Gundrum is erratic. He changes his mind a lot. One day he'll go into the Eye and never come back, like all the others.'

A shadow fell across the table. The man with the half-melted face stood over them, the burnoose dangling on one shoulder. He stabbed a finger at Rugolo.

'You mean to go into the Eye! I can see it in your mind. You are a fool.'

He swept on before Rugolo could reply. Kwyler poured himself another slug of the liqueur. He smiled sourly. 'Another dissatisfied ex-partner of Gundrum's,' he said. 'He's giving you good advice, though. Forget about doing business with Gundrum. You don't want those dream-gems. And definitely forget about the Eye. Death is a blessing compared with what can happen to you there.'

He raised his goblet in a brief toast. 'Still, what's the good of talking to you? You don't believe me. That eager look you've got in your eyes, I've seen it before. Too many times. Me, I'm sick of the whole business.'

'Then why are you still in it?' Rugolo asked him.

'At first it was for adventure, and an easy way to make a living. But now...' He knocked back the liqueur again, and seemed to pass into another realm.

He's addicted to it, Rugolo thought.

Too many people were telling him not to go into the Eye. Rugolo was cynical about such warnings. Nobody around here acted from altruistic motives. If they were trying to frighten him off, that meant the Eye was a good place to go, and easier to deal with than they claimed.

'When Gundrum comes back tell him I want to talk to him,' he said.

Kwyler started mumbling. 'No, no, you don't want to see Gundrum. Gundrum is bad. He has crossed over. So has Aegelica. Has she been taking an interest in you? Watch out. It's all right for her and her brother. They're good at making agreements. Others end up like Foafoa. Go back to where it's safe! Space Marines. Emperor. Inquisition.'

The liqueur had obviously befuddled the little man's brain. Rugolo left him trying one more time, under the suspicious gaze of the barman, to pour from the clandestine bottle.

THAT NIGHT RUGOLO put the dream gem under his pillow again. He had been only partly joking when he had wished for a slave girl. Now that he knew it was possible, he willed himself to dream of one as he approached sleep.

As before, his dreams were unusually vivid. And at first he did dream himself into a harem, where scantily clad women danced and swayed to lilting music. Briefly he remembered that this was but a dream and told himself that one of the women would be his when he woke up. But then they all faded.

Now he was in a bazaar he had visited many years ago. It was on a very hot planet where life was only possible under air-conditioned domes and arcades. The cooled air currents made the canvas of the booths ripple. Occasionally a searing blast of hot air went blowing through the bazaar as one of the outer doors was opened, causing the cooling units to whine in protest.

Again Rugolo's dream was the fulfilment of a thwarted desire. Quite by accident he had come upon a memory-portrait in the form of a large enamelled brooch with a damascened frame. These were rare, made by some lost art, and few people even knew of their existence. In this case the portrait was of some high-born lady, though she must have lived centuries ago for the portrait was at least that old. She was in the bloom of her life, her oval face surrounded by dark curls, her large brown eyes regarding the beholder soulfully, her full bosom diaphanously clad in sensuously peach-coloured silk. As Rugolo gazed at the portrait, her memories came flooding into his mind. He glimpsed the life of the nobility, their great houses, their power, their wealth, their elegant social life. He felt he knew her friends as she knew them. He seemed to remember her upbringing, her childhood, her parents and grandparents. And what of the present? Who did she love now? The portrait artist could not, of course, reveal that. Yet there were hints, closed doors in her memory, which seemed to tell more than they were meant to conceal.

Unfortunately the stall-keeper knew the value of the brooch. Rugolo's attempt to buy it as cheap gewgaw met with no more than a patient smile. Rugolo offered more and more, until he had gone to more than he could actually raise, and still it was not enough. Rugolo had been forced to give up and go away in a fury, wondering if he dared come back later and steal the brooch – a question which contained its own answer, for the punishment of a thief on this harsh world was too terrible to think about.

Now, so many years later, he had a second chance. Once again the stallholder was demanding a price he could not pay, the same price he would expect to realise himself. So he hefted the portrait in his hand and thought fervently: *This is what I want.*

'Maynard! Wake up!'

Pelor Calliden's voice in his ear brought him out of the dream with a jerk. He opened his eyes and saw the *Wandering Star*'s cabin around him. Automatically he looked at the chronopanel. It was well after dawn. Calliden had dressed himself and was gesticulating nervously.

There was something small, hard and metallic in Rugolo's hand. He lifted it before his face, his eyes widening in wonder. A damascened frame, enamelled surface, oval face and soulful eyes! Already little flashes of imparted memory were flickering at the back of his mind.

Fully awake now, he drew a deep breath and held out the brooch for Calliden to see.

'Look, Pelor, look! I dreamt it! It's become real, just like the Space Marines game!'

The navigator glanced at the brooch. 'Very nice,' he said coolly. 'But I thought you might like to know that Gundrum's ship is readying for take-off.'

'*What?*'

Rugolo threw aside the pallet's covering and staggered to the main board. Calliden had already activated the viewscreen, rotating the view to where the rainbow ship was powering up, a steam-wreathed glow coming from its venturae.

Kwyler had said that Gundrum was erratic. Of course, Rugolo didn't know exactly what Kwyler's relationship with Gundrum was. Presumably Gundrum and his crew were going into the Eye to get more trade goods. If they expected to trade with Rugolo when they got back to Caligula they would be disappointed. Why buy from Gundrum if he could go to the source?

'Wait till he's gone,' he ordered Calliden. 'Then follow. Can you do that without him knowing?'

Calliden said calmly, 'I don't remember accepting employment with you.'

Rugolo groaned. He had been hoping to avoid this.

'You have your ability back, it's your duty to use it.' he said, hoping he sounded convincing. 'You're a navigator again. I suggest we team up together.'

'Not,' Calliden said firmly, 'if it means going into the Eye of Terror.'

'You know, you're too ready to be frightened by rumours,' Rugolo complained. 'The Eye isn't something supernatural – it's just a massive volume of space that's been hit by a warp-storm. Anyway, I don't believe for a moment that Gundrum is going deep into the Eye. He's found a planet on the fringe of it that trade goods find their way to, somehow, from the worlds inside. A world that nobody else knows about. He's on to something good, but he's too addle-brained to know it and he's not exploiting it properly. I'll show him what a real professional can do!'

Calliden ignored the boast. 'The trouble with you is, you've closed your mind to what evil forces exist in this galaxy of ours. Essentially, you lack imagination.'

The trader snorted. 'Listen, I've seen rather more of this galaxy than you have. I've seen aliens, visited worlds outside the Imperium. But I've never seen any daemons! And I don't believe they exist.'

'Not even the one you said was impersonating my mother?'

'Well, that was just–'

'To fool me?'

Rugolo shrugged off his embarrassment. 'Look, I'll grant the Emperor is a god, if you like. I can accept that. But nothing else.'

He paused. 'But for me, you wouldn't have recovered your navigator ability, and you can't be certain you're completely cured yet. You need me, and I'm not ready to go back to more civilised worlds yet. There's nothing for me there. I'm my father's son, a Rogue Trader, in spirit if not in fact. I vote for going on.'

Calliden licked his lips. He knew that Rugolo was playing on his sense of honour – applying moral blackmail, in fact. The trouble was that it was working. It was true what he had said. He had forced him to face up to his mother's ghost – if it was his mother. He had made a navigator of him.

On the viewscreen, the painted spaceship was suddenly enveloped in flame and superheated steam. A roar resounded through the hull of the *Wandering Star*. The vessel lifted off the ground, hovered above the field for a few moments, rotating idly as if turning in the wind, then jetted straight for the sky with a fading rumble.

'Make your mind up, Pelor!' Rugolo shouted. 'On to riches or back to defeat!' He was like a child looking forward to a special jaunt.

There was no time for reflection. Calliden could follow a trail through the warp if it was made recently enough, but tracking a ship through realspace to its jumping-off point was a different matter. The radiation from a realspace drive dispersed quickly.

He threw up his hands in resignation. 'Prepare for take-off.'

Rugolo grinned. While the trader strapped himself in, Calliden took the pilot's seat and immediately began warming up the prime mover. There was a hollow roar and a faint shiver ran through the ship's frame.

He took them surging into orbit, executing an outward spiral which took them steadily further from the surface of the planet. The painted ship had to be given time to get away, or Gundrum would quickly spot that it was being shadowed.

Before long the instruments detected the trail of ions, positrons and decay products revealing the recent passage of a realspace drive. Rugolo bent his head to the scryer, scanning ahead in the direction the trail took. A faint, moving spot appeared on it, picked out from the background of stars and receding rapidly.

'There it is. Gundrum's ship.'

Calliden nodded. 'We'll wait until it no longer shows.'

They now had the other ship's direction. It was following a shallow curve straight out of the system, at an angle from the plane of the planetary orbits. Calliden fed power to the drive again. The *Wandering Star* shot off in pursuit.

After five hours they had come to the edge of the region where the gravitational power of Caligula's sun prevented entry into the warp. Calliden pulled down the cocoon navigators used to pilot through the warp, and diverted power.

With a stomach-churning wrench, they were suddenly in the warp. The Immaterium. The Between. There were countless names for it. 'The Sea of Lost Souls' was the one Calliden did not like.

In the three-dimensional jungle which was how his mind saw the warp, it was as though Gundrum's ship had pushed its way through the foliage, flattening it slightly. He had only to follow this trail before the foliage closed in again, like going through a partly filled-in tunnel. It hardly surprised him that this tunnel went in the direction of the Eye of Terror.

The hours passed. It would be days, probably, before the painted ship reached its destination. In the meantime, they would both have to sleep. The ships of the Imperial Navy would never set out with only one navigator on board. For others, for free traders making a living with smaller spacecraft, the case was different. They could afford – usually could only find – a single pilot capable of steering through the warp currents. Some navigators took drugs to keep them awake for extended periods, but these were apt to cause hallucinations if used too often. Many a ship had come to grief as a result. Otherwise a navigator would park his ship in a dead spot in the currents while he slept, hoping it would not drift too far off course, or else allow himself to be carried sleeping on what appeared to be a smooth current, hoping not to be carried hopelessly off course. Either way, he did not dare to sleep for more than an hour or two at a time.

For Pelor Calliden the warp currents consisted of winds blowing through the jungle and stirring up the foliage. If the currents were violent the jungle itself would begin to move, boles and vast green ferns appearing to become uprooted and hurling themselves at speed through the Immaterium, together with the leering faces which from time to time showed themselves.

None of this concerned Maynard Rugolo. He could see none of it. At length he announced that he was tired and left Calliden wrapped in his cocoon. For privacy he retired to the living quarters proper which he had allowed Calliden to use. And he took the dream gem with him.

Smoothing out the bed and slipping the stone under the pillow, he settled himself down to sleep.

Did the gem stir up dreams as well as make them real? It was true that for the past two nights Rugolo, usually a sound sleeper, had dreamed more vividly than ever before. Now, minutes after he dropped off to sleep, he entered a stream of dreams which seemed to reel themselves off one after another, like sliding down a helter-skelter, and all in brilliant colour. At first they were pleasant. He dreamed of friends he had known in the past, of good times he had experienced, of the youthful voyages he had undertaken with his father. He dreamed of meeting a wonderful woman who became his adoring companion, almost his slave. That dream began to turn a little sinister when the women turned into Aegelica, the sister of Gundrum.

Then he dreamed that she produced a knife and used it to cut off both her breasts. The blood streaming from her mutilated chest, Aegelica threw back her head and laughed, waving her arms in the air. Her green eyes sparkled with a perverse pleasure. Then she was gone. Rugolo found himself plunging through a verdant jungle of monstrous, unknown plants. He did not know it, but it was the same jungle Calliden saw when he looked into the warp. Faces leered from it. Impossible-looking creatures peeped between the stretching boles and the shivering leaves.

Rugolo came to a clearing. It was at that point that the dream turned into a nightmare. A creature waited for him there, a creature such as he had never imagined, a creature compounded out of the most vicious parts of every predatory animal. A huge raptor's beak jutted from a narrow bossed face with staring avian eyes. There were four legs with razor-sharp talons apparently designed for kicking and disembowelling. And more limbs that were a cross between human arms and avian wings, spreading metallic-looking feathers which glittered red and gold, ended in long pincers. That was not all. The creature had a tail which lashed from side to side and carried a sting the size of a power sword, while from muscular shoulders sprouted long tentacles equipped with rows of suckers. But worst of all, it spoke to him.

'Ah, Maynard Rugolo,' it purred. 'How could you have been so foolish? It is tiresome to feed on dead meat. Come, be a tasty morsel for me. Let me feed on you while you are alive. Let me suck the entrails from your belly and the thoughts from your brain.'

Rugolo's legs seemed made of lead as he turned and fled in panic. Fungi squished and popped underfoot, puffing out clouds of spores which surrounded him like a fog and made it difficult to see. Looking back, he saw the monster which knew his name ambling after him in leisurely fashion, gaining on him without effort. The terror and helplessness which overcame him made him shriek uncontrollably. He seemed to have no strength. He moved as if underwater, his feeble limbs failing to answer the urgings of his brain.

'*Maynarrrd…*' purred the voice from the great beak. It seemed to be right next to his ear. He felt the hard beak itself nuzzle him. A tentacle touched his shoulder. A hefty pincer stroked his face, and a great acid stench made him retch.

It was as his panic reached its pitch that a desperate thought came to him, a last ray of hope in his distress: *This could be a dream. A nightmare. I can escape if I make myself wake up. Otherwise–*

His shrieking had stopped. His terror had struck him dumb. Now he tried to shout out again, but all that came was a feeble croak. He tried again, and heard a wailing unsteady voice that might – or might not – have been his own, echoing through the blinding spore-fog.

'*WAKE UP! WAKE UP! WAKE UP!*'

He was trying to force his eyes open, making them bulge desperately in what he hoped was his nightmare. It was as the sharp beak dipped down to his soft bulging abdomen and began to caress it preparatory to feeding that there was a sudden snap in his consciousness.

HIS EYES SPRANG wide open. Sweating from every pore in his body, he was lying on his back on the divan bed attached to one wall of the domestic cabin, staring up at the dim mottled ceiling.

'Thank the Emperor!' he breathed in gasps. 'It was a dream!'

'*Maynarrrd…*'

Rugolo froze. He did not dare look. There was only a single electrocandle burning, set at its lowest level, and most of the cabin was swathed in darkness. From the corner came a rustling, scraping sound. As his eyes turned, despite himself, in that direction, he saw a beak-shape emerge from the shadows, glinting briefly in the candlelight. It receded. Then it came into view again, and with it emerged the rest of the huge monstrous creature from the green jungle, its crested head brushing the ceiling, its repulsive bulk taking up the entire end of the cabin.

Now Rugolo lost his reason entirely. His insides turned to jelly, seized by an uncontrollable juddering. He became a terrified child, shrieking and crying in a confused babble as the Thing That Knew His Name advanced on him.

The apparition was as yet only half-formed, by turns fading, almost disappearing, only to emerge once more into near-solidity before becoming transparent again, as if it had not quite accomplished the transition from the dream-world which had spawned it. Wing-arms spread as though to embrace him like a lover, tail-sting waving back and forth, the cruel beak descended as if for a kiss, in order to feed on him.

Suddenly the door banged open. Pelor Calliden stood outlined in the rectangle of light from the control cabin, his face a spectacle of shock and horror as he beheld the scene.

'*Emperor save us!*'

Such was Calliden's abject terror that, like Rugolo, he was unable to move, and all that came from his throat was an inane, quavering wailing noise. Like Rugolo, too, his intestines were writhing in fear-driven pain as though an electric current ran through them.

He sagged. His vision darkened and consciousness almost left him. Then he stiffened. His warp eye seemed to expand and to become lustrous. He glared at the monster. In a bellowing voice quite unlike the frail tones Rugolo was accustomed to hearing from him, he propelled words at the creature as though they were weapons.

'IN NOMINE DEI-IMPERATURIS! TIBI IMPERO FOEDE DAEMON, NE NOS MOLESTES ITERUM! ABI EX LOC ET REDI EO UNDE VENISTE! VENI NUMQUAM AD MUNDUM MORTALIUM!'

The extraordinary beast reared up and advanced on Calliden. It flickered, almost vanished, then resurged with an incoherent roaring and cackling.

Again Calliden pronounced the resounding words of exorcism. The monster shivered, shook and quaked. The immense beak gaped and exhaled a glowing purple smoke that brought with it an indescribable stench, a combination of burning, corruption, rotting flesh, all mingled in some indefinable manner with the most enchanting aromas, so that one could not tell which were repulsive and which enchanting.

Then ragged holes appeared in what was left of the monster. It was disintegrating. With a sudden screech it collapsed inward as though sucked to a central point and was gone, leaving behind an unbearable stink and a sensation of intense heat which departed only gradually.

With a shudder, Calliden closed all three of his eyes. He sagged, gripping the doorframe, but lacked the strength to hold on to it and slid to the floor, where he began to sob, his mind numb with a terror so great that he wouldn't have thought it possible to feel it and still live.

Rugolo was still shaking and babbling incoherently on the bed. Minutes must have passed before Calliden could venture into the cabin – to discover that sanity had left the trader altogether.

'Help me, help me! Divine Emperor, Potens Terribilitas, Saviour of Mankind! Help me!'

Calliden reached out and slapped Rugolo sharply in the face. Then he forced him off the bed and half-dragged him into the control cabin, where he dumped him on one of the two chairs at the table, taking the other himself. Rugolo's hysterical prayers fell to an incoherent mutter. As for Calliden, his strength seemed to have left him. He was like a puppet with cut strings.

'What… what was it?' Rugolo mumbled. 'In the Emperor's name, what was it?'

'A daemon!' Calliden quavered. 'It was a daemon!'

Rugolo was still shaking uncontrollably. 'It's the jewel,' he confessed. 'I used the dream-gem. It came out of my dream!'

'We must destroy it. Go and get it.'

'I can't. I *can't*. I'm too afraid.'

'Where is it?'

'Under the pillow.'

Summoning all his remaining courage, Calliden rose and gingerly stepped into the living quarters. The deodorising unit, a necessary piece of equipment in any spaceship with a confined living space, was whining away energetically to eradicate the extraordinary stench exhaled by the warp-thing. The cabin had a hallucinatory quality, an unnatural depth which seemed to stare back at him, the walls glowing with an eerie life of their own, as if the daemon possessed an intensity of life and consciousness far greater than that of physical creatures, and its aura still lingered.

He lifted the pillow. Where the gem would have been lay a patch of blue dust. Perhaps it had crumbled when he banished the daemon.

He returned to the control cabin. Neither man spoke for a long time. Then, in a tone of quiet admonishment, Calliden said, 'You see, it's true. Daemons do exist.'

Abjectly, Rugolo nodded. 'I've been so foolish.'

'Yes, I'm afraid you have. 'No wonder Gundrum made off without bothering to talk to us again. Do you understand? He was making a gift of you to the daemon. It was about to feast on you, body and soul…

'The dream-gem is a conjuration device. Its purpose is to allow daemons to materialise, to come out of the Immaterium.'

Rugolo's normally ruddy complexion, already nearly as pallid as Calliden's, went grey. 'Thank the Divine Emperor you knew how to banish it!'

Calliden looked at him. 'Navigators have psychic powers, but not enough to exorcise daemons! I was like you, just shouting prayers in complete panic – in this case, a banishment formula I learned in navigator training. It shouldn't have worked. I think it did because the daemon hadn't fully materialised. It was partly a dream creature still.

'You were probably supposed to dream several more times before the daemon was able to manifest itself,' he continued. 'But you used the gem while we are in the warp. That gave it a chance to get through prematurely.'

There was in fact a little more to it than that, but Calliden was loath to discuss the private and secret knowledge of a navigator. He had employed the banishment rite as if by instinct. It was formulated in the arcane words of an ancient language, pre-Gothic, but he knew its meaning:

> *'In the name of the God-Emperor! I command you, foul daemon, trouble us no more! Quit this place and return whence you came! Come no more to the world of mortals!'*

It was ironic that Rugolo, who had been an unbeliever until now, had unknowingly spoken the truth about one thing. When he thought to see his mother pleading with him from outside the ship, it must have been a daemonic pretender after all. Somehow it must have sensed his weakness.

'There's something you had better know,' Calliden said. 'I heard it from my mother. The Inquisition kills anyone who has seen a daemon, or who they even suspect has seen one. That's how dangerous materialisations are. So don't speak of what just happened to anybody.'

Rugolo's teeth were chattering. Insane thoughts were going through his brain. Would the daemon still be there in his dreams when he went to sleep again? What would it be like to be eaten by it – *body and soul*? He seemed to hear its voice now, calling seductively to him, reassuring him, offering him – wealth! Riches! Power! Incomparable delights!

The culminating delight of all being to be devoured.

It came to him that he had a reason for continuing in pursuit of Gundrum. The fiend had tricked him! He could get revenge by taking away his trade! Terror and greed fought within him, twisting his thoughts insanely.

'We are in a realm of madness!' he shouted in desperation. 'You were right all along, Pelor! We must turn back!' He found himself repeating the words of Kwyler. 'To safety! The Imperium! Space Marines! The Inquisition!'

He looked around him in bewilderment, as if waking up suddenly. 'Where are we?'

'I've moored the ship in a dead spot. I was asleep when I heard you screaming.'

'Then take us back.'

Calliden nodded. He stepped to the control board and took the first pilot's seat. Before pulling down the navigator's cocoon he directed psyker power into his warp eye – and started back in shock.

The elaborate jungle by which he was accustomed to interpreting the warp was no longer there. Not as a jungle, at any rate. Or rather, it was a jungle torn to shreds and engulfed in a raging ocean typhoon. Shattered branches, shredded leaves, boles and boughs splintered and smashed; all surged and whirled together, interspersed with brilliant orchids and splattered blossoms, carried hither and thither in the turbulence of an angry warp torrent it was impossible to resist.

The *Wandering Star*, too, was part of that onrush. Calliden stared in utter helplessness, knowing there was absolutely nothing he could do. Like driftwood in a hurricane, they were being swept directly into the Eye of Terror.

SIX
FIRST BLOOD

LORD MILITANT Commander Drang's visit to Segmentum Pacificus was not in the least like conferring with his own admirals. He was not Potens Maximus here, but a brother commander from whom was expected the punctilious protocol of an honoured guest. His entourage, consisting of two hundred persons – not counting the servitors, the holomats and lexomats on permanent loan from the Adeptus Mechanicus – was conveyed in a fast space barge escorted by a flotilla of cruisers. Here was a whole battery of adepts. An inquisitor from the Ordo Malleus who had spent three days in the charnel hull of the nullship soaking up the psychic resonances still faintly detectable in the adamantium shell. An entire team of analysts led by a Magos Logis, who had pored over every word of Librarian Merschturmer's report, as well as visual and auditory records taken on board during the attack in the Eye. And as well as that, a team of military analysts who had assessed both the threat and how to meet it.

Like an ambassadorial mission, the flotilla descended through the endless panorama of docks and installations orbiting Hydraphur, a cathedral-towered spectacle which made the planet itself, two thousand miles below, seem small by comparison. This was the base of Battlefleet Pacificus – not quite on the scale of Drang's own Battlefleet Obscurus base, but still grand enough to stupefy. One of the major investments of the Imperium, it was a girdle of steel and adamantium massing billions of tons. Further the flotilla travelled, emerging from the inner edge of the titanic ring and descending onto Hydraphur. The cruisers hovered just outside the atmosphere while the fast command barge continued alone, sinking through the air envelope. Below, the planetary surface came swiftly into view, and here the grandiosity of the base revealed itself again. Whole continents were covered over with buildings – vast repair sheds, forge factories, cathedrals whose intricately decorated spires poked through the clouds, while on the oceans, too, floated gigantic fleet-servicing yards.

The barge swept down below the clouds until it approached an expanse of adamantium-reinforced concrete. Titanic slabs slid apart like mountains moving. Gently Drang's barge descended into the Pacificus Fleet's underground planetary redoubt.

Lord Militant Commander Invisticone had responded to the visit by assembling analytical teams of his own, who would now engage in debate, if not fierce argument, with those brought by Drang. In full ceremonial dress, including glittering diadem headgear, high stiff collar on which his head seemed to float, in the full splendour of his knee-length tunic glowing with icon flags and decorations awarded him in the name of the Emperor, he was cordial once the ceremonial litany was over.

'What a great pleasure it is to see you, commander. This reminds me of old times.'

'Myself also, commander,' Drang replied, the faintest of smiles on his lips as he took in the double meaning of Invisticone's words of welcome.

The Lord Militant Commander of Segmentum Pacificus did not have Drang's monocled sternness of feature. His face was expressive and affable. It was also criss-crossed with duelling scars, some of which he had carmined with red dye, and the largest of these, cutting a furrow across his left cheek, was picked out in tiny rubies.

Drang had given him that scar, when they were both young officers. Relations between them had not always been friendly.

* * *

'SO ARE YOU convinced of the necessity for action, my lord?'

'Oh yes,' Invisticone drawled. 'I was from the beginning.'

Deep in the redoubt, the two were seated at a banquet, together with three of Drang's retinue and half a dozen of Invisticone's admirals.

The banqueting table, set on a balcony, was overhung by a vaulted ceiling which also extended itself above the large hall the gallery overlooked. In that hall the visiting and resident teams of assessors sat two by two, poring over dimly flickering viewscreens, giving rise to a murmuring hubbub of argument. This was in one of the oldest halls of Base Pacificus, hung with ancient banners, lined with fluted stone columns, paved with worn flagstones. Its antiquity made the air itself heavy with dust motes. Glow-globes flickered, aged valves crackled, and from somewhere came the hum and click of power relays.

Invisticone ate expansively, glancing askance at Drang as he refused course after course and stoically consumed only a small amount of plain fare and just a single tiny glass of a liqueur so rare and expensive that a single bottle was worth the entire life's income of an industrial worker. Drang had clearly not changed his austere nature since Invisticone had known him in his younger days. The only thing he seemed to relish was the bowl of smouldering herbs placed before him, inhaling the fragrance deeply. He was very likely addicted, Invisticone told himself, though the man probably did not know it.

'There is only one thing that puzzles me, my lord commander,' Invisticone continued in a tone of polite irony. 'Is this matter to be *sub rosa*? You do not appear to have informed Terra of the nullship's findings, or of your intentions.'

Drang put down the engraved-gold smelling bowl. He almost glared at his colleague, the alien-manufactured monocle glinting.

'And why should we inform Terra?' he challenged. 'Are you not hungry for your just share of glory? Are we not invested with power incalculable? What need is there to trouble the High Lords, still less to go whining and grovelling to the Adeptus Terra as though we two cannot deal with matters? They would hardly thank us if we did, indeed it would cast doubt on our courage and initiative. Oh no, this is a Navy matter. What I plan is a surgical strike, conducted by us alone. Do the Imperial Guard commanders ask us to do their work?'

He paused to catch his breath. He had prepared this speech, anticipating Invisticone's concerns. 'I have invited you to share in this campaign because of our friendship, assuming that you would be honoured and eager to share in it. But also, of course, because of a realistic appraisal of the threat. Pacificus and Obscurus are enough. Should you refuse, Obscurus alone will bear the burden, and still emerge victorious.'

'Ah, I understand you,' Invisticone replied slyly. 'You wish to become known as the saviour of the Imperium.'

'Alongside yourself, brother commander.'

'Of course. To act alone would be to risk seriously depleting the resources of Obscurus.'

'Then our interests are identical. We serve the Imperium, we serve the almighty Emperor, and we earn glory thereby in addition.'

Invisticone sipped from his goblet, aware that his admirals were listening intently. 'Some would call it treason to keep this to ourselves. To keep a secret from the Emperor?'

'It is not a secret, and we keep nothing from the Emperor,' Drang intoned ponderously. 'The Emperor knows all. But He no longer speaks. He has not spoken for a long time. The High Lords of Terra cannot convene for every local emergency that arises. If we were to wait for that, we would be guilty of weakness. We would be derelict in our duty, and duty demands that we act. We must act! We must act now!'

A long, awkward silence followed these words, until Drang spoke again, in a different, graver tone that shocked them all.

'In any case, the tyranids might settle it all in the end.'

'And what do you mean by that, brother commander? The tyranids are awesome, but we have dealt with them before.'

'Yes, we defeated Hive Fleet Behemoth,' Drang granted soberly. 'But with difficulty. And then came Hive Fleet Kraken. Have you considered this, commander? Each tyranid hive fleet consists of millions of vessels. What if Behemoth and Kraken were but the first members of a swarm of such fleets, itself numbering millions, which even now is advancing on our galaxy? Nature's profligacy reaches its most monstrous proportions in the tyranid. Nothing the Imperium can do could stop such a horde. It would leave behind it a dead galaxy, every trace of life extinguished. Even the Chaos realm would be gone. The tyranid hive mind has no soul, no spiritual counterpart. When a tyranid fleet moves through the warp, it is like a wall erasing everything in its path. A tyranid super-fleet such as I have described would be enough to extinguish the accursed Chaos gods and all their subjects.'

'You paint a grim picture, my lord,' Invisticone murmured. He recalled that the Ultramarines Chapter of the Adeptus Astartes had captured a Behemoth tyranid ship intact, and study of it had revealed much. It was clear that the tyranid were not of this galaxy. They came from afar, and for all anyone knew had been migrating through space forever. Leaving a great trail of lifeless galaxies behind them, perhaps?

And who was to say that there was only one super-fleet such as Drang had so graphically imagined? Conceivably there was a stupendous number of those in turn. The tyranid might be the universe's ultimate life-form, depending on infinity itself to sustain its eternal existence. As each dead galaxy was left behind it would, in a few billion years, recover, evolve life all over again, ready to be harvested by some other tyranid super-fleet.

The tyranid themselves might be infinite in number for all anyone knew. In the face of such a vision the whole of mankind, even the Emperor Himself, seemed helpless and insignificant – a treasonous thought indeed!

Invisticone smiled. The depth of Drang's defeatism surely meant he was losing his grip. The nightmare he depicted, while possible in theory, was in his imagination only.

Also, to express such defeatist thoughts so openly was to seal his fate. The arm of the Inquisition was long, and sooner or later it learned everything. Drang, at some time in the future, would face arrest and execution.

It was not surprising, therefore, when he immediately recovered himself and produced a counter-argument.

'Yet if this were true, then the Emperor would know of it. Therefore we can have utmost faith that it is not true.'

Invisticone nodded, and decided to throw Drang a lifeline. 'We must exercise our minds and consider everything,' he agreed, 'even if it is only to dismiss it as false, as you say. Well, enough of that, brother commander.' He stared down at the heated debate taking place on the floor of the hall. 'Assuming those experts we have assembled can reach a common accord, I will agree to take part in the campaign – but only if we inform the Adeptus Terra of our intentions, and await the response of the High Lords.'

Drang was exasperated. He had hoped his rhetoric had persuaded Invisticone otherwise. 'And what if they delay, disagree, order further investigation?' He snorted 'We must use our own judgement! Otherwise we are not worthy of our rank. Lord commander, I cannot demand, and I will not plead, but–'

Invisticone was smiling as he interrupted. 'Then let us settle it in the old way, my friend.'

Now Lord Militant Commander Drang understood the true reason for his brother commander's objection. Invisticone was stroking the ruby-decorated scar on his left cheek.

After all this time, he wanted a chance to get even.

Drang himself no longer wore his duelling scars. They had all been removed, the skin smoothed out and perfectly healed. He regarded the sporting of such trophies as a sign of a truly immature disposition.

He rose and bowed slightly. 'Of course, brother commander. An excellent suggestion.'

INVISTICONE'S JACKBOOTS slapped on the floor of the practice hall even deeper in the redoubt, Drang's own footsteps following him.

In his heart Drang was not sure what the commander of Battlefleet Pacificus intended. Duelling among the younger officers had changed in recent years. It had acquired a more bitter rivalry than Drang and Invisticone had known, and was more vicious. Traditional cutlasses had given way to pistols of various kinds. The loser rarely escaped with his life.

Perhaps, he thought, Invisticone would like to kill him, too, even though their former enmity had turned to something near to friendship.

But Invisticone walked past the cabinets containing handguns of various kinds. At the far end of the hall, cupboard doors creaked, unused for a long time. Within was a range of matched cutlasses and shields. Invisticone invited him to choose his weapon.

Drang rarely smiled, but when he held a chunky cutlass in his hand, testing it for balance, a feeling of forgotten pleasure came over him, and his thin lips curled.

'This will do.'

There were no seconds; no subordinate could ever be called upon to judge an Imperial Lord Militant Commander. Drang and Invisticone were alone. Invisticone smiled too as he took up the matching cutlass and slipped an arm into the bands of a shield.

The cutlasses were vibroblades, an obsolete type of weapon but still used for duelling. Drang waited for Invisticone to switch on his cutlass's power and make it sing, so that even a modest gash could prove fatal. But he did not.

Or would he do so in a final act of treachery?

Invisticone was looking at Drang's turreted monocle. 'Are you sure that does not give you an unfair advantage, brother commander?'

'Only if we were battling at a distance of half a light-year, which I trust will never happen,' Drang responded ironically. 'I cannot remove it, as you may know, but have no fear. I am using normal vision.'

They took their places on the white stripes painted on the floor. Though still in full dress uniform, complete with decorations, and no longer young, the two men remained agile. Invisticone began with a feint, whirled, and attempted to surprise Drang with a slash towards his left side. The cutlass clashed against Drang's raised shield. Drang made a thrust from beneath it, was parried, then sprang back as Invisticone launched a furious attack, his blade flashing this way and that, blocked by Drang at every stroke. Clearly he had never allowed himself to get out of practice.

Drang recovered and returned the onslaught. For a moment the two were locked, shield on shield, upraised blades caught at the guard. With a mutual shove they sprang apart, each eyeing the other.

Then Drang heard a faint singing sound. Invisticone had powered up his sword.

Before he could respond, the Pacificus commander was upon him, laughing savagely, battering again and again at Drang's shield with apparent disregard for his own safety. The powered cutlass sliced and chewed through the metal shield which in seconds was reduced to a ruin.

So that was how it was to be!

Drang stepped back again, grateful that his adversary allowed him a moment's respite to divest himself of the shield, no more than an encumbrance now. Invisticone, with a dramatic gesture, flung his own shield to the floor with a clatter, raised his cutlass, and unpowered it.

'That's better! Like the old days!'

Ruefully Drang admitted that he had misjudged his colleague. Invisticone was right! Shields were for those who had no skill with a blade! Light flashed on the cutlasses as thrust met block, swipe met deflecting parry, feint met counter-feint, in a swirl of dancing motion that was two master swordsmen at full stretch. Drang felt himself forced back, the keen blade missing his face by a hair's breadth more than once. Unless he could dodge aside his back would soon be to the wall, and then Invisticone would have him at a severe disadvantage.

Then, for what must have been no more than a tenth of a second, he found an opening. His aching muscles sent the heavy cutlass flickering like a snake's tongue before it was deflected in a clash of ringing steel. A line of crimson appeared on Imperial Militant Commander Invisticone's right cheek, matching the furrowed scar picked out on his left. Invisticone stood stock-still, his blade still laying across Drang's after having knocked it aside.

Then he drew himself up and raised the cutlass vertically before him. 'First blood is yours, brother commander.' With a wry chuckle he threw the cutlass aside, letting it clang to the floor alongside his shield. 'It is decided.'

Drang laid down his weapon also. 'You honour me, brother commander.'

'And your destiny, it seems, is always to be decorating my face.' Whatever Invisticone's private feelings were at being bested by Drang yet again, he kept his voice even save for a touch of chagrin. Blood was flowing down his cheek. He wiped it off with a handkerchief of some rare silk, then took a styptic pencil from somewhere in his uniform and ran it over the new cut. The bleeding stopped immediately.

It was quite remarkable how symmetrically the wound matched the earlier one. When Invisticone examined himself later he would probably imagine the Obscurus commander had achieved the effect deliberately, which would be to overestimate Drang's current swordsmanship. Would he be awed at such skill, or resentful in the belief that Drang was toying with him?

Either emotion could have consequences when the time
came to draw up battle plans...

'Well, it is work for my cosmetician,' Invisticone went on. 'I
have some new gemstones, quite uncommon. Sanglets; a type
of bloodstone. They look exactly like drops of freshly shed
blood. I shall have them sewn into the wound. Or do you think
jewels of a different colour would better set off your earlier
handiwork? Sapphire blue, perhaps?'

Drang forbore from expressing his disdain for cosmetic
ostentation. It would give Invisticone an opportunity to tease
him over his alien monocle.

They left the practice hall. Waiting in the ante-room was a
joint delegation from the combined assessment teams. Two
evaluation officers, one wearing the badge of Pacificus, one of
Obscurus, both bearing viewscreens, came to the fore, leaving
a small knot of adjutants behind them.

'We are in agreement, my lords,' Invisticone's officer said
gravely, bowing to each in turn. 'After much argument, we
reach the same projections. Our regions are in peril.'

'Commander Drang would hardly have come here were matters otherwise,' Invisticone responded dryly. 'It now remains to
combine our operations.'

'That too is our conclusion, my lords.'

Invisticone nodded curtly and turned as if to make his leave,
when the officer spoke again: 'On one other matter we are
agreed – Terra must be informed of what is afoot.'

The commanders glanced at one another, and then at the
officers with looks which were icy. Both Drang and Invisticone
had carefully kept members of the Administratum out of their
assessment teams. Apart from specialists borrowed from the
Adeptus Mechanicus, all were naval personnel. So instead of
the monk-like garb of Adeptus Terra Prefects, the men who had
saluted them were variously apparelled in the epauletted uni-
forms of the Fleets.

Now that Drang had obtained Invisticone's co-operation in
the matter, these teams, including the tech-priests would essentially be in custody, denied contact with any other human
being or communicator. It would be the same with everyone
else who had played a part in the assessment project. As for the
nullship, it had been recovered secretly by units of Battlefleet
Obscurus and as far as either the Adeptus Mechanicus or the

Inquisition knew, had come to grief in the Eye of Terror. It now lay in a pore-like cavity deep within Cypra Mundi, Battlefleet Obscurus's base planet, and its location was known only to a few officers personally loyal to Drang and sworn to secrecy. The navigator who had heroically brought the ship out of the Eye had been quietly executed.

As for the bodies of the Space Marines, including that of Librarian Merschturmer, as well as the progenoid glands Merschturmer had removed, these were being retained in stasis, a discourtesy which would have infuriated the respective Adeptus Astartes chapters – had they known. Whether Drang ever would return them to their fortress monasteries was something which he had not yet decided.

Invisticone answered the staff officer's point in a voice that was suddenly gritty: 'This is a Navy matter! Terra will learn of events on the successful conclusion of the campaign and not before!'

The faces before them became stony and pale, as each man in his own time worked out the implications of these words for himself personally. Drang could not help but smile, and he added a comment of his own.

'Of course,' he drawled, 'If we should fail... Well, Terra will know of it soon enough.'

SEVEN
DEADLY DELIGHT

EVEN IN A HURRICANE, the steersman must do what he can. Pelor Calliden pulled the cocoon down. He placed his hands on the controls. He summoned all his psychic power into his warp eye.

'*Imperator, adjuva me,*' he prayed. But he could make no sense of anything. There was only the raging, shredded jungle, a thick green sea shot with brilliant colours, through which he could see nothing, and which carried the *Wandering Star* along with it like a piece of flotsam. All he could do was to try to keep the ship steady as it was dragged along. Despite warp currents not being material in any real sense, he had heard of ships being spun to destruction in such a maelstrom, torn apart by their own centrifugal forces

And indeed the *Wandering Star*'s inertial integrity field, necessary in any spaceship to protect crew and passengers from lethal accelerations and changes in direction, were having trouble coping. Rugolo, strapped into the co-pilot's seat, shouted in protest as he was flung about.

In panic, Calliden dropped them out of the warp. Instantly, there was an audible rustling on the outside of the hull. Their eyes snapped to the external viewscreen.

There was nothing to be seen except a mist or fog, through which vague patches of light suffused. Rugolo diverted his gaze to the star tabulator, the navigational device which should have told them where they were. It, too, was confused, unable to recognise anything in the murk, its significator plate flickering out a succession of failed identifications.

They had materialised inside the thick dust cloud on the edge of the Eye. That was the cause of the rustling they could hear. Their manic warp speed had translated itself into a real-space velocity that was a solid fraction of the speed of light. The dust was impacting on the hull, racing over it as if the ship was flying through a sandstorm.

Abrading the adamantium shell, wearing it away. Dust bullets, given extra mass by reason of the relativistic effect, punching their way through the outer shielding, which was worn and weakened by age and use anyway.

Promptly Calliden dropped them back into the warp and concentrated again on holding the ship steady. And now he discovered for himself another phenomenon known to navigators, one he had heard of but never experienced before: the frightening moment when 'the allegory', as it was called – the means, private to himself, by which each navigator's mind interpreted the warp – broke down and was replaced by something else.

His subconscious could no longer see the warp as a colourful jungle. The warp storm had chewed that image into extinction. Briefly he was bewildered, having nothing to hold on to, nothing by which to exercise whatever feeble control he could over the *Wandering Star*'s movements. The inertial integrity trembled. Rugolo hollered as they felt the ship tumble over and over, though in fact the real rate of tumble was probably hundreds or even thousands of times per second.

Calliden did not hear his friend cry out, and was not really aware of the spinning sensation. He had other problems. It was his first real experience of what the cocoon was for. It was not truly necessary for piloting or navigating; one could manage either without it. The cocoon was purely for the navigator's protection. As Calliden's mind struggled to grapple anew with the impossible, his body went into convulsions, jerking uncontrollably this way and that. The cocoon wrapped itself more tightly around him, gently restraining him, preventing the wrenching spasms of his muscles from breaking his bones.

It happened then. Something was emerging from what had been an incomprehensible tumult, something that would enable him, partially at least, to get his bearings again. Figures. Faces. A three-dimensional sea of faces, millions of faces – grotesque, grimacing, some human, some half-human, some like the faces of beasts combined and mingled together, faces of all sizes, some bigger than the *Wandering Star* itself.

The faces swirled and flowed, delineating the mad flow at the edge of the great warp storm known as the Eye of Terror. But that was not all. The faces were changing, transforming into a huge multitude that was one face over and over.

His mother's face. Millions of times over. And to the faces were added his mother's body, apparelled in every form of dress he had every seen her wear, or else naked – a shocking sight, to see his own mother naked! – swaying, cavorting, beckoning to him, dancing, grimacing as if in enticement. And among these endlessly duplicated mothers of his, there came squeezing through, as if pushing up from some fluid substratum, horrific-looking daemons, with which his mother began performing a multiplicity of obscene acts, leering mockingly at Calliden all the while.

The warp entities had again read his mind. Once more they were attempting to throw his emotional instability at him. At first it worked. Briefly Calliden closed his warp eye in anguish, believing that this truly was his mother, multiplied and reproduced in the hell to which she had been condemned, made to couple with daemons for all eternity. The ship began to tumble again, and this made him pull himself together, realising that what he saw was but images taken from his own private nightmares. He forced himself to look back into the warp, attempting as best he could to stabilise the vessel.

The infinity of writhing figures had vanished. Suddenly the turbulence had come to an end. The *Wandering Star* was being carried along on a steady course. Calliden guessed that if he were to drop out of the warp now, he would find himself on the other side of the shield of dust which surrounded the warp-storm, turning the stars within it as seen by the naked eye – from the planet called Apex V, for instance – into a misty nebula.

But he did not do so. His subconscious had given up trying to interpret the warp by means of allegorical scenes. The insane region within the Eye defied all such exercises. Instead he saw what appeared to be an entire vast universe of roiling, writhing, twisting curves in hundreds of colours, woven throughout a black immensity. But this was hardly an immensity as the mind could normally conceive it. This was an incomprehensible madness.

He groaned aloud, his mind threatening to sunder. Then, just as he despaired, he began to understand what was happening.

He was seeing in eight dimensions!

He had been subjected to training exercises such as this in the Schola Navigationis – stretching the mind beyond the three-dimensional world of ordinary sense perception. It was said that only people with the navigator gene could really do this, and then not always.

Calliden was entranced. It was as though his brain had switched over into a new mode of seeing the spiritual realm – the warp *as it really was*. No warp entities were visible. Everything was purely abstract. A great loom of psychic-spiritual forces.

Scattered through the vastness, vanishing into immense distances, were what appeared to be dark curving chasms, holes of negative existence. He understood these to be stars together with their attendant planetary systems, islands of matter surrounded by gravity wells, places where – in the normal galaxy outside the Eye of Terror, at any rate – the warp drive would not work, and daemons could not directly manifest themselves. How things went here, Calliden could not say.

He twisted his head, looking for something else. Yes, there it was, filtering through the multidimensional chaos, faint, very faint and intermittent, much fainter than the stars of the Eye when seen from Apex V, but still visible, if only just. A pure white light, reassuringly pristine, peaceful and holy. There it was, even here... The saintly light of the Emperor.

The Astronomican. Calliden had never been so glad to see it. While it still shone in his vision, however dimly, he would never be completely lost.

Then, looking ahead, he saw among the labyrinthine curves a shining dot of a pearly hue, travelling ahead of him. He knew that hue. It was the signature that warp screens gave, seen from the outside. Almost certainly, it was Gundrum's rainbow-coloured ship. Excitedly he relayed the information to Rugolo.

'This gives us a chance. Gundrum – or his pilot – must know the way out of here.'

'Can you drop back so he doesn't see us?' Rugolo enquired anxiously.

'No, we're being carried headlong.'

Rugolo grunted, staring at the screens. They showed nothing but grey blankness. As far as the scanners were concerned, there was nothing outside the ship, not even space.

'Perhaps they can't see us anyway,' he murmured. 'According to Gundrum he doesn't have a navigator. That sister of his does it.'

'I don't believe that.'

Gundrum's ship seemed to be as much out of control as the *Wandering Star*. Usually it was possible to leave a warp stream and proceed to a planned destination. A navigator would not dream of entering a current so fierce that he lost the ability to change direction. That Calliden had done so within days of reacquiring his navigational ability was something he had difficulty in explaining to himself. He looked again at those dark patches of nullity which, in the warp, betokened the presence of matter in realspace. They looked as though it would be possible to travel to any one of them in a straight line, but he knew that the impression was an illusion. There was no such thing as a 'straight line' in the warp.

As yet the *Wandering Star* was only on the outer rim of the great Eye of Terror warp storm, being borne along its periphery like a leaf caught up in a whirlpool, and ahead of him Gundrum's ship was being carried along in the same manner. Further in there were probably more flurries, more irresistible turbulence as one crossed from one stream to another. But Calliden was not thinking about that. He did not want to venture any further in. At the moment he was wondering how, visible Astronomican or not, he was going to get out.

There must be a way, he told himself urgently. Gundrum had managed it.

He frowned. A well of nullity was looming up. An island of materiality, towards which the current was taking them. But something was wrong. As the great glow of nothing engulfed them… it vanished. Instead, a white sun blazed forth. Calliden glanced at the detector displays, at the gravitic entabulator, the radiation entabulator, the visual display, all set in their ornately engraved oval brass frames. A planetary system was set forth. Four worlds, one close and coming closer. Calliden shook his head. With his warp eye he could still see the screens of the painted ship. It looked as though the warp current was going to smash it into the planet. And the *Wandering Star* would not be far behind! It didn't make sense. The warp drive shouldn't work this far inside a gravity well. For that matter, a warp torrent shouldn't be able to flow through it, either.

Rugolo was mumbling to himself. He turned to his navigator in bewilderment. 'Are we still in the warp, or out of it?'

'We're in it, and we're not in it,' Calliden muttered, equally befuddled. 'No, that's not right. We're in the warp and in real-space!'

Panic came into Rugolo's voice as the implication of what he was reading on the tabulators struck him. 'If we hit that planet…' He gulped. 'Get us out of here, Pelor!'

Calliden was already struggling with the controls in a desperate attempt to alter course. It was no use. The only thing he could possibly achieve would be to put the ship into a spin which would tear it to fragments. Personally he preferred to smash into the planet with a velocity that would instantly convert it and its occupants into plasma. For the ship to disintegrate first would dump them alive in the warp, prey to daemons!

'It's no use,' he sobbed. 'Pray to the Emperor! Pray for the salvation of your soul.'

Rugolo slumped in despair. For his own part Calliden felt too numbed to pray. So this was the end! He cursed himself for having listened to the fake Rogue Trader, someone with the stamp of failure written all over him. Miserable as his life was before, at least it was life.

While these thoughts went through his mind he noted that the environment open to his warp eye was again changing, becoming even more difficult to apprehend. A warp-realspace overlap! To the eight dimensions of the warp were added the four dimensions – three spatial and one of time – of ordinary space! Twelve dimensions in all! Impossible even for a trained navigator!

Could the entities of the warp understand such an environment? If so, they had intellectual powers far exceeding the human. It was far too complicated for Calliden to grasp. He whimpered, eyes rolling in his head, and gave up trying to interpret it. The great loom-like scheme surrounding him collapsed. Instead he became aware of the white-hot sun casting flares into a space that was oddly coloured, a dark violet shot with faint streaks of light rather than the ebon-black space he was used to, and of the planet towards which they were hurtling, looming ever closer.

Where was Gundrum's ship? Had it already met its doom? No, there it was! So close they could have seen it with the naked eye! How was it they had closed the distance? How could the other ship have slowed down, in defiance of the warp current?

He estimated they were less than a minute away from impact with the planet. Calliden could think of only one thing to do. He shut down the warp engine and attempted to drop back into realspace.

A violent lurch threw them both forward. The breath was knocked out of Rugolo. Calliden, tossed about in his cocoon, felt something like a hammer blow in his head, and then lost consciousness.

WHEN HE CAME ROUND, Rugolo was slumped in his harness, still dazed. A whistling, rushing noise invaded the cabin, emanating from the outer hull. The *Wandering Star* was no longer in space. It was speeding through the atmosphere of the planet it had been rushing towards, flying through the air on stubby wings and steadied by the automatic pilot.

Calliden was astounded. How could the ship have decelerated sufficiently to negotiate the atmosphere in so short a distance? It should have fallen like a flaming meteor and ploughed into the surface in seconds, its exploding engines creating a crater miles across. He spotted Gundrum's rainbow ship, soaring swiftly ahead of them.

Calliden felt a stirring beside him. Rugolo was recovering. The trader took stock of the situation quickly, without bothering to ask how it had come about. His eyes gleamed as he spotted Gundrum's ship. 'Don't lose sight of them!'

Calliden had taken over from the automatic pilot now. He eased their speed as he saw the other vessel do the same.

Gundrum's ship dipped and went gliding down to a land and seascape far below.

There was something curiously limpid about the atmosphere. It didn't seem quite like air, more like transparent crystal. There was no trace of a cloud layer. The glowing surface lay completely bare in the light of the sun.

Both the painted ship and the *Wandering Star* were flying like atmospheric craft rather than landing directly using their realspace main motors. That was standard when a moderately sized spaceship entered a planetary atmosphere on automatic, such as if the pilot was unconscious. Whoever was piloting the painted ship flew with flair and verve, even recklessness. The vessel snaked and jinked and dived for the surface. Calliden wondered briefly if it was trying to lose its pursuer – but no, that would be impossible without cloud cover. More cautiously, he followed, being less familiar with atmospheric flying, strangely enough, than he was with flying through the warp. Soon the two ships were racing less than half a mile above a nearly flat surface. The planet seemed to have no mountains, no hills, no valleys. It was patchy, water and land mingling together in strips and rivulets. There were no definite seas or land masses. The colours were pastel: blue, green and pale pink. From here, two hundred miles under the air blanket, the sky showed itself as a deep azure, scattering the light of the dazzling white sun. It all looked perfectly normal, a habitable planet such as might have been of interest to the Imperium – were it not within the Eye of Terror.

An expansive plain came in sight, carpeted with greenery. Gundrum's ship had slowed so that its wings could scarcely provide enough lift to stay in the air. It tilted. A manoeuvring engine showed a hot white light, as bright as the sun overhead. Gracefully the vessel set itself down.

There was no point in trying to be discreet. There was nowhere to hide. Calliden carried out the same manoeuvre, landing no more than half a mile away.

The two waited to see what would happen next. Rugolo was tense. He felt trapped in his own ship, where a daemon had entered his dreams and nearly materialised. He seemed to hear its enticing voice calling to him still. It was not lost on him that, despite changing his mind, he was still being forced to follow his original plan to follow Gundrum, as though drawn by some fateful compulsion.

There was no movement. After more than an hour, a port opened on the hull of the multicoloured ship and a ramp uncoiled.

And that was all. No one emerged. Another hour later, and two carts, hauled by beasts of burden of some kind, appeared on the edge of the plain in the distance, accompanied by about half a dozen humanoid figures. As the party slowly approached the painted ship it could be seen that the carts were piled high with cargo. Rugolo's eyes gleamed.

'Trade goods! This must be Gundrum's source!'

Eyebrows raised incredulously, Calliden rounded on him. 'Are you mad? After what happened to you? You can think of anything but escape?'

Rugolo was not listening. He turned up the magnification, primarily to look at the contents of the carts, then drew back in surprise. Calliden followed his gaze.

The people walking alongside the carts were… not people at all. Their form was humanoid, but not human. Their skin shimmered with colours, like the scales of fish. Their limbs were unnaturally short and stubby. Their faces, if they resembled anything, were like the faces of frogs. Nothing about them, except for their upright and four-limbed form, which made them only vaguely man-like, suggested a human descent.

'Aliens!' Calliden exclaimed.

It made sense, Rugolo thought. The Eye of Terror dated from the twenty-fifth millennium, no earlier. There must have been alien-inhabited worlds as well as human colonies in the region when the warp storm blew up. And they were still here. He chewed his lower lip. Calliden, of course, was naive. Raised to think of aliens as evil, he probably would be shocked to know how many alien-manufactured goods free traders brought into the Imperium, not to speak of Rogue Traders.

'Well, I sold an alien trinket to an Inquisitor once,' he admitted aloud. 'Though I'm not really sure he was an Inquisitor.'

He heaved himself out of his chair. 'Stay here,' he said as he left the cabin. When he returned, it was to show that he had been to the ship's armoury cupboard. He was carrying two small laspistols, not military issue but manufactured for civilian use, with mother-of-pearl handgrips and damascened barrels. He offered one to Calliden.

'Hide this about you somewhere. It's fully charged.'

Calliden had extracted himself from the navigator's cocoon, which he had rolled up. He stared at the mother-of-pearl stock without touching it.

'What are you planning to do? Kill Gundrum and steal his trade?'

'Not a bad idea, but impracticable. What would happen if you tried to take us back to the Imperium?'

'That's easy to answer. A warp stream runs right through this planetary system, and we're stuck in the middle of it. If I try to steer us out, the ship will be shaken to pieces.'

'Exactly. But Gundrum must know a way out, or at least his sister does – whatever you say, she must be a navigator. We have to do a deal with him. We've no choice.'

'Aegelica can't be a navigator *and* Gundrum's sister as well,' Calliden pointed out. 'If she were, Gundrum would be a navigator too. I don't believe she's a navigator anyway. I'd know if she were.' He paused. 'How can you possibly trust Gundrum after what he did? Bringing down a daemon on you? Probably using an alien artefact into the bargain.'

There was a silence.

'We don't really know if it was meant to happen,' Rugolo said shortly. 'Perhaps it was my fault, for using the dream gem in the warp, like you said, with daemons nearby. Perhaps the gems are harmless otherwise.'

Rugolo's mind was in a whirl. The daemon's attack was receding in his memory, as if it had been no more than a nightmare. His original plan was nearing fruition!

Calliden sighed with despair.

The alien carts had pulled up some distance from Gundrum's ship. A knot of people descended the ramp: Gundrum, Aegelica, Foafoa and Kwyler. Rugolo thrust the lasgun at Calliden again. 'Take it, it's for our protection.'

Without enthusiasm Calliden accepted the weapon, inspecting it briefly and placing it in an inside pocket. It was slim, designed to be inconspicuous.

They left the cabin, climbed down from the port and stood in the shadow of the stubby wings, looking towards the rainbow ship. Calliden, having already performed the ritual of protective sealing at the base of the *Wandering Star*, was nervously intoning one warding-off-evil prayer after another, a navigator's litany.

Rugolo glanced at the greenness carpeting the plain, which he had taken it to be a variety of grass or moss, forms of verbiage common on many worlds. It was neither. It more resembled green pond-slime, and was smooth and slightly slippery underfoot.

The air had a cool, wine-like quality which was delightful to breathe, and was perfectly clear, so that even distant objects were sharp to the eye. But as Rugolo turned to speak to his partner he noticed something odd. The air seemed to ripple as he moved, as though it were a liquid. A movement made him look up. A number of silvery creatures were gliding above his head. Not winged creatures such as birds or bats but, to all intents and purposes, fish, moving with leisurely sinuous motions, waggling semi-transparent fins. In other words, swimming.

How could a fish swim through the air? Rugolo took a deep breath and waved his hand to and fro. Despite its odd rippling quality, the air seemed no denser than that which human beings normally breathed.

Calliden quickened the pace of his incantations when Rugolo pointed out the air-fish to him, making the Sign of the Emperor allowed only to navigators. He would be convinced, of course, that the phenomenon was unnatural. Rugolo cast his mind about for some non-magical explanation. Perhaps, he thought, the creatures had bladders filled with light-than-air gas to make them float. But they seemed too small for that and were moving too quickly. The small motions their fins made would have served to propel them through a liquid, but not through thin air.

He reached out to grab one as it came near. It flitted away and evaded him, angling upwards.

He returned his attention to the scene near Gundrum's ship The draught animals, four-legged, striped green and yellow, but with faces resembling those of gorillas, had been unhitched and the wagons unceremoniously tipped up, spilling their contents onto the ground in twin heaps. The visiting humans had begun sorting through the piles, examining object after object.

Rugolo touched his companion on the arm as a sign to follow and set out. As the pair approached, Gundrum straightened.

'By the roots of my desire! My good friends, the traders from the straight places! Yes, we have seen you following us! But why? *Why?*' A weird glaring expression, impossible to read, possessed his bony features. 'What irresistible desires do you come here yearning to fulfil?'

All eyes, alien and human, were on the two now. Rugolo's gaze roved briefly over the piles of goods on the green-coated ground. There was little there that he could recognise.

'So this is the source of your merchandise,' he ventured.

'Oh, no-o-o… We have never been here before. We never know where we are going when we set out for the great and glorious Eye of Pleasure… or the Eye of Terror, as cowards call it. We go where our lords will us.'

This statement alarmed Calliden. 'You don't know how you got here?'

'The roots of my desire brought me here. The delirious Lord of Pleasure brought me here. The winds of fate brought me here. Did I not tell you that space is different here in the great storm? Here you do not fly by instruments. You do not fly by looking at what is around you. You navigate by *faith*. Faith in your desire. Here, everything responds to that. Is that not so, my sweet little sister?'

Gundrum place his arm around Aegelica's bare shoulders. She writhed with apparent pleasure, pouting coquettishly. 'Oh yes, dear brother,' she breathed in a warm voice.

As if at her behest, a warm breeze blew over them, dispelling the chill of the air. Calliden recalled the strange behaviour of both Gundrum's ship and the *Wandering Star*. A shiver went through him. Could it be that some strange power – the warp itself, in some way – answered to a pilot's emotions and wishes? Picking out a destination in response to desires, perhaps even subconscious ones, and taking him there?

The idea was both sinister and alluring. He wove a further protective warding sign, at which Gundrum laughed. The frog-faced aliens blinked.

Gundrum's words went over Rugolo's head, however. 'You made a promise, Gundrum. I'm expecting you to keep to it.'

Aegelica was stroking her brother's back. 'You did make a promise, Gundrum… but who to? Ask him if he used the dream-gem.' She addressed Calliden. 'And you might be the one who owes the debt...'

Calliden's paleness went even beyond his usual pallor. He thought he understood what Aegelica meant. Rugolo, however, obviously took a different meaning. He began to speak angrily.

'Yes! That damned stone you gave me had something wrong with it! I was nearly killed!' His voice dropped. 'I suppose you do know how to get back to Caligula?'

Gundrum laughed loudly. 'I travel on the roots of my desire! I throw myself on the whims of the gods! You, however, were drawn along in my wake. You are a piece of flotsam, now. Your only hope is to embrace the great Dark Lords, the Ruinous Powers.'

The pair recoiled at this. Fiercely Calliden gripped Rugolo's arm. 'This is an insane world! And here is an insane man, telling us to abandon the Emperor!'

Kwyler, now dressed in some loose sort of jerkin, had been sifting through the alien articles. He glanced towards them before apparently losing interest, and resumed what he was doing. Foafoa, on the other hand, had become agitated. He was clenching his fists and stomping to and fro.

'Kill them, Gundrum! They are after our business! Why else did they follow us? Kill them now!' He rounded on Rugolo. 'I told you to stay out, didn't I? I've dealt with people like you before, so I have!'

Involuntarily Rugolo's hand crept towards where he had secreted the laspistol. While this happened he could not help but notice an increasing number of fish-creatures gliding through the air around them. It was almost as though the entire gathering of humans and aliens was at the bottom of an ocean, with shoals swimming hither and thither.

Foafoa noticed his involuntary movement. He grabbed him by the arm. *'Mind what you're doing, friend!'*

Humming and laughing to himself, Gundrum had begun to perform a disjointed dance. Aegelica too gave a trilling laugh as she stepped gracefully forward, easing Foafoa aside merely by brushing her hand on his bicep.

'How crude you are, Foafoa! Wanting to kill people by breaking their bones, stabbing and blasting them.' Her voice was warm and caressing, and her green eyes hypnotic as she looked upon Rugolo with fondness and admiration. 'Foafoa, you have no finesse! Here, my friend, let me give you a better welcome.'

Calliden felt helpless, overcome with dread. He felt sure something awful was about to happen to his friend. He watched in a trance as Aegelica halted in front of Rugolo. She was swaying slightly. The trader was in even more of a trance, staring with enchantment at the movements of her lithe body. Her eyes became saucer-like, taking on a hue of a deeper green than before.

Then the horrible thing happened. Her body changed like some monstrous orchid suddenly putting out new growths. Long, saw-toothed, crab-like claws sprouted where her delicate hands had been. Her feet, too, became elongated, and two-toed like those of a giant eagle. A long, tube-like tongue extended from her mouth. And, most grotesque of all, from her firm, fleshy rump sprang a thick, flexing tail, ending in sharp barbs.

Astonishingly, Rugolo did not appear to find any of this repulsive. He was trembling with excitement. Calliden reached for his weapon, but in a single swift bound Foafoa was behind him, clamping his arms in big, strong hands. Calliden could hear him hissing with quiet laughter. Aegelica took a strutting bird-like step. Those awful claws reached out and seized him, as though he were no more than a morsel of food she was about to tear apart. But the touch of those razor-sharp chitinous claws only made him delirious with pleasure. He moaned and reached out with a shaking hand, longing to touch her breast, while the tongue which was like a hollow tendril swayed towards his mouth. Still holding him by one claw, she released him with the other, using it to stroke and tease his body, causing him to lose all control and sag, while his eyes rolled up in their sockets and he whimpered in ecstasy.

It was eerie to see how much this terrifying spectre was still Aegelica. Wild delight came to her face. She raised one foot in a quick motion that was not quite human, placing the big claw against Rugolo's belly. Calliden saw that with one slash she could disembowel him, and very likely was about to do so. He struggled vainly to break free of Foafoa, unable to reach the weapon in his inside pocket.

'Maynard, wake up! She's a daemon! Use your gun!'

It was no use. Rugolo was beyond recall, pleasured beyond any self-restraint he could muster. Calliden opened his warp eye, even though it was hidden by the bandanna he had donned before leaving the ship, and began to intone the exorcism prayer he had used before. Foafoa instantly clamped a hand over his mouth, holding him close to his body with the other arm, so that all that came out was a muffled gurgle.

Unwilling to see what he was sure was about to follow, he cast down his gaze. In so doing he was witness to something unexpected. The slimy greenness on which they stood shimmered, and was gone, clearing as if in a sudden chemical change. Replacing it was a flat shiny surface, almost colourless, like the surface of a still stretch of water.

Too late, Calliden discovered that it was water. He instantly sank into it, as did Foafoa and the entire tableau. Rugolo and the hideously transformed Aegelica, the cavorting Gundrum, Kwyler, Calliden in the grip of Foafoa, the painted spaceship, the aliens, their carts and animals and the piles of merchandise, all descended like a mass of rubbish thrown into a pond.

The water closed over their heads. Calliden felt Foafoa release him. He tried to strike out for the surface, but could not. The water seemed thin and unresponsive to his swimming strokes or the kicking of his legs. Down and down he went. Looking up, he saw the roof of the 'ocean' receding beyond reach and experienced the stifling panic of imminent drowning. Then his feet touched a surface. His heart bursting, he looked about him and saw that the scene of moments before had remained almost intact, but translated to the ocean bed.

Rugolo and Aegelica had separated. Like Calliden, Rugolo was holding his breath and floundering. The aliens simply stood passively as before, undisturbed by what had happened. Gundrum and his party, albeit that they claimed to be strangers to this place, were waving their bodies from side to side in apparent enjoyment, their faces wearing whimsical expressions.

No sand had been thrown up by their impact. The surface on which they stood was firm, carpeted with rush-like growths on which the bulk of the painted spaceship rested nearby. Here, too, were fish, flitting here and there. The water was limpid and transparent, the sunlight penetrating it easily. Calliden could hold his breath no longer. He let go, resigning himself to the end.

But no bubbles came from his mouth.

By instinct he expanded his lungs. He felt liquid fill his mouth, pour down his throat and infiltrate his lungs. The water was not cold, only pleasantly cool, even refreshing. He no longer had any sense of suffocation. He expelled the water from his lungs, drew in again, and then was breathing normally.

Breathing water.

Calliden waved his hand though the water. Though it did not have quite the same consistency he would have expected, it still resisted the movement more as like a liquid, not as air would.

Aegelica was turning somersaults in the air, giggling, swishing her tail from side to side. Gundrum continued his peculiar jerky dance, laughing as he did so.

'Did I not tell you? Nothing can be taken for granted in this realm! You are on a planet where air and water are the same!'

Calliden looked around for the *Wandering Star*. Yes, there it was, some distance off, also on the sea bed. He supposed breathing water might be possible if it had a very high oxygen content dissolved in it, but that did not explain fish which swam through air, or for that matter how Gundrum could talk underwater so intelligibly, instead of having the words come out as a series of gurgles.

Or land that betrayed them by suddenly becoming ocean!

Land, air and water were all interchangeable!

With poise and delicacy Aegelica set her feet on the waving green rushes. She flicked aside a fat fish covered in iridescent red scales which had crossed in front of her face, and set her sights on Rugolo once again. Her voice seemed even warmer as it was transmitted through the liquid medium.

'Pleasure and pain are the same. Pain is pleasure, pleasure is pain… Come, my dearest one, my beloved Maynard. It is my will to pleasure you to death…'

Standing there, currents of water wafting in and out of his lungs, Rugolo waited in anticipation, longing for the deadly crushing caresses of Aegelica's crab claws. Calliden stared too, no longer thinking of rescuing his friend. Instead he was hoping, fervently, that once she had put Rugolo to his excruciating, ecstatic death, she would do the same for him.

Rugolo went limp as Aegelica seized him. With the buoyancy of the water, it took her no trouble at all to lift him off his feet with one claw. Her long tube-like tongue began to play with his face, his neck, his ears, drawing loud moans from him that were embarrassing to hear.

Her left claw had gripped him under his right arm. Now her free claw clamped itself onto his left thigh. Gently, playfully, she began to flex both claws, bending him a little. She was preparing to tear his leg off.

'No!'

Calliden came out of his mad, erotic trance. He plunged his hand inside his black tunic, noticing for the first time that it was wet through. Out came the laspistol. Calliden was unused to wielding weapons. It took him a moment or two to wrap his fist around the handgrip, release the safety, aim, and press the firing stud.

Steam bubbled all along the length of the laser beam as it hissed through the water. But it failed to reach Aegelica. Instead, it struck a fish, nearly a yard long, which at that moment glided between them. The fish exploded as the water in its body turned to steam. Fragments of flesh, skin and bone drifted to the sea bed.

Foafoa roared in indignation. He seemed not to move, but suddenly a weapon was in his hand, buzzing savagely. It was a shorter version of a chainsword – a chainknife, as long as a butcher's cleaver, and Calliden immediately imagined its teeth ripping through his flesh. He was terrified. He whirled round to bring the laspistol to bear, but didn't get in a shot. The chainknife cut right through the little gun, severing the emitter barrel and charge chamber from the stock, and nearly taking his thumb with it.

Foafoa laughed, waving the buzzing knife tauntingly in front of Calliden's face. 'That deserves a slow death, navigator!'

Then Calliden heard a long, lingering, agonised scream. It was not one of pleasure. It was one of realisation. Aegelica had begun the process of dismembering Rugolo. As he felt the painful wrenching of his joints, reality had returned to the trader. Yet, incredibly, that scream ended by turning into one of appreciation and gratitude, as Aegelica's heady hallucinatory powers took hold of him once more.

'AEGELICA! THAT'S ENOUGH!'

The cry came from beyond them. The voice was Kwyler's. He had ceased from sorting through the alien trade goods and had stood up. From beneath his robe he had produced a weapon far bulkier than Calliden's discreet little pistol. Calliden had rarely seen its like. It had a fat barrel, a cylindrical fuel flask, and a shoulder stock as well as a handgrip, although Kwyler was ignoring that and wielded the gun like an ordinary side-arm.

Flung aside by Aegelica, Rugolo lay sprawling and groaning. With a look of glee Aegelica whirled to face Kwyler, her wide saucer eyes staring, her transformed limbs thrown apart as if in welcome. Calliden was not sure he had identified Kwyler's gun correctly, until there came a vivid flash and a brilliant gout of energy brighter than any flame, and water boiled so furiously that the scene was near to being obscured until the roiling bubbles lifted themselves towards the overhead surface. It was a melta gun, also known as a fusion gun or a cooker, far more awesome than an ordinary flamer, firing a short-distance blast of sub-molecular thermal energy.

Aegelica took the blast full on. As it engulfed her she gave vent to an ululating soprano scream that went rising and warbling in a prolonged aria, a celebration of pain and delight and shock and gratification. She should not have been able to utter any sound at all. She should instantly have been reduced to molten slag and steaming vapour. But when the scene cleared, Aegelica was still there – not the crab-clawed, eagle-toed daemon now, but the fetchingly attractive woman she had been before.

'Aaaagh!' Smoke rose from her chest and belly as the energy of the melta gun dispersed. 'Do it again, Kwyler!'

Kwyler, however, was directing the melta-gun's barrel elsewhere. 'Drop the knife, Foafoa,'

He trained the gun on Foafoa and Gundrum in turn, one after the other. Gundrum stopped his dancing. Both stared at the barrel of the melta with something like fear. This at least told Calliden that neither was a daemon, unlike Aegelica.

Foafoa did not obey Kwyler's order fully, but with a flick of his wrist the chainknife was silenced and disappeared into his clothing.

'What ails you, by my roots, Kwyler?' Gundrum said in a lugubrious voice.

'I've come as far as I can, Gundrum,' Kwyler said wearily. 'You're all getting worse and worse. I'm quitting, going back with these others. Get aboard the ship and leave, all of you.'

Foafoa grimaced and roared, '*Traitor!*'

Two things began happening at once. The water in which they were submerged swirled, making the shoals of fish eddy. And the back of Foafoa's head also swirled, puckering until it formed a face – the face Rugolo had seen in the drinking hall on Caligula, which he had taken to be a hallucination caused by the peculiar liqueur Gundrum had served him.

Now he knew he had been wrong. It was real.

The snub-nosed, old-young visage sought Rugolo out where he lay on the sea rushes. The high, squeaky, voice screeched, '*I told you not to come! I told you! I told you! Now you're trapped! Now you belong to Chaos!*'

'Oh, Kwyler,' Gundrum said, in the same doleful tone as before, and ignoring the awful transformation as though it were perfectly normal, 'you have cut off the roots of your desire! What will you do now? How will you find your effervescent delights without us to guide you? You are lost! No more lemonade for your soul!'

With a sudden sloshing sound, the breathable water in which they were immersed drained away. The rushes, by some self-magic, transformed themselves into the same green slime the space travellers had stood upon before.

Calliden found he was again breathing air.

But still the fish swam around them.

The plain had not restored itself as formerly. It was, instead, a mixture of dry areas interspersed with meandering streams. The *Wandering Star* stood nearby.

Foafoa was glaring at Kwyler with hatred. He seemed unaware of the second personality expressing itself out of the back of his head. The exhortations from the rearward-pointing face reached fever pitch, then Foafoa's head wobbled as it forced itself further out with an immense effort. A pair of shoulders appeared. Two small hands freed themselves and pushed back against the edges of the hole now showing in Foafoa's skull. An entire human form was emerging. The abdomen and legs came free. A complete individual, resembling nothing so much as a year-old baby, but with an adult if dwarfish face, slid down Foafoa's back to stand on the rushes.

It was not completely independent. An umbilical cord led from the navel and back into the gap in Foafoa's head. Having been so horribly 'born', the baby-dwarf tottered towards

Rugolo, the cord lengthening and maintaining its grotesque connection. Soon the creature was trying to coax Rugolo to his feet. 'Are you all right?' it enquired plaintively. 'Can you stand up?'

Foafoa still behaved as though completely unaware of this repulsive extension of his being. He looked questioningly at Gundrum, who shrugged and threw up his hands.

'Come, my dearest and most delectable sister. Come, my ardent and trusty fellow-traveller. Let us be away!'

He turned and walked towards the painted ship with a peculiar high-stepping gait. Aegelica, who had been making mincing faces of invitation at Calliden, blew kisses as she followed. Alongside her walked Foafoa, the umbilical cord stretching behind him.

And now the knot of aliens, who throughout had remained immobile, even their animals reclining before the emptied carts, became animated and panicky. They went running after Aegelica, their arms held out beseechingly, calling out in gurgling voices. Turning on them with a look of contempt, she flung out her arm in a gesture of dismissal and marched to the ship.

For bizarreness Foafoa's departure far exceeded hers. As he was about to mount the ramp to the ship's port the umbilical cord reached its full extent. Suddenly it contracted. Foafoa staggered back only slightly – but the effect on the baby-man was much more dramatic. He went hurtling through the air and was jammed back into Foafoa's skull with a loud *schlucking* sound, disappearing in seconds. The hole in Foafoa's head had healed before he even reached the port, the skin smoothing over, the bristles of his cropped hair regrowing, so that there was nothing to show that the appendaged manikin had ever shown itself.

Rugolo came to his knees and began gibbering incoherently, his eyes glazed, all intelligence gone from them. He had been attacked by daemons twice in one day, and his mind had broken. The spectacle caused something in Calliden to snap, too, bringing him out of the numbness which had overtaken him. He held out his hands to the clear, open sky.

'*By all that's holy, this can't be real! It can't be!*'

'It's real,' Kwyler answered him curtly, replacing the melta gun in its harness. 'Move back, unless you want the backwash to catch us.'

His warning helped bring the navigator back to his senses Rugolo proved impossible to rouse; he had retreated into some private hell of his own. Calliden forced him to his feet and dragged him away. Had Gundrum's ship been a crude planet-to-planet vessel, relying solely on a reaction motor, nothing could have saved them from its exhaust as it took off. But it was not. Like every other interstellar craft its mass was reduced by controlled inertial fields. An incongruously small thrust was enough to lift it off an Earth-sized planet. Splashing over the wet ground, they felt a wave of heat hit them as white brilliance surged from the ship's twin venturae. It accelerated, became a dot, and then vanished.

Rugolo had stopped gibbering now. He was crooning to himself instead. They splashed their way through a shallow pool towards the *Wandering Star*. Suddenly a noise made Calliden look back. Having been rejected by Aegelica, the frog-faced creatures were crawling all over one another, gripping each other tightly until they were one heaving mass. They appeared to be in a mating frenzy. The beasts harnessed to the carts were aroused too. They threw back their heads and uttered chugging sounds.

The navigator turned away, choking back his revulsion. With difficulty he and Kwyler got Rugolo to the control cabin, where they laid him on the pallet bed. Calliden tried to speak to him, but got no answer. He didn't seem to know where he was.

'It's the horror of it,' Kwyler said in a neutral voice. 'Some people never recover. They go mad, and stay mad. Lucky it wasn't you. We need a navigator.'

Calliden rounded on him. 'Why did you help us? What do you want?'

Kwyler looked sour. 'I want to get out of this place, out of the Eye, and I hope you do by now as well. You're a fool if you don't. You will take me with you, won't you? I'd hate to be stranded here.'

He paused. 'As for why – I should have stayed away from Gundrum in the first place. That's all.'

Calliden cast him a suspicious glance and then moved to the utility cupboard and rummaged around until he found Rugolo's apothacarion chest. It was not well-stocked. But he found a little box of Calming Balsam which, if used with the proper invocations, could sometimes relieve mental stresses.

He applied the yellow cream thickly to Rugolo's forehead, muttering the appropriate spells. It appeared to have some effect. Rugolo's eyes closed. He fell into a deep sleep.

He turned back to the Eye trader. 'What was that… that thing that came out of the big man's head?'

'It's not a thing, it's a person. His name's Gidane. One of our group, originally. Foafoa was always bullying him, always dominating him, until in the end Gidane was absorbed by him altogether.' He shuddered. 'That's the sort of thing that can happen in the Eye. Gidane was a friend of mine,' he added, as if by way of explanation.

Calliden found Kwyler's explanation so repulsive that he couldn't even to react to it. It was too much for his imagination.

'Tell me about Aegelica,' he pressed. 'I know she's a daemon. But why does Gundrum call her his sister? And she call him her brother?'

'The original Aegelica *was* Gundrum's sister,' Kwyler told him. 'The daemon possessed her, though she was far from unwilling. Aegelica still exists, I think, but her personality is buried, subservient to the daemon's. There are so many kinds of daemons, but this sort is known as a daemonette, a child of Slaanesh. Aegelic has kept the name; a little joke on her part.'

'Slaanesh? What's that?'

Kwyler made a wry mouth. 'Do you really want to know? Slaanesh is one of the lords of Chaos– yes there really are Chaos gods, are you happy to know that? You shouldn't be! This one is the god of decadence and unbridled pleasure. The creatures on this planet seem to worship him, at any rate. A Slaanesh power must have led Gundrum here – through Aegelica, of course. She acts as his pilot, though as you've guessed she's not a navigator. She doesn't need to be, here in the Eye. The warp is her natural environment.'

'What did the aliens want from her?'

Kwyler sighed, as if having to explain things to a slow-witted child. 'Their price for the goods they were offering was to be pleasured to death by Aegelica, just as your friend nearly was. They are incurable hedonists.'

'How can you know that? Gundrum said none of you had been on this planet before.'

'It's quite obvious that they are worshippers of Slaanesh,' Kwyler said, sounding contemptuous of Calliden's ignorance, 'and that they know Aegelica is His daemonette. A Giver of Indescribable Delight. A Bringer of Joyous Degradation. Your friend might understand those titles, after what he's been through.'

'But the aliens already knew what Gundrum wanted. They came to him with carts loaded up.'

'That's how things work in the Eye, often. It's useless trying to explain it.'

A groan came from the pallet. Rugolo was waking up.

'Aegelica! Aegelica!'

Calliden hurried to him. 'It's all right. She's gone. She can't hurt you.'

Rugolo raised his head from the bed. His eyes were mazy, as though he were struggling to return to reality. 'You don't understand! I wanted it! *I wanted her to do it to me!'*

Calliden's abdomen crawled as he remembered how, quite against his will, he too had been inflamed with a desire to experience dismemberment by the daemon-transformed woman.

Lurching from the pallet, Rugolo turned his face away from the other two, trying to hide his humiliation. As he did so his gaze fell on the external viewscreen. The frog-people had finished their mass mating. They stood around among the trade goods that had been strewn around. He looked to the trade goods that now were strewn about on the ground. Among them were dozens of crystals about the size of a man's head. They seemed to fizz and sparkle, as if charged with energy. One by one they were popping and disappearing with quiet explosions, leaving sherbet-coloured smoke.

His eyes gleamed. 'Trade goods… they'd be worth something if we could get them back to the Imperium.'

'You haven't got what the aliens want in return,' Kwyler informed him dryly.

'You don't give anything to aliens. Aliens are owed nothing. 'You take. We've got weapons.' This was a lesson he had learned while travelling with his Rogue Trader father.

Kwyler appeared unimpressed. 'Forget about robbing them. They may not be as helpless as they seem, and right now they're frustrated and annoyed. You have a more pressing problem. Getting out of the Eye, which I strongly urge on you as a course of action.'

Rugolo was no longer sure he wanted to get out of the Eye. It was a fascinating realm. It had pleasures to offer, new ways to live…

Suddenly the edge of the strip of dry land where the aliens were situated gave way. Aliens, trade goods and carts were all tipped, plopping into the water and sank from sight.

'Well… we can breathe underwater…'

'Wake up, Maynard!' Calliden shouted. 'You're not thinking straight! Your mind's being affected!'

Rugolo shook his head, as if trying to throw off a mental miasma. He muttered to himself.

'Think straight! Forget Aegelica. Daemons–' He turned to Kwyler. 'Can you help us get out?'

Kwyler spoke succinctly. 'We go out by the same means you came in. You followed Gundrum, right? You were carried along by the wake his ship left in the warp, in fact, as he said. That won't work in the warp normally, but this isn't just the Immaterium. It's also the Eye, where everything is driven by the Chaos powers.

'So we do the same again. Follow Gundrum until he leaves the Eye. Aegelica always finds a way out. Their wake can carry you, as before.'

'What if they spot us?' Calliden said.

'Gundrum's not interested in you. He never meant to do business with you in the first place. Giving you that gem was his idea of a little joke – as well as to curry favour with his masters, of course, though that's always an uncertain thing. Apart from that, he's not particularly vindictive.'

'Not vindictive?' Rugolo said vacuously. He appealed to Calliden. 'I can't make any decisions, Pelor. I'm confused. What shall we do?'

'You're not making any decisions anyway, Maynard,' Calliden told him firmly. 'You're not mentally competent just now. We are leaving, and we are leaving straight away.' He took one last look at the totally flat land-and-seascape. A wind began to ripple the surface of the otherwise calm water below them. He didn't like it here.

'Lay on the pallet, Maynard,' he said. 'Take-off might be a bit rough for you, but you can take it.'

He gestured Kwyler into the co-pilot's seat, then stationed himself at the controls, pulling down the navigator's cocoon.

Minutes later a hissing cloud of steam billowed where the pond had been, condensing and forming a fogbank from which the spaceship, venturae still blasting, emerged and went surging towards the sky.

ONCE ABOVE THE atmosphere, Calliden observed the same strangeness in his surroundings that he had seen before. Space was not quite black. It was shot through with shades of dark blue – indigo, purple, violet – which wavered as though it were a heaving sea.

The tabulators failed to pick up the radiation trail of the painted ship. Calliden pulled the warp lever. There was the familiar lurching sensation as the screens came on and the ship was phased out of realspace… except that there was no proper division between realspace and the warp within the Great Storm. The twelve-dimensional complexity of the combined realms ranged all around him, confusing him, driving him to the edge of insanity. He knew he would have to simplify his mental environment if the cosmic loom was to be comprehensible. At length, by a supreme effort of will, he managed to 'collapse' one dimension after another, until, to some extent at least, he was able to distinguish one direction from another.

And now he could spot the rainbow ship's trail, in the form of a long-drawn-out nacelle or tunnel, a bending of the abstract curves that, for him at the present time, represented the warp.

The warp torrent had already seized the *Wandering Star* and was propelling it along at enormous speed. The star which was sun to the world they had just left was already far behind. He had only to guide the ship into the tunnel-like deformation, and he was sure to stay on Gundrum's trail.

He spoke to Kwyler. 'Why is Gundrum's ship so strange? That odd shape, and its colours. Is it of alien manufacture too? Eldar, maybe?'

It did have the typical smooth Eldar look about it, he told himself. And Gundrum had sold a wraithguard.

'No, it's Imperium-made, believe it or not. It's mutated. Once it looked not too different from yours – a rustbucket of a scow, if you'll pardon the comparison, but let's face it, your merchantman isn't the latest model straight out of the fabricator's yard either. The Eye is a place of changes. Gundrum's ship got made over, so to speak – all in a minute or two.'

'Were you there? Did you see it?'

Kwyler nodded. His face became dreamy. 'There were these rainbow clouds, drifting about. No, not clouds exactly. More like patches of coloured light. One of them passed through the ship. When it had gone, well, she was as you see her. Everything inside is really pretty, too. Completely redesigned furnishings. Though mechanically she's pretty much the same.'

A thoughtful silence met his words. 'None of us were aboard at the time,' he went on. 'I've often wondered what we'd look like if we had been.'

Again there was silence.

'That was a Tzeentch world,' he finished.

Neither of the others asked what *Tzeentch* meant.

A glowing dot came into view in Calliden's warp vision, the signature of warp screens in action. It was Gundrum's nameless ship. He reminded himself that if he could see it, then it was likely that Aegelica could see the *Wandering Star*.

Then the dot disappeared. Seconds later, they hit turbulence.

There had been no warning! No way to avoid it! Rugolo and Kwyler yelled as the ship spun, once again exceeding the capacity of the inertial stabilisers. Calliden thrashed about in his cocoon harness, the incomprehensible and contradictory signals reaching his brain translated into epileptic seizures – the reason the cocoon was there.

Even in the training simulators, he had not experienced warp chaos like this! He was dazzled, unable to act, caught in a labyrinth-maze-skein-jungle-vortex-tangle-tumult-ferment-pandemonium.

Absolute disorder!

He did not know how long it lasted. He could not say, later, whether he had done anything to preserve the ship, or whether it had survived the raging cataract purely by luck. But, at some time or another, the *Wandering Star* was shot out of the turbulence like a squeezed pip.

Before he could take stock Calliden had first to stabilise the ship. How to correct a spin in twelve dimensions was a daunting problem. Calliden ignored all questions and appeals from the others.

An hour later, he felt he had done what he could. Only now could he dare transfer them into what passed for realspace in the region, wherever that was. All he knew was that there was no longer any sign of the painted spaceship. And that they were further in to the Eye. Much further. The ship was still being swept along by the storm, of course, carried along as part of the great circular motion that enclosed in its compass thousands of worlds, like a daemonic hand enclosing a pocket universe.

To get his bearings, Calliden threw back the warp lever.

This time the transition was smoother, less of a jolt. All three occupants of the *Wandering Star* looked at the scene through the external viewer.

Splendour.

During the millennia of its existence, the warp-storm had not only shaped all psychic life within it. It had caught up the stars themselves, reordering them into new formations. A huge spectacle of clusters and starstreams, interspersed with vast veils of dust and gas, met their gaze.

Space itself sparkled with colours – the colours of the warp!

For Calliden himself, there was something else the others could not see. Although he was now looking though his 'visual' eyes, his warp eye was still open. This would not have brought him much by way of perception in normal space. But here – faces. Flickering in and out of existence. Hideous faces.

He was staggered. How could there be faces tens or hundreds of light-years across?

That, however, was not what frightened him most – not that, or the fact that he had lost all sight of Gundrum. He struggled out of the cocoon, pushed his way up out of the pilot's seat, and held out his arms to Rugolo, an appalled expression on his face.

'Maynard! We're lost! We're lost! We'll never get out! I can't see it!

'I can't see the Astronomican!'

EIGHT
THE HIGH LORDS SPEAK

DRANG VISITED THE bodies of the vanquished Space Marines. He could not help himself. He was doing it every day. Down into the deepest excavations of the Segmentum Obscurus's planetary base, treading the dankest tunnels, dismissing the trusted, most fully oathed, most fully restricted personnel, coming to the storage chambers of the sacred relics of those whom, in his closest thoughts, he admired most of all: Space Marines.

He had seen Space Marines before, but rarely, and even more rarely had he seen them in action. He had spent his life in the Fleet, which provided transport for the billions-strong Imperial Guard. The Adeptus Astartes chapters, to give the Space Marines their official name, had their own vessels to carry them between the worlds.

What little he had seen of them had given him a lifelong fascination. Each one was a super-man, as though belonging to a different race altogether. Biologically enhanced, given extra organs, much larger than an ordinary human being, having a lifetime measured in centuries; their very existence made Drang feel puny by comparison.

There were something like a million worlds in the Imperium. In all, there were only about a million Space Marines too,

organised into around a thousand chapters of a thousand warriors each. One Space Marine per planet – and yet it was
enough. The Imperial Guard held the Imperium together, but it
was the Adeptus Astartes which defended it against its enemies.

Drang peered through the transparent wall of the stasis
chamber. Many of the bodies were too burned and butchered
to be recognisable. Others still seemed to exude might and
strength, even in death – especially the librarian, who had survived the attack in the Eye of Terror for a short while. Drang
could see the black carapaces which had been melded with
their rib-cages, enabling them to function in the vacuum of
space.

It was not lost on him that these supermen had been vanquished by other Space Marines – *Chaos* Space Marines. Those
Marines, furthermore, would have belonged to the First
Foundings.

Yes, there was depth upon depth to the history of the
Imperium, which few knew about. As a Lord Commander of a
Segmentum, one of only five, Drang had been able to learn
much. The First Founding had produced even tougher warriors
than those of the present-day. Their seed-genes had come
directly from the original Primarchs, the laboratory-created
progenitors of all Space Marines past and present.

That had been ten thousand years ago. And yet First
Founding Space Marines still lived, there in the Eye of Terror,
protected from the passage of time by the insanity of Chaos,
with its power to transcend physical laws.

Drang looked upon those faces in the stasis chamber, those
that had not been blasted away or sawn off. What faces! Such
grimness! Such endurance! Such fearlessness!

A rattling sigh escaped Drang's throat. *If only I could have been
one of you!*

He thought again of those First Founding Marines, and of
everything they had accomplished. There was a reason why the
present-day Marine chapters were limited in size. It was to prevent the possibility of their turning on the Imperium itself. The
First Founding had been far more numerous, organised into
entire legions. Inevitably this had ended in a huge civil war, in
which legion fought legion, tearing the Imperium apart.

How could it have been otherwise? thought Drang. The
Imperium was the greatest example of large-scale organisation

the galaxy had ever seen – thank the Emperor! What was the point of such organisation if it was not put to some use? Why have fleets of battleships and destroyers, why have gigantic armies, why have the greatest armoury ever to be assembled, and then do nothing with it all? The urge to engage in full-scale conflict must have been irresistible.

Just as it was with him. When the news had come out of the *Ocularis Terribus* of the fleets of battleships being constructed, a force big enough to challenge the Imperium, he had exulted.

That was the true reason he had taken steps to prevent this news reaching Terra. For a decade now he had commanded Battlefleet Obscurus – a frustrating, fretful time! Acting as ferryman to the variegated hordes of the Imperial Guard. Engaging in the occasional skirmish with assorted aliens. Punishing the occasional recalcitrant world. *When he had all the tools for a mighty war!*

Drang had been fearful that the High Lords would rob him of his adventure. That they would be cautious, or produce devious plans, or give orders to other battlefleets and command Segmentum Obscurus merely to stand by as a reserve – or that they would simply refuse to accept the findings of the nullship.

It had been a gamble on his part, one which had failed. Drang did not expect to live long enough to take his fleet into battle now. He took his eyes away from the stasis chamber and tilted his head, almost as though he could actually peer through the roof of the square-sided corridor. Which, in a way, he could.

He was looking through his implanted monocle. He knew that many rumours circulated concerning his prosthetic, though no one had ever dared to ask him for the facts. He had claimed to be able to see half a light-year away through it, *in present time, not taking into account the passage of light itself,* and that was true. But it was not all.

The true story of how he had acquired the monocle was not quite as dramatic as some of the rumours averred, but it was mysterious enough. He himself did not know its origin. It had been sold to him by a free trader who claimed to have obtained it from an alien world beyond the reach of the Astronomican. Drang had paid a high price, but the cost to the trader had been greater. Drang was possessive. He did not want anyone else in the Imperium to own a similar device. He had killed the trader, and all his family, and all his associates. Then he had used Naval Intelligence to trace the trader's past movements, killing everyone he had had dealings with. The trail had indeed led to the edge of the Imperium, but then, quite unexpectedly, had backtracked into Drang's own Segmentum Obscurus, where it had petered out.

He had never discovered all the monocle's powers, but he did know that it could see into the future.

And he knew that he was doomed. Someone was coming to him. Someone whom he, for all the security he had at his command, would not be able to stop. It was to be a woman, to add to his indignity. He could see her now: a shadowy, willowy shape, as if at the end of a tunnel.

He knew, too, that she would not be long in coming. It could even be today! Many a night he had spent mulling over his foreshadowed doom, searching for a way out, but the monocle offered none. All that was left was cold frustration. That, and the determination to achieve glory first.

No, let it not be today! *Mighty Emperor, give me victory!*

But in any case… Briefly he looked back at the brutal faces of the dead Space Marines. 'Take comfort, Drang,' he muttered to himself. 'Die as they died!'

His boots clumped and clanged on the metal floor as he retraced his steps. At the end of the corridor he pulled open a clashing bronze gate and entered a tube-car. The transport shot him through the bowels of Base Obscurus.

Eventually he emerged at a gallery overlooking a glass roof. Beneath that roof, ensconced in individual cubicles, were all those imprisoned as part of his secrecy measures: members of the Adeptus Mechanicus, psyker specialists, cyber-modified computators, as well as all the support staff, even the caterers, that made up the evaluation team.

Guards stood on the gallery at fifteen-yard intervals. Drang waved one aside and stood on his podium. From here, anything he said would be conveyed to all the prisoners. He clenched his fists.

'WHICH ONE OF YOU WAS IT?' he bellowed.

They all looked up, some in fear, some with curiosity, some with resigned patience. Servants of the Imperium were used to brusque treatment.

In truth, it was unlikely any of them had found the opportunity to pass information out of the base. Invisticone must have been sloppy. Unless... unless it was someone on Drang's own staff. Dark thoughts of revenge bubbled in his mind.

With a gesture of disgust he left the podium and returned to the tube car. Minutes later he was in his own office, where he sat down to compose himself. It was unsettling, not knowing when the assassin would show up. He expected she would belong to the Callidus Temple, a specialist in stealth and cunning.

What if he were to succeed in defending himself, and kill the assassin, unlikely though that event was? After all, he was forewarned, which was surely an advantage. Would the Officio Assassinorum decide against sending another of their number? The temple master would not think of his operatives as expendable.

No, he would be unable to do that. If what Drang had heard was correct, assassinations were ordered directly by the High Lords. An order from that level could never be rescinded.

A deep tone sounded, startling him. It was the door's annunciator, indicating that someone wished to enter. What, did an assassin knock politely and wait for permission before committing murder? An astonishing notion! Realising the absurdity of it, Drang bade them enter. The door hummed aside. But it was only his adjutant, Captain Jesa, bringing the day's order sheet for his attention.

'All right, Jesa, be quick about it. I'm feeling impatient today.'

The door closed again with a quiet thump.

'All things require their own time, my lord,' Captain Jesa replied politely.

It was such an unusual thing for his adjutant to say – indeed, it was such an insubordinate thing to say – that Drang froze. Suddenly he realised that he was alone with Jesa. With a shout, with a touch of a key, he could bring security men rushing into the room, or he could fill it with sleep gas. But he knew that would not save him. Not from a Callidus assassin.

Slowly he rose to his feet. As he did so, Captain Jesa's stiff black uniform shivered and disappeared. His face melted. Before Commander Drang there now stood a comely young woman in a form-fitting black body-suit. Around her waist was the white sash of the assassin. Her hair was a compact mass of dark curls. Her face was oval, her eyes dark and soft. It seemed inconceivable that her life was dedicated to delivering death in a thousand different forms.

'Polymorphine.' The word sprang unbidden from Drang's lips. It, too, was a specialisation of Callidus assassins, enabling them to modify and mould their physical forms. She must have taken on Jesa's form, including his uniform…

No, that didn't make sense… Drang was annoyed with himself, recognising that his thoughts had become confused when faced with imminent death.

In a musical voice, she spoke. 'Not polymorphine, my lord commander. Something much simpler. A holographic image, that is all. Quite sufficient for a temporary disguise.'

She tapped a tiny medallion on her chest: a holographic projector.

'And what of Captain Jesa?'

She looked at him apologetically. 'Sometimes the way to a target must be cleared.'

Damn her! Did she really have to kill poor Jesa? He had liked the man. He was his favourite among all the adjutants who had served him

'So what's all this talk?' he ground out. 'Get on with it!'

The smile she gave him could easily have been mistaken for friendliness.

'Were I of Venenum or Eversor, you would have been dead the moment I came through the door. I have been sent by the Callidus Temple. We have a particular role: to take vengeance upon traitors.'

With a graceful gesture she indicated the room around them. 'None of your surveillance or recording instruments work. None of your warning or help-summoning devices work. Everything has been neutralised.'

Now she turned to him. Her voice became firm and admonishing. 'There is something else about the Callidus Temple which you must know. A Callidus assassin can kill a traitor only after explaining his errors and crimes to him.

'Your crime is twofold. You have concealed a threat to the Imperium from the Senatorum Imperialis. And you have planned large-scale military operations without reference to the Senatorum Imperialis. These treasons are the reason why you are to die.'

Drang still spoke in a grating voice. 'I know what I have done, and what I have planned. These proceedings are tiresome. Do what you have come to do!'

'I already have done so. Now I bring a message from the High Lords. It is this – in short, they approve of your plan. They order the commencement of the campaign. But the start of a campaign is not the time for a change of commanders. Therefore you, Lord Militant Commander Drang, together with Lord Militant Commander Invisticone, are ordered to go into the *Ocularis Terribus* as commanders of your respective fleets. Your deaths are deferred until your return, and are *sub rosa*, matters for yourselves alone.'

To lead a military expedition under sentence of death! Drang found a grim satisfaction in this idea. His thin lips formed a smile of pleasure. His only worry was that the Callidus assassin might interpret this as a sign of relief.

But she had not quite finished. Her eyes went to the carvings of lord militant commanders of the past which decorated the wood panels of the room in a procession of Drang's predecessors. 'One more thing, my lord commander. Should you perform your duty fully and return to face me again, you will die with honour and your name and face will be added to the proud record of Segmentum Obscurus. It will never be known that you died at the hands of the Officio Assassinorum. But should you default and flee, even after a successful conclusion in the *Ocularis*, then no honour will be accorded you. Your name and person will be expunged forever from the Imperial record. Future generations will never know you existed.

'And let me warn you, you will still not escape me. I am of Callidus, sworn to vengeance. I *will* find you.'

Her lips became full and red and formed a sensuous smile. Her eyes held a soft lustre. He saw that she was looking forward to killing him: a fine figure of a man, noble-born, high in the ranks of the Imperium, obdurate and brave. How could an assassin succeed who did not find pleasure in his or her work? She was like a lover who was promising him a future tryst.

'You will die by means of a poisoned needle. You will feel intense pain for about three seconds, and then will be no more. Take this. Keep it with you at all times.'

She held out her hand. In her black-gloved fingers was a card from the Emperor's Tarot: the Assassin card. A slim figure kicking, punching, chopping, shooting, stabbing, a gyrating whirlwind whose weapons changed from instant to instant.

She touched the medallion on her chest. In no more than a second or two, she appeared to be Captain Jesa again. In Jesa's baritone voice, she spoke. 'Thank you, my lord.'

The door swept open, and closed again. Drang rushed to follow her, peering into the corridor in both directions. It was empty.

He burst into his adjutant's adjoining office. It, too, was deserted. She had killed the good Captain Jesa elsewhere. If, indeed, she really had killed him, as she claimed. But it was unlikely she had lied. She had no need. Her *modus operandi* was easy to discern. The good Captain Jesa had died simply to remove the possibility of his being seen in two places at once.

The lord commander returned to his desk. He called through to the security officers. 'Drang. Has there been a breach in surveillance to my office?'

The reply from the surveillance servitor crackled back through the speaker after only the briefest pause: 'No, my lord.'

'Who has entered my office during the past ten minutes?'

'Only you have entered your office during that period, my lord.'

'Replay the last ten minutes.'

He sat watching the playback. It showed only himself, sitting alone at his desk studying a report on recent Fleet manoeuvres. No one else came in.

So. The young Callidus woman had been able to disrupt his office's electronics and leave a clear record.

But of course. Were Drang not a lord militant commander, he might never have heard of the Assassin's Office. In any political system, the best technical equipment went to the secret organs of the state. And the best equipment of all went to the Officio Assassinorum.

LORD MILITANT Commander Invisticone's visitation from the Callidus Temple lacked some of the charm and romance of Drang's. Earlier that day he had briefly attended a passing-out parade of Battlefleet Pacificus's newest intake of cadets, fledging officers, none over seventeen years of age.

It came as a slight surprise, therefore, when one of those cadets appeared in his private quarters that night, as he was enjoying, for the hundredth time, *Imperium Commander*, the most famous work by the military dramatist Willhelmis Swordkiller. That the cadet had penetrated his personal security, with its depth of five levels, machine and human, was slightly shocking. That the young man appeared in his apartments stark naked was, for Invisticone, marginally more so.

After assuring him that his visit was not from passionate motives, the young man delivered basically the same messages which had been given Drang. Comparing the Callidus assassin with himself at the same age, Invisticone could not help but be impressed. Hardly more than a child, but with a self-assurance, a knowledge and ability, belonging to a man with much experience behind him. A faint half-smile hung permanently around the youth's round face. He would always know exactly what to do. It was a tribute to the training given by the Officio Assassinorum.

Damnation! Drang had got him into this!

But there was no way out, Invisticone had the good grace to see that. What could he say to this smiling naked boy with the nerve of a Space Marine?

Well, there was one thing...

'Might I be granted a final request when we get back, young man? Any chance of a final bout with Lord Militant Commander Drang? He is a very old friend of mine. I would dearly love one last opportunity to run him through with my sword.'

NINE
BATTLE BETWEEN
THE STARS

'PREPARE TO ENGAGE! Suit up!'

In the bowels of the battle-barge, Sergeant-Brother Abdaziel Magron of the Dark Angels bellowed the order to his fellow Space Marines. His company of fifty had waited patiently, chanting a prayer while listening to the ear-splitting discharges of the great lasers whose turrets sprouted like warts all over the exterior of the vessel.

The barge was a hurriedly converted freighter. There was no way, down here in the hold, to tell how the attack was going, except when the craft juddered and its adamantium-reinforced steel howled in protest at receiving incoming fire. Once, distant hoarse shouts had been heard, followed by a loud hissing and whipping noise, a sudden sense of decompression, and the slam of emergency bulkheads sealing off a hull breach. The order given Magron could mean anything: the barge was being boarded, *they* were to board an enemy space vessel, or they were being sent down to the interstellar planetoid that was under attack. If the last, then the earlier laser bombardment had failed to destroy the rebel base.

None of the hugely bulky, genetically enhanced warriors, bearing the gene-seed of Primarch Lion El'Jonson, was so undisciplined as to ask questions. The order itself was enough. Each man strode to the cubicle where his personal power armour was stored. It was but the matter of a minute to insert himself into such armour. Neural connections to the spine and the brain snapped in place. These ensured that in terms of movement, strength and enhanced perception, wearing such armour was like having a new war-body, an artificial extension of a marine's already superhuman toughness.

The company was lucky. These were the new Mark Four suits or 'Imperial Maximus' suits, a considerable improvement over the standard Mark Threes, using lighter, harder material. It was the first power armour in which the helmet actually moved with the wearer's head. The dark green of the armour, the livery of the Dark Angels, appeared even darker in the dim electrolumen as, bolters at the ready, the company assembled in the hold, a hulking army – literally an army, since fifty Space Marines was worth a regiment of ordinary soldiers. Company markings, campaign badges, as well as the Imperial eagle on each breastplate, all gleamed in bright yellow as they caught the light.

That eagle, sign of allegiance to the Emperor, was now an even stronger bond than before, if that was possible. Magron knew that there burned in the heart of every brother Dark Angel in the hold the same absolute faith in the Emperor as burned in his. And besides that, the same hatred. For an inexplicable fate now called on them to fight the worst of blaspheming heretics – fellow Astartes, Space Marines who had painted out that eagle from their own armour, defied their vows and rebelled against the God-Emperor! Such stupefying treachery was beyond understanding. Such apostasy was beyond forgiveness. The only possible response was implacable hatred. Sergeant Magron took comfort in knowing that at least no Dark Angel would ever commit such a betrayal. The Dark Angels were renowned throughout the Adeptus Astartes for their religious zeal. It was inconceivable that a brother would ever forget his holy purpose.

There were lift tubes to take them to the assault craft on the deck newly welded to the outside of the barge. As they were about to file into them, there came a shuddering shock and a spurting of hot smoke. The wall where the tubes were installed buckled, rendering them useless. Magron barked orders, his

voice carrying through the comm-link in each man's helmet.
The troop leaders knew what to do. Bolters banged, their shells
exploding against a metal partition and demolishing it to
reveal the emergency exits. There was a *woosh* and a tugging as
the hold was evacuated of air. They had broken through to the
decompressed part of the ship.

This action might well be resulting in the suffocation of any
crew members who had so far failed to don space gear, but that
could not be helped. Gigantic boots tramping and kicking
through wreckage, bolter shells blasting aside any impediment,
the Dark Angels found their way to the outer hull and the
nacelle containing the assault craft, rocket-driven rafts open to
space.

Waiting for them was their lieutenant, cloaked over his
armour. He beckoned to them, one gauntlet grasping the rail of
the nearest raft.

Sergeant Magron now could see for himself why the lieutenant had given the order to deploy. He had fought
engagements in space before, but then there had always been
a sun at the heart of the system. Here the scene was lit by
starlight from the massed stars of the galaxy, the nearest of
which were light-years off. Blotting out a patch of that light
was a planetoid about the size of Jupiter's small inner moon,
Io. How it had got here – whether by escape from some planetary system millions of years ago, or by forming in interstellar
space in some freakish manner – no one would ever seek to
know. Its value was strategic: it was roughly equidistant
between a number of settled star systems, and so was an ideal
place for a military base.

Long before the rebellion, the World Eaters Legion had taken
possession of this lightless, frozen world and had excavated a
stronghold deep within it. But now the World Eaters were
among the blasphemer traitors. They had transferred their allegiance to Horus, the renegade warmaster and therefore were
anathema. To seize or extirpate the interstellar base was the
Dark Angels' objective.

A battleship, three cruisers and any number of improvised
spacecraft had formed a staggered crescent around one half of
the ancient planetoid and were sending massed laser fire slicing
into its surface. Nothing else would have sufficed for the task;
thermonuclear bombardment would no more than have

dented the blacked-out landscape. Only high-density lasers carried enough energy to dig through the planetary crust and penetrate the mantle beneath, carving up the little world as if it were a ripe melon.

The battleship – recommissioned as the *Imperial Vengeance* – was at the centre of the crescent, a huge cathedral-like form shrouded in intricately worked turrets. Most of the planetoid's defence lasers must have been put out of action in the first salvo; only a few brilliant beams still stabbed upward from their armoured keeps, wavering to and fro in search of targets. Just the same, the scratch fleet's commander had miscalculated, for the battle crescent was already being broken up, under attack from another quarter. Round from the other side of the planetoid, ascending from what must have been subterranean hangars secretly excavated, had come a fleet of heretic ships the Imperial planners had surely believed to be elsewhere!

Now the two forces were manoeuvring, the Imperial fleet forced to defend itself even while keeping up the laser bombardment of the minor world below. Plasma drivers ripped through the ether, tearing ships apart. The vast bulk of the *Imperial Vengeance* hove close by, blotting out the stars, a gargantuan turreted shape gouting plasma as well as planet-targeted lasers, smaller rebel ships gathering round it like sharks round a whale, while in its shadow the battle-barge seemed no more than a beetle.

The cloaked lieutenant was ignoring the bulking, blazing battleship, the flashes of battle visible over a range of thousands of miles. He was pointing down towards the World Eater planetoid. Brother-Sergeant Magron switched to visor magnification and directed his gaze likewise.

Combat assault craft, small, lumpy images even at maxmag, were rising from the surface of the planetoid. World Eater Space Marines, ready to take on even a battleship in close order combat!

Such crazed courage did not surprise Magron. The World Eaters were infamous berserkers, at the forefront of all the campaigns in the Great Crusade. Their love of carnage and destruction was excessive even for Space Marines. It was said that the Emperor himself had censured them for their savagery, as well as for their practice of turning recruits into murderous psychopaths by the use of brain surgery. Sergeant Magron's hatred for the traitors was tempered by the knowledge that they were also the worthiest adversaries he had ever faced.

The lieutenant's instruction was simple: 'Neutralise those transports!'

Magron bellowed into his helmet microphone, aware that the whole company had heard the lieutenant's order, and had also seen what their sergeant had seen.

'Embark and attack!'

The response was an eager roar from fifty throats: *'IT SHALL BE DONE, BROTHER!'*

Rocket-rafts shot out from the deck nacelles, making for the assault pods which were climbing up from the planetoid and bearing on the battleship. Spotting their approach, the pods swerved, changed course and jetted to meet them. The World Eaters never refused a challenge!

Once the great battleship had dwindled there was a sense of coldness and desolation, as though they were in the midst of a vast undiscovered cave. The far stars were frigid, indifferent and unreachable. Sergeant Magron was aware of this utter bleakness in the brief period while the assault craft approached one another – then it was gone.

They were three on three: three rocket-raft and three carrier ascent pods capable of climbing up a modest gravity well such as might be possessed by a moon or an asteroid. As if by prior agreement they picked one another out. Rafts and pods collided with a crunch and went spinning through space jammed together.

The ascent pods differed from the rafts only in having a more powerful engine and protective cowl at the front. Bolter in one gauntlet, chainsword in the other, both Dark Angels and traitor heretics clambered to get at one another. Magron was taken aback at the lack of any tactical sense on the part of the World Eaters. Something had happened to them since they turned traitor; they had become a mob. Whereas the Dark Angels fought with discipline, co-ordinating their efforts and listening to the orders barked by their sergeant, there was no such organisation among the rebels. Each Traitor Marine fought on his own, apparently consumed with frenzy, and forgetting all the battle drills for which the World Eaters had once been famous.

Theoretically this would have given the Dark Angels an advantage. Instead they were taken by surprise to be plunged into a chaotic scrum. Neither side was equipped with suit jets. Each warrior had to find a foothold amid the tangled remains of the carrier assault craft to avoid being knocked into space by an exploding or ricocheting bolter shell, and could advance or retreat only with caution. The Dark Angels did retain one advantage, however: the World Eaters were mostly encased in the old Mark Two power armour, more likely to be ruptured by a bolter round or opened at the joints by a chainsword.

Amid the flashes of distant laser beams, under the glimmer of starlight, the Marines fired, grappled, clashed. Some were flung into space where they slowly receded, trying to fire bolt after bolt back at the battle scene as they spun round and round. Armour cracked and opened, allowing the entry of the next bolter round which would turn the suit into a container of bloody mush. Chainswords snagged one on another as combatants sought to thrust, parry and find a weakness where plate met ceramite plate.

Magron had already disposed of three traitors when he came face to face with a World Eater bearing the markings of a sergeant, like himself. For a moment or two the combined discharges of a whole bank of laser cannon threw the scene into vivid relief. Magron saw that the hated rebels had indeed discarded the Imperial eagle, painting it over. Instead the World Eater bore, on the breastplate of his armour with its traditional chapter colours of white and blue, a strange symbol, crimson in colour: an X-shape transecting three horizontal bars, the upper one broken.

He had no idea what this sign represented, but for anyone to deface or cover over the emblem of the Emperor and His Glorious Imperium drove him to an extra fury. He switched to rapid fire and aimed a barrage of bolts at the offending bonded ceramite, even though it was the strongest part of the traitor's armour. So concerted was this shock-train of explosions that the World Eater sergeant was propelled backwards and lost his foothold on the wreckage of the assault pod. But before he could be thrown out of reach of any solid object he had recovered himself, seizing an upright grip-rod.

His next reaction came as a total surprise. Magron had been unable to glimpse the other's face, hidden as it was within the visored helm. Now the rebel sergeant reached up with his chainsword hand and used two fingers to unsnap the fastenings, remove his helmet and fling it down to where it lodged in the wreckage! With a puff, air was whisked from inside his armour, instantly freezing to a frosting of glittering crystals in the sunless cold of space.

Magron found himself staring at the bared face of the World Eaters sergeant: a beastlike, feral face with bared teeth, craggy brow half-buried in campaign studs, the face of a frothing madman, screaming soundless words of defiance.

The Dark Angel could not understand such an action. True, a Space Marine could survive exposed to space for a while, though in some discomfort – but who would so expose his head to bolter shot and ripping chainsword, for no reason?

Not only the sergeant appeared to have gone mad. Others were following his example, discarding their helmets to grimace and mouth in hard vacuum. Were it not for the lack of air to carry it, a discordant concerto of harsh battle-screams would have greeted the struggling Dark Angels.

Were the World Eaters now so thirsty for blood that they would offer their own to their enemies? The Dark Angels launched themselves with renewed confidence, sure that the traitors' foolhardiness had sealed their doom and that the affray would soon be over. Strangely, it was not so. Not only had their recklessness heightened the World Eaters' berserker rage, it was as though some sorcerous mystical influence protected their exposed heads. Again and again the broken bodies of Dark Angels were despatched, to hover lifeless near the assault craft, while the World Eaters, daring their enemy to kill them if they could, adroitly dodged bolter shells and turned aside chainswords.

Magron went after the sergeant, determined to rip through that manic rebel head. If only he could wipe out Primarch Angron's entire gene-seed! In mock welcome, the traitor sergeant held out his arms, grinning insanely, eyes gleaming. Then he pointed his bolter overhead and loosed off a volley in sheer delight, waving his chainsword with abandon.

Magron took a risk. He kicked himself off from the raft and sailed towards the World Eater, temporarily abandoning his foothold, at the same time loosing off a volley aimed at the other sergeant's bolter. To his gratification it was torn out of the traitor's gauntlet and sent spinning off into space. He anchored himself again by wedging his right boot under a warped handrail. He raised his left gauntlet to point his bolter directly at the other sergeant's exposed face. The World Eater, with eerie soundlessness laughed back at him, daring him to fire.

Magron put up the bolter. He had promised himself to use the chainsword.

The rebel sergeant also seemed to relish the challenge. He edged forward, more cautious now, the speed-blurred edge of his own weapon held before him. Expertly he flicked his gaze over Magron's Mark Four armour. Demented he might be, but he was no fool. He had tested the Mark Four's capabilities in the last few minutes, and had learned much.

It was at that moment that Magron noticed something happening on the planetoid below. A glow was emanating from it, becoming brighter and brighter.

Despite the raging space battle ranging over the planetoid, the Imperial task force had managed to sustain the laser barrage. Now it was working, and what was more, it was working better than its directors had planned. The beams had scythed through the planet, had cut aside the crust and had delved deep into the mantle in search of the deep keeps. And now, what had not been intended – they had penetrated to the hot liquid metal core of the planetoid.

The little world was not like other planets and moons. It was alone, lacking a parent sun or brother worlds to flex it with gravitational tidal forces. So it had never been tempered by a dynamic environment. It had never been forced to settle and cool into long-term stability. Now it was paying the price for its aeons-long inertness. The pent-up power of the core, which had lain quiet for so long, encased in its thick shell of rock, was roused. It seethed and moved. And it had more than its own energy now. The high-density lasers had added theirs to it, turning it into a bomb.

Already partly disintegrated by the barrage, the planet exploded.

It all happened tremendously fast. The core glowed and swelled, lighting up the darkness, demolishing the crust and mantle and hurling their fragments outward mingled with sprays and streams of flaming, molten iron, a vast outpouring of high-velocity matter and total destruction.

Sergeant Magron's visor temporarily turned black to protect him against the glare. His momentary blindness left him prey to the World Eater. With a grinding, whining sound the other sergeant's chainsword buzzed against his ceramite armour, trying to saw through the plate abutments. He brought his own chainsword up and, more by luck than skill, turned the traitor's ravening sword-teeth aside, only to have him attack the armouring of his power cables.

When his visor cleared, the first thing Magron saw was the ruddy face of the World Eater sergeant, mouth exultantly agape, as if revelling in the annihilation of his own base. A red glow suffused the scene, coming from the still-expanding mass of the exploding planet below them. Magron staved off the World Eater's next rush, at the same time snatching glances around him. Several of his brothers had been despatched during their sudden blindness, betrayed by their own equipment. Some of the Traitor Marines, however, had met the glare unprotected and were dazzled, unable to see clearly.

The strident voice of the lieutenant came through his communicator from one of the other rafts: *'Brother Sergeant! Brother Angels! Our end has come! Pray for your souls! Pray to the Emperor!'*

The first wave of that explosion began to reach them, the smaller fragments, the gravel, the tiny shards of rock, that had been flung outward at higher velocity than the more massive pieces of the disintegrated world. It was a preliminary warning of the greater flood of stone and metal that was coming. Magron heard a rattling against the exterior of his armour. Too late, he realised he had allowed his attention to be distracted. He was open to the traitor sergeant's next lunge.

Then a rock the size of his fist took off the World Eater's head.

Similar missiles were slamming into the assault carriers, wrecking them completely, shoving them back towards the World Eaters' original destination, the *Imperial Vengeance*. Marines of both chapters were crushed as high-velocity rocks smashed into them, cracking open their armour, flinging them into space broken and crippled.

Even that was but a foretaste of the deluge to come, the broken-up masses of the one-time planetoid's crust and mantle, the still-molten spilled core, the raving glowing vapour, which now overwhelmed the space battle which was still in progress, spouting plasma and laser fire even in the face of the catastrophe. Aghast, Sergeant Magron watched as a huge chunk of black basalt, as big as the *Imperial Vengeance* itself, struck the task force's turret-encrusted capital ship. The impact shattered them both. Fractured adamantium, twisted metal, broken rock and superheated steam receded into the darkness in a writhing turmoil.

Something crashed into the assault craft and carried it away into the darkness too, away from the great torrent of debris that smashed both spacefleets to nothing. Had Sergeant Magron not been a Space Marine the initial impact might have killed him instantly, but he *was* a Space Marine, with his specially hardened body. So he survived, to be briefly carried along in the wreckage until he became dislodged from his footing and went flying off, spinning slowly end over end, the stars apparently spinning about him.

For a long time faint glimmers – chunks of basalt, globules of cooling metal or fragments of spaceship – went sailing by at the edges of his enhanced vision, against a background of spiralling stars. Finally there was nothing. Nothing to show that there ever had been a solitary interstellar planet, or a base buried deep within it, or a task force, or a battle in space. No voices, whether friend or foe, loyalist or traitor, came through his communicator. No one else had survived to answer his calls. He was adrift in space, with no other human being within ten light-years.

He was utterly, completely alone.

TEN
THE GREAT INVENTOR

'SKREAAAK!
 'Skreeaa-aa-aawk!
 'SKREEAA-AAW-AAAW-KK!
 'SKREEAA-AAW-AAAW-KK!'

The Chi'khami'tzann Tsunoi – or greater daemon of Tzeentch, or Feathered Lord, or Watching Lord of Change, to name but a few of his countless titles, though his *own* name was known only to himself and to the highest, most exalted of the Chaos Gods, Tzeentch, he of indescribable majesty and cunning, source of the Feathered Lord's secret name and also of his very being – spread his wings and flew through the serried heavens of the warp. His feather-edged form glittered with a million colours, sharp and flashing. His long neck craned this way and that as he descended through the countless levels of the Immaterium. His staring eyes, deep with wisdom, scanned glory after glory, bathed in supernal light that would have blinded any mortal creature, revealing gorgeous palaces, relentless conflicts, plots and counter-plots; all were naked to the probing gaze of the Watching Lord of Change.

Yet all this splendour, of a scale greater even than the galaxy it enshrouded, was non-physical. Its substance was that of thought, emotion, intention, disembodied consciousness. The bodies of its creatures, their towering palaces, the paradises, the purgatories, the places of abomination, were only apparent. In truth nothing was there but psychic force.

There was another realm, a seemingly dark realm, towards which the Feathered Lord now descended. The realm of matter. The non-physical Immaterium and the physical Materium had a terrible hunger for one another. Every physical being longed for the freedom and ecstasy of the unfettered spirit. Every spiritual being craved after a physical existence so as to fully realise itself. Some cosmic law kept the two apart. Yet it was possible – it *would* be possible – for them to combine in some monstrous new birth. Only the fact that there existed in the physical realm a god as powerful as the Chaos gods prevented their joyous victory.

'*Skreaaak!*
'*Skreeaa-aa-aawk!*
'*SKREEAA-AAW-AAAW-KK!*
'*SKREEAA-AAW-AAAW-KK!*'

The servant of Tzeentch, the Great Conspirator, opened his cruel, curved beak and once again gave vent to his frustration and his joy. Apart from his secret name, which would give anyone who learned it power over him, the Feathered Lord had of course names given to him by his fellow daemons. One he hated: Weaver of Stratagems that Fall Apart. Others he carried proudly: The Finder of Ways. The Great Inventor.

The Great Inventor! The Chi'khami'tzann Tsunoi was an inventor indeed! His fame would resound forever in the new world that was to come!

Two wars lay ahead. One was to defeat the God of the material galaxy who kept the Ruinous Powers at bay. After that would come a greater war: the Great War to decide which of the Chaos Gods was to rule the Materium!

That God would be Tzeentch! The Master of Fortune! The Architect of Fate!

What other rightful ruler was there? Only Tzeentch had the Promethean mastery of *foresight*. The rule of Nurgle would cause the whole galaxy to collapse in a morass of disease and decay. Slaanesh could look ahead only to organise ever greater excesses of depravity and dissolution. Khorne, the Blood God, was contemptuous of forward thinking altogether – looking

ahead was for cowards. He lived only to kill, slay and slaughter, without regard for consequences, only for the honour of
battle. Just the same, an ally was needed. An ally, to be betrayed
once his usefulness was over.

The Feathered Lord swooped down towards what appeared
as a dark, uneven wall or floor. It was the realm of the
Materium, a vast unshaped mass as seen from the outside, a
realm which had only three or four dimensions, as compared
with the many and varying dimensions of the warp. A daemon
who was strong enough could look into that strangely con-
stricted realm, sometimes, but generally he was barred from
entering it. However, the Chi'khami'tzann Tsunoi flew down to
where the darkness cleared a little. This was known as the Door.
Behind it lay a limited region where a daemon could materialise. Elsewhere he could do so only with extreme difficulty
and the help of a mortal.

Standing near the entrance, as if to deny access, was a
Khak'akaoz'khyshk'akami, a Bloodthirster, a greater daemon of
Khorne. His crimson fur, eternally dripping the blood of the
slain, was but partly hidden by brief but richly decorated Chaos
armour of black and red, the uplifted triangular shoulder-
plates embossed with the shapes of skulls. His membranous
black and crimson devil-wings were folded behind him. Iron-
black horns ranged above his dog-like face with its glistening
fangs. In his left hand the great daemon held the stock of a
wicked whip capable of reaching far, and in his right was the
carved bone haft of an axe blessed by Khorne, the black blade
struck with a single rune. The Chi'khami'tzann Tsunoi knew
well to be wary of that axe. It had another greater daemon of
Khorne imprisoned within it.

The Bloodthirster spoke in a voice like that of a barking dog:
'*We cannot be allies if I can defeat you.*'

The Feathered Lord carried only a runesword and he did not
even draw it from its scabbard as he alighted. It would avail
him little against the axe-daemon. Besides, his real weapon was
magic.

The energy of the warp shimmered as the Bloodthirster
moved his lithe-muscled body, as though he was surrounded
by a fluorescent liquid. The whip snaked out and coiled into a
knot-like skein, seeking to entrap the Feathered Lord and render him prey to the black axe. The Lord of Change uttered a

purring sound and waved a taloned claw. Warp energy congealed into a ribbon of light which laid itself along the writhing whiplash turn for turn. The whip seemed to collapse, to turn back and become limp. The skein of light then disengaged itself and spiralled around the Bloodthirster. With an angry growl, the Khorne daemon slashed around him with his war-axe. A weapon inhabited by a greater daemon has power even over magic. The light crackled, broke apart and fled.

'Now...'

Cracking his whip once more, the Bloodthirster flexed his body and whirled the battleaxe over his head. 'Eye of Tzeentch, *I know your name!*'

The lie was intended to startle the Feathered Lord, to put fear into him and render him open to the Bloodthirster's onrush, even if only momentarily. The Chi'khami'tzann Tsunoi cackled with amusement. What simpletons the servants of Khorne were! To think a Lord of Change could be deceived so! He crooned soft syllables, the etheric equivalent of spell-runes. The baleful black blade aimed at his craning neck slowed, as if hacking through thick tar. The daemon within strained to add its strength to the Bloodthirster's, groaning audibly as if it sought to be free. For some moments the axe hovered, moving neither one way nor the other.

Suddenly the Khorne daemon withdrew the weapon. Throwing down his whip, he made the sign of blood-honour.

'You are worthy, Eye of Tzeentch. But that does not make us *comrades.*'

The Lord of Change clucked and cawed. In the warp there was no friendship. Though emotion was the warp's chief constituent, that emotion was raw and primeval. If friendship had any counterpart, it was the Khorne sense of battle companion.

'We are not finished yet, Drinker of Blood. We will stage the contest. If I win, you will give me what I want. If you win, I will give you a dozen worlds of your choosing.'

'I am to trust a servant of the Great Betrayer?'

The Chi'khami'tzann Tsunoi's beak clacked shut. He turned his head from side to side, studying the berserker image of the Bloodthirster with his stony gaze. It was common for greater daemons of different lords not to understand one another's motives, despite their high intelligence. The one exception was a Feathered Lord, practised in studying the hopes and fears of every living thing, whether of the physical world or the Chaos Realms.

'Yes, you are to trust a servant of the Great Betrayer. To betray visibly is to destroy one's own plans. To betray without reason is foolishness.'

The Deathbringer of Khorne, accustomed to turning his huge axe on his own followers in his bloodlust if the enemy should all be slaughtered before his berserker rage was slaked, moved threateningly on hearing this. He seemed to suspect he was being insulted.

'Come!' he barked, in a voice that was a challenge. 'We go to the contest!'

The two spread their wings, one feathered, one membranous.

It is an advantage of being a greater daemon that the quality of size, the greatest of restrictions placed on merely physical beings, means nothing. Size is a property of matter only. The disparate pair, allies of convenience if events fell that way, flew through the Door, the narrow pass through which all this time the forces of Chaos had been trying to overcome the Materium. Spread before them was what, in comparison with the galaxy in its entirety, was but an antechamber. Still they could fly here, for the space of the warp and the space of the physical world overlaid one another here, like oil spreading and swirling on water, creating rainbow colours. This was what some mortals called the Eye of Terror, and for rainbow colours there was the suspension and warping of physical laws, making new types of worlds possible.

The two great daemons flew through entire star clusters which for the moment were smaller than they were. They adjusted their size, dwindling as they approached their destinations. Each selected a suitable planet from their respective domains. They moved those planets away from their warming suns – it did not matter, the planets did not freeze; instead their atmospheres were heated by friction as they moved through the ether-like warpspace-realspace overlap. They brought the planets close together and drew out from the surface of each a long tongue or causeway so that they met and welded together. Here, then, was the field of battle: a verdant bridge between two worlds, lit by a glowing sky, blasted by hot winds, crackling with incessant lightning.

And on each of these worlds the war hosts were already assembled. Officered by daemon princes, its leading standard bearing the Eye of Tzeentch, raising aloft every magical emblem, herded by Chaos champions, half the population of the world belonging to the Chi'khami'tzann Tsunoi, armed and trained, mutated into their war roles, proceeded forth on to the battle-bridge.

Officered by daemon princes, its leading standard bearing the crossed-bars emblem of Khorne, skull-filled banners dripping blood, herded by Chaos Champions, half the population of the world belonging to the Khak'akaoz'khyshk'akami, armed and trained, mutated or else mutilated into their battle roles, proceeded likewise.

Far above, seated on floating thrones of gold and silver, the greater daemons directed the game, relaying tactics to their captains.

The war hosts of millions met. At first it seemed as if there was no strategy at all. The forces milled together, those in the rear pushing those in front further onward, so that in the crush half a million in each army were trampled to death by their own side. The slaughter of the slaves of Tzeentch was great, for the conscripts of Khorne, raised since birth to regard maddened mass murder as the highest form of human achievement, laid about them with insane ferocity, and were apt to strike one of their own number with each backstroke of an axe or sword.

Saliva foamed from the snout of the Bloodthirster as he beheld the great slaying. Three million enemy dead within the hour! A massed roar of impending victory rose through the lightning-seared air, joining the gory stench which now permeated the atmosphere.

'*BLOOD FOR THE BLOOD GOD!*'

Then the strategy of the Feathered Lord came into play. His opening gambit had been but a sacrifice with which to rob his opponent of all caution. Now he gave cool instructions to his princes. He had placed the more disciplined of his forces in the rear. Their columns opened, diverged, began to manoeuvre, weaving through the rampaging berserker mobs. Magic, now, began to prevail over brute force of will, spell-blessed weapons over the warrior craving to kill. The Khorne horde became fragmented, squashed together in clumps, adding its blood to the blood that had already turned the pleasant verdure of the interplanetary bridge into a sticky red swamp.

The Khak'akaoz'khyshk'akami spread his wings and they quivered as he hovered over his throne, bellowing commands to his marshals below. Rage and frustration convulsed him. The confused clamour which drifted up from the battlefield was to him like a bitter wine that he must quaff and choke on. Were it not in breach of the agreement, he would have leapt down into the scene and laid about him, a titanic monster crushing minuscule human beings by the thousand.

His battle direction had its effect. The host from the Khorne world – a glowering, turbulent planet, unlike the bright, dazzling, sizzling sphere from the Tzeentch demesne – rallied, succeeded in disengaging, and so gained a respite. Khorne, too, could manoeuvre, though with less subtlety, in the pursuit of blood and bleached skulls, if defeat threatened. For a while the two armies circled around one another on the vast plain, like two serpents preparing to mate or strike. Then, with a massed cry, a great roar of bestial savagery, the Khorne horde charged.

The onrush was designed to overrun the enemy at one pass. The Feathered Lord let his beak gape, his long, thin tongue loll, a yawn not of *ennui* but of languid interest. He had anticipated this. The host of the followers and slaves of Tzeentch was pressed, yielded, gave up blood and torn flesh and hoarse screams of agony, hacked bone and armour flying in all directions. It was impossible to move without treading on severed limbs and spilled torsos, so that the warriors slipped and slid on wrenched-out hearts and livers and entrails.

But the Feathered Lord's calculation had proved correct. His war-host had absorbed the push, and now the two armies were a melee in which any further orders from above, any bellowed commands from the daemon prince generals, went largely ignored. The perfect situation for Khorne, one might think! But no; the Chi'khami'tzann Tsunoi's preparation was complete. The Khorne horde had lost its impetus. Not only that, but in the earlier second stage of the battle, carefully crafted by the Feathered Lord, the Bloodthirster had lost many more millions than he had noticed. He was now outnumbered. The Watching Lord of Change had successfully taken advantage of his impetuousness.

By now fifty million or more had died, two thirds of them of Khorne, a hundred million more left for dead. Slowly, like a mass of amoeba, the roiling, raging conflict was moving, creeping towards one edge of the interplanetary bridge. There was no way that those who reached it could save themselves. Once they were pushed over the border by the pressing mass, the gravity which acted on the bridge itself was no longer present. First thousands, then millions, fell flailing into space. A few, those with daemonic protection, managed to stay alive without breathing; the vast majority were lost. And sooner or later they all were attracted by one planet or the other, and plummeted in flames through the respective atmospheres.

Despite the apparent loss of control over the bloody struggle, the Feathered Lord still had a tactic in progress. As the murderous morass moved it had wheeled, so that the greater number of those who toppled over the edge were Khornites. At length the Khak'akaoz'khyshk'akami slumped in his throne.

'You have won the game,' he conceded in a grudging growl. 'The armoury hells are yours. And I shall join with you in what is now *our* war.' Contemptuously he gestured to the planetary bridge. 'Let the killing continue. Kill them all. I shall punish my princes myself, in our Chaos realm, for suffering defeat.'

The Feathered Lord cawed softly in pleasure and acknowledgement. He did not, of course, disclose his opinion that the defeat of this Eater of Gore and Flesh had been a foregone conclusion. It would only anger the son of Khorne, whose unsubtle brain, in any case, would have been unable to follow such indirect reasoning.

The Bloodthirster had defeated himself, without knowing it. The lure of a major war against the human Imperium which Chaos would, for once, win, had sabotaged the way he had played the war game. He had *wanted* to lose.

An exhausted exultation had gripped the battle scene. During the course of the battle the linked worlds had rotated around their common centre of gravity several times, and many days had passed in continuous strife, without sleep or rest. The greater daemons flew off across the warp, leaving the bridge intact. The joined worlds would now whirl through space together everlastingly, like a dumbbell, magically lit and warmed. It would have the same effect as placing a stick to connect two formicaries. Half the population of each planet was still intact. Long after the battle was finished, those populations would continue venturing across the bridge into each others' worlds, the ingrained glowering warlust of Khorne meeting the traditional magic and manipulativeness of Tzeentch. Invasion and counter-invasion. The war would be unceasing and unending.

Off across the region of the Door they flew, their wings wafting on the warp. They found their direction, and flew deep into a spreading gloom and darkness, a stygian abyss where writhing black vapours shut off the light of any surrounding star. Round and round they flew, spiralling inward, until a faint redness became visible in the distance.

The Khak'akaoz'khyshk'akami's forge hell-worlds came into view, worlds which – like many in the Door, the Eye of Terror – would not have been possible elsewhere in the galaxy. Twelve vast pits or funnels floated in space, arranged radially like the spokes of a wheel, mouths facing inward to the hub. Every pit was planet-sized: five thousand miles across at the mouth, fifteen thousand miles deep, extending into the darkness. No sun or nebula illuminated them. There was no need. The yawning mouth of each vast pit glared with a red glow and gave off infernal exhalations, like burning smoke.

The craggy outside walls of the hell-pits glimmered only faintly in the gloom. Coming closer to one of the hell-worlds, what looked like clouds of gnats or dust could be seen. Closer still, and it emerged that the mouths of the funnels were exhaling not just lurid smoke but weapons. Weapons by the billions, as well as armour. Swords, hammers, spears, pikes, war-scythes, war chariots, motorised armoured vehicles, bolt guns, flamers, plasma weapons, artillery, spaceships, attack aircraft, all the arcane, semi-magical weapons used within the Eye of Terror, lasguns, dirks, daemon-guided missiles, all drifting and spreading into the darkness of unlighted space.

The Khak'akaoz'khyshk'akami's forge worlds. As befitted Bloodthirster crudity, they churned out stupendous quantities of armament willy-nilly, without regard for requirement, collection or logistics. Nearly all of it would drift off into space and be lost. But more would always be there, if they should be needed.

The Khak'akaoz'khyshk'akami enlarged himself and flew to each of the dozen hell-funnels in turn, banging its outside with the flat of his warblade, causing it to vibrate.

He barked out a message which carried through the warp to go ringing into each Hades-like interior.

'SLAVES! ETERNALLY DAMNED! YOU HAVE A NEW MAS-TER! ENDURE HIS TORMENTS AS YOU HAVE MINE!'

The Deathbringer was formally handing over the worlds to their new lord. But first the Great Inventor had to inspect his new property. He flew into the mouth of the nearest funnel, adjusting his size as he did so.

The interior stretched away and dwindled into the far distance. The whole of it was filled with a cacophony and a fiery ruddy glow and a stench composed of sulphurous fumes and the smoke of blood. The toiling millions – or perhaps billions; they had never been counted, the individual worth nothing – laboured on the inside surface amid seething seas and torrents consisting of boiling blood and molten sulphur. The directors were daemons, the slave-drivers Chaos renegades. The Great Inventor was met by a daemon prince, who bowed with great reverence, though he could hardly have been pleased to have been abandoned by his lord and patron and consigned to the aegis of another Chaos Power.

The prince had cast off his Chaos armour. This was not a place where he would need to fight, and naked he could better show off his Chaos gifts. His oiled leathery skin gleamed in the furnace heat. His horned head, with eyes as fiery red as the scene behind him, sported a nose and mouth that had grown together into a single snout, while his arms, each with two elbows for greater agility, ended in bear-like paws, one of which gripped a whip adorned with barbs. His legs were of living metal, a truly fitting mutation for the supervisor of a forge world.

He left the rostrum on which he stood and led the way to an air chariot. 'Allow me the honour, most respected lord, of showing you the facilities.'

The Great Inventor had to shrink himself still further to stand on the chariot's ornate platform, and even then he dwarfed the daemon prince who ordered the vehicle – once a living being, now a dragon-like machine – into motion. They flew over the steaming landscape, ignoring work parties suddenly engulfed in lava streams, ignoring the screeches of those drowning in molten sulphur, or the despairing screams of those sent to scoop up vats of liquid metal from the high-temperature seas who instead lost their footing and tumbled from the crumbling headlands and floated on the glaring surface as charred slag.

A dozen times they alighted so the Feathered Lord could be shown examples of foundries, rolling mills, factories and workshops. The naked slaves – they weren't allowed clothing, protective or otherwise – made terrified obeisance when the greater daemon appeared. Sometimes the Feathered Lord was displeased and ordered entire continents scorched. Becoming a little anxious at this, the princely supervisor of the hell-world proudly showed him the punishment pits, where those who failed to meet their production quotas were put to endless torment – by burning, by racking, by the slow slicing of internal organs – in the huge torture dungeons. They stood, taking in the wailing, the fearful gibbering, the pain-filled howling, which echoed between the stone walls.

'No unsatisfactory slave is allowed to die until every last drop of agony has been extracted from him, Most Glorious and Noble One,' the daemon prince assured him, in a tone at once servile and boastful.

The Feathered Lord cast his unswerving gaze on the supervisor. 'You do not know what dungeons, what devices, what facilities for *everlasting* torment exist in the Tzeentch heavens, should you not serve me well,' he informed the Khorne-appointed daemon prince coldly.

He flew out of the gaping mouth of the redly glowing hell-pit and into the next one, and so on, until he had finished his inspection of all twelve. Then he rejoined the Khak'akaoz'-khyshk'akami.

'They are suitable. They will serve.'

'Then as we are to be companions at arms...' This was the moment the Bloodthirster had been waiting for. He peered from beneath his jutting brows, struggling with unfamiliar concepts. 'Tell me why you want these worlds of mine. Is it true what you told me? That you have found a way to *create matter*?'

'My great invention! Am I not the Great Inventor?' The Chi'khami'tzann Tsunoi could not resist the boast. The name given him by his fellow daemons was well deserved. He, and he alone, was to become the favourite of the highest of the Chaos Gods! The most favoured of Tzeentch!

His neck craned and his beaked head with its multicoloured crest waved this way and that. He opened wide his beak, raising it to the heavens. His psychic voice cawed loud enough to echo throughout the Door.

'*I CAN MAKE MATTER!*'

The Bloodthirster responded with a doubtful growl. 'Let me see this marvel.'

The Feathered Lord held out a talon. He murmured words of power, deep magic. His mind became still as ice, calling on the multi-layered spells nested and imprinted in the warp, beyond mortal comprehension. Spells that had taken millennia to form.

'When we materialise in the Materium, or even in the Door, we must borrow the matter to do it, and that is hard,' he clucked softly. 'That is all our difficulty. That is why we cannot burst into the Materium and mould it to our will! But this is not borrowed matter. This is *new*.'

A wavy, serrated blade had appeared in the Feathered Lord's talon: a short sword, one of the sinuous emblems of Tzeentch struck on its side. It gleamed with a blue sheen in the garish red light from the hell-pits.

'A new age dawns.'

He withdrew his talon, leaving the weapon floating in space. The Bloodthirster seized it, hefted it, testing it. His wolfish face twisted in amazement.

'And now,' the Great Inventor said, 'I will take my tools.'

He made a convoluted sign. He purred words of power. He exerted his will.

The forge hell-worlds were sucked straight into the warp.

ELEVEN
THE BYSSOS

THE IMPERIAL RECORD had no figure for how many nullships had been sent into the Eye of Terror during the last fifteen millennia, but the number certainly amounted to several thousand. It did, however, say how many had come back out: no more than one hundred and ninety-eight. Even this was inexact, for some expeditions, such as that organised recently by Technomage Ipsissimus, had been mounted in the utmost secrecy and were never registered in the archives.

In all that time, the surviving probes had succeeded but sketchily in their chief task, that of charting star formations within the Eye, altered beyond recognition as they were since the day when the warp had exploded into realspace. The incomplete charts which had been built up had never been made available to the houses of the Navis Nobilite. They were accessible only to the Inquisition's innermost daemon-hunting arm, totally unknown to society at large and calling itself the Ordo Malleus, and to the secret offices of the Naval Segmentae.

So it was that, as he looked out over the Eye of Terror, Navigator Pelor Calliden saw nothing he recognised. None of the star clusters, none of the stellar formations, none of the familiar mapped shapes and patterns of glowing dust and gas, that he had come to know from his years of poring over and memorising the great star charts which were the holy writ of the Navigator Houses, appeared before him. The only things that were familiar – and what shocking familiarity it was! – were the human faces which flickered in and out of existence, each measuring hundreds or thousands of light years across by the look of them. Yet he was not sure they were *really* human. They looked... *changed*. He was not sure, either, whether they were not just an illusion produced by his own bewildered vision, for after a few minutes they faded.

He sat, numbed, until gradually his panic swelled and overwhelmed him. He looked behind him to where Maynard Rugolo lay on the pallet, a restraint strap across his middle. The trader's eyes were glazed. He had not answered Calliden's frantic cries, seemed not even to have heard them – either that or the news they had brought were the last straw which had driven him over the edge into insanity, for he seemed to have withdrawn into himself.

Calliden turned pleadingly to Kwyler who occupied the second pilot's seat beside him.

'What shall I do? I can't see the Astronomican. I'm lost!'

The bland-faced Kwyler, dressed in his voluminous striped blouse or jerkin that was almost like a robe, grinned and nudged his arm. 'Use faith!'

Calliden threw his head down and covered his face with his arms. 'I can't! The Emperor has deserted me!'

Kwyler sniggered. 'Not in the Emperor, you fool! He can't help you here. Just *faith*.'

Slowly Calliden disengaged himself from the cocoon. He rose, retreated from the flight panel, and sat down at the table, the arched roof of the cabin curving over him in the dimness. His warp eye seemed to have lost its lustre. His shoulders slumped.

'I don't have faith. We're finished.'

'Of course you do, you're a navigator.' Kwyler retorted. 'How can you not have faith?'

'I worship the Emperor!' Calliden protested. 'You want me to pray to daemons! I can't do that.'

Kwyler waved a hand. 'No, no, you don't understand. Not faith in a god. Just *faith*. Faith that you can get where you want to go. It's the best way to navigate in the Eye. It responds to psychic forces.'

Dolefully Calliden shook his head. 'The Emperor is the only light,' he intoned, quoting Navis Nobilite liturgy. 'The Emperor is a sun above all suns.'

Kwyler smiled twistedly. 'You're in the Eye of Terror now. Here, let me give you some help.'

He reached into his loose garment, from which he had earlier produced the plasma gun, and brought out a small curved bottle of ribbed glass, russet in colour. Taped to it was a tiny goblet, no bigger than an acorn.

Calliden recognised it as identical to the liqueur bottle Gundrum had produced on the frontier world. The experience then had frightened him. It had been unexpected, an invasion of his private person, a momentary loss of control which he did not like. He shrank back as Kwyler unstoppered the bottle and carefully tipped it, having first detached the acorn-sized cup. A slug of sparkling syrupy liqueur crawled from the neck of the bottle and filled the little glass to the brim.

Kwyler handed it to him and made an odd remark: 'Get him inside you. He'll give you your courage back.'

Reluctantly Calliden accepted the glass and stared into the little blob of thick liquid with its subdued but ever-changing colours. He felt as though Kwyler's words had impelled him to drink despite himself. He raised the minute goblet to his lips. The liqueur seemed to crawl on to his tongue of its own volition, and again he felt the bewildering succession of tastes, as though every flavour he had ever experienced was being played back to him. He was not even aware of swallowing, but the liqueur was sliding down his throat. As soon as it reached his stomach the savage electric shock jolted through his every fibre. His nerves were on fire. He felt exultation, as though new life had awoken within him. The grimness of his situation had been replaced by a confident expectation of the future. It was as though gloom and darkness had been replaced by iridescent hope.

While he experienced this slow, irresistible explosion, Kwyler was also taking a slug, straight from the bottle. He closed his eyes, as though listening deep within himself.

'By the Emperor,' he groaned, apparently speaking to himself, 'I hope we find the place soon. This is my last bottle; I've got to get more. Why was I such an idiot?'

Calliden had not known the stuff was addictive. Was Kwyler regretting his actions in rescuing Rugolo from Aegelica's attentions? It seemed so. This knowledge made Calliden additionally uneasy.

Wiping the neck of the bottle, Kwyler was looking at him, watching the effect the liqueur had on him. 'There's only one place you can get this stuff,' he said casually. 'A planet Gundrum goes to. Most of his goods he gets from there; don't listen when he tells you about having extensive contacts. He relies on his sister.

'So, you know what to do now? Do what Aegelica does. Fly by *faith*. Follow her trail. She leaves a strong one, I can tell you that. No, I don't mean a warp trail. I don't even know if that will work here. Follow *her*. You've been doing it all along, though you probably don't know it.'

He said this last with a wry smile, then reclaimed the goblet from Calliden's limp hand and turned aside. 'Better give your friend a drop, too, or he'll never regain his proper sense of himself again. This is the last either of you are getting, though, till we get a new supply.'

An unexpected disappointment came over Calliden. The electric sensation was already beginning to fade, provoking the hope that Kwyler would share the remainder of the bottle and repeat the thrill. Nevertheless he felt vibrant. He watched as Kwyler lifted the trader's head and gently applied the freshly filled acorn-cup to his lips. Rugolo swallowed, then went rigid. In one sudden movement, he threw off the restraint strap and leaped from the pallet, eyes blazing.

'By the Divinity! We're not finished yet!'

'Of course not,' Kwyler murmured. 'By the Divinities.' He turned to Calliden. There was a new look in his eye. 'Why do you wait? Follow Aegelica! I need essence!'

Calliden hurried to his cocoon.

Throwing the warp lever, he prepared to do as Kwyler had bid, and try to navigate without the Astronomican.

At first the *Wandering Star* was caught up in a fast-flowing stream as before. Normally Calliden would have frozen with fright. That he did not do so had something to do, perhaps, with the liqueur – essence, Kwyler had called it. He realised suddenly that there was something in what Kwyler had said. Navigation in the warp *was* an act of faith, even with the

Astronomican. Formerly he had always associated this with faith in the Emperor, which was every navigator's creed. But there was something more. Something internal to the individual. A sort of confidence that he *could* succeed.

Calliden stared ahead, seeing here and there the peculiar areas of darkness which betokened stars or clusters of stars. Not that that meant much. Line-of-sight was of little use in the warp. The navigator gene did more than give one warp vision. Its other gift was second-guessing, an instinct for how to get from here to there in the shortest time. It would surprise many, Calliden reflected, to learn to what degree the traffic of the mighty Imperium depended on this instinct.

The warp whirlpool smoothed out a little. They were beyond the first barrier, where the turbulence was greatest. And then the incredible happened. The whine of the warp engine died. The engagement lever clicked back, *by itself*. The ship had dropped spontaneously out of the warp.

Calliden sat bewildered, looking out again at the vast extent of the Eye with its glittering stars – most unusual in their colours, he noticed now – embedded in space which, though dark of course, was not nearly as dark as the space of the rest of the galaxy, but glimmered with transient colour, as if a thin sheen of oil had been poured on ebony and was diffracting the light of the stars themselves. In fact that space was not black at all. It was nearer to blue, as he had noticed before.

'Something's wrong with the drive,' he said in a quiet, quavering voice. A warp drive was the most thoroughly tested, most solidly designed piece of equipment in the entire Imperium. It was almost unheard of for one to fail. But if it did…

'The drive's all right,' Kwyler told him from the nearby co-pilot's chair. 'You don't need it, that's all.'

Slowly Calliden turned his head to stare at Kwyler, his warp eye gleaming as though with malevolence. What the little man had said made no sense.

'Engage the realspace drive,' Kwyler told him, 'and hold on maximum acceleration. You'll see what I mean.'

Calliden spluttered. 'You're mad. Your brain has turned to mush. At realspace velocity it would take us thousands of years to reach even the nearest star.'

Unperturbed by the insult, Kwyler smiled. 'Try it.'

Calliden took his hands from the controls and sat back, the cocoon enwrapping him like a shroud. 'I refuse to behave so foolishly.'

From behind him came a shuffling. Rugolo had left the pallet and staggered up to the control board, placing his hand to lean on the back of Calliden's chair. His eyes still had a slightly insane glaze to them but also an excitement, as if of a new adventure. He seemed almost drunk. For a few moments he gazed at the external screen, which showed the weird sight of the Eye fitting cleanly within the screen's rococo oval frame.

'Do as he says, Pelor. He knows more about this part of the galaxy than you do.'

Stubbornly Calliden folded his arms. For an answer, Rugolo did what he had done on the night of their first meeting. He reached past Calliden and engaged the realspace drive.

It burst into action with a coughing roar, quite unlike the smooth and ghostly whine of the warp engine. Calliden reached to turn it off again, but Rugolo kept his large, sturdy hand on the brass control handle, preventing him. Clenching his teeth with annoyance, Calliden perforce took over the trim controls, not willing to see the ship fly unguided through space.

'Maximum acceleration,' Kwyler stressed. He was not smiling now. The look on his face was one of grim satisfaction, as if showing them something incredible which he did not himself understand.

Which indeed he was. There was no sense of acceleration in the little cabin. The ship's own inertial field was easily able to handle realspace forces of that kind. The three men each kept his eyes on the velocity tabulator. It had two readings: one in miles per hour, and one, rarely referred to, in fractions of the velocity of light.

It was being referred to now. The performance of the *Wandering Star* was beyond belief, far outdoing even what the ship could have achieved when brand new. The first dial whirred until it became a blur. All eyes were on the second reading.

'Captain!' Calliden yelled – the first time he had acknowledged Rugolo's right to be so called. 'We have exceeded the speed of light!'

Nonplussed, Rugolo took his hand off the engine lever.

The tabulator continued to climb.

'We are doing warp speed in realspace,' he said with a puzzled frown.

'Not realspace exactly,' Kwyler reminded him. 'This is the Eye of Terror, where the warp and realspace overlap. This particular phenomenon has appeared only recently, though, perhaps in the past year. We're in a region of the Eye where the overlap has changed its nature. Warp and space have become welded or stuck together somehow, fused rather than simply overlapping. The result is you can have star-to-star travel with just an ordinary drive. Extraordinary, isn't it?'

He shrugged. 'The Eye is full of surprises. Don't expect this one to last, though. It's temporary, I imagine.'

'You don't need a navigator at all,' Calliden said dully. 'Anyone could do it.'

'I wouldn't say that. The warp is still involved. You still need that *faith*. It might look like you can go from alpha to omega in a straight line, but you can't, not always.'

Just the same, if the whole galaxy were like this the Navis Nobilite probably wouldn't exist, Calliden reflected. More than that, the Imperium wouldn't exist either. Other races, lacking the navigator gene, would also be able to steer their ships over long interstellar distances. The advantage enjoyed by the human species would be gone.

The tabulator continued clicking up figures. Calliden was amazed. The *Wandering Star* was now travelling at nearly a hundred times the velocity of light! It was impossible. In normal space no ship, even with the most powerful engines, had ever managed to accelerate to more than one half the velocity of light, and even then the friction due to dust and gas – unbelievably tenuous though the matter in the interstellar medium was – had proved so destructive as to tear such a ship apart. Yet Rugolo's cargo carrier, a battered scow, moved smoothly with no hint of any drag on the external hull!

Kwyler broke in on his pilot's delirium. 'Go easy. Remember what you're about. *Follow Aegelica*. She's out there, leaving a psychic trail for you to follow. She even *wants* you to follow her.'

Calliden scarcely heard him. The *Wandering Star* went scorching through space, faster and faster. He could hear Rugolo breathing heavily behind him. The experience of seeing stars whiz by like snowflakes in a blizzard was so exciting that he could scarcely contain himself.

Kwyler's voice rose to a shout. 'Slow down! You're taking us too far! We'll–'

A violent jolt flung them all forward, so that Rugolo catapulted over Calliden's shoulder and ended up sprawled on the control panel, bruising himself on the protruding instruments and levers. The *Wandering Star* resounded like a gong.

The view on the external viewscreen disappeared. The screen was blank. They were in the warp.

And quite unaccountably, the realspace drive had shut down and the whine of the warp engine resumed. On the control board, from which Rugolo was extricating himself, the two levers had moved themselves.

How had this happened? Had Rugolo's collision with the panel moved them? Had the sudden jerk of the ship jolted them into new positions?

Or – Calliden hardly dared think it – had the ship itself responded, as if it were a living thing?

The Eye wrought changes, Kwyler had said. And if it could change an inanimate object like the *Wandering Star* so, what might it do to Rugolo and himself?

Kwyler was still shouting, trying to rouse him. 'You've taken us over the edge! Out of the region I told you about! Turn round! Take us back!'

But Calliden could recognise nothing around him. Without the Astronomican, he might as well have been in pitch darkness. Where was galactic north, south, east, west, zenith or nadir? How could he turn round when he didn't know which way he was pointed?

He closed both his warp eye and his realspace eyes. For a moment it was as though he had fainted. He lost conscious of the cabin and his two companions. Deep down within himself, he heard a voice speaking to him, urging him, warning him: *Get out, Pelor. Get out of this place. Get back to the normal universe!*

His mother's voice!

Except that this time he knew it was not really his mother, and not any deceiving daemon either. It was his own subconscious, trying to warn him, using a voice it knew he would listen to.

He opened his warp eye again. There was no jungle, no curves and skeins of multidimensional space, nothing at all that made sense, except that a powerful onrush had seized the *Wandering Star* and was hurling it onward. How far had they come? It was impossible to know. Thousands of light years, perhaps. The warp engine was idling, having no effect in the Chaos stream. Kwyler was still yelling at him and thumping him on the arm. Rugolo had retreated back to his pallet.

He had to do something to get his bearings, Calliden decided. Here no stars were visible. Everything was one dark, roiling mass. Perhaps if he could see stars in realspace he could guess the direction they had come from.

He pushed forward the warp lever.

The transition was instant, but still there were no stars. In fact, he was not sure they were back in realspace, until he looked at the viewscreen and saw the image there. Kwyler saw it too. He sucked in his breath.

'No... no...'

What was on the screen Calliden could see with his warp eye too. A huge, black, boiling, circular patch of space through which vomited a flood of even darker blackness such as he had never imagined before. This was not the blackness or darkness that came from the absence of light. It was a positive thing, like a solid substance or active force, ravening, raving, seeking to overcome everything. There was no sound, of course. But Calliden's navigator's imagination had manufactured one, and he heard the cosmic eruption as a rumbling, a roaring, a shattering and cracking as though the universe itself was coming to an end.

It was the vastest thing he had ever seen. The impression of huge size it gave was like nothing else. In comparison, the *Wandering Star* was no larger than an atom.

Kwyler stared at the phenomenon, stunned and frightened. 'By all the Gods!' he exclaimed. 'By the Emperor! By Tzeentch! By Slaanesh! By Khorne and Nurgle, we are lost! We've come five thousand light years! It's the *Byssos!*'

Calliden scarcely even noticed Kwyler's blasphemy in grouping the divine Emperor with strange names he had never even heard of. 'What did you say it is?' he stuttered.

'The centre of the Eye! This is where the energy of the warp pours through, more concentrated than anything you've seen!

Get us out of here if you love the Emperor! If that stuff touches us there's no guessing what will happen!'

Was this the secret of the Eye? A hole punctured in the fabric of materiality for the forces of madness to pour through? Kwyler was right about the effects of such a violent concentration of Chaos. It would twist reality beyond comprehension, but that would hardly matter as warp energy that furious would spin the ship to fragments anyway.

He heard his mother's voice again, sounding as if in his vitals: *Get out of here, Pelor. Get out now!*

The Byssos, as Kwyler called it, had at least given him a point of reference. He dropped back into the warp. Curiously, the Byssos was not visible here at first. The warp stream which had been carrying the *Wandering Star* – and which possibly was one of the great torrent's tributaries – had occluded it. But now the stream was slowing and breaking up as it met similar currents to form, finally, a horrendous vortex, and the awesome maw was revealed.

Calliden knew he would not be able simply to turn the ship round and head back upstream. The warp drive would make no headway against such a powerful flow.

He attempted an arabesque manoeuvre, weaving in and out of the flurries surrounding the mighty Byssos, like a moth trying to survive a raggedly blowing gale. The cabin swayed to and fro, caught in the raging forces.

Flee! Flee! Flee!

Eventually he was able to put some distance between themselves and the supernatural hole in space, and then the ship seemed to get caught in one of the fast jets put out by the Byssos. A cold, malevolent wind was blowing through him, a wind of the warp, not merely as a psychic mirror to the material universe, but as a ferocious invading power. Calliden did his best to hold steady as this baleful pupil of the Eye of Terror receded behind them.

Where would they come out? He could only hope they would be deposited back in the same region from which they had so precipitously departed. Kwyler was looking relieved but tense, licking his lips, his face pale.

'Think of Aegelica,' he advised. 'Picture her in your mind. Feel her presence. You can do that, can't you?' Sarcastically he added, 'I'm sure she made an impression on you.'

Calliden found the instruction unnerving. Gundrum's dae-
mon-infested sister was not someone he wanted to think of at
all, let alone follow her psychic trail as though it was a spectral
umbilical, to wherever it might lead.

'What if I just keep going?' he challenged. 'We got close to the
centre of the Eye. If I keep going we should reach the periphery
sooner or later. Maybe we can get through to the outside.'

Kwyler gave vent to a sarcastic laugh. 'Stop daydreaming, my
friend. You know better than that. You know you can't travel in
a straight line here. *You're in a warp hurricane.* You'd only be
chasing your own tail. As for getting through the boundary, you
won't manage that either, without Aegelica – unless you want
to try making it through the Cadian Gate, which is just as hard
to find, and patrolled by Chaos ships as well. Fancy meeting
one of those?'

'No.'

'Then use your navigator's senses. Forget the Emperor. Find
Aegelica!'

A groan came from the pallet. 'Aegelica! Aegelica!' The name
was uttered with a mixture of dread and longing. Calliden's
skin crawled. How could he take Rugolo back to *that*?

He wondered again why Kwyler had acted as he did, in
defending them from such a horror, when all he wanted now,
it seemed, was to get back to the source of his addiction again.
He could only suppose the addiction itself had robbed him of
his reason, leaving him at the mercy of his impulses.

Looming far off he saw warp-traces which indicated stellar
formations, and some patterns that he did not recognise, sug-
gesting structures that certainly would have been impossible in
normal space. He felt no wish to investigate. He was doing as
Kwyler had said, flying on instinct, doing what he had always
done but without the Astronomican, without the Emperor,
homing on the signature not of a star or group of stars but on
an individual with very strange qualities.

The fast jet on which they travelled dispersed itself into the
substance of the Eye. Calliden reduced warp velocity, Hours
passed, and then the *Wandering Star* jolted violently once again
and the tumultuous view of the warp disappeared, to be
replaced by the transparent deep blue, shot with colours, that
they had seen before. The warp drive faded at the same time as
the realspace engine coughed into life, both without any

intervention from Calliden. It was eerie to be piloting a ship which seemed to have a mind of its own.

Kwyler was looking about, manipulating the viewscreen. 'We have to look for the Rose Cluster,' he said.

'What's that?'

'Believe me, you'll know it when you see it.'

Calliden didn't need the viewscreen. In this part of the Eye his warp vision gave him a clear view. They were travelling faster than light but he restrained himself, not wanting to make the same mistake as before. Everything was unfamiliar. Far off, he saw what might be the physical counterparts of the strange figures he had seen in the warp. It was hard to make out what they were, unless they were simply dust veils.

A planetary system loomed up. He slowed further and steered close to take a good look at it. Its sun was huge, except that it was not what he would normally think of as a sun. It was not spherical but a flat disc, in colour a brilliant shimmering green. There were at least twenty planets, each a different colour – mauve, russet, lemon yellow, magenta – but they were not arranged as planets usually are. Instead of being roughly in the same plane, their orbits criss-crossed at all angles, like the electrons of an atom, and sometimes more than one planet shared the same orbit.

Then something appeared which caused Calliden to sit stock-still with shock. A figure was flying through the system, and it was bigger than the planets themselves, bigger than the disc-shaped green sun. A vaguely humanoid figure but crimson-furred, with a ferociously fanged, dog-like head, eyes glaring like pits of blood from beneath jutting brows, the head topped by great angled horns plus a twisted unicorn horn jutting from the crown. The creature was flying by, flapping vast membranous wings which put a dozen planets in shadow with each pass. It wore brief but ornately worked armour down to the waist, glinting red and black, close-fitting except at the shoulders which were protected by raised and extravagantly worked pieces. The curve-bladed battle-axe it carried in one great hand, holding the haft loosely as it flew, was bronze-black and vaster than any weapon should be. A supernatural energy seemed to flow and crackle through the unbelievable apparition, making it more solid-seeming, more real, than any natural creature.

'What– what–'

Calliden stuttered until his mind found a rational explanation. 'It's a hallucination. Can you see it, Kwyler?'

Though frightened, Kwyler was not quite as astonished as the navigator. 'It is real,' he said quietly, his mouth dry. 'A daemon, one of rank too.'

Now something happened which confused Calliden at first. The apparition seemed to be retreating. Too late, he realised that in fact it was approaching, but dwindling in size at the same time.

The daemon seemed angry. It flew alongside the *Wandering Star*, no more than twenty times the size of the spacecraft now, glancing at it sidelong with its smouldering eyes, wings beating majestically.

'How can it use wings to *fly in space?*' Calliden queried hysterically.

'It flies on warp currents. Be careful. Don't do anything. Perhaps it will go away.'

Calliden shrieked and pulled on the controls as the warp entity, in a sudden rage, swung round and lashed out with the battle-axe, itself larger than the starship. The *Wandering Star* jinked aside, narrowly missing being crushed by the blow, then sped off.

The daemon did not follow. The spaceship was too minute to be worth the bother, no more significant than a gnat. When last he looked Calliden saw the immense Chaos creature, system-sized again, taking his frustration out on one of the circling coloured worlds, batting it sidewise with the flat of the battle-axe and sending the broken pieces hurtling into the disc-shaped sun.

For the very first time the navigator felt that now he truly understood what it was that the divine Emperor was striving to protect the human race from.

Briefly he wondered if the smashed planet had had a human population.

MULTIPLE MULTI-COLOURED suns fled past, some misshapen, some ring-shaped, some joined together in complicated patterns by filaments of light and fire, some surrounded by what looked like intricate decorations made of gold and silver and brass. There was no consistency; no two were identical. It was a storm-enwrapped minor universe in which the normal laws of physics did not count. The will and imagination of daemons counted for more.

'The Rose Cluster,' Kwyler kept saying. 'Look for the Rose Cluster.'

Calliden found it, coming at him from the darkness and distance, and despite everything that had already happened, he gasped with wonder.

'Maynard!' he called. 'Come and look at this!'

The trader staggered from the pallet where he had been lying and peered out blearily. His arms dropped limply. His jaw sagged.

The Rose Cluster was, as its name implied, a large cluster of stars. Typically these were globular and contained thousands, sometimes tens of thousands of stars. In that respect, the cluster was unremarkable.

Except that all the stars were an entrancing pink colour. And the entire cluster had the shape of a rose. It was all there, the curving petals, hundreds of light years across, picked out in sheets of stars and glowing gas – also pink – the petals foliated one within another, layered down to a softly blazing heart. Some mighty daemon with a sense of beauty had crafted this. Calliden powered the telescope, feeding its image to the viewscreen. One of the stars forming the cluster appeared before them. It, too, was in the shape of a rose, its radiant plasma magically suspended to form identical layers of soft petals.

'Every single sun in there is the same,' Kwyler told him. 'And that's not all. Every one of the planets in there is shaped like a rose too. Thousands upon thousands of them.'

'Is Gundrum in there?'

Kwyler shook his head. 'No, we use this as a signpost. But they are nearby. Can't you sense her? You ought to by now.'

He pointed to a reddish-brown dot of light just to the left of the Rose Cluster. Evidently it was not part of the cluster proper, for it had been missed out by whatever magic had created the floral miracle.

'That's the star. It only has one planet. That's where we usually finish up. That's where Gundrum's trading post is.'

'How can you be sure they're there now?'

Kwyler uttered a short, explosive laugh. 'Because you brought us here, navigator! How else do you think you found it?'

Although Kwyler could just as easily have done so, Calliden guided the *Wandering Star* towards the undistinguished sun. When it billowed into view, it was revealed as swirling and moody, an angry, muddy brown sphere shot through with flashes of red. Its sole planet was not hard to locate. It orbited close to its primary and no sister planets showed up when he set the tabulator to search for them. A sun with only one planet was extremely rare in the rest of the galaxy, and usually resulted from some cosmic accident which had destroyed the rest of the planetary system. Remembering how he had seen a daemon casually destroy a planet only a short while earlier, Calliden could but speculate on what might have happened here.

He didn't know how much it might be due to suggestion on Kwyler's part, but he did indeed seem to feel an insinuating presence in his mind. Aegelica, she of the barbed tail and long pincers in place of hands. She seemed to be smiling at him, laughing at him. The memory of what she had nearly done to Rugolo came bursting into his imagination. Somehow it made him feel dirtied and depraved.

He parked the ship in orbit and studied the world below. Like its sun, it had a turbulent appearance. Boiling cloud hid its surface, shot through with lightning flashes. But Calliden's attention went to a most unusual feature. Perhaps a dozen spiky towers stuck out from the planet, protruding not only above the cloud layer but above the atmosphere as well. They gave the planet a stellated appearance, like a seed pod equipped with spines. The spikes must each have been a thousand miles tall. From their tips jagged streams of energy occasionally streamed, linking the spikes together in transient patterns.

'What are those?' Calliden asked Kwyler, indicating the spikes.

'Just mountains.'

Calliden shook his head. 'Mountains that high are physically impossible.'

'You are forgetting where you are.'

Fascinated, Calliden sat watching the discharges from the incredible towers. It was hardly correct to call them mountains, he thought. They were too slender. Slim columns of rock a thousand miles tall–

Kwyler broke into his thoughts. 'Well, pilot, take us down. I'll guide you in to Gundrum's camp.'

Puzzled, Calliden said, 'Isn't that fraught with danger? Our plan is to follow their spaceship out of the Eye. We should stay hidden. I doubt they'll spot us here in orbit.'

For an answer Kwyler reached into his jerkin and fetched out the liqueur bottle. He tapped its side, showing how little liqueur was left.

'I've come to collect some of this, remember.'

'Would you endanger us all for that? Be reasonable.'

The tips of Kwyler's fingers sneaked back towards the opening of his jerkin. For a moment Calliden feared he was going to bring out his melta gun. But no, he realised, he would never be so foolish as to discharge its deadly energy in the small cabin. It would vaporise them all. Not, of course, that he could believe Kwyler would turn on them like that.

'You owe it to me,' Kwyler said sullenly. 'Where would you be without me? Let's go down. I told you, Gundrum won't hurt you.'

Rugolo was also looking down on the spiny planet now. Calliden sensed a struggle going on in him, a struggle concerning Aegelica. His eyes were avid, but his face was pale with fear.

Aegelica...

The navigator thought he heard Rugolo whispering the name, though in fact his ears had not picked up anything. He was detecting or else subconsciously guessing Rugolo's thoughts.

Suddenly the trader seemed to snap out of his reverie.

'It's too risky. We'll stay parked here in orbit, then follow Gundrum's ship when it takes off. If you want more liqueur you can buy some from Gundrum back on Caligula, if he brings any with him. Provided he'll sell it to you now, that is.'

'Very well... captain,' Kwyler said, snarling his disappointment.

'How long is Gundrum likely to stay here?' Calliden enquired.

Kwyler shrugged. 'Not long. A day or too, perhaps, Imperial time. Of course, you're only supposing they'll head back to Caligula. Perhaps Aegelica will take it into her pretty head to explore the Eye a little more.'

Rugolo remembered what Kwyler had said earlier, about Gundrum having mainly one source of supply. The addict was pathetically trying to influence his decision.

He nodded. One got used to waiting on a spaceship. 'We'll set the close-range scanner to ring an alarm when it spots an object rising from the planet. Meantime let's get something to eat.'

Rugolo prepared a meal in the tiny galley from desiccated vegetables and dried fruit. Kwyler, as he had been doing all along, took occasional furtive sips from his ribbed bottle, not offering any to the other two.

Fatigue took its toll. Rugolo retired to the rear cabin. Calliden threw Kwyler a blanket, then lay on the pallet to get a few hours sleep.

IT MUST HAVE been an hour or two later that a swaying motion brought him gradually to consciousness. The cabin was in darkness except for the emergency electrolumen, which was never switched off, casting the palest and most subdued of blue light. He raised his head and looked to where Kwyler had settled himself by the far bulkhead, but failed to see him in the near-darkness.

He became aware of a susurration, a low whispering noise – the sound of an atmosphere rushing past the outer hull! As noiselessly as he could, he eased himself from the pallet and saw the dim glow of instruments on the control board. Outlined against that glow was the hunched form of Kwyler.

He must have kicked the ship from orbit by using momentary, near-silent nudges from the close-manoeuvring engines. On the external viewscreen, thick brown cloud was boiling past the sensors. They were flying through the atmosphere, like an aircraft.

Kwyler was taking them down on to the Chaos planet.

TWELVE
IN THE ROSE CLUSTER

THE VIEW OF the sky from Rhodonius 428571429, whether by night or by day, was beyond compare. By day it was dominated by Rhodonius's rose-tinted sun, enwrapped in its own radiant pink petals, the nearer stars of the surrounding Rose Cluster showing through a pale mauve sky. The night display was even more gorgeous. The whole cluster became visible against a purple background, stars and glowing gas sheets laid out, layer after curved layer, surrounding the planet with endless shells of shining pink veils. The overall view was the same from all the planets within the cluster, all of which were designated Rhodonius followed by a number. It was said that each number represented just one barb on just one feather of the Great God Tzeentch.

As far as Rhodonius 428571429 went, the specific form of the view also depended on where one stood, for there was no single skyline Each petal of the planetary rose was a landscape, and petal arced over petal, allowing light to permeate sufficiently to cast a rosy glow on the lower levels, the pink quartz-like rock of which they were composed singing faintly on a high, sweet, crystalline note.

Captain Zhebdek Abaddas, late of the Dark Angels Chapter, eternal enemy of the Emperor and everything the Imperium of Mankind stood for, looked out upon the wondrous sight from one of the planet-petals of the second layer, the lip of a higher quartz canopy soaring above him. The sun was setting amid a fiery glow and the greater rose of the star cluster was swelling into its full splendour. This was the time of day when he paused in remembrance of the beloved Warmaster Horus, who should have replaced the Emperor and ushered in a new age of glory.

He remembered, too, his own spiritual preceptor, Commander Luther, presumed killed in the great final battle on the Dark Angels' home world of Caliban. Though there was a distant rumour that he still lived, Abaddas did not believe it for a moment. Had Luther survived, he would have gathered all the scattered Angels together under one banner, here in the Imperium of Chaos.

His daily reflections finished, Captain Abaddas addressed himself to donning his armour once more. This was also the time of day when he shed that armour for a while, though it became harder and harder as time went by. He had come to see the armour as *himself*. To be without it meant more than to be naked. He no longer recognised himself as a body of flesh and blood.

It had changed much since it had first been fitted for him. The armour-forgers of the Adeptus Mechanicus who had wrought it would scarcely recognise it as their own work now. All the old symbols had been replaced, but that was the least of it. The power suit, of a bulky, squarish shape, the most cumbersome type of Space Marine armour of its era, was as though it had lain for centuries in some chemical-laden bath and had grown coloured crystalline excrescences, mutating the former clean ceramite lines into curlicued intricacy.

Such an explanation was not so far from the mark. The power suit was ten thousand years old – or, from another standpoint it was only a hundred years old, for time did not proceed in a straight line in the Chaos realm. It had indeed mutated as though it were a living thing, armour and wearer growing together, changing together, tending towards the point where they would at last become a single entity. Captain Abaddas knew the day would come when he could no longer bring himself to remove it.

Chaos armour.

Seeing that he had finished his meditations, his body-slaves scurried forward and with the skill of long practice began fitting his craggy body with its bleak face, so unused to expressing anything now, into the mass of altered metal, ceramite and machinery. This was not as difficult as it once might have been. Though his body still carried all of its Marine's modifications, it was relatively unchanged by Chaos gifts, for he worshipped no particular Chaos power. The mark of Chaos on him showed chiefly in his strength of will.

Abaddas stood amidst a meadow strewn with roses of all sizes and hues. His habitation was a cabin carved from the trunk of a giant rose tree. His personal retinue fended for themselves in the rose forest which lay deeper in the gap between the planet-petal on which he stood and the petal arcing overhead. The Angel Captain's domain – that is, the territory where all feared and obeyed him – consisted of these two petals and the petals on either side. Though he could exert his will over more of the planet if he had a mind to, which he sometimes did.

His moustachioed seneschal approached. He wore body armour consisting of carved plates of blue feldspar and a helmet of hard rosewood. He carried a halberd. All this indicated to Abaddas the nature of the message he was bringing.

He bowed. 'Master, we have located the intruders in the forest.'

By now the body-slaves had fastened on Abaddas's helm, with its prow-like visor. He had access to all his suit-enhanced senses, which went well beyond those of a Space Marine of the human Imperium. He could see the seneschal's feelings as clearly as he could see the man's face, playing over his body like the changing colours of a chameleon. The seneschal was feeling resolute, confident in his commander, excited at the thought of conflict.

But also, of course, afraid as much that he might be sacrificed in Abaddas's battle plan, as he was of being killed by the enemy. Abaddas grunted to himself. An unmodified human being was a patchwork of emotions, any one of which could betray him. There were only two ways to extirpate fear: brain surgery, or to receive the favours of Chaos. Abaddas had not felt fear for thousands of years.

His hollow voice boomed from his helm. 'How many hours' march?'

'Perhaps two, master.'

'Call Sergeant Arquid and his war parties together. We will attack tonight.'

'Yes, master.' The seneschal bowed again and departed.

The body-slaves, their task done, backed away with heads lowered.

Abaddas began to check his weapons: chainsword, bolter, streak gun – a Chaos weapon that did not work outside the Eye of Terror, once presented to him by a daemon prince as thanks for his part in a campaign.

When he had finished he again became lost in thought, standing as still as a carved statue while the rose sun vanished and the Rose Cluster took possession of the sky. Captain Abaddas sometimes felt lonely for the company of his own kind. Oh, he had met other Traitor Marines – there were perhaps a quarter of a million of those in the Eye – but in all his wanderings, he had never met another Dark Angel. For all that he knew for certain, he might be the only battle-brother to have been cast here, on that terrible day when they had all been drawn through the warp and scattered across the galaxy. Once he had heard news of another, but had never found him; eventually he had concluded that he had but heard some story about himself.

The Dark Angels captain had not been in the Rose Cluster for very long. He had wandered all over the Eye of Terror, always alone, witnessing countless marvels and offering his services to one prince after another. War was constant in the Eye; his power armour was scorched and scored in testament to the action it had seen. But he had found it easy to cow the inhabitants and carve out a territory for himself. A true warrior should always have slaves.

A puissant daemon of Tzeentch had transformed the cluster originally, magically imposing the rose theme upon it, but had left it more or less open, so that Chaos renegades of all kinds were attracted to it. Lately worshippers of Khorne had been swarming into the system, always ferocious, always destructive, coming only to slay. Abaddas had heard that a war was now being fought between the Cluster's patron and a greater daemon of Tzeentch, so he regarded it as an act of courtesy to oppose the invaders, especially if they threatened his own domain.

The seneschal returned with Captain Arquid, while upward of two thousand men he had trained under Abaddas's supervision began filtering from the edge of the rose forest on the limit of the meadow. Arquid was a Chaos renegade, not native to the Eye, who had fought as a mercenary on the fringes of the Imperium before being swept into the warp-storm aboard a crippled warship. Life here suited his adventurous nature perfectly. One side of his face had been ruined by a flamer blast and never repaired – reconstructive surgery was one service the Eye did not offer. A crimson cockscomb replaced the hair on his head, the only visible favour of Chaos he had received so far. He wore chain mail and a metal breastplate, but disdained a helmet, the better to show his mutation. Thrust into his swordbelt in cavalier fashion were two laspistols.

Of Abaddas's small army, several hundred were adventurers like Arquid, the remainder conscripted locals, some of them wearing blue feldspar armour like the seneschal's – for there were no metal ores in the crust of Rhodonius 428571429 – but many were clad only in their usual clothing of woven rosewood fibre. Weaponry was various, ranging from slug guns, flamers and laspistols to quartz axes, spears and pikes.

Moved by the shouting and cursing of the corporals, they formed up in massed columns, holding aloft their banners decorated with garish designs in vermilion, purple and black, mostly designed by Abaddas and incorporating or redesigning a number of well-known symbols of the Dark Powers. Many of the banners bore a portrait of the power-armoured Abaddas himself, sharp-edged visor jutting forward, bolter and chainsword at the ready, as though about to steamroller over the viewer. In these parts a Space Marine sworn to Chaos was a figure to strike terror, a fact consciously exploited by Abaddas.

Now he stood before them, legs astride, massive powered boots trampling the roses. He delivered a brief address, his amplified voice booming over the assembly.

'A foul enemy has invaded our fair realm and is encamped in the wood. An enemy who will take more of your daughters, kill more of your sons, than I have. We go now to destroy and humiliate him, not to preserve your families and your farms, not from fear of me, but

*because only in this way do you please the Gods. Throw yourselves on
the enemy! Any who shrink face THIS!'*

He raised the chainsword and let it buzz for long seconds,
waving it in the air. When first he began to press the local people into military service he had sometimes killed all the
survivors after a battle, in the interests of morale. Subsequent
recruits showed a little more backbone as a result.

He finished with a fervent prayer: *'LUTHER, LEAD US!
HORUS, BESTOW YOUR BENEFICENCE!*

*'Sergeant Arquid! Double time! I give you one hour to get through
the forest!'*

Arquid bellowed commands. Furling the banners for ease of
travel, the war party tramped at a run across the meadow and
entered the forest, forming columns which passed easily
between the boles of the giant rose trees. Sunset was giving way
to night now. As the temperature fell the quartz song dropped
a tone and became louder, a sultry blue note. The underside of
the vast overarching planet-petal arced far overhead like the
roof of a giant cave, but the foliations of the cluster's stupendous interstellar rose still showed through hazily, as if through
a luminous screen. The rose forest, with its great blooms –
which were larger than a man, and which gave off a heady,
powerful scent – never knew darkness, only a purple twilight.

Abaddas did not trouble to ask himself how a raiding party
from another world had managed to lodge itself so deep in
between two petal-landscapes. He thought he knew.

After nearly an hour he ordered a slowing of pace and sent
scouts ahead. Their reports brought no surprises. With his
enhanced senses he could already hear where the Khorne force
was, encamped in a hollow, holding a noisy revelry. He could
also see the glow of their fire, reflecting off the shiny stems of
the rose trees.

He called a halt and advanced alone, for all his bulk moving
quietly with his powered tread. The invaders had not posted
sentinels, which was typical of followers of Khorne and their
contempt for caution. He was able to hide himself in a rose
thicket and look down into their camp.

Rosewood blazed cheerily, casting a bright light over the proceedings. The hollow was a large one, amphitheatre-sized, all
of the rose trees having been cut down to make space and
thrown onto the towering campfire. Abaddas guessed that

about a thousand warriors were sprawled around it. He cast his senses beyond the camp, and thought he saw the outlines of the landing craft which had brought them here. The starship that had transported them might still be in orbit, though that was unlikely. Its restless captain would already have gone off elsewhere, promising to come back sometime.

He gazed overhead, searching the roof-sky. There it was. A gap, through which the Rose Cluster shone through with greater clarity. The Khorne worshippers had blasted their way through the upper planet-petal, boring into the rose planet like a devouring worm.

He knew full well how it had been done, using an explosive that combined daemonic power with nuclear fusion, able to aim the detonation in one direction and punch a clean hole through a quarter of a mile of quartz in complete silence. He had seen it done before, though trapping a minor daemon inside a fusion bomb was not easy.

He turned his attention to the camp. A glaring, manic Khorne totem had been erected in the firelight, overlooking the scene as though it were fully conscious – which it probably was. He saw that practically all the warriors were Chaos renegades who had received mutations. Common were dog-like heads; arms mutated into swords, battleaxes or spiked clubs; scorpion tails; tongues that spat poison darts. About a hundred had apparently received their Chaos rewards in common. They all had insect faces, with transverse mandibles powerful enough – Abaddas had seen this mutation before – to bite through steel.

And among them were a few great champions, grossly transformed, more monster than human, whose every step and gesture radiated violence. There appeared, however, to be no Chaos Marines.

The Khorne worshipper knew by now that there was an enemy force in the forest. They had captured one of the scouts, and a number of the forest dwellers. A space had been cleared before the totem. The prisoners had been stripped and given blades. This was the only sort of sport Khorne worshippers liked. Grey-faced, the captives were required to fight for their lives against opponents chosen from the bestial horde.

But the Blood God's sense of honour still prevailed. Abaddas tuned up his hearing and heard, through the celebratory howls and grunts, the conditions of combat being stated. The captives could strike on any part of the body, but their Khorne adversaries could disembowel only.

There were maybe fifty prisoners but the entertainment lasted only minutes. Intestines spilled in red mounds upon the bloodied ground, accompanied by dying shrieks. There was no mercy for those who, seeing what fate had in store for them, refused to fight or else begged to be spared. One slash across the abdomen was the only response.

From among the crowd, inane, near-mindless creatures began to lap the blood and gobble up the steaming guts. They had once been human but were now deformed beyond description, scuttling on all fours, comical in their grotesquery were it not so horrible – Chaos spawn, champions of Khorne whose careers had ended in uttermost degradation due to having displeased their master in some way. Knowledge of this likely destiny was one of the reasons why Abaddas had declined to dedicate himself to any particular Chaos power, for all the gifts such worship might have brought him.

He turned his head back in the direction from which he had come, amplifying his voice and calling, his words roaring through the purple forest and making the fleshy petals of the big roses tremble.

'ADVANCE!'

And he leaped straight down into the Khorne worshippers' camp.

'Blood for the Blood God!' he growled, the amplifier still full on. His chainsword sent blood and shredded flesh spattering across the camp. His bolter blasted out shell after shell as he waded into the press of bodies. He saw looks of admiration on faces that were obliterated a split-second later. His armour became outlined in a crescendo of laser and flamer fire. Impotent spears glanced aside from his narrow-angled visor. Chaos champions fought among themselves for the honour of being the first to confront him, only to fall with hoarse cries of fulfilment, vanquished by a worthy warrior.

Sergeant Arquid at its head, Abaddas's small army was soon pouring into the amphitheatre, banners raised. Normally it would have been no match for the Khorne berserkers, despite outnumbering them two to one, but Abaddas had already turned the tide in their favour. Brandishing a laspistol in each hand, Arquid stood back to back with Abaddas, coolly picking off those attacking him from the rear, watching in amusement as the mortally wounded proudly displayed their sacred mutations in their final agonies, calling on Khorne to witness their end.

A more equal slaughter began. The insect-headed mutants, in particular, proved adept at biting off faces, heads and limbs. The air became filled with a hubbub of howls and chitterings, hoots and squeals, growls and hoarse screams, as well as neighs of abject terror from the more fainthearted among Abaddas's recruits. On the edge of his vision he saw some sneak away. He marked them down for exemplary execution later.

His death-barrage had emptied his bolter's magazine, while at the same time reducing the Khorne force by about a third. Rather than spend seconds replacing the magazine he slapped the weapon to its holster-clamp and seized the streak gun in his gauntlet.

Its appearance was unusual for any kind of gun. The muzzle was a slot whose width was five times its height, enwrapped in a decorative serpent of gleaming electrum. As soon as he took hold of the handgrip he felt the gun connect with his mind. Like much that was Chaos-crafted – especially weapons – it was partly physical, and partly psychical. Only the very strong-willed could use the streak gun. Its backlash would engulf a weak-willed user along with the target. Abaddas's armoured forefinger wrapped itself around a trigger that might have belonged to a muzzle-loaded arquebus on some backward world.

A striped streak, a rashered ribbon, a stretch of pulled candy, a length of taffeta banded in orange, mauve and brown, rippled from the horizontal slot and went zipping around the encampment. It seemed to have an attraction for heads, of whatever description, while avoiding those belonging to Abaddas's men. Abaddas felt the shock of concussion on mind after mind.

The streak gun was a terrible weapon. It attacked, not men's bodies, but their *souls*, forcing them to experience in one flash every moment they had ever lived, at the same time filling them with self-hatred. The soul fled the body in horror, finding itself in the warp, to be feasted upon by some daemon or other as it saw fit.

The psychic streak targeted the most mutated first of all. These were especially vulnerable, forced to see themselves through normal eyes, as they were before falling to the twisted visions of Chaos. Their horror knew no bounds. Pale bodies fell suddenly lifeless to the floor of the forest. Dropped weapons clanged and thudded.

A Khorne champion with a fanged wolfish face and shaggy mammoth fur, otherwise naked, scornful of any protection, his only weapons a modestly sized axe in one paw and a dirk in the other, roared his outrage on seeing the streaking blasts flying about and felling his battle companions.

'*Dishonour, dishonour! No blood! No blood! There is no honour without blood!*'

The naked champion's prime Chaos gift was one of spirituality, the gift of unalloyed bravery. And indeed the streak gun was a weapon which no true follower of Khorne would have used. Abaddas averted the muzzle as the champion sprang at him. His respect for a champion of Khorne, whose battle record must have been long and glorious, was too great.

On the other hand, he was not tricked into thinking how foolhardy the Khorne champion was to attack an armoured Space Marine with such puny weapons. If they were daemon-blessed, they might well be capable of biting through ceramite, flesh and bone in one stroke. Abaddas's power suit hummed as he turned this way and that, deflecting the creature's axe with his buzzing chainsword. Suddenly he lumbered forward, forcing the shaggy-furred champion against the press of bodies struggling behind him. Momentarily the servant of Khorne was thrust off-balance, the razor-sharp axe wavering in the air. Abaddas stepped in. The fanged head was ripped from the champion's shoulders and went flying through the air, dripping gouts of blood on to the combatants below.

Abaddas found time to look around him in satisfaction. Despite having to recruit some unsatisfactory material – the inhabitants of the rose planets were not as warlike as he would have liked – the forced training was producing results. The invaders were being slaughtered.

Then a noise came from overhead, a humming, a whining, a clattering. Abaddas saw bulky shapes descending, having entered through the hole punched in the planet-petal above.

Then he understood his mistake. The encampment he had attacked was but the vanguard of a larger invasion. Possibly the

Rose Cluster in its entirety was suffering encroachment by a space-borne, Khorne-worshipping horde.

And indeed, as the newly arrived landing craft *crumped* into the rose forest, crushing blooms so that the sweet, fresh smell of rose essence mingled with that of animal-like sweat and spilled blood, he saw how makeshift they were, welded together – perhaps even bonded together by magic – from roughly cast plates that were lumpy and misshapen, hardly given time to cool as the metal ran from the furnace. They had been put together in some haphazard workshop, perhaps even on a starship.

And they were not even designed to take off again. They fell apart on landing, their hulls collapsing and banging to the ground, reduced to scrap. From their crammed interiors flowed crowds of frothing beastmen, falling and tripping over one another in their eagerness to kill. Blood flowed, too, from the dismantled landing craft, as well as butchered bodies carried along by the crush. Fighting had begun inside the carriers during the descent, even though there had been no room to move.

An endless torrent of such drop pods seemed to be falling through the purple twilight. Abaddas had no great loyalty to Tzeentch. Mainly he had thought to defend his own little demesne as a homage to the greater daemon who ruled the Cluster – paying rent on his holding, as it were. But it was unlikely that an incursion on this scale could be resisted.

For the moment, at least. Things would be different, he told himself, when the Great Night came. Which would be soon.

He bellowed the command to withdraw. A few, those in whom the bloodlust had taken hold, seemed reluctant, willing to face certain death in the excitement of battle. But they obeyed. What remained of his force melted away among the rose trees, a terrain they knew better than the invaders did, filtering back towards the openness of the clear sky.

It was impossible to say for certain which way the worshippers of Khorne would go, but the fact that they had used a daemon-fusion device to drill their way into the planet indicated an intention to march further into the interior of the world. In the narrower spaces between the more closely wrapped planet-petals were unknown tribes and kingdoms, prospects for gore and adventure so beloved of the Blood God and his minions.

Dawn was close when they regrouped and returned to the meadow where Captain Abaddas had his hermit-like cabin. The more badly wounded had been carried through the forest. These were laid down on improvised beds of piled rose petals, and Abaddas found time to attend to them with healing spells he had learned during his time in the Eye.

Meanwhile Sergeant Arquid formed up the rest to await their lord's pleasure. Abaddas's voice was more subdued as he addressed them, praised their courage and discipline, and uttered brief words of appreciation of the fallen. There was also a more demonstrative duty to attend to. A few of those who had fled had also returned, dazed and confused. Others, those who still had wit enough to remember Abaddas's warning, had stayed in the forest.

Well, the Khorne worshippers would deal with those soon enough. Abaddas ordered the cowards lined up, and asked them if they understood the penalty. Their eyes widened as if they had forgotten, but none protested, none struggled, none tried to escape. Of all the billions of human beings who lived in the Chaos realm, there were few who failed to understand the arbitrariness and absoluteness of their rulers. They bowed their heads in abject obedience as Abaddas's chainsword sliced through neck after neck and body after body slumped to the rose-strewn ground.

'Go to your villages,' he told the silent watchers, some of whom had just seen their own relatives executed. 'We will soon know if the invaders come again.'

They departed, the badly wounded calling out their gratitude as they felt the healing spells take effect. Abaddas's body slaves crept forward. They knew he would want to inspect his armour after an engagement. He allowed them to remove it, then checked its exterior for damage and carefully tested all its systems, inspecting the diagnostic runes one by one. They brought sweet-smelling oils, all rose-based, and cloths with which he cleaned off all trace of dirt and blood. Then he polished each plate, each embellishment, each emblem until all shone as before. Such work a Space Marine must do for himself. It would insult his armour, his chapter and his deity to leave it to slaves or servants.

The rose sun was rising, the Rose Cluster fading, as he was fitted into the power suit again. He dismissed the slaves and prayed, addressing first Luther, then Horus, to know if he had acted right, delving deep into his mind to listen for any answer.

As he turned towards his hut his glance went to the brass-coloured beastship lying on its belly in the shade of the rose trees, partly supported by squat reptilian legs, its earlier torpedo shape mutated into a gnarled, knobbly form, a cross between a felled tree trunk and a striated reptile, snout raised as if eager to launch itself into space. It was his means to leave Rhodonius 428571429, should he need to.

Returning within his hut, he checked and cleaned his weapons. The one piece of furniture in the hut was a huge, straight-backed rosewood chair, taking up about half the space. It was in this chair, fully armoured, that Captain Zhebdek Abaddas of the Dark Angels spent much of his time. There he ate, slept and thought. He sat in it now, rested for a while, and then contemplated the future.

It was at about mid-morning that villagers came and sought out the seneschal, who did not dare to disturb the revered Space Marine. Some hours later Abaddas emerged. He had decided to check out the beastship.

The seneschal bowed. 'Lord, the villagers have news.'

'Are the invaders coming this way?'

'No, my lord. Something else.' The seneschal gestured to the party of five villagers, who were dressed in simple woven smocks, and indicated that they should speak.

At first they remained dumb until urged in a sterner tone by the seneschal. 'Lord Abaddas, we have found something, lying on the meadow outside our village.'

Although he himself had instilled it in them, Abaddas felt contemptuous of their cringing attitude. 'Well, what?'

'He is not moving, lord. We think he is dead.'

'Dead? Who is dead?'

Again they seemed reluctant, until Abaddas raised his ceramite-clad arm in a threat to crush all their skulls. The bravest of them spoke up.

'A Space Marine, my lord.'

THIRTEEN
THE LONG SLEEP

ALL THAT SERGEANT Abdaziel Magron could hear in the confines of his power suit was the sound of his own breathing. Many long hours had passed since the joint destruction of both the rebel World Eater base and the loyalist task force, including the battleship *Imperial Vengeance*.

The stars wheeled sedately around him. He was spinning helplessly, aware that rescue was impossible. After a long time he realised that he still clutched his chainsword in his gauntlet, though he must have unpowered it at some point. In resignation, he placed it in its scabbard-clasp.

It was inevitable that a man of deep religious convictions would reflect on the course of his life in such a situation. Life proper had begun for Sergeant Magron at the age of seven, when he had been taken from his home world of Duthovan, a wild world of stormy seas, thunderous skies, mountainous archipelagos and strong-muscled men who had learned to navigate their entire planet in flimsy catamarans. The strength and boldness of the Duthovans was famous. It was what had brought the Dark Angels' recruiters there, in search of future legionaries.

Abdaziel Magron's training had begun immediately in the fortress-monastery on Caliban. He could not even remember now what his native name had been. By tradition Dark Angel novices took new names. But of the three hundred boys in his intake, he alone had survived the rigours of that early training. He had then served for twenty years in a scout company, attached to the Luther Regiment – a signal honour, for the Luther Regiment was the most respected of all the nineteen regiments in the Dark Angels chapter.

It was in a scout company that a prospective Space Marine proved his worth, often sent into the thick of battle wearing only light flak armour, despatched on the most perilous of missions completely alone. It was the most testing ordeal that a man could be put through, and the fatality rate was high. A thousand scouts had been inducted along with Magron. Only six survived to eventually become Space Marines.

The day he was selected was the most glorious of his life. Then had begun the biological enhancement: the additional organs; the additional glands to increase his weight, strength and stature; the enhanced senses; the implants to allow him to interface with his power armour; and above all, the gene-seed to allow it all to work, taken from his spiritual leader, Primarch Lion El'Jonson.

Then, also, he had been fitted with his power armour. How deferential had been the armourers who had adjusted it to his individual person! How they had admired him! Now he was a Space Marine.

That was when the *real* training had begun. Everything else was but a preliminary. It had lasted ten years. Yet the most important aspect had been the religious side, in Magron's estimation. Without religion, without total devotion to the Emperor, a Dark Angels Space Marine was but an unfinished thing.

Which was what made the defection of entire legions of Space Marines to Horus the Warmaster, once the Emperor's most trusted companion and friend, now the greatest of archtraitors, so incomprehensible to him.

A procession of visions welled up in Sergeant Magron's memory, like a panorama which he panned from one end to the other through the two hundred and thirty years of his life. The campaigns in which he had served, the battles in which he had fought, from one end of the galaxy to the other! He had even stood alongside the legendary Luther, the legion's second-in-command, as a companion in arms. And he had been in the presence of the legion's blessed leader, Primarch Lion El'Jonson himself!

Yet his most precious memories were of the religious cere-monies and the occasional large-scale festivals, all devoted to veneration for the divine Emperor. Such veneration was the core of Brother-Sergeant Abdaziel Magron's being. As he drifted in total solitude, a row of silver campaign studs dinted into his forehead, his greatest regret now was that he was out of the fight, and the traitor legions were still undefeated.

His reflections finished. The distant stars still wheeled past his visor, as they would for all eternity, leaving him with but one more duty to perform.

A Space Marine's life did not belong to him. It belonged to the Emperor. No effort had been spared to make him what he was. Therefore he was expected to preserve himself whenever possible, in all conditions. So it would have been a dereliction of duty for Sergeant Abdaziel Magron not to follow the one option still remaining. He activated the suspension-of-anima-tion membrane in his brain.

Of all the implanted organs which made a Space Marine more than a man, the sus-an organ was perhaps the least used, but he used it now. One by one it closed down all his biologi-cal and psychic functions. His heart slowed, then stopped. His metabolism reduced itself to zero. All his muscles became qui-escent. His nerve and brain cells ceased firing. His whole body was blanketed with an electric field to kill any bacteria which might still be alive, and then that field was switched off.

In such a state a Space Marine could survive for centuries. In Magron's case the survival period was to be extended indefi-nitely. His power suit responded to the sus-an signal by testing its own physical environment. It discovered that environment to be hard vacuum, particularly favourable for long-term stor-age. It therefore arranged for the evacuation of air from the suit. It shut down all its own functions, allowing the near-total frigidity of interstellar space – the closest thing to absolute zero – to permeate the body of Abdaziel Magron. The Dark Angel was now essentially no different from any other lump of mat-ter drifting between the stars.

ELSEWHERE, THE HISTORY of the Imperium continued. The war of the Horus Heresy ground on. The Dark Angels Chapter itself was cleft in two by the conflict – incredible though that would have seemed to Sergeant Magron – with the trusted but treacherous Luther siding with Chaos. The Emperor met the daemon-possessed Warmaster Horus in single combat, defeating him at the cost of such dreadful injuries that only everlasting imprisonment within the Golden Throne could preserve his life. Hardened though he was, Magron would have wept had he known what had happened.

Centuries passed, and stretched into millennia. The vast task of reconstructing the Imperium went patiently on. The Adeptus Astartes was reorganised. Planets were scoured, sacrificing countless billions in a sacred effort to rescue the purity of the human race. The dreadful forces of Chaos were driven out, able to take refuge in the Eye of Terror only because the depleted loyalist forces were insufficient to eradicate them completely. As for the Emperor in his Golden Throne, the palace surrounding it expanded until it covered an entire continent. The Cult of the Emperor became the religious mainstay of the galaxy.

Of all this the de-animated Space Marine knew nothing. His inert body drifted slowly, aimlessly. Every few centuries, answering to some vestigial function, the sus-an membrane stirred and began to restore mental awareness to the frozen brain.

Sergeant Magron would find himself dreaming. He would even wake up blearily and see glimmering stars wheeling past his visor as before, and enter into reveries of remembrance for what seemed like ageless periods but were in fact only a minute or so at a time, while membrane and suit, using the last few ergs of energy still remaining in the power pack, tested the environment and decided that the time to reawaken had not come yet, if it was ever to come, and put him back into death-like sleep.

In this way Sergeant Magron reviewed his life yet again. He even recovered memories of his infancy on Duthovan. He relived his most dangerous mission as a scout, trekking across a desert to gain intelligence on a band of orks. He was captured by them, tortured for days and left for dead, later revived by Chapter apothecaries by means of treatment almost as painful.

He relived the engagement in the deep tunnels of a world without any external atmosphere, inhabited by aliens who had preserved their remaining air by retreating into the crust of the planet. To be trapped ten miles down amid the collapsing tunnels of a doomed alien warren was a nightmare, even for him.

Particularly vivid was the dream in which he and one of his battle-brothers, a Captain Zhebdek Abaddas, had been the sole survivors from an entire company dropped on a death world in an attempt to recover Standard Template Construction material from a crashed Navy ship. A dreadful episode! The planet boasted monsters able to crush Space Marine armour like an eggshell, and almost impervious to bolter fire or anything else. Others of the company had sacrificed themselves to give him and Abaddas a chance of reaching the wreck. This had spurred them on against impossible odds.

The dream faded, to be replaced, later, by another. He could not know, of course, that sus-an was preserving him for thousands of years. It seemed to him that the periods of oblivion were brief. Yet all unknown to him, something was changing. Though the nearest stars were light years away, even at those immense distances some minute gravitational influence was exerted. Given sufficiently long periods of time, a small object begins to weave a course among them. The Mark Four armour, with its frozen occupant, traversed light-year after light-year, steadily gaining velocity.

Close to ten millennia passed, at the end of which time the now-defunct power suit became lost amidst a huge shell of gas and dust having the appearance of a vast nebula.

Obscured within that nebula lay a huge swirl of stars and star clusters. Strange indeed are the ways of the warp. Somehow it had influenced Magron's millennia-long drift. Somehow it had attracted his inert form. Now he was being drawn through the suffusing outer garment of the Eye of Terror. Once within, he moved more swiftly, this time in defiance of the laws of physics. Further centuries passed, in which the warp nudged him into the great warp-storm's whirlpool motion. It seemed as though the souls of brother Dark Angels were calling to him, drawing him on. To and fro he wavered. Then he seemed to head straight inwards, until he came to a particular star cluster, strangely shaped.

Being de-animated, he could not see that impossible shape. Or the equally impossible shapes of the stars composing it. Or, as he came among them, of the planets circling those stars.

By now he was moving with the speed of a spaceship. Yet, from no evident outside cause, he slowed. The light of a strange sun was warming the casing of his armour. Gradually, degree by degree, his body emerged from a temperature low enough to liquefy helium.

Gently, he came to the edge of an atmosphere, belonging to a planet that was not a planet but whose surface was foliated into great curved awnings coloured rose-pink, each one a continent. Sergeant Abdaziel Magron should now have fallen through that atmosphere like a flaming meteor, armour and man burning up together. He did not. He drifted gently down, as if being lowered on a bed of rose petals, and after many an hour came to rest on a pleasant meadow. The impossible sun was in the sky. A warm breeze, laden with perfumes, wafted over the suit as it lay upon its back.

And now the only function remaining in Magron's body, a function belonging to the sus-an membrane itself, came into play. It was able to sense that the Dark Angel was once more in a friendly environment, or at least one in which he could survive. It began the process of reanimation.

This itself took a fairly long time. The human body, even a superhuman body, could not be started up in an instant. It was not like switching on an engine. Magron's muscles trembled ever so slightly as his somatic cells came alive. Liver, intestines, kidneys, spleen and pancreas came into readiness, as did all the extra organs implanted in him more than ten thousand years ago. Nerve cells began firing. Faintly at first, his two hearts began to beat, and his Space Marine blood, far more efficient than that of a normal human, began to flow through his veins. His brain cells began firing, preparing the ascending reticular system to arouse the frontal cortex. This did not happen immediately. For some days Magron lay in a coma, and days after that he spent in dreams weirder than he had ever experienced.

Then Magron woke up. He was in complete darkness, and unable to move, so that at first he believed he was dead, a disembodied spirit drifting through the sea of souls.

The reason for his immobility was simple. So long had been Magron's sojourn that his suit's power pack had drained itself of all energy. His helmet's sensory devices no longer had power by which to function and were dead, unable to supply signals to his brain. The coils and cables for moving the heavy suit were equally inert. The abutments between the armour plates had become stiff, making it impossible to move the suit at all by muscle power alone.

But one thing eventually convinced Magron that he was, after all, alive. He was breathing, and therefore had a corporeal form. This was due to the foresight of the suit's designers, for the pump which should have fed him oxygen was also dead, and in a completely sealed suit he would have suffocated where he lay, once the oxygen stored in his liver ran out. Therefore, thousands of years before, when the energy reading of the power pack sank to near-zero, the suit had carried out one last tiny action with its final few ergs. It had opened up an orifice to the outside, just large enough to allow Magron to draw in breath should he find himself in an oxygenated atmosphere.

He had, of course, no idea how much time had passed. He did not know where he was or how he had got there. He had not expected ever to be revived, and as no one had communicated with him or rescued him from the depowered suit, he now expected slowly to starve to death.

Entombed as he was, he neither saw nor heard anything around him, though the air he breathed was pleasantly perfumed. So he did not know that denizens of the remade planet had found him, had walked all around him, and had recoiled in horror at the hated Imperial eagle which was still discernible on his breastplate through all the erosion wrought by his long sojourn. They knew that this was a Space Marine, albeit an enemy Space Marine. So in the end, making obeisance, showing cringing respect, they took the news to another who bore the same colours, though hardly the same emblems.

The Fallen Angel took his time travelling to the place. He looked carefully over the recumbent figure, reading everything the suit's emblems and sigils told him, including the Dark Angel's identity. He also recognised the type of armour the Space Marine wore. It belonged to the same era as his own.

Outwardly Captain Abaddas expressed no surprise. The fantastical was not surprising in the Eye of Terror.

But inwardly he was astonished. The power armour's external skin was strangely scored and pitted, as though it had spent long centuries naked to space. Otherwise it was unchanged, in stark contrast to his own. This was no Chaos Space Marine.

He could hear the suit's occupant breathing.

'Raise him to his feet,' he ordered.

This was a difficult task. Ropes were required. But eventually the bulky figure, a very emblem of warrior might, had been placed upright. The power suit did not collapse. The stiffness of its plate abutments was sufficient to hold it erect, as Captain Abaddas had guessed.

He walked around the stiff figure. Coming to the rear, he saw that the solar converters at the back of the hulking shoulder mouldings were covered in a thick layer of dust which had been attracted there by the electric charge on the silicon panels. He barked orders. Someone fetched a soft cloth and cleaned the surfaces until they gleamed ebony black.

Slowly, a trickle of energy fed through to the sensory systems. Dimly at first but growing stronger, Sergeant Abdaziel Magron began to see.

Captain Abaddas waited patiently while the storage charge built up, before he spoke.

'Do you know me, Brother-Sergeant Magron?' he enquired in his hollow voice. 'I am Captain Abaddas, of the Third regiment.'

A voice, gruff, weak, disbelieving, muffled by the Space Marine's helm – there was not yet enough power to work the external speaker – came through the breathing apertures opened by the suit.

'Brother-Captain Abaddas... is that really you? What has happened to you?'

Abaddas repeated his question. 'Do you know me, brother-sergeant?'

'I know you, brother-captain,' Magron whispered faintly.

'Then let me help you, brother.'

Captain Abaddas placed his hand on the emergency charge port on the sergeant's backpack. There was a fizzing and a glow as he delivered power into the drained storage unit. Creaking at first, the suit came to life.

'Come with me, sergeant.'

And Sergeant Abdaziel Magron of the Dark Angels Legion stepped towards his new future.

It was as though the two met fully armoured on a battlefield. Magron experienced a flashback. He could not help but be reminded of the time he and Abaddas had stood together on a death world, expecting never again to see Caliban or to receive benediction in one of the fortress monasteries.

Abaddas had not been armoured then as he was now. Magron was able to recognise his power suit as originally a Mark Three,

designed mainly for boarding actions and tunnel fighting;
Magron had worn one himself, in the bowels of the de-atmos-
phered alien world. The Mark Three was especially
brutal-looking in its appearance, with its thick wedge of a helmet
and its additional frontal armour plates. But the suit worn by
Abaddas had been transformed somehow. It was as if the external shell had become an organic thing and begun to sprout
cancers, putting out multicoloured growths. A stag-like structure
extended from the top of the helmet. The Imperial eagle was
gone from the breastplate, as was the regimental badge from the
right shoulder casing. Both had been replaced by curious designs
he did not know. The chapter badge remained, but it had been
oddly distorted and elaborated, as was Abaddas's badge of rank.

They stood outside a wooden cabin which apparently was
the captain's quarters here. A Space Marine was tough-minded,
able to adapt to changing circumstances, but this was the
strangest place Magron had ever been in. The ground was composed of a pink crystalline substance which, however, was
carpeted with a mossy or crystalline growth of the same colour
and translucency. It was also strewn with roses which appeared
to grow straight out of that crystal ground, without benefit of
any bush. Not far off lay the margin of a forest which again
sported roses, but of immense size.

The overhead panorama offered what was the real enchantment. Half the sky was open and clear. Evidently Magron was
in a star cluster, for stars shone through even in daylight. The
sky was pale mauve in colour, almost white. Halfway up from
the horizon there shone a pink sun. Shaped like a rose.

And the other half of the sky... It was like an awning, a solid
structure, also pink. Magron guessed it was of the same substance as the ground. But it cast little or no shadow, apparently
offering no resistance to sunlight. Even a few stars could be
seen through it, though faintly.

Altogether, this was a world of magical beauty. Sergeant
Magron had no idea how he had arrived here. But it was his
duty to report to Captain Abaddas – if this was, in truth,
Captain Abaddas.

He spoke up. 'Captain, why are you armoured? Is there an
engagement?'

'Engagement or no, I remain armoured,' came the enigmatic
reply.

Magron hesitated, then continued.

'Captain, may I see your face?'

A sardonic chuckle came from within the sharp-edged helm. 'Do you suspect that I merely impersonate your brother and superior officer? That I have stolen his armour? Very well, Sergeant Magron. Be reassured.'

Abaddas reached up, unfastened the clamps of the encrusted helm and removed it. His square-jawed, bleak face stared out from between the hulking shoulder encasements.

Magron studied that face carefully. It was much as he remembered, and of no greater age, but bleaker and more impassive, as if the officer had forgotten how to use facial expression. There was, too, despite its stony quality, an almost unnatural vitality, a glaring sense of will-power.

'Do you remember when we stood together on the death world, brother-sergeant, with a whole company lost?'

'Captain,' Magron burst out, 'why do you not wear the Imperial eagle?'

'I will explain presently, brother-sergeant. First, make your report. How did you come to this world?'

'May I remove my armour, captain?'

Abaddas stood unmoving for a moment or two, as though the request surprised him. Then he turned his head and uttered a call in a low, hallooing voice. From the fringe of the rose forest his body slaves ran forth, heads low. In clipped tones he ordered them to assist Magron. They slunk to him like curs, aiding him to strip himself of the power suit until he stood on the rose plain in his black, one-piece utility garment. Their demeanour was certainly nothing like that of the servitors who would have performed the same service on Caliban. Magron swayed slightly now that he was divested of the support of the suit. His bodily functions were still struggling to return to normal after the sus-an.

'Now, sergeant. Your report.'

Magron related everything that had happened: the destruction of the World Eaters' interstellar base along with the task force sent to neutralise it, how he had been cast adrift in space and had gone into sus-an. He knew that almost a hundred standard Imperial years had passed since then – that was when his suit's timer had ceased functioning – but nothing else, especially how he came to be lying on this pleasant world.

Abaddas was not entirely pleased to hear the story. He had hoped that Sergeant Magron had found his way into the Eye of his own will, a newly committed Chaos renegade. Instead, his continued devotion to the Emperor and his hatred of the rebels were both clear from his words.

Just the same, his arrival could be no accident. The siren lure of Chaos, spreading through the warp and through all space-time – especially in the period of the rebellion – had drawn him here. And for Magron and Abaddas, who were possibly the only two Dark Angels in the Eye, to have met up in this manner could not be coincidence. Abaddas believed that it was his will and his need for the comradeship of another Dark Angel that had brought the sergeant here.

'Tell me, brother-captain,' Magron said, 'how long have I been in suspended animation? Where are we now?'

Captain Abaddas thought long before he replied. His main care had to be for his brother Dark Angel's salvation, to bring him on to the right path and away from his misguided loyalty. This was going to be difficult. While Sergeant Magron was fighting the renegade World Eaters, Captain Abaddas had been on Caliban, listening to the inspiring words of Luther, hearing how Primarch Lion El'Jonson had betrayed them and had stolen all the glory for himself.

Abaddas was not Luther. He did not have his ability to persuade men out of even their deepest convictions. A certain amount of guile was going to be needed. And what was truth? What was falsehood? Where Chaos ruled, one could not always say which was which. And where time was concerned, whose time should he use as an answer? Magron's, or his own?

'Time does not mean what it did,' he said at last. 'It is no longer the tyrant it was. One could say that the events you speak of took place about two hundred years ago.'

This puzzling response caused Magron to frown. He looked again at the alien device on the captain's breastplate, as if the inkling of an awful possibility was beginning to penetrate his understanding.

'Then the foul rebels are long ago crushed,' he stated, as if daring Abaddas to say otherwise.

And Captain Abaddas then took a decision. He was recalling the advice he had once received from one wise in the ways of Tzeentch.

Tell the truth only if a lie will not serve.

'Brother-sergeant,' he said in a voice of command, 'give me your bolter and chainsword.'

Magron took a step back, not liking this order from one armoured as Captain Abaddas was, lacking the Imperial eagle. Abaddas glowered.

'Sergeant,' he added in a more conciliatory tone, 'you are still suffering from the after-effects of sus-an. Your judgement is not to be depended on. Before I explain your situation, you will surrender your weapons to me. Or have you come to the stage where you will disobey an order from a superior officer?'

This rebuke had its effect. Magron reached down to the discarded power armour, unclamped both bolter and chainsword and threw them at Abaddas's feet.

'What I have to tell you,' Abaddas said, in slow measured tones once this was done, 'will be hard for you to accept or even comprehend. Therefore prepare yourself. The rebellion led by Warmaster Horus succeeded. The Emperor is dead, killed by Horus himself in single combat, though Horus too died of his injuries. Lion El'Jonson is dead. The Chaos powers, if you know what those are, rule the galaxy.'

A Space Marine can be put to the extremities of torture, physical and mental, and scarcely flinch. He can face horrors that would send ordinary men insane. But as Sergeant Abdaziel Magron heard these words the world went dark before his eyes. He felt himself tremble. He might have fallen in a faint, had not Captain Abaddas, power fibres whining softly, stepped forward to support him with his huge gauntlets.

'Stand on your feet, Space Marine. You must endure the worst.'

Magron groaned. He cursed himself for having gone into sus-an. To be revived in a galaxy without the Emperor!

Horrible! Unbelievable! Impossible to bear!

Stricken, he looked into Abaddas's flinty grey eyes.

'Who is Emperor now?'

The first hint of an emotional reaction flickered on Abaddas's face. 'What need have we of an Emperor?' he roared. 'We have the Chaos Gods!'

Magron had heard of these. Chapter chaplains had delivered sermons on them when the rebellion broke out. The greatest threat mankind had ever had to face. Malevolent intelligences from beyond the physical universe, worse than the worst of aliens, bent on subjecting mankind to the most abominable and unimaginable perversions and degradations. Against which the Emperor was the only shield!

'And our... chapter?' he quavered.

'It still exists, sergeant. We are still brothers.'

He paused, as though weighing the words he was about to speak. 'I, too, was faithful. I slew many of my battle-brothers who had pledged themselves to the Warmaster. Now do you see why I demanded your weapons of you, sergeant? At one time to hear what you are now hearing would have caused me to launch myself at the speaker with everything at my disposal. Only at the end, with the Emperor already dead, was I able to see the truth. The Emperor was denying mankind its destiny for the sake of personal power. Warmaster Horus made the ultimate sacrifice so as to free us.'

'You speak blasphemy, captain!'

'Once it would indeed have been blasphemy. Now it is historical fact.'

Abaddas gestured to the glowing rose sun and the rose-pink canopy spread across half the sky. 'Look about you. Look what we can achieve now the Emperor's restrictions have been cast off. The ability to shape worlds! To climb to heaven! Men may become as gods, if they have the nerve! There is nothing now that may not be accomplished.'

Abaddas was using his emotion-sensing Chaos gift to observe his brother Dark Angel closely. A pre-heresy Space Marine's emotions were stripped down and finely honed. Essentially he had only two: determination, and allegiance. Determination to overcome every enemy, and allegiance to the Emperor and His Imperium. Worship of the Emperor had been more strongly inculcated in the Dark Angels than in any other legion. Abaddas could see, as clearly as he could see the rose-strewn quartz meadow all around him, the black despair that was engulfing Magron on hearing of the death of the Emperor and the destruction of His cause. It passed over his whole body like a boiling dark cloud.

It was inevitable that eventually he would discover that his captain had been lying to him. Abaddas's task was to ensure that by then he would approve of the intention behind those lies. Magron's devotion had to be redirected. It needed a powerful focus, if he were to come to hate and revile the Emperor in the Golden Throne. He would have to be seduced into the service of one of the Ruinous Powers.

Abaddas already knew which one it would be. Magron would accept no other. Khorne. God of battle. God of honour. *God of blood.*

He felt a presence and glanced above. Sergeant Magron followed his glance and recoiled, doubting his sanity. For a fleeting moment he had thought to see a face, spanning the entire visible sky – a dog or wolf's face with glaring red eyes, topped with a three-horned helmet, the middle horn like a unicorn's horn.

The vision gave him the feeling of being an ant trapped in a jar, while some far huger animal looked down on him. He would have taken it for a hallucination, another after-effect of the sus-an, had not Captain Abaddas evidently seen the apparition too.

'*What was that?*' Magron barked.

'A Chaos being,' Abaddas answered, his tone unperturbed. 'A greater daemon; they are the only ones can adopt any size like that. This planet is finished. We had better leave. You will find much to give you satisfaction in your new life, brother! Get back into your power suit and follow me.'

Magron stared at him. 'May I remind you, captain, that you have renounced your vows to the Emperor, vows which we both swore. By what right do you command me?'

'You can please yourself, brother-sergeant,' Abaddas said, replacing his helmet, his voice changing as he did so, now issuing from the external speaker. 'But a strategic withdrawal is what I strongly advise.'

He lumbered off towards the large metallic structure Magron had already noticed lying sprawled against the fringe of the nearby forest. Magron looked up a second time and spotted a scattering of glints against the pale mauve backdrop. He did not need to be told what *they* were: drop pods.

He had reinserted himself into the recharged armour, without any help this time, when one of the pods, a very roughly made affair indeed, banged down on to the meadow and fell apart. From the wreckage rampaged a nightmare mob such as Magron had never seen before. At first he thought it a motley collection of vicious aliens – some in the weirdest of armour, far stranger than Abaddas's, some naked, some wearing criss-crossed straps of cured hide from which hung severed heads, limbs, torn-out hearts and livers, some draped in bloody entrails, some slashing themselves so as to luxuriate in blood as they ran. Then he realised what they were.

Mutations. Probably they had all been human once.

As he looked on the snarling animal faces, the chittering insect faces, the grotesque bodies, that were running towards him, stumbling, pushing one another over in their haste, Sergeant Magron felt chilled to his soul. The Emperor dead. The galaxy given over to Chaos! Yes, there was beauty in it, the planet on which he stood gave testament to that. But the chaplains had been right, too. There was foulness and degeneracy.

Captain Abaddas paused to turn and fire a storm of bolter shots at the onrushing crowd, creating carnage. Another drop pod smashed itself to pieces further off, and then another. Magron retrieved his own bolt gun and chainsword – though the latter was probably drained of power – and set his suit in motion, following his battle-brother, who climbed through an opening in what Magron took to be a brass statue of a large but loathsome beast, and beckoned him to follow.

Bullets from primitive stub guns rattled off his armour as he seized hold of the edges of the opening and hauled himself through. The opening sealed itself seamlessly behind him, as though the skin of the structure had merely flowed into itself.

He found himself in a roughened, lumpy interior. The beast-shape appeared to have been cast in one piece in a mould, but to have been done roughly, the interior swirled with once-molten metal. The space was long and narrow, giving the armoured men just about enough room to stand. Light came from redly glowing patches in the roof, and from two thick windows forward.

These were where the eyes of the reptilian beast would be. They admitted light on to a shelf or sill supporting a cursory set of controls, consisting of two or three moulded brass handgrips surrounded by a low rail, like that of a tray. The arrangement confirmed to Magron that this was a vehicle of some sort. There was no place to sit, however, either at the controls or anywhere else. Wherever the vehicle took one, one travelled standing.

Hammers, axes, claws and fists began banging and scratching on the hull. There was a concerted howling of frustration and hatred. Other attackers, having climbed up the front legs somehow, snarled through the forward windows, attempting to smash the steelglass – or whatever substance it was – with any weapons they wielded or else with their own demented-featured heads. Because these were windows and not the usual view-screens used in spacecraft, Magron had assumed that the odd vehicle was an aircraft of some sort, able to fly through the atmosphere only. He was wrong. Standing in the nose of the craft, Abaddas wrenched two of the controls. The beastship let out a roar. Magron was bemused to see the interior of the hull flex itself, as though the metal were flesh. Then it leapt into the air, dislodging the bestial invaders which clung to its lumpy surface.

Looking past Abaddas and through the round window-eyes, Magron saw the pale mauve sky turn a deep purple in which the delicate pink petals of the sun blazed. Abaddas flipped the beastship round, allowing Magron a view of the planet below them. He was amazed to see the same figure of a rose basking in the pink light of the rose-sun. And all around them spread great sheets of stars and gas which, Abaddas assured him, were formed into an even vaster rose, the Rose Cluster.

'How is it possible?' Magron breathed, returning his gaze to the strange form of his one-time comrade-in-arms in his multi-coloured, Chaos-mutated power armour.

'I told you. We have the power to shape worlds! The intelligence which created this marvel must have liked roses.'

Magron wondered whether any segment of the old Imperium would be recognisable to him now. Perhaps it had all been reshaped, even the stars rearranged.

'What sort of intelligence accomplished this?' he asked. 'A man, or a... a Chaos power? A daemon, as you said?'

Abaddas gave a sardonic chuckle. 'What difference does it make? I told you, men can become like gods now. Anything is possible for us! Our infancy is behind us!'

He took his hands from the control levers and turned to face Magron, the sharp-angled wedge of his helmet tilting downward slightly as if to regard him with a steely frown.

'This is what the Emperor denied us, sergeant. He was like a parent who would not let his children take their place in the world, for fear of what might happen to them. To justify his restrictions, he demanded worship. But the children were made of sterner stuff. They revolted, and became free!'

'And that swarm of mutations we have just left behind us?'

Abaddas was silent for a spell, thinking how proud Magron would be when he received his first Chaos rewards, foul and monstrous though they might seem to him now.

'You are still in the Emperor's nursery, sergeant,' he said, his voice becoming softer. 'You wish to limit freedom to what the Emperor would find acceptable. Later you will think differently. But enough of that. You were born for war, seasoned and modified to be a warrior; even the Emperor fitted you for war and offered you honour and glory. Here, in the Chaos realm, *you shall have war!'*

It would have suited Abaddas just as well to have quit the Rose Cluster and seek adventure elsewhere. But his care for Magron stayed him. The Rose Cluster was about to be engulfed in a conflict. Magron's progress would be the swifter if he were drawn into it.

He steered the nose of the beastship into the Cluster. There was no need here for the detailed calculations and headings accompanying space travel outside the Chaos realm. Tzeentch was the lord of ways and courses. Magron heard him intone the resounding, unintelligible words of the Magical Spell of Destination The beastship roared quietly, like an animal warning off rivals from its territory. Abaddas took his hands from the levers. The beastship would find its own way now, guided by the warp itself.

He turned his attention to helping his brother Dark Angel check his power suit after its long sojourn in the void. There were many adjustments to be made. It was a miracle that it was so undamaged, so undecayed, after so long a time – much longer than he had led Magron to believe.

No, he corrected himself. It was design, not accident. The design of Chaos!

He made the same point to Magron. 'You have been sent to me, brother-sergeant. How do you imagine you came to be lying on the meadow on Rhodonius? Did you expect ever to be revived, after going into sus-an in interstellar space? No, you expected to drift in the void forever. The Chaos Gods have helped you and have shown you the respect due to a warrior. Do not spurn their beneficence.'

'I cannot disown the Emperor! I am sworn!'

'All vows are dissolved when death intervenes,' Abaddas reminded him. He held out his gauntlet for Magron's chainsword, recharged its stacked-atom power and tested it for efficiency. It still worked, but the usually vicious buzz was ragged.

'The motor needs retuning,' he observed. 'We will find a tech-wizard.

'I can do it myself,' Magron responded grumpily. He checked his boltgun and bolt pistol, and found both in working order but the ammunition degraded. He accepted fresh magazines from Abaddas.

'Now you must rest, brother-sergeant. Your body needs to recuperate from sus-an, and trials lie ahead.'

'What is our heading, brother-captain?'

'We go to another star in the Cluster.'

It puzzled Magron that Abaddas was still fully clad in his extra-bulky Mark Three power armour with all its Chaos excrescences, as though unaware of how confined his movements were made. He had not even removed his helmet, which Space Marines often did even in the heat of battle.

Magron had piled his own equipment at the rear of the narrow cavity. As far as he could judge this took up about half the length of the peculiar craft. From the rear came the growling, roaring sound of the engine.

Magron lay on his back on the metal floor. Although the captain's advice was good, he decided not to go into sleep proper. Instead he used the catalepsian node implanted in his brain, which made it possible to rest half of his brain at a time and so stay alert.

Several hours passed. Magron, feeling rested but still full of bewilderment and grief, rose to his feet. Abaddas stood silently in the nose of the ship, looking out. The soft roar from the engines could still be heard. Through the windows, he noted that the stars of the cluster seemed to be moving visibly, which should not happen at realspace speeds.

'When do we go into the warp, captain?'

Abaddas turned ponderously to glance back at him. 'We are not going into the warp. We are already travelling faster than light.'

Magron stared at the stars again. They were flowing with a fluid motion, their colour changing as they passed by, phasing from violet to red.

'Yes, you think it impossible,' Abaddas said gruffly. 'Contrary to the laws of nature. Well, what did I tell you?'

'Is this how all star travel is accomplished now?' Magron asked. 'Throughout the galaxy?'

Abaddas decided to tell the truth for once. 'No,' he admitted, 'only in a limited region, and that but recently. I do not know why. But I think one of the great daemon-lords has devised it as an aid to space travel. As you can see, it is far easier than journeying through the warp.'

Magron asked himself how it was possible to see stars at all if one outran the light they shone by. Trying to look into the warp with one's physical sense of sight – though few had ever tried it – yielded nothing, just blankness.

'You speak of daemons…'

'It is just a name for the intelligences which aid the Chaos Gods.'

A star loomed up out of the close-packed field of stars that comprised just one astronomically vast petal of the cosmic rose. How the ship had found a way to it Magron had little idea, for Abaddas had appeared to do little by way of navigation. Now, however, he grasped the brass handles again. The ship veered and slowed. The bubbled, roughened walls of the interior creaked and bent slightly. Astonishingly, the control sill of the ship bore no instruments that Magron could see, no star tabulator to locate their position or magnifier to examine the worlds of the planetary system. They might as well have been sailing a raft through a group of islands, without even the help of a compass.

They were approaching a planet superficially identical to the one they had left, its surface foiled in shining petals, at least on the sunlit side. Abaddas steered them towards the crown of the rose, and here was something new. At first it seemed like a sparkling diamond or dewdrop. Then, as they descended, it revealed itself as a city of huge proportions, perched athwart the tightly clustered rose petals, with towers soaring upward. Magron felt as though he did indeed look down on a simple flower, in whose folds tiny civilisations dwelt.

The beastship sank among those towers, and their true stature revealed themselves. Magron peered through the window eyes, entranced despite himself. This was not like the grim cities of the Imperium he had known; it was a fairytale city, resplendent in the pink sunlight.

The beastship grounded itself on a broad plaza. The side of the vehicle flowed open, revealing a broad view. There was a crowd on the plaza, but Magron took little notice of that at first. His gaze was on the city beyond, with its graceful towers, its arcades and boulevards, its delicate stonework and solemn temples.

Abaddas interrupted his reverie. 'You have a decision to make, brother. As I had, long ago. The age you have known has ended, and our chapter has survived the transformation into a new age, albeit scattered far and wide. You must adapt to the new universe. Look, see what is coming.'

He pointed a gauntlet, indicating the sky. What appeared to be metal motes were glinting far above. Rapidly they grew and it became clear what they were.

An invasion fleet was descending, though without any semblance of order. A motley collection of hundreds or even thousands of craft hove into view, many resembling the beast-ship but larger, their twisted, gnarled metal shapes like cast-offs from some furnace or forge, but all showing an unnatural influence which could not have been the work of man. Ships with kicking monster legs, ships with gesticulating arms and tentacles, ships with bestial faces that grimaced.

Ships that spewed blood on the fair city below.

'This star system is being invaded,' Abaddas told Magron. 'I go now to join this city's defenders. The choice is yours. I beseech you to remember our brotherhood. Remember our defeated Emperor, if you will. But if you remember these things, then remember also that I am your captain! Armour yourself, and follow me!'

Abaddas's words flashed reminiscences into Magron's brain. How he had admired this stern, impassive Space Marine officer! The episode on the death world – then, Magron had accepted that they were doomed like the rest of the company, the expedition a failure. Not so Abaddas! The cool, implacable captain had found a way not only to survive but to complete their mission as well!

In truth, Abaddas had left him no choice at all. Magron hurried to don his armour. Abaddas did not wait for him. He departed.

Magron soon followed, re-checking his weapons as he did so. Bolter, bolt pistol, chainsword, shortsword – the one weapon he had not thought to inspect, but he examined it now for straightness and keenness of edge. As his armoured boots crashed on to the broad esplanade Abaddas casually reached out, demanding the blade from him. With one swipe he dashed it against a nearby marble statue of some alien winged creature.

The blade shattered into a dozen pieces. A hundred centuries in the near-zero of interstellar space had weakened it, as the Chaos Marine had surmised. He reached into his suit-scabbard and handed a replacement to Magron.

'That would not have served you. Take this.'

Magron accepted the blade. It was wavy, with eerie hues running along its sinuous length. Unfamiliar runes were engraved on both sides. The hilt was cast as a serpent, which made him reluctant to grasp it. Nevertheless he placed it in his scabbard.

For the first time he examined the crowd assembled on the plaza. There were knights, warriors, fighting men, in all types of armour or none at all. Nearly all, Magron noted, were abnormal in some way. The city was evidently stricken with a disease which caused congenital deformities. It would have been cleansed in the old Imperium. Many people, however, were unarmed and seemed normal. And these were now running in terror as the ships descended, seeking to hide in the magnificent buildings lining the square.

A knight in armour of gleaming beetle-blue called out to Abaddas. *'DO YOU FOLLOW TZEENTCH – OR KHORNE?'*

Abaddas bellowed in response: *'I fight for Tzeentch!'*

It was clear now that the invading fleet was putting down over a wide area. Artillery pieces were flinging aloft blue laser blasts and seething plasma balls, trying to destroy the tumbling invaders before they landed. Only one craft made for the plaza, and that was a huge flying edifice, crowned with towers like a cathedral and seemingly built of sparkling white stone. As it settled, a droning could be heard from inside it. Huge timber doors swung open. A congregation had been at prayer – and now it emerged.

It looked, at first, like a pageant of banners, for every armoured member of the throng carried such a blazon over his head, held up by a pole fixed in place to the armour's backplate, after the tradition of the Adeptus Astartes. Magron had no time to inspect those banners, except to note that their designs were lurid and alien-looking. In addition there were monstrous-looking creatures, each one different, some on mounts equally monstrous.

Tramp, tramp, tramp. Those in armour disembarked in a disciplined troop. To his shock, Magron saw that it was like Space Marine armour, but grotesquely altered as if fashioned by some demented armourer, even more so than Captain Abaddas's.

'Do you still hate traitors, Brother-Sergeant Magron?'
Abaddas challenged. 'Then take your revenge on these, for they
are Marines of the Alpha Legion – *among the first to declare for
Horus the Warmaster!*'

Magron stared. He now recognised the Alpha Legion colours.
He also saw, on some of the banners, the same X-shaped emblem
with three horizontal bars he had seen when fighting the World
Eaters. Rage filled Magron's heart. Bolters were now barking, creating carnage among the knights and warriors who rushed
forward in a vain but valiant attempt to drive off the invaders.

He let out a shout: 'FOR THE EMPEROR!'

Side by side again with Captain Abaddas! Though his cry
went unnoticed in the rising tumult, Magron strode onward.
His bolter voiced its savage bark. The first bolt ricocheted
among the bizarrely armoured enemy, doing little damage. He
would need to get closer.

He loosed a short burst. He heard the explosions but saw
nothing. The shells had disappeared into a sudden darkness.
He switched his suit-senses to other wavelengths, but again saw
nothing.

For a few moments the darkness continued, and in it the
noise of the battle died away. Then vision returned, but not to
the clear rose light from before. The scene seemed frozen, the
armoured warriors as if caught in amber, set in a dull, muddy-
brown light that was the only illumination. Sergeant Magron
looked up. The sun was still there, but it had changed. No
longer was it a wonderful glowing pink, It had darkened to the
same burnt brown colour. The fleshy-looking petals were shriv-
elling and collapsing in on themselves, turning almost black
and becoming dimmer and dimmer. This should have revealed
the Rose Cluster in its full splendour, but it did not. Only the
background of stars beyond the Cluster remained visible. Of
the Cluster itself, nothing could be seen.

On the plaza, near-darkness descended again. Sergeant Magron
felt the paving stones beneath his boots shudder and crumble. He
heard a titanic crumpling sound from far off. Looking around, he
dimly saw the planet-petals which had clustered round the gorgeous city collapsing and turning into cinders.

He spoke into his comm-link. 'Captain, what is happening?'

Abaddas replied sourly. 'The Great Night is coming.'

FOURTEEN
LIFE-ESSENCE

TOO LATE, PELOR CALLIDEN realised that he had forgotten to carry out the sealing ritual on closing down the control panel. He had neglected to put his right palm on the sealing rune and intone the formula of protection. Had he done so, anyone trying to fly the ship illicitly would have found it rebellious and difficult to handle. As it was, Kwyler was piloting with expert ease.

How could he have been so remiss, Calliden asked himself? *Something* must have nudged his mind into forgetfulness. Perhaps the same *something* – awful thought! – that had guided him here.

What to do? There was no sense of motion within the *Wandering Star*, buffeted though it was by the turbulent atmosphere. Just the same he felt it might be dangerous to tussle with Kwyler for control.

Silently he crept into the rear cabin and shook Rugolo awake. The trader groaned as he emerged from his slumber and scratched his black goatee beard.

'What is it?' he mumbled.

'We're landing on the planet! Kwyler hasn't played straight with us.'

Calliden couldn't read Rugolo's expression by the light of the emergency electrolumen, but he heard a sharp intake of breath. The trader sounded frightened.

'Stop him, Pelor!'

'I can try, but we might crash.'

Rugolo groaned again and heaved himself to his feet. He went lurching into the front chamber, his hand hitting the illumination bar on the wall. Light sprang into the cabin.

'What are you doing?'

Kwyler cast a sneaking glance back at him, then reached for the little ribbed bottle that stood on the control board. He put it to his lips, gulped, then offered it to Rugolo.

'Only one swallow left. Take it.'

Automatically Rugolo accepted the bottle, then stood and stared at the screen over the control panel. The boiling brown clouds parted. The surface of the planet was revealed, in a sepia glare seeping from the low cloud cover.

The planet was a gallimaufry, a jumble of tumbled images. Streams of fire, glittering waterfalls, poured from the turbulent clouds. A strange yellow lightning – if indeed it was lightning – criss-crossed the gap between cloud and surface, creating an impression of transient giant figures stalking the landscape, flickering in and out of existence. Were they real, or an optical illusion? Rugolo assumed the latter, for Kwyler steered the ship straight through a huge bearded figure which stretched from the ground to the clouds, waving a hammer, that had suddenly appeared in their path.

Calliden knew better. During the instant when the cargo ship had entered the giant's midriff he had felt a psychic shiver that was not imaginary. The planet was producing transient beings, generating them from the cloud-to-ground energy discharges.

'Look out!' Rugolo screeched. A huge stone structure had suddenly loomed up, not transient this time but solid and permanent. It was a vast castle, miles high, its battlements merging into cloud. There was no way that Kwyler could avoid it.

He did not even try to. The *Wandering Star* plunged straight into the massive stone pile. Glimpses of interior apartments, halls and stairwells zipped past. Then they were out the other side.

A ghost castle! Calliden thought.

'Take us back up!' Rugolo ordered sternly. But before he knew it, he had put the liqueur bottle to his lips and tipped it up. The small amount of spirit left in it crept down his throat, creating the blessed explosion that spread through every cell of his being. '*Aaaaagh…*'

It was like being reborn. The terror Rugolo had felt on learning what Kwyler had done – the terror of meeting Aegelica again – evaporated, especially when he realised that Kwyler's motive was only to get more of the liqueur sooner. And what was wrong with that?

Calliden crept forward, studying Kwyler's hands on the controls. He felt disappointed that none of the liqueur was left for him. Didn't he deserve some too?

He shook his head, trying to clear his brain. The atmosphere was awash with psychic forces, he could sense that much, and they were affecting his judgement. He felt an urge to open his warp eye, but desisted. He feared what he might see.

He returned his attention to the phantasmagoria that was hurtling past them. The immense bulk of one of the great atmosphere-piercing mountains slid by, its lower slopes clad in real trees as well as what looked like buildings. The flickering lightning was creating a strobe-like effect, making him feel slightly nauseous. Rugolo staggered forward. For a moment, it looked as though he might try to wrench Kwyler from the controls. Then he drew back, as if realising how dangerous this would be. He seemed slightly drunk.

They had decelerated and were close to the ground now, racing over what appeared to be an industrial area, with smoke rising from sheds and furnaces which flickered in the strobing lightning. Then something happened which struck terror into Calliden. The terrain ahead of them swelled up, forming a vast head and shoulders struggling to emerge from the landscape. A huge hand shot out and seized hold of the *Wandering Star*.

Despite the instant dead stop, the occupants of the craft remained steady on their feet. The inertial control which made space travel possible was able to handle the forces involved. The sound of the engine could still be heard. They found themselves looking straight into the face of the… *thing*… that held them.

Was it a spirit of the planet itself? Sticking out from its bare skull were spikes, much like the mountain-spires visible from space. Its visage was a parody of a human, with round staring eyes, a toothless, drooping mouth and a hooked nose. It grinned inanely as it stared at the cargo ship, moving its head from side to side. This was no mere apparition. The ship was held firmly in the massive fist.

The thing opened its mouth, a red cave leading into a deep gullet, eyes bulging in anticipation. Nose first, the ship was pushed towards the gaping lips.

Then Kwyler gave a sudden flick of the guidance levers. They shot out of the earth-giant's grip and were away.

'Ha, they're not as dangerous as they look,' he said casually.

Rugolo was silent, numb with shock. Not so Calliden: 'Take us up, Kwyler. It was going to eat us. *Take us back up!*'

'It's all right. We're just about there.'

'This is insane.' Calliden decided he must act. Kwyler was not wearing the seat restraint. He attempted to push him aside and grasp the controls. But Calliden was puny physically, unused to physical conflict, and Kwyler, despite being small, had a wiry strength. He hung on despite all Calliden's efforts, yelling at him to let go. Calliden was desperate. He yanked with all his might, trying to turn the nose of the ship spaceward. Kwyler yanked in the opposite direction, while Rugolo roared in alarm and threw himself into the fray.

The end result was that Kwyler's head hit the control board. The view-screen, had anyone been looking at it, was a flurry. They heard a loud prolonged grinding noise as the ship hit the ground and went sliding a long distance, throwing up mounds of earth, before slewing round and coming to a stop, the engine giving out a coughing, protesting note.

Calliden reached out and punched the rune to switch it off, silently but feverishly reciting the Canticle of Damage Limitation, from the Navigator's Catechism.

But the prayer came far too late, as he saw from the board's glowing sigils. The *Wandering Star* was old, and not very sound structurally. Rugolo had never had the money to renovate the gradually weakening hull. The impact of the forced landing had wrought damage everywhere.

The viewscreen was shattered, but that did not stop them from seeing outside. Just below the buckled oval screen was a rent which clearly went through all three of the hull's layers. Through it, they could see earth and uprooted ochre-coloured vegetation.

Calliden scanned the damage sigils again, his heart sinking. Rugolo would have tools to repair minor damage, but this was not minor. The damage to the hull was bad enough, but the warp screens were ruptured too. Repairing those was a task for a tech-adept.

The *Wandering Star*, even if it could take off again – which Calliden doubted – would never make it out of the Eye of Terror.

'MY SHIP! MY SHIP! It's all I had left!'

Maynard Rugolo's grief was real. He, Calliden and Kwyler stood on a mound of deep brown soil that had been thrown up by the *Wandering Star*'s crash-landing. The furrow it had dug stretched away into the distance. As for the ship itself, its vanes had all been torn off and lay scattered alongside the furrow. The hull which loomed over them like some enormous beached sea monster was dented and crushed, the gargoyles obliterated.

The low clouds boomed, pouring down their glowing streams The lightning-like energy criss-crossing the gap between cloud and land spat and crackled, the spectral figures the strikes created dancing over the landscape and seeming to mock them all.

Calliden thought Rugolo's emotion misplaced. The issue was not the loss of the trader's property. It was how they were going to escape this mad and nightmarish region. His mind turned to thoughts of Gundrum's painted spaceship.

The air was restless, buffeting them with hot gusts. Wildly Rugolo looked about him. 'There are people on this planet. I saw buildings on the way down. They could help us hoist the ship upright, seal the rents–'

Calliden shook his head. 'Unless they know how to repair and tune warp screens, forget it. In fact, forget it even if they *do* know. Everything and everyone in the Eye is tainted with Chaos. I'm not going into the warp with screens that haven't been dedicated to the Emperor.'

Kwyler grunted, shaking loose his long jerkin. Calliden glimpsed the melta-gun hidden inside it. 'Well, don't blame me,' he said. 'I would have got us down in one piece, nose up. Let's go and see Gundrum.'

'*Go and see Gundrum*?' Rugolo response was a disbelieving shriek, a frenzy of fear and protest. '*Aegelica's with him!*'

Kwyler stared hard. 'Do you want to spend the rest of your life here? We have to persuade Gundrum to take us back out of the Eye.'

The thought of a journey in company with the daemon-possessed Aegelica made even Calliden quake.

Rugolo rounded on the navigator. 'This is all your fault! It's all happened since I met you! I should have known better than to team up with a psychotic navigator!'

He halted in mid-tirade. He knew he should not blame Pelor. His own recklessness, surely, was more to blame. But he was wishing himself safely back on Gendova, even though stranded and without a navigator. Where, he reminded himself, he would have lost the *Wandering Star* in any case, to pay off a debt to some piffling local merchant. What ignominy!

Rugolo almost preferred things this way. If it weren't for… The flickering half-seen giant figures, the constant booming, the luminous sepia light, were sending him into a trance. The booming was forming voices, shouting out something to the landscape below! But what? He couldn't tell. He shook his head, trying to clear his brain.

Kwyler pointed. When it crashed, the *Wandering Star* had been brought to a halt by a rise in the ground. Three figures had appeared at the top of this rise, and were looking down on them – Gundrum, Aegelica and Foafoa.

The rugged, burly Foafoa was glaring fiercely. Aegelica, still clad in her brief basque, was smiling and not looking at all threatening now. As for Gundrum, he looked even more extraordinary, even more angular and gesticulatory, than before. Somehow he seemed to have grown an extra foot in height – or was that a trick of the light?

They set off down the slope. Calliden saw Rugolo go green and break out in a sweat, sagging with terror. Kwyler put out his arm to stop the trader from running in panic back into the *Wandering Star.*

The trio halted some yards away, no more than glancing at the bulk of the crippled cargo ship in whose misty flickering shadow they now stood. Gundrum smiled as if in quiet satisfaction, his pale lips barely moving. Aegelica laughed, a trilling contralto sound, as if in pleasure and welcome. Foafoa, on the other hand, stamped his feet and beat the air with clenched fists. Then, his tantrum over, he threw back his head and howled with laughter.

Kwyler stepped forward to meet them. 'I am come to offer contrition, Gundrum,' he said.

Gundrum raised his eyebrows more than seemed physically possible. 'And to tickle my sister again with your melta-gun, which I see you still have on you, Kwyler? By my roots, by my words, by my twisted thoughts and simple innocent deeds, what do we have here? A ship on the rocks, and a crew in trouble.'

Rugolo and Calliden both shrank as his gaze lit on them. It was impossible to tell what was going through his mad mind. Then he waved a negligent hand at Rugolo and turned to the grinning Aegelica.

'Do you still want him, sister?'

Rugolo gagged, bent over, and vomited up what he had eaten earlier in orbit. Calliden, himself paralysed with fear, would have moved to assist him, but instead it was Aegelica who did so. Shocked and bewildered, he watched as she placed an arm round his shoulders, wiped his mouth with a kerchief she took from her bosom, and murmured words of reassurance. Strangely, her words seemed to calm him. He smiled and thanked her, a gesture which convinced Calliden that his partner had indeed lost his reason. She fell back, continuing to look on him sympathetically.

'Well, what is it you want, my old friend?' Gundrum asked Kwyler.

'A slug of essence, for old times' sake?' Kwyler's demeanour was begging.

'Lemonade for your soul? Do your roots thirst for nourishment? Come, then. Let bygones be bygones!'

He turned and led the way. By his fierce expression Kwyler indicated to his companions the necessity of following. They mounted the rise, and found themselves looking down on a broad shallow valley through which meandered a narrow river, gleaming like tarnished metal in the subdued light.

Upcurrent was the river's source, a fiery cataract cascading down from the cloud cover, by some alchemy becoming water by the time it reached the valley.

There lay Gundrum's painted spaceship, looking sleek and shiny, quite unlike any ship of the Imperium. A few hundred yards further off began a sprawl of buildings lining the nearer river bank, constructed – it appeared – of burnished brass, their piled-together outlines wavering and winding. Smoke, steam and puffs of coloured powder gusted from vents in their upper surfaces. One building spanned the stream. Much larger than the others, it had three chimneys putting out a grime of smoke and red sparks.

The scene was unmistakably industrial, and had the look of being an outlying part of a larger town that was out of sight. Kwyler had said that Gundrum got his trade goods mainly from one place. Could that place be as small as this? A row of workshops, rather than a whole planet? It made sense. Perhaps Gundrum had chanced upon the place early in his wanderings, and since then had kept to the same route. It could explain why he had managed to survive in such a very dangerous part of the galaxy.

They descended into the valley. A small pavilion of vermilion velvet had been set up between the painted spaceship and the river bank. And, for the first time, Rugolo and Calliden saw other human beings. A line of half a dozen men was being conducted beside the river, linked together by iron neck-bands, hands tied behind their backs: slaves. Their guards, a party of four, wore plain ochre tabards and leggings of a leathery material. They carried gold-coloured weapons, guns of some kind, with flanged muzzles and twin stocks, one for steadying at the front, one with a trigger at the back – much like Kwyler's melta-gun.

The prisoners' subdued clothing of black and brown seemed familiar to Rugolo. As they drew closer one spotted Calliden and seemed to recognise him. His pale, despairing face came suddenly alive with desperate hope.

'Help us, sirs! Please!'

'He's from Gendova!' Calliden exclaimed in surprise. 'Do you remember? He was one of those who tried to kidnap me. How did he get here?'

'They're *all* from Gendova,' Rugolo said, placing their style of clothing now. 'It looks like they got into the Eye after all.'

Aegelica's trilling laughter rang out again. The guards hastened the pace, forcing the slaves towards the buildings in the near distance.

'Come, my friends!' Gundrum boomed, his voice mingling with the ever-present rumbling coming from above. 'We will drink a toast!'

With a graceful, extravagant gesture, he invited them into the pavilion. Calliden could not explain to himself why he and Rugolo accepted that invitation, willing to share the interior with Aegelica. The former episode seemed like a dream; she now exuded a sense of utter harmlessness. Inside, a round table stood on three curved legs, with three straight-backed chairs arranged around it. On the table were two of the cask-shaped liqueur bottles, one a sombre brown in colour, the other a faintly glowing orange. Foafoa declined to enter the tent. He stomped off towards the rainbow spaceship. But Kwyler almost ran into the dimmed interior. He sat down at the table, snatched up a bottle, then as if remembering himself, put it down again and stared at the tabletop with a strained expression.

'I always knew you would find a way to rejoin us, Kwyler,' Gundrum said lugubriously, pouring from the orange bottle into a tiny glass.

'Yes, of course you did,' Kwyler admitted.

'So let us drink to it. Only a local vintage, I'm afraid.'

'We'll do better tomorrow, eh?' Kwyler grabbed the glass Gundrum offered and let the thick liqueur slide down his throat. A look of relief and ecstasy transformed his face. He sat there with eyes closed, listening deep into himself.

Gundrum poured out thickly oozing drops for Rugolo, Calliden and himself. His own seemed to go into his mouth without the glass touching his lips at all, the slug flying into place of its own accord.

'Is it not a strange thing,' he said, with a note of satisfaction, 'how those wishing to trade into the Eye find their way here, to this little place? What could account for it?'

'What indeed?' Aegelica said in her pleasant contralto. She reached out, took the other bottle, the brown one, and unstoppered it. She did not bother with a glass. She lifted the bottle above her tilted head and poured the entire contents into her mouth. The liqueur flowed like a glacier, like syrup, straight down her throat without her having to swallow.

Rugolo remembered her long tubular tongue when she had been daemon-transformed. He imagined her extending it into the bottle to withdraw the last of the liqueur. But she did not. She seemed entirely normal now. She flung the bottle down into the scraggy vegetation which made up the floor of the tent.

She sighed. 'We must get something better than this, dear brother.'

'We shall, dearest one. By the roots of my desire, we shall!'

Rugolo swallowed his little glassful, seeing Calliden do the same. He felt the now familiar electric delight and power suffuse all through him, stopping his thoughts, turning his feelings around, filling his inner consciousness with sparkling colour, making him feel immortal and invincible.'

He gasped. 'How long before one becomes addicted to this, like…'

He hesitated, then said it anyway. 'Like Kwyler?'

'One is addicted already,' Gundrum assured him. 'One has always had this addiction; it is not something one needs to acquire. The liqueur is an essence – the essence of life. You like being alive, is that not true?'

Gundrum poured into the three glasses again, then spoke to Kwyler. 'This one bottle will not last us long enough. Go to the distillery and ask for what they owe me. They will know what I mean.'

Kwyler hastily swallowed his slug of life-essence, greedily prised the bottle from Gundrum's hand and served himself two more which he swallowed quickly, one after the other. Then he nodded, rose, and left the tent.

THE LEVEL OF THE remaining bottle quickly fell, and with it so did the sense of danger and the natural fear on the part of Rugolo and his navigator. Aegelica seemed to have been made sleepy by having drunk an entire bottle by herself. She lay down, relaxed and appeared to have fallen asleep.

Gundrum looked down at her, his expression softening, which on his hard, angular face looked comical. 'My dear little one,' he said huskily. 'See how peaceful she is. Yes, I know you have seen a different side to her, which has made you afraid, but look at her now. You see her as she was when young, before we learned to enjoy the changes of this region. An innocent, harmless young girl.'

They could not tell if he was celebrating or lamenting her daemonic possession. Perhaps, Rugolo thought, the daemon had left her. He hardly cared right now. He couldn't understand now why he had let Calliden talk him into making escape from the Eye their first priority. He felt strong and ambitious. The loss of the *Wandering Star* was only a setback. They had made it into the magical realm, with its magical products! All he had to do was find some way of obtaining those products, then find some way of transporting them… He reminded himself that all this required the co-operation of Gundrum, and that was uncertain.

'I have lost my ship,' he said. 'Will you take us out of the Eye? I can still be useful to you, once I get another. I seem to remember we had an agreement.'

He threw in the last as a make-weight. Gundrum had never been serious about that, if Kwyler was right.

He frowned. Wasn't there something else? Something about a jewel? Funny, the thought seemed to evade him, like something he had dreamed.

'Certainly I will take you,' Gundrum said. 'Both of you. When we make our way out, that is. We may visit elsewhere first.'

'And what can I do for you in return?'

'I am sure you will be able to pay for your passage.'

The liqueur bottle was empty now. The light in the tent was fading. Gundrum stood, leaning over Rugolo and putting his face, with its flaking parchment-like skin, close to his. 'You have pleased me, though you know it not. You have shown the energy and enterprise to get deep into the enchanted realm. Not many do that. You deserve a reward.'

The two travellers found themselves both repelled and hypnotically attracted by Gundrum's presence and also by his words, which seemed to open up new vistas. Rugolo realised that this little world, bizarre though it was, was unlikely to be Gundrum's sole source of merchandise. From somewhere he had got the eldar wraithguard, for one thing.

Perhaps it was the liqueur – they had both drunk nearly a third of a bottle – but they seemed to be seeing everything through new eyes, through someone else's eyes. Perhaps the liqueur caused mild hallucinations, Calliden thought. Many stimulants and beverages did that.

'The young men who passed by must have done the same,' Calliden pointed out. 'We happen to know where they come from. Why are they prisoners?'

'A sad tale,' Gundrum said. 'Criminals and fools, far out of their depth, financed by some unscrupulous business magnate who also provided them with a kidnapped navigator. They managed to follow our trail, as you did, but were taken as slaves by this planet's natives. I can do nothing for them, even if I wished to.'

Calliden jumped to his feet on hearing this. 'A navigator? Where is he?'

'Dead, I fear. He was still aboard their vessel when–'

'Where is their ship?' Rugolo pressed.

'Eaten,' Gundrum said after a pause. 'There are earth-giants on this planet, who rear out of the ground and devour anything that comes by, especially if it is made of metal. But don't worry, we are safe here.'

A strange sound came from outside. They followed Gundrum out of the tent and saw a trail of natives pulling sledges over the buff-coloured turf from the direction of the workshops and distillery. The sky still boomed and flashed its continual lightning – though it was probably not lightning, Calliden thought, but connected in some manner with the energy sizzling between the tips of the spire mountains – but the light had fallen somewhat. Night was a long time coming on this planet, the sunlight spreading through the cloud layer and past the terminator line. True darkness probably didn't come at all. The energy discharges would see to that.

The leading sledge-hauler, wearing the same dull-coloured tabard and leggings as the slave guards, greeted Gundrum. 'Here is your payment, as agreed.'

Payment for what? Calliden thought. *Slaves?* But if so, how had Gundrum obtained them? His own story made more sense.

Gundrum gestured them closer. The first half a dozen sledges were filled with hundreds of liqueur bottles, products of the distillery. He pulled out four, then handed two to Rugolo and two to Calliden.

'The rest are for export,' he announced. 'If we revive our former agreement, perhaps you can help me distribute them, to our greater profit.'

'My fortunes will have to revive first,' Rugolo murmured, half to himself.

Gundrum was off examining the rest of the sledges. Calliden took Rugolo by the arm and pulled him back.

'What's the matter with you?' the navigator hissed. 'Why did you let that girl touch you? She's daemon-possessed! Don't you remember what she nearly did to you?'

Rugolo's response was glassy. 'I don't think she has the daemon any more! She's really nice!'

Calliden sighed and drew away. He too had felt Aegelica's exciting magnetism, her seductive charm even. But another part of him had recoiled as though from a poisonous snake, and that had been before her daemonic transformation on the fish planet.

Rugolo willingly obeyed when Gundrum beckoned him over to take a look in the other sledges, offering to show him the output of the workshops ranged along the river. In spite of his essence-drunkenness, Rugolo was disappointed by the contents of the first sledge he came to. Gundrum proudly displayed an assortment of metal dishes, bowls, plates trenchers and goblets, ornately adorned, often eccentrically shaped, but otherwise unremarkable.

'What's special about these?' he asked peevishly. 'The like can be purchased in any bazaar of the Imperium!'

Gundrum laughed in delight. 'So you might think! But nothing made by an artisan of the Imperium compares with what you see here. Whatever is eaten from these vessels is twice, three times, five times as delectable!'

Rugolo blinked.

'I see you do not believe me, friend,' Gundrum said, his normally exulting, hooting voice becoming mournful again. 'These will excite you more, as you seek to peddle your wares among the curious and the lovers of the exotic.'

The second sledge was stacked with cases of various sizes. Gundrum unfastened the clasps on one. Inside, nestling amid a white downy packing, lay a cylindrical instrument three or four inches long, pewter-coloured, dotted with studs. Carefully Gundrum lifted it out and handed it to Rugolo.

'Look through this. Tell me what you see.'

At one end was an eyepiece. A telescope? Rugolo placed it against his right eye, squinting the other and peering into the cylinder.

He saw nothing until Gundrum applied his long fingers to the row of studs, manipulating them in some way. Suddenly a scene sprang into view. He was looking down on a city of the Imperium from an aerial viewpoint. It was easy to recognise the massive, brutal architecture with its florid decoration, the great buttresses which held up the oversized structures, the grime and grimness…

He moved the instrument and found he was panning across the planetary surface. Even on the far horizon the city still extended its excesses, but mixed now with belching smoke and flame from factories and forges.

He could not name the city. There were a million like it. Gundrum touched the studs again. The scene shifted. He was looking down through a transparent dome that floated in space. Gundrum twisted a milled ring on the scope. He seemed to pass through the dome and to see the wondrous habitation within, as unlike the Imperium as it was possible for anything to be, for elegance and beauty. And the people who inhabited it – no, they were not people, exactly – they were too tall and graceful, and their faces had an alien cast...

'Do you remember the wraithguard?' Gundrum murmured in his ear. 'It was made in a place such as this. These are eldar.'

Rugolo continued to gaze in fascination. Then he removed the instrument from his eye, and shrugged.

'Interesting, but hardly worth coming into the Eye of Terror for. It is simply a viewing device with a number of scenes and images stored in it.'

'No, it stores nothing. What you see is happening now. You are looking through the warp, at things far off.' Seeing Rugolo's scepticism, Gundrum said, 'Look again.'

The instrument was warm in Rugolo's hand. He put it to his eye again.

He was looking into the interior of what at first he took to be the largest cathedral imaginable. The vaulted roof was so far overhead as to be obscured by condensed water vapour – clouds inside a building! Crowds of robed priests and acolytes thronged the nave. The aisles were flanking ranks of banners – torn, tattered, but still glowing their ancient colours – a hundred yards in height. Multihued light filtered, gleaming on slowly moving murals depicting battle after battle.

The huge building buzzed with a febrile sense of activity. There was none of the calm of prayer and contemplation. Rugolo himself turned the magnification ring now. He seemed to progress down the nave towards the far chancery. Guarding the sanctuary there stood two Titans, the greatest war machines that could be used on land, which he had seen up to now only in Imperial Guard propaganda, one on either side, power fists raised as if in salute. And beyond, in the sanctuary itself – a shimmering golden globe, surrounded by a forest of cables and hoses so numerous they almost occluded it, bracketed by field generators, both the source and the focus of all the excitement in the vast...

Rugolo snatched the instrument from his eye.

It could not be! It was impossible! *He could not be looking into the Emperor's throne room!*

Gundrum relieved him of the warp telescope, replaced it in its box, and the box in the sled. 'Take these things to my ship. Foafoa will direct you how to place them in the hold.'

He turned away, then stopped, frowning upwards. From the distance, sliding through the lightning, three vehicles were flying low. They were more like boats than aircraft, with curved prows and lacking canopies, their cockpits open to the sky. Brief wings, more like vanes, angled sharply back. As they came closer faces peered down over the sides. The craft circled the spot twice, emitting a noise rather like that of buzz-saws, spitting sparks from their rear ends, and then gently settled on the ochre turf.

'Ah, more visitors!' Gundrum declared vigorously. 'So many visitors! Who will be next?'

The local merchants – or were they merely artisans? – had stopped hauling the sleds and now looked on with numb foreboding as half a dozen warriors piled out of each airboat, variously armed, clad in makeshift armour of overlapping metal plates fastened on with straps, metal helmets more resembling skullcaps strapped to their heads.

The warriors all bore the same mutations. Their eyes sprang from their sockets on stalks which swivelled this way and that. Their ears had become bats' ears, long funnels which cast about in all directions. Their mouths were extraordinary, extending three quarters of the way round their heads, so that when open they looked as if their heads had been axed almost in half, and filled with spike-like teeth. Their arms were too short, only half the length of a normal man's, but this was made up for by long, bony fingers which wrapped themselves round their weapons like tentacles.

Their leader, his rank advertised by three froth-like yellow plants fixed to his helmet and his billowing red breeches, took a brief glance at the rainbow-painted spaceship, nodded to Gundrum in familiar fashion, then addressed the hauler of the leading sledge in a whining, snarling voice, more like the voice of an animal that had learned to speak.

'Our master, the high and lordly daemon Spittingbottom, likes your liqueurs. He wishes to possess your distillery.'

The crimson-tabarded industrial worker kept his head bowed. 'Sir,' he said respectfully, 'we serve the daemon Mouldergrime, who already owns the distillery, and also likes the products of our labours.'

'Pah! And how does he treat you, this great Mouldergrime?'

'Very well. We live in peace and raise our families. Of course there are the sacrifices at festival times. At the Festival of No Food we must hang up all our five-year-olds and disembowel them. At the five-day Festival of Eat Nothing we burn our four-year olds alive. But these festivals come only every two years, and it is a welcome sacrifice to make to Mouldergrime, for all his blessings to us.'

'Pah! Your Mouldergrime is niggardly! What has he done for you? You look the same as you always did! Spittingbottom will let you keep your children. All he demands is to eat your wives! And if you serve him well, eventually you will look like us!'

The local man's head sank even lower, as did the heads of all his fellows. 'We cannot speak against Mouldergrime, sir.'

'No matter. As you know, on the other side of this world Spittingbottom has possession of one continent and Mouldergrime the other. Tonight they are holding a contest on the island of Grossgrease, to see whose champion can eat the greatest mass of worms and thus expel the greatest weight in dung. If Spittingbottom wins, he has the distillery and this town with it. I come only to prepare you for your change of masters. Have plenty of essence ready!'

With a ferocious gesture the squad leader ordered his men to the airboats, which took off and buzzed their way back the way they had come.

Gundrum, however, continued looking upward. 'It often follows their wake... Yes, here it comes. It is close, and low, and coming near. Follow me, you two,' he said to Rugolo and Calliden, 'and see what happens. This may be to your advantage.'

He set off in a jerky run, his arms waving as though not properly fixed to his body, making his way up the shallow slope of the valley. More slowly, the other two came after him. They saw now what he had been watching for. Making its way through the air, advancing majestically through the crackling criss-crossing energy, was what at first looked like a patch of multi-hued mist. Gundrum paused at the top of the rise and waited for them to join him. Below was the crippled *Wandering Star*.

'Once my ship was a common scow, like yours,' he told them. 'This world's *magic* is what has made the difference. Watch.'

It was like seeing a rainbow that had gathered itself up and become a scintillant giant amoeba whipping itself through the air. It became less misty and more well-defined as it came closer. As it came on it engulfed Rugolo's starship, a rolling amorphous shape that filled half the field of view. Rugolo's heart leaped. His ship would be magically restored! The hull glowed and sparkled with all the colours that the rainbow cloud carried along with it.

And then fell to pieces.

He gaped. The rainbow cloud was ascending skywards again now as it met the rise in the ground, its lower edge missing them by a good margin. It left behind a broken and sagging mass of crumpled metal.

Gundrum grunted. 'Not to be, evidently.'

He began walking down the slope. Rugolo followed him despondently, leaving Calliden at the top of the ridge. Gundrum picked up a piece of metal from the collapsed hull, showing it to him. The rainbow cloud had done more than just wreck his ship. The metal gleamed dully with oily colours.

'This scrap at least is worth something,' Gundrum told him. 'Everything on the worlds within the Eye of Terror, even metal, is soaked in the forces of Chaos. Metal from outside has a novelty value. It is touched by Chaos when given the rainbow treatment, of course, but in particularly pure form.'

This was the most sensible speech Rugolo had heard from the Chaos trader. He threw down the lump of rainbow metal.

'Bad luck,' Gundrum said. He looked at Rugolo with something resembling sympathy. 'Let's go back to the tent. You look as though you could do with some more essence.'

Rugolo did not have the heart to refuse. They rejoined Calliden and strode back.

AEGELICA WAS STILL sleeping, unaware of the visitation by the servants of the daemon from the other side of the planet. The trio opened one bottle of liqueur, then another. Each bottle, it seemed, contained essence of a different colour. Whatever the distilling process was, it was very individualistic.

Gundrum seemed ready to show a more human face. He described some of his travels in the Eye, though clearly he was leaving out some of the more bizarre details. After the second bottle was nearly finished, Calliden asked him a serious question.

'Do you believe in the Emperor?'

'Ah, our beloved Emperor,' Gundrum rejoindered jovially, 'who holds together the human race and has charge of our souls. Of course.'

'Then don't you ever feel that what you are doing is wrong?'

'Wrong?' Gundrum made an exaggerated grimace and relapsed into his former mode of speaking. 'Oh no, oh oh! Oh no, oh oh! By my wordiness! Oh oh! I do not care about all of that. The priests will tell you everything is evil except the Emperor. Aliens are evil. Chaos is evil…

'How are aliens more evil than us? They are simply creatures, as we are. No, it is all the same to me. The Emperor is not captain of my soul.'

Calliden's normally pale face went even paler. Even Rugolo, elevated as he was to a state of near-ecstasy by the amount of liqueur he had drunk, was shocked to the core. He had never before encountered a man of such total amorality. True, he had traded with aliens, but like everyone else who did so, he believed deep down that he was doing something wicked – had even revelled in his sin. Murderers, thieves, swindlers and heretics – they all acknowledged the Emperor in their hearts. A man without even this elementary moral sense was incomprehensible to him.

Embarrassed, he changed the subject. 'What has happened to Kwyler? He did not return with the merchandise.'

'Unable to tear himself away from the distillery, no doubt!' Gundrum sighed. He let out a roar. 'Sister!'

Aegelica woke up and looked about her sleepily. Her appearance was girlish and innocent. It was hard to believe she was the same person they had first met, or who had attacked Rugolo in such ghoulish form.

'Go into the town, find Kwyler and bring him here.'

She went obediently out into the darkening gloom. In a little over half an hour she was back, without Kwyler but carrying yet another small ribbed bottle.

'Kwyler sent this,' she said.

'Ah!' Gundrum seemed pleased. He took the bottle from her hand, unsealed it, then poured into the acorn-sized glasses. The liqueur was a quite bright yellow, and poured more easily than usual, seeming thinner.

Gundrum sniffed it, then sipped rather than take it straight down, rolling it around his mouth before swallowing.

'Hmm. New. Not given time to mature. Raw, but refreshing. A brave little essence, I'd say.'

'Bottled only hours ago, is my guess!' Aegelica giggled.

Rugolo and Calliden sampled theirs. It had, as Gundrum had said, a raw flavour. The taste-assault on their tongues was more limited, but sharper. As it went into their stomachs there was the usual explosion, but with an extra excitement to it.

Rugolo grinned inanely, and took some more. 'I *like* this!'

Calliden too liked it. He reached for the bottle.

Then he noticed that Aegelica had changed since she made the trip to the distillery. The withdrawn, slightly pathetic innocence was gone. Here was the magnetic, vampiric Aegelica of previously. Her eyes had widened, become rounder and greener. Her exposed skin had firmed and glowed. She had moved to Rugolo and was tugging his goatee beard with one hand and running her finger nails along his neck with the other. The look she was giving him was ogling and predatory.

Calliden rose to his feet. 'Get away from her, Maynard,' he said raggedly.

And that was all either of them knew.

RUGOLO BECAME AWARE of the noises first. It was a while before he could open his eyes. There was a shuffling of feet, and the mutter and murmur of voices. And there were other sounds: an intermittent hissing, like a slow-acting piston; liquid, bubbling and pouring.

Everything echoed, as it would in a large metal shed, which proved to be the case when the trader opened his eyes. He was lying on his side on a hard floor. His hands and feet were tied together. Calliden was in the same situation a few feet away. Both had been stripped of their laspistols.

He became aware of a face looking down at him. 'Ah, here we are, then.'

The man was clad in drab blue coveralls tailored from some rough material. A workman. But he did not look unkindly. He called over some others, who helped Rugolo and Calliden to a sitting position, leaning against the wall of the shed. It appeared to be next day. The flickering brown daylight came through openings in the roof.

The shed was crammed with equipment. A small furnace was being stoked, sending thick smoke up a flue. The regular sighing sound came from an elaborate contraption, at the centre of which stood a fat yellow cylinder into which a piston was being pushed at intervals, and from which escaped gusts of powdery vapour. The contraption was connected to the inlet valves of a row of half a dozen vats arranged along the shed. These vats in turn had outlet cocks leading to storage cylinders lining one wall, one cylinder per vat. Rugolo guessed they were in the distillery which spanned the river. But why?

The workman spoke to him. 'So nice to see people from the outside. Hard to get good raw material, you know. I expect you want to know how it's done, don't you? It's a dipping process to begin with, you see. Then there's the rendering down. Well, you can see for yourself. Here are the people who came in before you.'

Calliden hissed words at Rugolo. 'That last bottle must have been drugged.'

Rugolo became aware of an acrid smell. It came from a vapour being exhaled from the vats. And now he saw 'the people who came in before you', being led in, chained together. The Gendovans. They looked around themselves in bewilderment, then began struggling as the iron collars were removed and they were hung upside down by the feet from a movable belt, fitted with pulleys and running the length of the shed. When they each found themselves suspended over a vat the screaming for mercy began.

It was to no avail. The belt was lowered. Each Gendovan, flexing desperately, disappeared into his vat. Half a minute later he came up again, spluttering and dripping, wailing with protest until he went down again.

Squatting down beside Rugolo to make himself heard over the screams, the distillery worker continued explaining the process, in the same friendly, informative tone. 'The dipping has to go on for quite a while, you see. It's like making candles, except in reverse. Instead of putting tallow on the wick by degrees, the soul is gradually leeched out of you, if you like, all the psychic content going into the liquid. Oh, that liquid is the secret of this business! No one else knows it, not on this world, not on any other! Well, I'm not saying any more about that, am I? That's our trade secret. What's it like? Well, I'm not going to say you'll enjoy it. You feel like everything's being drawn out of you. It's quite uncomfortable. But after a while you hardly know where or who you are, so they say. It's all gone into the solution. Then with the last dip they leave you there and you stop breathing. The rendering down begins then. There's lots of chemicals and hormones and things, like memory molecules out of your brain, all those things go into the brew too. Then we draw you off to clarify. After that it goes to the still to be sublimated, then to the casks for maturing.

'Been in this job all my life, I have, ever since I was a boy. Proud of the work we do here, I am. Best liqueurs in the galaxy! And this is why: they are essence of human being. Could there be anything better?'

Having finished taking pride in his craft, the distillery worker heaved himself to his feet and wandered off to be about his duties. Eventually the Gendovans had ceased their struggling and were left for an hour or two totally submerged.

Rugolo and Calliden now appreciated the full extent of Kwyler's treachery. *This* was why he had brought them here: to be rendered down and distilled for the delectation of others.

But where was Kwyler? Back with Gundrum, presumably. He had only left the tent – on Gundrum's orders, they recalled – to arrange for the drugged essence.

'*This* is Gundrum's real business,' Rugolo said through gritted teeth. 'He isn't trading out of the Eye so much as trading in! He brings people here to be turned into liqueur!'

'Why would he need to do that? There are people here already.'

Rugolo thought about it. He remembered what Gundrum had said about local vintage. What he had said about the value of metal from outside.

'Everything here is corrupted by Chaos, including people – people most of all. People from outside the Eye of Terror, uncorrupted, untainted, must make a superior product.'

'People like us, you mean,' Calliden added mournfully.

Rugolo noticed him staring at something. He followed his gaze. Underneath one of the vats, perhaps accidentally kicked there, was an object he recognised. Kwyler's melta-gun.

Now it was their turn for the vats. 'We can be of use to you!' Rugolo yelled eagerly as the workmen approached. 'I'm a trader! My friend's a navigator! Take a look at his warp eye! We can bring you better material than Gundrum can! We know where to get lots of people. We won't charge much – *just give us a chance!*'

His increasingly frantic babble was ignored. His last pleas came as he found himself looking down into the murky evil-smelling surface of whatever concoction it was accomplished the absorption of a man's essence – his nature, his life's experience, his very soul.

With the rattling of a chain, they were dunked into the brew. It felt oily, seeping reluctantly through their clothing. It stung Rugolo's skin. He held his breath, but somehow it got into his mouth and his nostrils, making him choke. He seemed to be there for an eternity. Psychically he felt little – perhaps just a sense of melting away at the edges – but then this was the first dip.

The chain rattled again as they were hauled free of the liquid. The more sensitive Calliden had not held out as well as his partner. He came up blubbering and twisting from side to side.

'I can't stand this, Maynard! I can't! I can't stand it!' His voice rose to a shriek as they descended again. 'Help me! Help me! *Mother, help me!*'

Unlike Rugolo, he had suffered more from the psychic effects of the dipping process than the physical. It was like being pulled apart from the inside, the absorbing fluid causing his psyche to seep out of him as though by osmosis. It caused a pain that went beyond what he had ever experienced before. He threshed about in the vat, trying to scream with his mouth full of the filthy-tasting liquid, feeling it enter his lungs.

Then he heard a calm, cool voice. *'I'll help you, Pelor.'*

His mother's voice!

He could feel her presence in the vat with him. His eyes were closed, but he clearly saw her face, her dear face, as she tried to comfort him.

The rope holding him to the overhead belt snapped. He doubled up, rolling about in the bottom of the vat. The ropes tying his hands and feet seemed to have been weakened and made slippery by the oily absorption brew. They were slipping off as he struggled.

He was free. He reached up and gripped the lip of the vat.

COMING UP AFTER his second dip, Rugolo quickly became aware that something had happened. Calliden was no longer his dipping companion, no longer hanging beside him from the overhead belt. Instead he was on the floor of the shed, wielding the melta-gun. Its sub-molecular flame whooshed and roared ahead of him, vaporising men and charring plant and machinery, sending out a wave of heat which he could feel even where he was.

Any it did not catch scattered and fled through the openings at the far end. Calliden wasted no time in finding the pulley that worked the belt and lowering Rugolo to the floor. After some difficulty he undid the ropes.

Gasping with relief, Rugolo clawed sticky, smelly fluid from his face.

'How did you manage that, Pelor?'

Calliden sobbed. He threw himself on Rugolo's shoulder. 'It was my mother!' he howled '*She* released me! It's real after all! My mother is in *Hell*, Maynard!'

Rugolo pushed him off and gave him a quizzical frown.

'Clearly,' he said, 'it's an advantage to have a mother in hell, if you're in the Eye of Terror.'

He snatched the melta-gun from Calliden. 'Come on, let's settle accounts with Gundrum. We need his ship, after all.'

Calliden stumbled after him. 'You might kill Gundrum and Kwyler, but you can't kill Aegelica with that thing. You saw what happened before. And anyway, we can't get out of the Eye without her.'

Outside the shed, men were running past. But it was not because of the melta-gun. The airboats had returned, landing just beyond the line of workshops. The troop leader from before was firing two crude slug pistols in the air, discharging messy gouts of flame and smoke, and urging his bizarrely mutated men on.

'Daemon Spittingbottom owns this town and distillery!' he roared triumphantly. 'His champion defecated as much as a hundred ton megastegasaur could! Bring out your wives! Spittingbottom is hungry!'

He spotted the drenched, oily-faced escapees from the vats, and pulled up sharp. 'What are you doing? You are outsiders! You are bottles of essence! Get back with you!'

Rugolo did not know how much fuel remained in the melta-gun's reservoir. He displayed the weapon to the ruffian, hoping he would recognise it for what it was. A calculating look came to the troop leader's face, his eyestalks wavering from side to side. He turned to his men, and made a bowling action with one arm. 'On! On to the distillery!'

Rugolo continued as fast as he could along the river, Calliden in tow, to discover that a few of the mutants had been left behind to seize the painted spaceship. They were pinned down behind their airboat, as were Gundrum and Foafoa, crouched by the scarlet pavilion, exchanging laser with musket shot. There was no sign of either Kwyler or Aegelica.

The quickest way to the starship was straight through the middle, between the two parties and into the line of fire. Rugolo beckoned.

'When I say so, run for all you're worth,' he said to Calliden.

So far they had not been spotted, and they were to far away for the range of the melta-gun, though worryingly, in range of Gundrum's laser. Rugolo took a deep breath.

'Now!'

He set off at a run. When he had covered half the distance, Gundrum turned and looked at him with a ludicrous exposition of surprise. He let fly with a badly aimed laser shot. Rugolo answered with a brief squeeze on the melta-gun's trigger, the stock at his shoulder. There was a hissing as the blast of sub-molecular energy superheated the air through which it passed. He twisted round to let off another blast in the direction of the airboats. The melta-gun was a short range weapon and he was still too far off to do any real harm, but through the haze it created he saw Gundrum fall back, raising his arms as though to ward off the heat. Foafoa, however, took the opportunity to launch himself across the gap towards the mutants. Unwittingly Rugolo had given him covering fire.

He and Calliden ran through the same swirling haze of still-hot air, feeling their skin burn. In seconds they were past the small pavilion. Rugolo glanced round and saw Foafoa, close by the airboats, laying about him with his laspistol, the bright beam darting here and there.

A white-blue beam hissed past Rugolo's ear. He whirled round. Gundrum must have gone round the other side of the pavilion. He was standing on the ramp leading into his spaceship, both man and machine rearing over him presenting the same odd, angled appearance.

Rugolo dodged another laser shot and then, putting the melta-gun's stock back to his shoulder, marched challengingly on. He was close enough now to be able to vaporise Gundrum. Realising this, the trader pointed his laspistol at Calliden.

They came to the foot of the ramp. It was a stand-off. With a glittering smile Gundrum looked sidelong at Rugolo, daring him to squeeze the trigger, knowing that his dying act would be to drill the navigator through the heart. His face lit up with delight, as though an idea had struck him.

'By my roots, by my words, by my secret desires, what will you do? I will be gone, your navigator will be gone. You will have to team up with my dear demented sister!'

His eyes swivelled, looking towards the airboats. Rugolo did likewise, making sure to keep Gundrum in view. His pistol's charge run low after killing half a dozen mutants, Foafoa had thrown down his pistol and drawn a short curved sabre from a scabbard strapped to his thigh. At that moment a musket ball took him in the chest. He staggered back, and fell. The mutants were on him in a moment. His own sabre was used to slash and slash at him, cutting his torso to ribbons.

What happened next made Rugolo sick to watch. As the now dead Foafoa lay there the back of his head opened and his twisted companion, Gidane, emerged. The baby-sized midget got to his feet and toddled towards the painted ship, arms held out imploringly. The umbilical cord which attached him to Foafoa had been cut by the sabre. It trailed behind him on the turf, its end bloody. The grotesque thing did not get far. One of the mutants picked him up and held him before his face, his oversized mouth gaping in pleasure. The mutant seemed to think Gidane a baby. He started kissing him and licking him with a broad green tongue, while Gidane made faces of disgust and puked his protests.

'May I suggest we go inside?' Gundrum said quietly. 'Gidane has found someone new to care for him, I think.'

That suited Rugolo. Weapons still trained on one another, they mounted the ramp. After a nod of permission from Rugolo, Gundrum pressed a stud which raised it and made it flush with the hull.

They were in an elevator. With a whine it took them up, slid smoothly to a stop, and opened on to the ship's interior.

The first thing Rugolo saw was Aegelica. She was seated on a piece of furniture unfamiliar to him, not a chair but a stool which was able to swivel on a pedestal, a facility which she obviously liked, for she was turning herself playfully from side to side. She hunched herself up on seeing them and smiled invitingly.

'How nice to see you again!' she said to Rugolo. 'Your name's Maynard, isn't it?'

Rugolo didn't recall ever telling her his name. Perhaps the daemon in her had plucked it out of the ether.

They had entered what was a common arrangement in a small trading ship, a combined flight room and living accommodation. But its style was totally alien. Instead of the cluttered intricacy which was the norm everywhere in the industrialised Imperium, it had clean-swept lines, a streamlined look, like the external lines of the ship itself. There were no nooks and crannies, no protuberances and florid decorations, and the colours were pastel and uncomplicated. Rugolo would never have been able to feel at ease here. It was a perversion. A product of Chaos.

Gundrum spoke softly. 'Do you realise you have made a mistake? You have given me the advantage. If I kill your navigator now, will you really fire that melta-gun in such a confined space? You would cook us both, as well as turn this control room into slag.'

'I won't care in the least about that,' Rugolo said confidently. 'I'm ready to do it anyway.' But he noted that Gundrum had left Aegelica out when describing the gun's effects.

'Where's Kwyler?' he demanded.

Aegelica giggled. 'He's on board.'

Rugolo allowed his glance to locate the flight panel. Apart from the lack of runes and ornate decoration, it was standard.

'Pelor,' he ordered, 'get over there and take us off this damned planet!'

Gundrum still kept his laspistol on the navigator as Calliden obeyed, seating himself at the strangely bare control board. The view-screen, of an unfamiliar square shape, flickered on and the ship's engine roared smoothly into life.

They lifted away, through crackling lightning and transient virtual figures, through the boiling brown cloud layer. Calliden put them in parking orbit, looking down on the spiky planet which surrounded itself with a tracery of flashing energy.

Without warning, Gundrum put up his laspistol. 'It is time for a truce,' he said imperturbably.

Calliden was reluctant to put up the melta-gun likewise. He kept it pointed at the Chaos trader.

'Bring Kwyler here,' he said. 'I want to pay him back for the drugged liqueur.'

'There was no drugged liqueur. It was Aegelica who put you to sleep. She can do it now, if she wants.'

Rugolo gawped.

'Show him, Aegelica.'

Aegelica batted her eyelids at Calliden. He slumped suddenly unconscious, his head hitting the control board. She blinked again. He recovered, looking around in puzzlement.

Rugolo was appalled at the realisation that he was powerless. Gundrum had been playing with him. He put up the melta-gun.

'What do you intend to do?' he asked.

'Go back to Caligula, with our cargo – or perhaps further off.'

It had been Rugolo's intention to go further than Caligula too, if he could. He had been plotting to steal Gundrum's ship and goods for himself.

'As for Kwyler,' Gundrum went on, 'don't blame him too much. True, he betrayed you, but he couldn't help himself. He rescued you at first, remember. That was genuine. But poor Kwyler is a man with no consistency, a weak person. He found he couldn't do without the liqueur. So he brought you to us as payment.'

'You betrayed us too,' Rugolo pointed out.

'*We* betrayed you?' Gundrum performed the unnaturally high lifting of his eyebrows again. 'What did we owe you? Let me confess that at one time I had it in mind to spare you the vats. We are both traders, after all. If the rainbow cloud had restored your ship to operational status, I would have let you go on your way. But–' he shrugged with an exaggerated angular jerk of his shoulders – 'it was not to be. And you are valuable, after all, coming from outside the Eye. Those who make their *own* way here are most valuable of all. They are of the best quality, much better than those who are brought here as captives. That is why Aegelica leaves a trail for them to follow.'

Rugolo pondered. 'Where *is* Kwyler?'

For answer Gundrum pointed to a small, bare, round table. On it was a stoppered liqueur bottle of a yellowish colour. It was the same one that Aegelica had brought back from the distillery.

'You have been drinking him!'

Rugolo and Calliden both stared, aghast.

'*That* is Kwyler?'

Aegelica trilled. 'Part of him, at any rate. The rest of him is in the cask, maturing!'

'He had betrayed and abandoned *us*, remember,' Gundrum put in. 'We could not have that, by my roots! But a fitting end, don't you think? Kwyler knew he would end up in the bottle sooner or later, I don't doubt.'

Aegelica stood. 'Let us be going. brother. Make amends to these two fools. Take them with us.'

'Just as you wish, sister. You were ever soft-hearted.'

She gestured Calliden out of the pilot's seat and seated herself in his place, setting up the board for the journey. Her movements were assured; it was clear she was an accomplished pilot. Rugolo began to feel relief, mingled though it was with distrust. Without Aegelica they would never be able to leave the Eye, and here she was offering to take them herself. But was it the woman or the daemon making that offer?

Suddenly she looked up at the viewscreen, her hand making an adjustment. 'Brother, see!'

All eyes went to the viewscreen. It showed a big dark patch, surrounded by stars and glowing dust.

'The Rose Cluster! It has vanished!'

Gundrum moved closer, his tall form bending and peering. 'No, it is still there. See, it occludes the stars behind it. It has gone dark, that is all.'

'Yes, I see it,' Aegelica murmured. 'The cycle has turned. This is a good time to be leaving, brother.'

She gave her attention back to the pilot's instruments. She was turning the ship around, preparatory to setting out. The swirling brown and red sphere of the spiked planet's sun hove into view on the screen.

Calliden and Rugolo both went rigid with terror. The sun convulsed while an angry-faced head and shoulders poked out, looked around itself briefly, then withdrew, the sun closing up after it to swirl red and brown as before, a turbulent ball.

If Gundrum and Aegelica had noticed the vision, they made no comment. Aegelica yanked a lever. The painted spaceship shot off, leaving the sun with its solitary planet behind.

Then she gave out a high-pitched cry.

'Brother! We are out of control! We are falling! Something has hold of us – I can't pull out!'

On the viewscreen all stars disappeared. There was only a glimmering blackness. They were falling. Not onto the spiked planet. Not into its angry sun. They were plummeting deep into the darkness that was once the Rose Cluster.

FIFTEEN
THE WORM IN THE ROSE

THE GREAT ROSES were withering on the stem of Chaos. The rose-shaped suns, the rose-shaped planets, writhed and turned black, stricken by a dreadful canker. Everywhere visions of beauty and harmony erupted into foulness. Pale, glimmering worm-shapes sprang from between planet-petals now gone putrescent, turning everything they touched to slime. The once enchanted landscapes became covered with wriggling, slithering, rustling masses of noisome, loathsome insectoid and reptilian creatures. The human inhabitants, with their formerly peaceful natures, became growling brutes obsessed with a hatred for everything living.

A glorious example of Tzeentchian change! The Great God's followers all roared their approval!

Utter darkness had descended. There was silence. Sergeant Abdaziel Magron of the Dark Angels Chapter, unable to see in any frequency his helmet had available, felt his captain's gauntlet clank against his armour, steadying him. 'Wait a few moments, sergeant.'

Now his visor was bringing something to his senses. Not light exactly; no, not light. Blackness that was visible. Black light. No-light. A nullity that showed itself.

Magron looked overhead. An ebony sun sat in a jet-black sky. A sun that *glowed* with utter darkness, washing the landscape with negative light. How could such a contradiction be?

In that Cimmerian nothingness, Magron could see Captain Abaddas, though not in the same way that he had been able to see him before. He could even see the colours of his armour, like enamel glowing dimly from black depths. The city around them glowered in the black light, too, but it was changing. The sparkling minarets and elegant belvederes were collapsing and heaving, twisting into ugly grotesqueries, rough-hewn caves and misshapen piles.

Darkness entered Sergeant Magron's soul. All in the plaza – both the invading Alpha Marines and the confused mob of defenders – had paused, as if frozen, during the Rose Cluster's descent into utter darkness. Now they began to move again. Although Magron had invoked the Emperor in his battle-cry, he now forgot even that. Battle rage possessed him. Had no others been present, he might even have launched himself at his captain.

The knights and warriors of the city, despite being better armed, were no match for the Alpha Legion Marines who in little time waded in blood, gore, crushed armour and splintered bone as they continued their joyous advance. They disdained to use their bolters which they left clipped in their holsters. Instead they restricted themselves to power-maces and hammers, all the time emitting a concerted drone of prayer to some unimaginable Dark God, a chant which rose and fell, becoming ever more fervent as the slaughter progressed.

All Magron could understand of this chant was that it spoke of blood, of death, of crushed skulls, of gifts of carnage to the lord whom they addressed. He would not have known them for Space Marines at all, had Abaddas not told him so. But some indistinct sense of honour made him put up his bolter too. A figure confronted him whose armour was metamorphosed beyond recognition. The helm had become the head of a wrathful hook-nosed bird, shrouded in thick hair, surmounted by two huge curlicued horns with tips pointing forward. The main body of the armour was an embossed mass, damascened with scenes depicting butchery and bloody sacrifice, which somehow seemed able to project itself into the visible darkness like a hologram. A power-maul in one hand, power-hammer in the other, the Chaos Marine took a step back in confusion at seeing armour that was unmutated and untouched by Chaos. Then his maul met Magron's chainsword and his hammer swung towards the other's helmet. Magron raised an arm to deflect the hammer blow. The strength of the shock on his ceramite vambrace was a surprise to him. He charged, intending to rush in to wreak whatever damage he could with the edge of his buzzing chainsword – and was flung back by an unexpected force.

Captain Abaddas's voice sounded in his ear. 'Do not call on your dead Emperor, sergeant – he cannot help you. The Alpha Marines are aided by the Chaos Gods. Call on the same! Call on the Changer of the Ways!'

Abaddas's words should have been barely comprehensible to the Dark Angels sergeant, but somehow, they were not. Sergeant Magron knew now that the Emperor was dead. He knew that lofty Chaos Gods now ruled the universe – and that a pact could be made with them! It was as though a tendril had penetrated his mind, like the pale worm-shapes that, at the coming of the Rose Cluster's sinister night, were emerging from the slimy landscape.

His rage and bloodlust curdled into a manic resolve to call on any power, no matter what, that would help him to triumph. He roared once again at the top of his voice: 'CHANGER OF WAYS! STRENGTHEN ME!'

This was more than a heartfelt ritual. It was a cry from the soul. A feeling of fresh potency flowed through him. He resolved to see the face of the Alpha Marine who had nearly bested him with daemon-assisted weapons. He drew his bolter and aimed a rapid close-range volley at the bird-shaped helm. The Chaos Marine staggered. The weird helmet cracked, then shattered.

The face that stared out at Magron was a bloody skull with round, bulging bloodshot eyes. It was not a face he could make any sense of, a face without humanity – but inexplicably Magron found it admirable and even enviable. He fired a single shot which shattered the skinless head. Putrid brain matter, green in colour, spattered in all directions. Slowly, with the majesty of a colossus, the bulky form of the warrior fell.

Grimly Captain Abaddas smiled to himself. Sergeant Magron's first step on the path of devotion to Chaos had been when he had come floating down unharmed, wafted by some mysterious warp influence, on to the surface of Rhodonius 428571429. Now he had taken his second, more corrupting, step.

Fighting in the black light was strange, like fighting in a trance. A dim tumult surrounded Magron. Wheeling around, he searched the darkness for another opponent, another enemy to kill. Abaddas was wrestling hand to hand with an Alpha Legion Chaos Marine, each preventing the other from using his weapons, their power armour whining and humming. Magron strode behind the Alpha Marine and applied his chainsword to where he knew it would be most effective – the gorget where the helm connected with the trunk of the power suit. Chaos armour was no different. After some resistance, his chainsword broke in and bit deep. The foul Marine's head flew off.

Captain Abaddas raised his gauntlet in salute.

Magron exulted. It did not matter that victory lay with the invaders, who now walked knee-deep in piles of butchered bodies. Battle was glorious!

Captain Abaddas's calm, incisive voice came to him. 'We have done what we can, brother-sergeant. We are outnumbered, now. Let us withdraw.'

Magron did not want to obey him. He wanted to continue fighting till meeting certain death at the hands of the Alpha Marines – just as long as he could take some of them with him. But he still had the discipline of a Dark Angel. He could not disobey a superior brother officer.

Both men took their bolters in their gauntlets, letting off scattered shot to cover their retreat. To Magron's surprise Abaddas did not make his way back to his beastship. He backed towards the edge of the esplanade and to the slumped and distorted buildings there, which would give good cover should the Alpha Legion pursue them.

Magron found it odd to see masonry which had flowed and reformed itself like some uncontrollably cancerous protoplasm. Once in one of the side streets, the black light became more like ordinary darkness, the glowing ebony orb of the sun out of sight for the moment. He reached out a gauntlet and stroked a wall. It was hard but rough, reminding him of badly poured, unsmoothed concrete.

And then, in the blink of an eye, the negative light vanished. A ruddy radiance fell on the ruined city. Moving out of the shadow, they saw that the sun had changed again and was a glaring bloody sphere.

But that was not all. That sun was but a small ball, flanked by two truly enormous figures. Magron stared in total disbelief. This could not be real. It had to be a hallucination on his part.

Both vast beings were winged, but otherwise were totally unlike one another. On the left, a vaguely humanoid bird-like beast, crested and feathered, beaked and taloned, with plumage of glittering, changing hues. On the right, a majestic, fearful, wolf-faced, triple-horned, man-like thing, its brief armour decorated with skulls, carrying a huge war-axe and a lash. Both looked down on the world with hard shining eyes which carried cunning, knowledge, and power.

It was difficult to estimate the extent of their enormity. If they really stood by the sun, as they seemed to do, then they would have to have extended tens of millions of miles. But it could be they were nearby, perhaps just above the atmosphere, and so only some hundreds of miles in height.

Cumbersomely, Captain Abaddas was sinking to his knees, as were all the Alpha Marines and the few surviving defenders, faces raised to the twin manifestations.

'Kneel, sergeant!' he barked. 'This is not a vision. It is not a projection. It is real!'

Magron froze. To kneel before the powers of Chaos? What would the Emperor have thought of him!

'*Kneel!*' Abaddas's voice became harsher. 'Did you not call on the Changer of the Ways? See how quickly your prayer has been answered! Do not insult the servants of the Dark Gods!'

The dead Emperor receded in Magron's mind as he looked on these exemplars of the new universe. He realised now that what the captain had tried to tell him was true. Here was power such as he could never have dreamed of.

Slowly he bent his knees and joined Abaddas in homage.

THE BIRD'S BEAK opened, and a gigantic purring voice boomed down on to the surface of the planet. Magron did not even ask himself how that voice could carry through the vacuum of space. Such rational questions had no place here.

The greater daemon's words carried a persuasion and a compulsion that brooked no doubt.

'A GREAT PROJECT IS AFOOT. A PROJECT FOR WHICH MY FRIEND THE KHAK'AKAOZ'KHYSHK'AKAMI AND I ARE IN ALLIANCE. YOU ARE NEEDED, MY SUBJECTS, MY LITTLE ONES. COME! THERE IS WORK FOR YOU TO DO!'

The daemon made a slight gesture with his clawed hand. It was as though gravity had been reversed for the common inhabitants of the city. They went tumbling skyward in a great crowd, kicking and wriggling. At a height of about a quarter of a mile, they disappeared.

And not just in the city, although Magron and the others present could not know it. All over the planet, and on countless planets of the star cluster, where the two greater daemons, unimpeded by the normal laws of space and time, were appearing simultaneously, billions were similarly being dragooned into service in the Chi'khami'tzann Tsunoi's forge hells.

But not so any champions of Chaos, any Traitor Marines, any who had received marks of favour. The two daemons, friends of convenience, whirled and flew off, their forms dwindling into space. Captain Abaddas rose to his feet and pointed an armoured finger to Magron's left shoulder pauldron.

There, shining like gleaming quicksilver, was a sinuous sign which had not been present before. And the Imperial eagle on his breastplate was gone.

'You have done well, brother! Those are signs that you have been recognised. Serve Chaos with all your heart and you will receive many gifts.'

The Alpha Legion Marines, left with an empty city, were marching, still chanting, back into their cathedral-ship. 'They go to continue the war elsewhere,' Abaddas informed Magron. 'It is being waged all through the star cluster.'

'Then were the two beings we saw… Chaos Gods?' Magron asked, still stunned with the wonder of it.

'No, they are greater daemons, one an agent of Tzeentch, the other of Khorne.'

Magron recalled that these were the names used by the Alpha Marine when challenging Abaddas. 'If they are allies, why do their adherents fight one another?'

A short, humourless laugh came from the captain's helm. 'This is not the world you are used to. Everything is arranged differently. When daemons converse, their words form a miasma which breaks out into warfare between their followers.'

The cathedral starship lifted off and was gone. Now something new was happening to what had been the rose planet. Around the ruined city, the curled and blackened remains of the clustered planet petals had still been visible once there was light, rearing into the sky. Now they crumbled altogether and vanished. The distorted city, too, collapsed and seemed to bury itself in the ground beneath. Soon there was only a bare landscape, dotted with suddenly erupting volcanoes and lashing trees of some alien kind, all in the bloody glow of the red sun. That, and the products of the recent slaughter in terms of butchered bodies.

The Chi'khami'tzann Tsunoi's magical influence had left the star cluster, leaving it to revert to its former natural state, as it had been before the onset of the warp-storm known as the Eye of Terror. Except, of course, for its human populations, which in some cases replaced the alien populations that had been there before.

Captain Abaddas looked around him, as though surprised by the change.

'I brought you here to meet someone,' Abaddas said eventually. 'Come with me.'

They set out on foot across the barren landscape. As they walked, Abaddas began to explain about the Chaos Powers.

'There are four main Chaos Gods,' he said. 'One of them you want little to do with – *Slaanesh*, a god of unbridled sensuousness and perversion. He is not even connected with humanity but with an alien race called the eldar. *Tzeentch* has the greatest wisdom of all, and is the unsurpassable master of magic. Then there is *Khorne*, the Warrior God. *Nurgle* is perhaps the strangest god of all to understand, for he spreads disease and contagion, but through him one can learn to endure any misfortune.

'Each of these great lords has an unknown number of greater daemons, which are like lesser gods, to do his bidding, as well as ranks of lesser daemons, and of course human champions who can in time attain the status of daemons themselves. Men can become as gods, immortal and with divine powers.'

Magron harkened to this account of the pantheon with fascination.

'The crime of the Emperor,' Abaddas added cautiously, 'was to try to deny mankind this advancement and keep it only for himself.'

'Which of the four powers do you worship, captain?' Magron enquired, after he had let this sink in.

'I do not devote myself to any one master,' Abaddas replied. 'It is not necessary. For you, however, attachment to a single god is the quickest path to the joys and glories of Chaos.'

'And which…?'

Abaddas was silent for a moment, as if ruminating. 'I know your qualities, brother-sergeant. A warrior of your worth should submit himself to Khorne, the War God. In service to him you will find fulfilment beyond measure.'

They walked for some time in silence. 'Brother-captain,' Magron then said, 'I beg you, tell me of the last days when, you say, our chapter was all but destroyed.'

Abaddas hesitated, reluctant to do this. But he decided that prevarication would only make Magron suspicious. He began to mix truth with lies.

'We fought hard, and to the last,' he said. 'In the end what was left of our chapter retreated to Caliban and came under siege by much greater rebel forces. The Emperor was already dead by then.'

He paused, genuinely recalling the titanic struggle. 'Such was the ferocity of the battle that Caliban itself was reduced to a fragment, held together only by the defence screens of the central fortress monastery. You will be surprised, sergeant, when I tell you which chapter led the besiegers.'

Magron waited for him to continue.

'The Word Bearers.'

For all that his outlook was beginning to change, Magron was shocked to the core. The Word Bearers were the only legion of the Adeptus Astartes who possibly exceeded the Dark Angels in religious zeal. Their very name was a byword for missionary passion. In the Great Crusade they had brought worship of the Emperor to every planet they conquered, erecting cathedrals and monuments everywhere. This was the first he had heard of their defection. Communications had been disrupted during the rebellion, and news had travelled slowly.

'Yes, those most dedicated to the Emperor were among the first to abandon him,' Abaddas continued sombrely, 'a loss of faith which paradoxically grew out of their religious fervour. The Word Bearers came to realise that the Emperor was not worthy of worship. He was only a man, and a fallible one at that. They now worship the great Chaos Gods with the same dedication they once gave the Emperor, completely and entirely.'

The two power-armoured Space Marines continued striding over the landscape. Abaddas knew that Magron was struggling with himself. But Chaos was aiding him, was helping him to find the way. More help would come soon.

'I hope you find this story instructive,' he said after a while.

'Who is it we are going to meet now?' Magron asked.

'A chaplain of the Word Bearers.'

While they journeyed, the Rose Cluster's Great Night slowly returned. The sun turned black. But this time the negative light it emitted mingled with the fiery glow from the numerous volcanoes. The mixture of black and red light was more than usually eerie. Evidently the Chi'khami'tzann Tsunoi, the daemon of Tzeentch who had created the Rose Cluster, had only interrupted the rose cycle in order to make his dramatic appearance. The cycle was now imposing itself anew on the planet's original nature.

Hours passed as they made their way across the grumbling landscape. Occasionally dim stooped figures, missed by the greater daemon's levy, crept by in the distance.

'The chaplain's shrine is not far off,' Captain Abaddas announced eventually.

He stopped. A towering shape had come into view. It appeared to be a spaceship, but it was of unusual design, a leaping, streamlined shape. In the black light, streaks of sombre colour ran over it. And at its foot, a grisly scene.

SIXTEEN
THE BATTLESHIP
RECTITUDE

RIVET GUN STRAPPED to his thigh and tool belt clinking, Repair Mechanic Third Class Gragsch knelt alongside the secondary ancillary transformer, one of a row of fifty that he had been trying to service. He placed his ear to the casing and listened intently. He shook his head. Everything had been tuned, worn parts replaced, but still the output was not smooth.

Gragsch's world was a cluttered cavern, one of many in the vast innards of the Gothic-class battleship *Rectitude*. Riveted and blackened pillars criss-crossed it. Hoses, cables and data ribbons turned it into a jungle. Pipes ranging in diameter from one inch to ten feet snaked their way through the gloomy space. At either end lay a confused melange of companionways and tunnel entrances.

The floor ran with oil and green fluid. The only illumination was a red glow from the roof lamps. Noise was constant. Hissing, clanging and clanking, drilling and banging, and the persistent roaring of the far-off drive engines which made the cavern shake. Gragsch had known no other world than this. He had been brought aboard at the age of six, contrary to regulations, by his parents who had been junior ensigns. For some reason unknown to him, they had been executed the next day

and the *Rectitude* had set off with the young Gragsch still
aboard. Engineering crewmen had taken care of him, and had
trained him as he grew up. Much older now, his face was
grimed and twisted. He had never been off the battleship, and
did not even know that it was the flagship of Battlefleet
Obscurus. He had little knowledge of the outside galaxy. When
the discharge of the *Rectitude*'s mighty weapons resounded
through the inmost chambers, he rarely knew whether the warship was engaged in a battle, an exercise, or was test firing.

His ignorance was not unusual. Many among the lower-rank-
ing crewmen had forgotten any other environment.

He trudged his way to his supervisor.

'Magister, I can't fix Number Five. Better call a tech-adept.'

The supervisor, who had been watching his efforts from the
gallery, shrugged, nodded, then barked into a speaking tube.
Shortly a tech-adept clad in a hooded work-suit decorated with
arcane symbols appeared. He listened to Gragsch's grunted
report, bent over to stare at the casing of the transformer, then
reached into his work-satchel and brought out a little pot of
sacred red paint and a brush. Carefully he calligraphed fresh
hex signs on the casing, at the same time reciting a religious
formula in a loud voice. Then he stood back.

Suddenly the transformer was humming smoothly. Gragsch
applied his test gauge and grinned with pleasure. The machine
had been cured.

Without a further word the tech-adept stalked off, stepping
with dignity through the muck on the metal floor to climb a
companionway. At the top of the ladder he cleaned the oil off
his boots and entered a liftway to a somewhat more orderly
level, that of Engineering Co-ordination and Control.

The disordered jungle of engine rooms and machine shops
he had just visited extended for a full Imperial mile, and that
did not include the massive drive engines, both warp and realspace, which occupied the aft mile and a half of the Gothic
battleship. Engineering Co-ordination and Control took up a
smaller space. The ceiling was low. Instead of the cacophony of
the lower decks, the hiss of air purifiers and the click and hum
of tabulators mingled with the sweet smell of incense drifting
from the nearby shrines. Something like a hundred tech-adepts
attended the long bank of gold and electrum framed read-
screens, speaking tubes at their throats.

A fleet officer was collecting the hourly report. Unlike those who had to go down into the bowels of the battleship, he was immaculate in his high-collared, square-shouldered, dark blue greatcoat, in his black jackboots, black cummerbund and black holster. A starburst medallion dangling from the braids on his chest showed that he belonged to one of the hereditary Fleet Families. Embroidery on his left sleeve indicated his rank and his assignment to the Engineering branch. A scabbarded power cutlass was strapped across the small of his back, a sure sign that the *Rectitude* was shortly to go into action.

Accepting the small read-plate, the officer took a lift which whooshed him half a mile towards the upper deck. He paced a corridor lined with armed security men. Then he entered the bridge of the flagship.

Even here, the countless sounds of the battleship's functioning were heard. The bridge was a broad crescent more eerie in many ways than the dungeon-like engineering sections, especially now that the combined battlefleets were preparing to enter the Eye of Terror. Lord Militant Commander Drang, resplendent in full combat uniform, including a peaked hat able to become a full space helmet, prosthetic eye glinting, strode to and fro. An admiral stood at attention behind him, facing the view-screens. A whole battery of specialist officers – gunnery, tactics, evaluation – were seated at comm-desks.

The usual tangle of hoses and cables looped and sagged from the ceiling. The usual friezes of protective runes and grimacing gargoyles glared from the walls in the dim, uneven light. In the centre were five throne-like chairs. Clamped in them so completely that they almost disappeared were five venerable navigators of enormous experience, clusters of ribbed hoses spraying from their headpieces and leading to various pieces of equipment. To their rear were five smaller restraint chairs. In them were held primary psykers of the most sensitive sort, made completely immobile. These had been obtained with some difficulty, for they were regarded as expendable – as were the navigators for that matter. They were not expected to survive what might face them in the Eye of Terror. Adepts from the Schola Psykana attended them, monitoring the potions fed into their bloodstreams and eavesdropping on their trembling psyches.

The curved forward wall of the bridge was an array of view-screens, some oval, some octagonal. One of these showed the main deck of the *Rectitude* as it speared through space, four Imperial miles long, bearing ranks of Cobra-class destroyers, Ravager attack ships and Doomfire bombers. It was also possible to see the superstructure and outrigs of the massive ship, the intricately crenellated towers, the gargoyled casemates and buttressed sponsons which bore the battleship's mighty weapons.

Apart from the craft arrayed on the flight deck, cruisers and frigates clung like barnacles to the sides of the flagship, while, moving under their own power, brute ramships and heavy battlecruisers flanked the huge vessel in all directions. The remainder of the combined fleets would have been invisible to the naked eye (though not, of course, to Drang's monocle). The screens, however, annihilated distance and brought the formation into view. Drang's and Invisticone's flagships were the twin prongs of a vast echelon in the form of a forward-pointing cone.

The two fleets had come out of the warp to create the formation. Travelling at sub-light speeds, they were now in the entrance to the Cadian Gate, which led into the Eye. The planet Cadia lay behind them. The formation was ready to drop into the warp again.

Drang had already stood on the open deck and used his monocle to probe ahead. There were Chaos ships guarding the other end of the Gate – there always were – which might attempt to attack them in the warp. This rarely succeeded. Ships usually had to emerge into realspace in order to fight.

Still, he was glad they were there. They would give warning to larger forces in the Eye. Elements of the fleet he had come to destroy would be able to deploy and fight.

There was no glory without battle!

On his personal screen there appeared the scarred and decorated face of Invisticone, his fellow commander, smiling ironically. 'All is in readiness, brother commander. Will you give the signal?'

'I will indeed, brother commander.'

Drang raised a finger. The admiral standing behind him bellowed an order. A signal flashed out from the flagship.

The entire formation dropped into the warp and raced through the Cadian Gate.

* * *

WITH A CRASH that rocked space, the attack fleet emerged within the Eye of Terror, spontaneously quitting the warp. Every single warp engine died, without reason. The psykers moaned. The engineers looked at one another aghast. This was a totally unexpected disaster.

And yet the fleet still sped on, at something like warp speed. An impossibility! Staring into a void that was not *quite* the space it should be, that was bluish rather than black, using all their skill and instrumentation, the adepts soon found the answer.

'Revered commander, this is not realspace as it should be! The speed of light is infinite here! We are travelling at translight velocity without the benefit of the warp!'

Drang and Invisticone were both of them mentally agile enough to understand this news. 'A Chaos modification,' Drang commented. 'Fascinating.'

How useful it would be if the Imperium could master this alteration of physical reality!

The small Chaos ships stationed near the Cadian Gate were almost casually dealt with, blasted out of existence as the fleet darted towards the five worlds where, according to the nullship report, the Chaos invasion fleet was being constructed. These were to be pounded from orbit and then overwhelmed by the half a million Imperial Guardsmen the fleet carried – the one addition the High Lords had made to Drang's original campaign plan.

The psykers, gagged to muffle their screams, were struggling and attempting to speak. The Schola Psykana adepts who read their minds – a safety screen against Chaos terrors – relayed a startling message.

There *were* no dockyards orbiting the denoted worlds. No enormous yards and factories on the planetary surfaces. The Navy had come to destroy what was simply not there. The psykers aboard the nullship had been deceived. They had picked up mental images only.

Momentarily Drang was stunned. He felt his dream of glory slipping away.

And yet… And yet…

His switched his attention to his alien-manufactured monocle. It had never yet proved false. Its vague beckonings of the future called him on. A huge battle!

But with whom, or what?

'Report on daemonic activity!' he barked.

The answer came soon. 'Less than would normally be expected for this region, commander.'

That in itself was suspicious. The five worlds were displayed onscreen. They formed a ring, all sharing the same orbit, which would have made a nonsense of celestial dynamics in the universe beyond the Cadian Gate. Each world had a different shape. One was elongated like a capsule, another cube-shaped with rounded edges, a third helical like a corkscrew...

Psykers and scrying teams reported human habitation, as well as daemonic presence. Drang consulted Invisticone and they came to a decision. After a brief but devastating laser barrage, half of the Imperial Guard regiments were dropped, divided between the five planets. Drang felt only a passing pang of conscience as he saw the swarms of pods rain down. Never before had a world within the Eye of Terror been invaded by the Imperium. The occupation would be brief and the guardsmen were ultimately doomed, though they did not know it. This was an exercise, an experiment. Any who rejoined the fleet when it withdrew would first be examined for Chaos contamination and then scoured, exterminated.

There was another advantage to the Great Inventor's welding together of warp and real space. As the velocity of light was infinite, communication was instantaneous. The fleet's farseer radars could see light-years ahead. The cry came from the tech-adepts and the Schola Psykana adepts simultaneously.

'Commanders! A huge battlefleet is approaching!'

Drang gave a shout of exultation. 'Onward!'

FOUR HUNDRED GOTHIC-CLASS battleships led the way, racing deeper into the Eye. A Gothic was so designed that, seen prow-on, the entire vessel appeared as a blazon in the gridded shape of the Imperial eagle, speeding inexorably. Accompanying the Gothics were heavy battlecruisers by the thousand, and as many ramships. Cobras and Doomfires launched themselves from the Gothics' decks. Cruisers detached themselves from the holding brackets.

To meet the challenge there sprang from the Immaterium nearly three hundred Chaos Juggernauts – built to the Great Inventor's own design as the answer to the Gothic – together with thousands of Iconoclast, Idolator and Infidel-class cruisers. All were driven by the pure white blinding light of heaven, a form of energy beside which the gouting plasma of the Navy's drives seemed dull and ineffective.

It was an illusion. Both sides had equal speed and manoeuvrability. The Chi'khami'tzann Tsunoi's plan was working well. First, the camouflage of the five planets to lure the forces of the Imperium into the Chaos realm. Then, a fleet forged from his great invention, newly created matter, to test the new strategy and weaken the Imperium's naval forces at the same time.

He had even created the arena for the battle by welding the warp and realspace together. But it had cost no small effort to field his battlefleet. He had drafted the extra workforce from the Rhodonius planets only hours ago, as the linear time of the Imperium would reckon it. But in the warp, where time meant nothing, they and their progeny had laboured in the forge hells for over a century. Some of their descendants now helped man the Chaos battlecruisers, in the service of their daemonic masters.

As the two huge fleets hurtled towards one another they opened up with vast lascannons. Ships were scythed open while the fleets were still far apart, spilling their contents in a spreading mist.

Then the fleets came together, discharging plasma cannons and plasma torpedoes. The truth was that the Chaos fleet was outgunned. The Lord of Change had not given the same attention to weaponry as he had to the ships themselves, delighting in their massiveness, like a child playing with the new toy – matter! But he knew something which the Imperium, as yet, did not. He had a different strategy: ramming!

Juggernaut and Gothic! A million tons meeting a million tons at a million miles per second! The flash produced by such mutual annihilation lit up the entire segment of the Eye.

After the first impact, which produced dozens of these flares, the two fleets reduced their velocity and engaged in more conventional manner. Ramming was in fact part of conventional tactics – all Imperial Navy ships had ram prows – but not at such velocity as to destroy the attacker as well. Laser, plasma and ram!

SMASH – HAMMER – SMASH – HAMMER!

Screech and shriek of tortured metal, rip of adamantium armour torn apart, millions of tonnes of incandescent wreckage exploding into space! The Brute ramships tore at the

Juggernauts like dogs worrying a stag, adding themselves to the deep-probing laser shafts and vaporising plasma. The Chaos ships rammed, too, whenever they could, unheeding of any damage done to themselves. If they succeeded in opening up a hull, hordes of beastmen poured across the gap.

Whenever a Chaos ship was destroyed or wrecked, a miasma of mindless, gibbering daemonic entities flimmered out of it and flapped about in space before fading back into the warp, as if slipping out of the very metal of the vessel.

As the battle progressed it spread over light-years. Despite the colossal destruction that had been wrought the Naval fleet was gaining the upper hand. It had maintained communications and still was able to deploy tactics. The Chaos fleet had not. Its Chaos champion captains were dedicated either to Tzeentch or to Khorne, and disdained to co-operate with one another. So it was entirely due to his own skill and daring when a champion of Tzeentch succeeded in dashing his Juggernaut into the side of the *Rectitude*, despite his ship's being disabled by a broadside of laser and plasma fire from turret and sponson on the approach. A deep wound was opened up in the side of the Gothic battleship. Baroque towers collapsed and tumbled away end over end. Crushed buttresses exploded. Sponsons contorted and broke away. Entire inner sections spewed, disintegrating, into space along with thousands of crewmen.

Among them was Repair Mechanic Third Class Gragsch, who up until that moment had not known for certain that the ship on which he served was in action.

The coral-like excrescences of the Juggernaut, too, collapsed, crumbled and broke away in whirling chunks. Engines silent, the giant hulks drifted dead in space, jammed together and spinning slowly, while savage warfare developed between the two crews. Lord Militant Commander Drang found to his grievous annoyance that all communications were down. He could not contact the remainder of the fleet – leaving Lord Militant Commander Invisticone in sole command!

A hiss and a ping warned that the bridge was bleeding air. Drang glanced at the widespread wreckage on the screens. He pulled down the peak of his cap, making it a space helmet, sealing himself from the coming vacuum. Seizing bolter and cutlass, gesturing to his officers to do likewise, he strode out to face the enemy.

* * *

IT WAS IN THE fourth day of the space battle, and now the Feathered Lord's secret showed itself.

His technique of creating matter out of the stuff of Chaos was not yet perfected. It was false matter, virtual matter. In this specially prepared part of the Eye of Terror such false matter could persist for days before it dissolved back into the Immaterium. Elsewhere in the Eye it might last for a few hours.

In normal space-time, it would shred and dissolve in minutes.

The Chaos battlefleet, built at the cost of such toil and suffering, had done what it could. The remaining ships, together with the scattered wreckage, faded away over a period of a day or so, leaving the human crews behind to perish in space. The Chi'khami'tzann Tsunoi was well pleased with the exercise. He had shown that he could create matter and take on the might of the Imperium, which could not be done any other way. He would perfect the method, make the false matter stable in any conditions.

Almost anything would then be possible. Battlefleets so huge they would overwhelm the human Imperium. Whole worlds brought into existence out of nothing.

Chaos would have triumphed.

ABOUT HALF THE FLEET, including more than a hundred Gothic battleships, was still able to get under way after the enemy disappeared. Despite the heavy losses, Commander Invisticone was satisfied with the outcome. The Chaos battlefleet had been decisively defeated and largely annihilated. Even had it still been present, it was no longer in a position to threaten any part of the Imperium. He assumed its gradual disappearance to be an admission of failure.

Another feature of the enemy's performance was not lost on him. Some of the Chaos ships had begun fighting one another, apparently quarrelling over who should engage particular targets. Chaos had revealed its greatest weakness.

The fleet regrouped. Scans were made for missing ships. A few were found and could be assisted. Most were either destroyed or out of range, and there was a limit to the amount of time that could be spent on rescue operations. The *Rectitude* did not show on any instrument sweep.

The fleet prepared to withdraw, first approaching the ring of five worlds which had been the original objective. From a distance of half a light year, contact was attempted with the signals units on each planet.

From four, no answer was received. The response from the fifth, the corkscrew planet, so alarmed the signals officers that they relayed it directly to Lord Militant Commander Invisticone.

He found himself staring into the face of a commissar. The man's appearance shocked Invisticone. His peaked hat was awry on his head. His stiff narrow greatcoat was unbuttoned and disarrayed. His eyes bulged. Sweat filmed his face.

'Help us, lord commander! For humanity's sake, help us!'

Invisticone's expression became icy. 'Where is your regimental commander?' he snapped.

'Insane! All who are not dead are insane! We are beset by daemons! Men should not have to die like this–'

Beyond the commissar, Invisticone saw the outlines of a room with curved pink walls. Suddenly the rear wall swelled. It became a giant leering face, green eyes diamond-shaped. A huge tongue licked out. The commissar let out a strangled shriek as he felt it wrap itself around him. Then the room blinked and changed. Invisticone realised it had become the inside of a huge mouth, jagged teeth where the far wall had been, a red tongue rolling the gurgling commissar around it.

He cut the connection and told the signals team to cease any further efforts at communication. Then he ordered one of his admirals to send a detachment to virus-bomb all five planets – not that that would necessarily be effective against daemons.

The victorious fleet set off for the Cadian Gate. Adrift deeper within the Eye, the *Rectitude* was still the scene of bitter fighting between Naval crewmen and the beast-horde from the now vanished Juggernaut. Lord Militant Commander Drang believed he had escaped the Callidus assassin. He was determined to die in control of his flagship, even though it was nothing but a dead hulk.

SEVENTEEN
'BLOOD FOR THE BLOOD GOD!'

CALLIDEN HAD BEGUN to realise that he, like Rugolo, was no longer quite sane.

They both were in a dream-like fugue, attempting to screen off reality – yet the world they faced was not reality at all. It was a warped perversion of everything they had ever known. Here they were in the lounge of a Chaos-transformed starship, piloted by a daemon-possessed woman who already had tried to disembowel one of them – yet they behaved as though they were in no danger.

His head in his hands, Calliden agonised over his mother. Rugolo had dismissed his claim that she had helped him struggle free of his bonds in the distillery. His version was that the ropes must have been loosened by the fluid in the vat, perhaps had not been tied properly.

Calliden knew differently. His mother's soul *was* in the warp after all, of that there was no doubt. He went through the possibilities. Perhaps it had been his mother at first, and then a daemon had impersonated her, but at the end…

Aegelica pushed herself back from the control board. 'A greater daemon is behind this,' she said. 'There's nothing I can do. We are being pulled into the Cluster by an irresistible force.'

'It is all dark, my dearest sister,' Gundrum gurgled, his eyebrows jerking up and down. 'Dark stars, that were ablaze with light!'

'They emit dark light, brother. It is a form of Chaos radiance.'

She joined them at the elegant table in the middle of the lounge. On it stood the liqueur bottle containing its lustrous yellow essence.

Gundrum picked up the bottle and gazed at it with an appreciative expression. Only a small amount of the liquid remained.

'Ah, Kwyler! Our good friend Kwyler! I was fond of him. And what better way to remember him than...'

Calliden took his head from his hands. He stared appalled as Gundrum unstoppered the bottle and poured the last of the liqueur into four tiny glasses. It emerged slowly and thickly, glistening in the light.

Pursing his lips, his eyes bulging, Gundrum swallowed.

'Aaah! Dear friend! So pleasant to know you again!'

He shivered and glanced with lugubrious surprise at the shocked looks of Rugolo and Calliden. Aegelica, meanwhile, sipped casually from her own glass.

'Drink! Drink! Have you not drunk of our friend Kwyler before? Do not insult him now!'

They lowered their gaze to the drops of life-essence Gundrum had poured out for them, anticipating the pleasure the unnatural indulgence would bring.

Gundrum was right. Resignedly, in an ironic valediction, they raised their glasses in a salute, then put the last of Kwyler to their lips.

THE PAINTED SPACESHIP curved down into the Rose Cluster as if in a power dive. Eventually it slowed and drifted. All the stars looked alike. Rugolo and Calliden gaped in fascination, unable to understand why those stars seemed so luminous when they put out no light. Gundrum's and Aegelica's explanations made no sense.

Aegelica took the controls again. She studied the tabulator briefly. They were in a planetary system, the local sun showing as a brilliant obsidian ball. Calliden expected her to attempt to fly out of the Cluster again to find a route out of the Eye. He had forgotten that such directness went against her method of navigation. She steered by faith, by feeling, by obedience to the strange ways of Chaos, and Chaos had directed her into the Cluster. Her emerald-green eyes became misty.

She made for the nearest planet. It loomed up, seemingly composed of jet or ebony, washed in the black light of the obsidian sun. As the painted spaceship whispered down through its atmosphere, glimmering red splotches came into view. The craft flew over a midnight landscape where volcanoes erupted like blowtorches.

Aegelica set the ship down gently. Calliden gave a cry of alarm when she pulled the lever to let down the ramp and open the port without checking the quality of the outside air. But no poisonous vapours or deadly spores drifted up the elevator shaft to invade the ship, only a sulphurous smell. Curiously they all followed her. She stood at the top of the ramp, looking over the desolate landscape.

'Bracing!' she breathed. She paced down the ramp, with a curious high-stepping tread, and rubbed her bare feet in the strange cinder-like soil, from which wriggling, worm-like tendrils were constantly poking and withdrawing. 'This is the place! Oh my brother, we enter the dark night of the soul! Pleasure beyond compare!'

She began to dance, waving her arms in the air, lurid flashes from the distant volcanoes giving her flesh a rosy glow amid the jet-black of the sun's illumination. Her face had come even more alive, her emerald eyes glittering. Rugolo shook off Calliden's restraining tug and followed her down the ramp. He was in a trance. Never had she looked more exotic, more magnetic, with her heaving bosom and full rump straining to burst out her basque. He held out his arms and walked towards her.

'No, Maynard! No!'

Calliden ran down the ramp, seized Rugolo and pulled him away. But Aegelica was not even looking at either of them.

'It is the black light, brother!' she trilled.

'By the roots of my desire!' Gundrum boomed.

Now she uttered a delighted shriek, and seemed to explode out of the bounds of nature. She became the daemonette again, the daughter of Slaanesh. Her green eyes grew slanted, more large and more saucer-shaped. Masses of green hair surrounded her head and shoulders. Her hands became long razor-toothed pincers. A long, thick barbed tail sprang from

the base of her spine. Her feet became two-toed eagle's
talons.

But it was in her beauty that the transformation was most
startling. It was a beauty to induce ecstasy in the beholder, a
beauty that was utterly irresistible and at the same time utterly
loathsome. Now Gundrum was standing on the cinders, staring
at his sister, entranced. The look on his face was extraordinary
even for him, as though he had ceased to be human altogether
and had been converted into some alien creature with a different set of emotions.

Then Aegelica struck him. With one pincer-like claw she
seized her brother by the neck. The other delicately tore away
his dark-coloured clothing and then began playing with his
exposed skin – stroking, teasing, cutting... ripping. Blood
flowed. With a crunch she snipped through ribs and removed
them, exposing lungs and heart into which her pincer playfully
delved. Gundrum put up no resistance, apart from flapping one
arm about ecstatically. He gave voice to a continuous ululating
hooting screech of agony, enjoyment and encouragement.

'Truly, sister, truly, is this what it had to come to? By my *roo-
o-o-ts*, sister-r-r, by my *roo-O-O-O-O-O-OTS!'*

Calliden still had the melta-gun. He whipped it out, despite
remembering what little effect it had had before on the daemon, intending at least to put Gundrum out of his torment.
Rugolo grasped the weapon, forcing the muzzle up. His face
was wild with passion.

'Leave her alone! It's my turn next!'

The burst of energy gouted into the air, momentarily outlin-
ing the scene in a white glare. In the same moment the
daemonic Aegelica raised a talon and elegantly tore open her
brother's skinny abdomen, then dipped inside and tickled his
intestines as though splashing her toes in water. With each new
sensation of pain Gundrum's shrieks became even more joyous.

Surely pain alone could not do that! What incredible
delights were being added by Aegelica to the unbearable sensa-
tions?

With one jerk she pulled out Gundrum's intestines in a
bloody tangle, wrenched out his still pumping heart and flung
aside his twitching mutilated body. She looked pleased with
herself.

'He goes to Slaanesh! What better gift could a sister give her brother?' In a nearly normal tone, she added, 'It's Gundrum's birthday!'

She came forward, reaching out with her still-bloody claw. 'Now... I like you, too, Maynard...'

Rugolo took a step back, then, with a shuddering sigh, stumbled to meet her. When Calliden tried to stop him he threw the navigator to the ground with a shrug of his shoulders, using sudden, surprising strength.

'Aegelica...' he groaned.

Calliden couldn't use the melta-gun on Aegelica without burning Rugolo. He fired it in the air again.

The resultant glare revealed two figures standing a short distance away, previously unnoticed in the negative light. Whatever was about to happen between Rugolo and Aegelica stopped. Something in the manner of the daemonic Aegelica seemed to change.

The two figures were huge and hulking, and wearing shining armour – shining even in the black light – which totally enclosed them, like spacesuits but much bigger. Calliden climbed to his feet. It took him some moments to realise who the newcomers must be. He had never expected actually to see such heroes of the Imperium, but he had watched Administratum propaganda dramas depicting their exploits. *Space Marines!*

At least, the one on the left looked like a Space Marine. Of the other he wasn't sure. It was as though a Space Marine's armour had contracted a cancer and put out uncontrolled growths. Two great horns projected over the helmet. Whorls and strange devices covered the rest of the plating.

Calliden turned to the Marine he felt sure must be a warrior of the Imperium. Indeed, he could just make out the Imperial eagle... He whipped off his bandanna to show that he was a navigator. 'Help us, sir! We are lost and in danger!'

Neither took any notice. They moved apart from one another, all their attention on Aegelica. From the helm of the cancerous quasi-Marine a strong, grim baritone voice issued. 'Beware! She is your enemy, a child of Slaanesh, a Giver of Indescribable Delight, a Bringer of Joyous Degradation! She will debauch you if she can. And do not be deceived by her lack of weapons. She has powers we do not.'

Aegelica walked past Rugolo. She jabbed a pincer towards Magron. Her voice was now spiteful as she spoke. 'Though he bears the sigil of Tzeentch, he is bound for Khorne. We do not like Khorne!'

Captain Abaddas raised his bolter. 'Do not waylay us, debauched one. I am sworn to help my battle comrade find his destiny. And though I remain human, I have some manner of gifts from more masters than one, and will not yield easily. So do not anger the Blood God by denying him a future prince.'

Aegelica's face contorted with fury. 'I do not want this carcass any more!' she spat.

She writhed, and suddenly was her human form again. But only for a moment. The daemon reappeared, but seemed to erupt out of the human woman like a snake sloughing off its skin. Suddenly there were two creatures, a naked human female who slumped senseless to the ground, and the basque-clad daemonette standing beside her, glittering, full of fatal loveliness and beautiful malevolence.

At Abaddas's signal Magron also pulled his bolter from its bracket. But the daemonette – she could not be called Aegelica now – did not attack. She raised both pincers in the air. 'I know who has brought me here! I have somewhere to go!'

There was another convulsion, a flash in the blackness. Suddenly, to the further astonishment of all but Abaddas, the female daemon was astride a mount. It was bipedal, with ostrich legs and a long reptilian-looking body covered in green and lavender fur. The steed's snout was long and tubular. From it a long tongue shot constantly in and out, like the daemonette's own tongue but larger.

'Away!' At her urging, the mount strode towards the distance at immense speed. Then it appeared to be climbing an invisible mountain, running skyward. It was impossible to tell what happened next, whether rider and mount merged into the black sky or merely vanished.

'It is a mount of Slaanesh,' Abaddas explained to Magron. 'A daemon of low rank, often ridden by debauched ones. Come, brother. We are close to the place.'

'Should we not succour these unfortunates, who have called on us for help?'

Abaddas looked at the surviving pair. It was obvious to him that they were from outside the Eye. Sometimes traders found their way in, looking for easy riches. Usually they got themselves into trouble, as these had.

Plainly the woman had given herself up to possession by the daemonette, allowing it to venture into the galaxy at large. It did not need a physical host in the Eye of Terror – it could manifest itself directly. But he could not explain this to Magron. He had given him a different account of things.

'Let others assist them. We are on a path of destiny. Come.' He strode off, Magron lumbering after him.

When they had gone Rugolo and Calliden crept to where Aegelica lay on the cinders. She was limp, and quite dead. Rugolo was bewildered. He remembered the uncontrollable erotic mania she had evoked in him. Yet the woman he saw now could never have done that. She was not even young. She was probably older than Gundrum, with sagging flesh in place of the former plump firmness. Her face was simply not the same face at all. The features were quite different, with none of the vampiric magnetism which the *other* Aegelica would have possessed, even in death.

Rugolo was reminded more than anything of a disappointed, ageing spinster. No wonder she had been willing to give herself up to possession by a daemon of pleasure.

They stepped back, averting their gaze from the remains of Gundrum. Mortified and ashamed, Rugolo looked up at the spaceship. Its rainbow hues had turned to striations in various shades of black – obsidian, charcoal, ebony, sable – in which murmurings of subdued colour could be discerned.

'We've got the ship,' he said. 'And Gundrum's trade goods! The liqueurs alone are worth a fortune! No one else will ever obtain any!'

Calliden stared at him. 'You can't sell those! They are made from murdered human beings!'

Rugolo raised his hands palms up and shrugged. 'Look around you! It's a tough universe, Pelor. Some good ought to come out of their sacrifice. You've got to pilot us back to the Imperium.'

'The Astronomican is not visible from here. I can't get us back. That's why we were following Aegelica.'

'Of course you can!' Rugolo urged. 'Remember what Kwyler said. Have *faith*. There's no one to help us now.'

'We ought to bury these two,' Calliden mumbled. He stepped back further from the corpses. Gundrum and his sister Aegelica had both paid the price for their involvement with the Eye of Terror. What foolishness…

Why was *he* here, he wondered. What affliction had led him here? Perhaps it had something to do with his mother. She had begun by pleading for his help, which he had been unable to give. But she had ended by helping him. It seemed as though a circle had closed. The thought made him calmer.

He cast his eye in the direction in which the two armoured warriors had disappeared. 'There might be someone who can help us,' he said. 'Those two are Space Marines, or at least one of them is. He wears the Imperial eagle. He must be here for some reason. Perhaps he has a ship with a navigator who knows a route out.'

'What about our goods?'

But Calliden was already stepping out over the cinders. Reluctantly, Rugolo followed.

A NEWLY-FORMED lava flow made a sludgy red river in the middle distance, pouring from the rough cone of a young volcano. Paradoxically its glow only served to obscure the structure ahead of the two Space Marines, which otherwise stood out stark and clear in the negative light.

It was a semi-circular colonnade. Arranged within it were four broad altars, each surmounted by a different grotesque idol, symbols of various kinds forming a backdrop. To one side of the colonnade stood a small stone building. A hulking human figure with a stern face sat on a stone bench before it. He wore a simple surplice of four colours: red, blue, yellow and purple. As Abaddas approached in his humming power armour he rose and made a sign of blessing, recognising the ex-Dark Angel.

'I bring you a supplicant, chaplain. Dedicate him. He is destined for the Blood God.'

Magron scarcely noticed his words. He stood transfixed, staring at the altars, fascinated by the aura of majesty and power the entire colonnade emanated. The figure on the left shone with an unnatural beauty which reminded him of the captivating daemon they had just encountered. It was bisexual, male on one side and female on the other. Two pairs of horns rose from flowing golden hair. The idol was clad in a fringed mail shirt, and held a jade sceptre in one hand.

On the far right of the colonnade was displayed an idol of absolutely opposite nature. A grossly bloated and decayed figure squatted on the altar, a pile of billowing flesh, narrow-eyed, huge-mouthed, unspeakably repulsive in expression and appearance, seeping green and yellow pus from ulcers, pustules and gangrenous lacerations through which necrous internal organs spilled. The constant seepage made Magron think the statue was alive at first, before he realised it was truly motionless.

He turned his attention to the inner pair of altars. Next to the disease-ridden idol, which he assumed to be of Nurgle, Lord of Pestilence, was a figure which in its own way struck him as almost equally ugly. A puckered face, lacking any neck, was jammed straight down on a pair of thick-set shoulders from which sprang curved horns. Some magic was at work: constantly changing faces crawled over the naked skin of the figure, leering and mocking. A vague phantasmagoria hovered around the idol's head, a confusion of momentary images.

But it was the fourth idol which riveted Magron's attention most. It stood out from the others for it was taller, seated on a weirdly fashioned brass throne which in turn rested on a mound of skulls. A muscular humanoid figure in elaborately worked plate armour, face half hidden by a winged helmet.

But what a face! Magron could see it well enough from where he stood looking up at it. A face of utter, bestial ferocity. The red eyes glared straight at him, demanding – and expecting – all his courage, all his martial ardour, and his unquestioned obedience. Here was a face to lead one to war! He suddenly felt as if everything in his life had been leading him to this moment.

The Word Bearer chaplain was speaking to Captain Abaddas. 'You bring a brother Marine, I see. But–'

'He is newly arrived,' Abaddas said, knowing that the chaplain recognised the almost unchanged antiquity of Magron's armour. He raised a gauntlet in warning. 'But speak no more of that, or he will turn aside from the ordained path. Prepare him for the dedication.'

Magron regarded the chaplain. He saw that he bore all the marks of a Space Marine: the hefting increase in weight and stature, the martial countenance, the campaign studs on the brow. He saw a darkening beneath the silky surplice, betraying the black carapace and welded rib cage.

Abaddas hoped he did not notice the chaplain's Chaos favours hidden below his surplice, in the form of tentacles tipped with articles of worship.

The chaplain stood up. 'Remove your helmet. The Blood God will want to see your face.'

Magron held back. 'I still feel some loyalty to the Emperor,' he admitted. 'And the new state of affairs seems to me disordered and without reason.'

The Word Bearer chaplain nodded, unperturbed by Magron's misgivings. 'It is customary at this point to say a few words about the step you are about to take.' He pointed a finger to the colonnade. 'Yonder are shrines to the four great Chaos Powers. The Word Bearers worship Chaos in its undivided entirety. So does your Captain Abaddas. But most men must serve one lord. As you must.

'You speak of disorder and needless bloodshed. It is true that the followers of Chaos commit gross excesses. But these only reflect the crudity and violence in the human psyche. Do you not see that the Chaos Gods are creations of human consciousness? It is all part of the evolution of the galaxy. It is a stage humanity has to go through to attain spiritual maturity. Any who hold back will *fail*.'

The Word Bearer's homily took away Magron's last doubts. He removed his helmet. The red eyes of Khorne bored into him as the chaplain ushered him towards the altar. Although this was only an idol, it was an idol in a world blessed with the energies of Chaos. The presence of the deity himself was in it, and Abdaziel Magron was face to face with the Blood God.

The chaplain began to recite a litany in a language unknown to Magron, a language with long liquid vowels. With each refrain, a blood-curdling growl came from the Blood God idol. Magron's brain blazed with a red mist. The promise! The promise of glory!

The chaplain broke off and spoke softly to him.

'For now you will remain unchanged physically. But your Lord will signal his willingness to accept you by means of marks on your armour.'

Instantly Magron felt as though he had been struck a ringing blow. A feeling of rage coursed through him. Thunder rumbled from the idol. He looked down at his armour plating. The

Imperial emblem was gone. In its place was the blood-red emblem of Khorne, three bars linked by a cross. And from each vambrace there had sprouted what at first looked like gouts of gore, but were in fact hook-like claws, clenching and unclenching as if hungry to rip flesh.

Leading him away from the altar, the chaplain spoke in a stentorious voice, using Imperial Gothic: '*DO YOU RENOUNCE AND REVILE THE EMPEROR OF MANKIND? DO YOU PLEDGE YOURSELF TO KHORNE AND EMBRACE HIS FAVOUR AND PUNISHMENT?*'

A tumult arose in Sergeant Magron's heart. Once he took this vow he knew that he would have finally turned his back on his old life and be forever Khorne's.

Something in him still resisted. There was an obdurate core which wished to die rather than change. He pushed this stubborn core away from him and opened his mouth to deliver the required response.

At that very moment he was distracted by a shout. A slim, black-clad figure was emerging from the blackness. It was the navigator he had seen earlier. A melta-gun dangled from one hand. Stumbling along behind him came his goatee-bearded companion, pleading with him to turn back.

Mentally unhinged as he was, Pelor Calliden had lost all caution and fear of death in his outrage at what he had heard. He yelled at Magron at the top of his voice.

'How can you take part in this blasphemy! You are a Space Marine! You are sworn to the Emperor! Where is your loyalty? Where is your honour!'

'It is *KHORNE* who offers honour!' Magron roared in retort, pleased at how offended he felt. 'You fool, your Emperor is dead these two centuries, killed by Horus the Warmaster!'

Captain Abaddas drew his shortsword and strode forward, intending to despatch the intruders forthwith, but Magron stayed him with an uplifted arm. 'Is that not so, captain?'

'It is indeed,' Abaddas rumbled. 'And these two have defiled a holy ceremony! Kill them for their presumption, sergeant. That is an *order!*'

In his panic at these words, Maynard Rugolo found his brain racing. He knew little of Imperial history, but everyone with any schooling had been told of the great civil war when traitors led by the vile Horus had attempted to usurp the Emperor. He looked hastily from one Marine to the other, and sensed from whence came the deception. He pointed to the warrior in the weirdly misshapen armour.

'He is lying to you! Horus was defeated and the Emperor still lives! We are in the Forty-First Millennium!'

'Kill the liar!' Abaddas boomed. But he made no move himself.

Magron turned to him. He looked as if a veil had been lifted from his eyes. Seeing that expression, Abaddas knew that the illusion he had lovingly wrought for Sergeant Magron had been dispelled, and that there was no longer any help for the Dark Angel. He put up his shortsword and drew his bolter.

Magron was remembering the sanctity of his years as a Dark Angel. His unshakeable faith in the Emperor flooded back to him. The scene around him, with its four Chaos idols, seemed suddenly evil and corrupt.

'What is the truth?' he demanded of Abaddas.

'The truth,' Abaddas said harshly, 'is that Khorne has drawn you to him. And you have robbed yourself of eternal life!'

In that instant, while Captain Abaddas aimed the muzzle of the bolter at him, the struggle for the soul of Sergeant Magron was over. 'I will not forsake the Emperor, living or dead!' he cried. 'But I will know the truth!'

He ran at his captain, deflecting the muzzle of the bolter as it barked its death-song. His rush was unexpected and pushed Abaddas off-balance. Both Marines crashed to the ground, crunching the cinders beneath them, and rolled so that they were face down, Magron on top. Power cables hummed. Ceramite plates creaked. Abaddas's *Armorum Ferrum*, as the Mark Three armour was sometimes called, had great strength, greater than Magron's Mark Four. Magron would not be able to hold the captain down. But he knew where the power cables were situated. Magron reached for his own bolter.

The chaplain stepped towards them. He intoned words and raised his hand in a magic sign. On the rise Calliden lifted his melta-gun and fired, hoping there was still fuel in the much-depleted reservoir. The chaplain span to face him as the searing super-heat engulfed him. But he did not burn, nor even fall. A protective bubble seemed to surround him.

Calliden fired again without pause. Then a third time, but nothing happened. The reservoir was empty.

The Chaos chaplain, a frightening super-human figure to Calliden and Rugolo, stood staring at his attacker with empty eyes, before toppling to lie still. Not even his surplice was charred.

There came a repeated loud barking. Sergeant Magron levered himself up so that the bolt explosions caused no more than scorch-marks on his own armour. Burrowing through the cancroid growths, blasting between the abutments of the heavy armour plates, the bolts severed the Mark Three's power cables, causing severe injuries to the hardened Marine body beneath. Abaddas was now as immobile as Magron had been when he floated down to the Rhodonius planet.

It grieved Magron to treat a brother Dark Angel so, but he had killed Space Marines before, and he was ready to do so again – if they turned against the Emperor! He unfastened and pulled off the other's wedge-shaped helmet. Captain Abaddas did not attempt to look at him. His face was as bleak and expressionless as always, as he endured his pain and his helplessness.

'Forgive me, brother – but I must know the truth!'

Rugolo and Calliden looked on in horror at what happened next. Sergeant Magron's powered gauntlet reached out and wrenched off Captain Abaddas's skull. He then leaned forward, craning his neck, and bit into the back of the captain's exposed, bloodied, living brain.

To them it looked like some dreadful obscene rite or act of cannibalism. They could not know that among a Space Marine's implanted organs was an omophagea, enabling him to absorb another person's memories by eating his brain tissue. Sergeant Magron wanted to gain information rapidly, and that meant eating such tissue while its owner still lived, desperate measure though that was!

They did not dare approach the location of the horrid feast or even speak in reproach. They backed off, and crept away.

CAPTAIN ABADDAS KNEW what was happening to him, although, the human brain possessing no sensory nerves, there was no sensation. He made no protest, however, as Sergeant Magron devoured his cerebellum. Soon he could not form words in any case. Mouthful after mouthful Sergeant Magron chewed and

swallowed. With each bite Abaddas felt his personality emptying, until there was only a vague presence without any
memory, a furtive whispering from the warp.

Then nothing.

Magron raised his bloody mouth from the emptied skull and
regained his feet. The omophagea was extracting memory at
speed. Magron went into a trance, sorting through the caval-
cade that was Zhebdek Abaddas's extraordinary life, letting it
reel past him in a confused jumble. At last he seized on what
he needed.

The Horus Heresy. Now he learned the truth of what had
really happened to the Dark Angels. And the truth was incredible. Even while Magron's company took part in the attack on
the World Eaters' interstellar base Luther, the Angels' second-
in-command, had persuaded the remaining garrison on their
home world of Caliban to side with the rebellion. Having now
experienced for himself the seductions of Chaos, Magron knew
that only a spiritual infection of that kind could have produced
such astonishing disloyalty. He lived as though the memories
were his own the bombardment by loyal Angels and the subsequent battle which had reduced Caliban to no more than a
bare rock.

Captain Abaddas had been among the traitors. Magron experienced with him his memory of being rescued by the Ruinous
Powers, sucked into the warp and deposited elsewhere. It was
Horus who had been killed, not the blessed Emperor. Of the
fate of Lion El'Jonson, Magron's spiritual preceptor, Abaddas
knew nothing. But the Chaos rebellion had not succeeded. The
galaxy had not been transformed into a Chaos realm. Chaos
dominated only a few small parts of it, such as the one into
which Abaddas – and Magron – had been drawn. There were
only a few Dark Angels – Fallen Angels, the renegades were
sometimes named – in the Eye of Terror. Most had been scattered throughout the galaxy.

It was a tragic tale, and one which filled Magron with wonder, especially when he learned of the span of time involved.
He had drifted in space for ten thousand years.

He also learned why Abaddas had been prepared to take
such trouble over him, to deceive and trick him on to what he
regarded as the right path. It was not just because they were
both Dark Angels. It was because they were Marines from ten

thousand years ago. He despised Space Marines inducted since that time as weak and inferior, superhuman though they still were in ordinary terms.

Magron checked the Word Bearers chaplain who had so nearly committed him to Chaos forever. He appeared to be dead. But now Magron saw the four tentacles beneath his surplice, each tipped with a different image.

He looked around for the two who had opportunely saved him from spiritual dissolution. They had gone. But he would need their ship, as well as a navigator, if he was to return to his Chapter.

He retrieved his helmet, relieved Captain Abaddas of his spare ammunition, and was about to set out when a movement caught his eye. Racing towards him on her peculiar fast-stepping mount was the female daemon he had seen earlier. He snapped out his bolter and let off a quick volley, fearing to let her too close. He had felt her terrible attraction once before.

The bolts exploded against her breasts and belly and did no harm. She trilled fetching laughter. 'Had I a mind, Sergeant Magron, I would pleasure you to death, as I have so many others. But that is not why I am here.'

Her contralto voice was warm and heady to listen to. How did she know his name? Her next words seemed to be an explanation.

'I have consulted with one who ranks higher than myself, a Keeper of Secrets who hears anything that is said anywhere, in any dimension. There is a mission for you to perform, sergeant. Don your helmet, for you should not show your face.'

She dismounted, and beckoned. 'Come with me, Abdaziel.'

The use of his first name made him distrust her all the more. But Magron replaced his helm, more for his own protection than anything. She could not arouse lust in him, for his modifications meant he had no feelings for a woman. But the sight of her plump buttocks and projecting barbed tail as she turned away from him produced the same fascination he had felt before. This was surely a daemon, with the power to enslave men's minds.

He took only one or two steps before the scene changed. The blighted rose planet was gone. The black light was gone. A great green plain stretched before him, and on it was an armed multitude, millions strong. He saw one or two Traitor Marines, their armour grossly and colourfully corrupted, but most were lesser warriors, hideously mutated, apparelled in hues that shouted and blazed, waving their weapons and roaring with joy.

He understood that in the space of a step he had been instantaneously transported to some other place. About half of those he saw carried the emblem he himself now wore, the emblem of Khorne. The rest carried, on banners, armour and clothing, various versions of the curiously curved and sinuous sigil he had seen during the attack on the rose city, and which Abaddas had told him was the sign of Tzeentch.

And indeed there loomed over the plain the two daemonic figures who had appeared back then: one a feathered monstrosity, the other a horned, red-eyed, wolf-faced warrior in black and red armour. They were no more than fifty foot tall now, hooves and talons planted on the turf.

He heard the feathered daemon addressing the throng, his purring voice reaching to every part of the field: *'We have victory! We have driven off the Imperium's best effort! The way is clear to a final victory – victory in the Long War!'*

A huge shout greeted his words. The daemon raised a talon, calling for silence. He began to speak of things Magron barely understood. Of warp-sourced matter from which a great battlefleet had been constructed; 'virtual matter', the daemon called it.

'Once my invention has been perfected and made stable,' he purred, 'there is no limit to what can be achieved. Battlefleets to overwhelm the human Imperium. Worlds created out of nothing, the duplication of worlds already existing. And what if we contrive to remove the Emperor and his palace and replace them with a replica under our own control?'

Magron struggled to comprehend. He had always understood that the warp and the physical world were opposites in every way – Materium and Immaterium. The daemon seemed to be boasting of a way to bring about the very overthrow of the physical world that Abaddas had described!

'But,' the daemon snarled, 'we must be patient. Patience is the mother of strategy. And how have we succeeded so far? By our pact! Between myself and my Bloodthirster brother!'

The other daemon glowered, as if he did not like being called a brother by the eagle-like Chaos being. The hand holding his great battleaxe twitched.

A kaleidoscopic flurry whirled around the head of the Tzeentch daemon. Had any been able to read that kaleidoscope – and none could – he would have seen that a large part of the Lord of Change's plan was to forge a long-term alliance between Tzeentch and Khorne. Between them they could crush the other two Chaos powers, as well as turn on the human Imperium once he had made virtual matter stable. When all that had been accomplished, of course, there would be no further need for Khorne…

Magron was getting an inkling that the pact of which the daemon spoke was crucial. Not everyone seemed to like it. The devotees of Khorne, in particular, were becoming restive, contemptuous of what they saw as a call for inactivity.

The Tzeentch daemon turned to his partner and let out a clarion call. 'Does our pact continue, brother?'

The Bloodthirster's reply was a snarling growl, uttered as if with surly resentment. 'Yes!'

A silence fell. All were looking up at the two daemons. Magron saw that this was a defining moment. If it passed without incident, the alliance would be forged. But the balance was fine.

Without even thinking he tuned his external speaker to maximum and roared out at the top of his voice: '*BLOOD FOR THE BLOOD GOD!*'

His voice echoed away in the aching silence. And then it was as if he had switched on an engine – an engine of war. He heard armour powering up. Weapons were raised again. He heard his cry taken up in an ever-expanding circle.

'*BLOOD FOR THE BLOOD GOD!*'
'*BLOOD FOR THE BLOOD GOD!*'
'*BLOOD FOR THE BLOOD GOD!*'
'*BLOOD FOR THE BLOOD GOD!*'

Weapons clashed, barked and spewed as the madmen of Khorne, unable to suppress their blood lust any longer, turned on their traditional enemies. The Bloodthirster shook himself and aimed a blow at his ally.

'To the Emperor and all his vassals with your clever schemes! Khorne does not wait for blood!'

The daemons commenced to fight, crushing hundreds beneath their tread as they stepped to and fro. The place of meeting had become an arena of battle.

For all the warfare he had seen, Magron had not encountered such rabid bloodletting as this. The turf almost immediately turned into a crimson quagmire. Three champions of Tzeentch rushed at him, eager to have the honour of killing a Space Marine of Khorne. He fended them off with his chainsword, stepping back meanwhile–

And was once again on cindery ground beneath a black sun. The clamour of battle had vanished as if with the snapping of a switch. A delightful contralto voice trilled at him. He turned to see the daemonette still waiting there.

'For hated Khorne to gain the alliance of the powers of Tzeentch would be bad for us of Slaanesh,' she told him. 'The Keeper of Secrets has advised me well. Your intervention has begun another war between them instead, one which will engulf the whole Chaos realm, if I am any judge.'

She approached slowly, reaching out with a long graceful pincer. 'Slaanesh rewards those who have served him…'

Magron stepped quickly away. 'No!'

'Then let your reward be to go on your way unmolested, Space Marine.'

Without another word, she regained her steed, mounted, and was off into the distance with its long-legged lolloping gait.

Magron was eager to reach the spaceship before it could take off without him. He hurried to the spot and found Rugolo and Calliden in the act of heaping coke-like dirt over the bodies of Aegelica and Gundrum, having scraped out shallow graves with fragments of rock.

They retreated nervously in fear of him but Magron would brook no argument.

'Come. We must return to the Imperium.'

'I can't navigate out of here,' Calliden protested. 'This is the Eye of Terror, a Chaos realm.'

'You came in, you can get out,' Magron told him bluntly. 'Have faith in the Emperor.'

Towering over them, he herded them into the ship.

EIGHTEEN
ABOARD THE BEASTSHIP

Sergeant Magron strongly disliked the bizarrely painted spaceship, both for its exterior and for its interior design and furnishing. It did not surprise him to be told that it was Chaos-altered. Such unnatural cleanness of line was an affront.

He had again removed his helmet but elected to remain suited. He stood at the rear of the cabin, looming over the frightened pair, the trader and the navigator. He was a Space Marine. They did not have the option of disobeying him or arguing with him. But there were things they had to explain. One was that, for the time being, there was no dropping into the warp, and no need to get out of range of the black sun.

Magron was soon able to see the phenomenon for himself as Calliden guided the ship through the Rose Cluster, the mysterious force which had drawn them into it no longer showing itself.

'This is a perilous region,' he said to Rugolo. 'Find spacesuits for you and the navigator, in case of attack.'

Rugolo did so, taking the opportunity for a brief exploration of his newly acquired vessel, and particularly of the contents of the hold.

He returned to find Calliden excited. They had cleared the Rose Cluster by several times its diameter. And he had found space trails, the equivalent of warp trails. Many of them, all leading in the same direction.

Magron recalled the daemon's talk of a big space battle. Had the Imperium really attempted to invade the Eye?

'Follow them,' he ordered. 'They may lead us to normal space.'

Calliden obeyed. The Eye, with its abnormal space-colouring, its formations of stars and gas-sheets, flowed past. He felt discomfited by the lack of a cocoon or of any of the usual iconography of a starship. The painted craft was almost a blasphemy, a denial of holiness.

A pleasant musical chime sounded from somewhere on the display, unlike any standard warning signal and confusing those present. Eventually Calliden discovered it was meant to draw his attention to the contact tabulator. A ship was approaching at great speed.

'Suit up,' Magron ordered when given the news. While they struggled into them, he stepped forward to watch the viewscreen. The ship came in sight, on the magnifier at first, but soon it hove to, broadside of them, looming over the little rainbow ship, and its gargantuan nature became evident.

It was a warship, a battleship of some sort, but it had been built in no yard of the Imperium. Its turrets followed some wild and insane plan, jutting out at crazy angles. Its prow was a huge mass made for ramming, though hammer-headed instead of wedge-shaped as if it was actually intended that the ship should destroy itself along with the enemy, although in fact it would have brushed aside the painted spaceship like a fly. It was, without doubt, a Chaos vessel.

Rugolo and Calliden stared frozen and Magron breathed a prayer as a weapons sponson rotated towards them.

But it failed to fire. Instead, an incredible spectacle played out. The immense warship began to disintegrate. Ragged holes appeared in it. Intricate turrets sagged, chunks and fragments floated away. The vessel appeared to be dissolving. In less than a minute it was like a carcass that had been torn apart by scavengers. Horrible to behold, thousands of its crew were deposited kicking and unprotected into the void, suffocating in droves.

Then something burst from a great holding bay in the warship's belly, a vessel itself as large or larger than the painted spaceship. It appeared as though made of shining brass, but looked more like a beast than a ship, a body of living metal that could flex and turn. A head section was inset with domed insect eyes of a purple colour – probably observation windows, Calliden thought. Stumpy legs splayed out from the main body or hull. It dove at the painted spaceship.

'Evasive action! Helmets on!' Magron barked.

It was too late. The brass beastship's attack was savage and swift, but it was not by the use of any weapon. Briefly its external skin swept across the view-screen, seemingly composed of metal that seemingly had been allowed to run and then set without benefit of a mould. Then there was a deafening crunching. The drive engine screamed, then stopped. All lights went out. The cabin began to collapse.

Calliden got the impression that the Chaos ship was devouring their vessel as though it were prey. There was a huge, confused convulsion. A chomping and crunching.

Then all was still. There was light again. He found himself lying on a warm, uneven surface. Rugolo and the Space Marine lay nearby. They were in a long cavernous space with dull yellow walls that were rough and lumpy. Fragments of the painted ship's interior were scattered and strewn throughout the length of the cavern – the smashed cabin, crumpled bits of the cargo hold, its bins and crates piled in a heap. There was no sign of a crew. It seemed the beastship had acted all by itself.

Calliden scrambled forward. He found himself looking through the purple dome-windows from the inside. He saw the wreckage of the rest of the painted spaceship: the crushed hull, the torn fins, the smashed engines.

Like some hungry predator, the beastship had devoured the tastiest innards of its victim, namely the accommodation and the hold, though how it had done so with no visible mouth Calliden had no idea. He glanced down. There was a recognisable if minimal control board. A quirky thought struck him. Had the beastship been in search of a crew? He heard a whining sound from the rear. It was a drive engine idling.

Rugolo was giggling inanely to see that the painted ship's cargo had accompanied them.

Magron strode over. 'Can you explain what has happened, navigator?' he asked of Calliden.

Calliden shook his head. 'Nothing makes much sense where we are.'

'Is this a ship? Can you pilot it?'

'I think so.'

Magron nodded. He had travelled in a beastship before. 'Then resume our course.'

There was no seat. Calliden would have to pilot standing. He took the controls.

The engine roared. The beastship shot forward.

THE FIGHTING ABOARD the *Rectitude* was over. The lacerated and shattered bodies of countless brute-men were being expelled into space, thrown through the rents and gaps in the hull of the battleship.

Inexplicably, the Chaos battleship which had rammed the *Rectitude* had melted away. The phenomenon would have to be the subject of analysis later. For now, the prime objective was escaping from the Eye of Terror.

Lord Militant Commander Drang, flushed with the excitement of the hand-to-hand struggle, had returned to the bridge to discover that the fighting had reached there too. His admirals and nearly all the bridge crew had died defending the navigators, without whom there was no returning home. One out of the three had survived. No one seemed to have bothered about the psykers. One had a smashed skull; the others were alive, but only as drooling idiots.

The Chaos ship had rammed a huge hole in the *Rectitude*. Commander Drang began receiving reports. The engineers calculated that a sufficient number of the main stems which transmitted force through the ship's structure were undamaged for it to stay in one piece during flight, provided weakened sections were cut away first. The warp screens were repairable. Power had already been restored.

The main concern was the drives. Work went on for three days. At last Drang was told what he wanted to hear. Two of the four realspace drives, and one of the five warp drives, were now working.

All of the navigators Drang had brought with him were special. They knew how to find the Cadian Gate.

The *Rectitude*, crippled but undefeated, got under way.

CALLIDEN FOUND THAT the beastship could achieve the same speed in the warp-realspace weld that the *Wandering Star* had.

But without the massed trail of the Imperium battlefleet, he would probably never have found his way to the Cadian Gate. Neither would he have dared go through it if it had not been for the Space Marine's insistence. He had fully expected to be set upon by Chaos ships. Whether it was because they themselves were travelling in a Chaos ship, or because the battlefleet – if Magron was right and there *was* a battlefleet – had already cleared the way he did not know.

One other thing bothered him. Did the beastship have a warp drive? There was a lever on the panel that might well engage one, but Calliden could not read the few runes and sigils that were on the board. They were unfamiliar, hard to look at. Chaos runes.

The beastship sped obediently through the blue-tinted space. It no longer showed any will of its own. Time passed. Rugolo slept, but Calliden and Magron did not.

Then the ship began to judder. Rugolo awoke, alarmed that it might be coming to life. But such was not the case. There was no speed tabulator to tell Calliden their velocity, but he felt instinctively that they were slowing, decelerating towards the creeping speed that light normally had.

Neither was there a viewscreen, only direct vision through the eye-light blisters. He peered through one of them. It was difficult to tell because of their purple tint, but he thought that the slight blue of space was fading back towards black.

Another judder, a violent one this time. They must be leaving the region of the weld.

It was time to jump into the warp. He took hold of the lever and pulled. Nothing happened. At least, nothing he expected. The lever appeared to work nothing. If there was a warp drive, it was inoperative.

A chill of fear struck through him. Stuck in interstellar space without a warp drive! But there was worse. A hoarse cry came from Rugolo.

He had put his hand against the wall of the beastship to steady himself. A strip of it had come away in his hand.

'It's no stronger than paper!'

In almost the same instant, the drive levers Calliden had been holding broke off, leaving him staring at them stupidly. He looked around at his companions. The ship was dissolving, breaking up.

'Helmets on!' It was Magron, shouting the order before slamming on his own armoured helm.

The process of dissolution was unbelievably rapid. No sooner had they snapped their helmets to the retaining rings in the suits they already wore than ragged holes appeared in the walls of the vessel. Air whooshed out. The matter of which the ship was made was curling and disappearing like paper in a fire.

In not more than half a minute there was no ship at all. Its three occupants, together with a few fragments from Gundrum's ship and most of his trade goods, floated in space.

The little group stayed together. There was nothing to make them drift apart in the short term. No one spoke. Rugolo and Calliden were too much in shock to do so. They stared at the huge swirl which the Eye of Terror warp-storm presented from here, the source of all their misfortunes.

As for Magron, he reflected that he had been in this situation before. Would he be drawn again into the Chaos realm? But he did not go into sus-an. Not yet.

However, this was not the end. An hour passed. Then a moving shadow cut off a patch of starlight.

For the second time, a giant warship came into view.

NINETEEN
ENDS & STRATAGEMS

THE SMALL CHAOS SHIP had been spotted as the *Rectitude* limped through the Cadian Gate. The battleship had immediately changed course, intending to vaporise it before it could reach the Imperium, only to see it spontaneously wither away as had the Chaos Juggernaut.

A party of loaders was despatched to haul in the detritus remaining with boarding gaffs. Two of the survivors were dragged through the clanging confusion of the largely wrecked space leviathan, still littered with signs of recent carnage, for interrogation by Naval Intelligence. They seemed unable to explain themselves at first, even when put on the porta-rack. Only when administered calming and mind-opening inhalants were they able to tell their remarkable story.

For the Space Marine it was a different matter. All stood back in awe of him. Lord Militant Commander Drang rushed to view him on hearing that he had been brought aboard. When he claimed to be a Marine of the First Founding from ten thousand years ago – a claim supported by the armour he wore – their awe increased a hundred-fold.

But that armour also bore the marks of Chaos. Naval Intelligence did not presume to carry out an interrogation, and there were none of the Inquisition on board. Sergeant Magron was stripped of his weapons and his armour, and locked in a specially constructed brig from which not even he could break out. Upon their return, he would be handed over to the Dark Angels Chapter of the Adeptus Astartes.

FED AND RESTED, Rugolo and Calliden were once again ushered into the presence of an officer belonging to Naval Intelligence. He was not either of the pair of officers who had interrogated them earlier. He obviously had needed to recover too. His arm was in a sling and a cloth poultice covered a gash on his head. His bearing was stiff, showing that he had other injuries. But he was immaculately turned out in tunic, britches and jackboots.

They had heard that the battleship would soon arrive at the base of Battlefleet Obscurus. The officer made them wait in silence while he read slowly through the interrogation report – not, they were sure, for the first time. Then he ventured an opinion.

'You both appear to be in something of a difficulty.'

Rugolo nodded, clenching his fist. 'I've lost my ship,' he said, putting a sob into his voice. 'I've lost everything I had! Of course, if you could return my merchandise–'

'Obtained within the Eye of Terror,' the officer interrupted in a clipped tone. 'You are aware of the penalties for such traffic?'

Rugolo had been hoping that the Navy, being a purely military organisation, would be uninterested in legalities. 'Well, er, no, not exactly…'

'And you, Navigator Calliden, you succeeded in finding a way into the Eye, and even managed to come back out again. An impressive feat.'

Calliden said nothing. The Intelligence officer leaned back in his chair, regarding them both with an unreadable expression. 'The Navy may be willing to give you a new ship,' he said to Rugolo, 'provided Navigator Calliden remains your partner.'

'*Really?*'

'Let me put it this way. You two have been through experiences which would have driven most men insane. Yet apart from a recoverable measure of psychic trauma, you are relatively unaffected. Perhaps because…'

He did not finish what he had started to say. In his view, the pair had survived simply because they were not intelligent enough to appreciate the full horror of what they had encountered.

'Naval Intelligence has a use for such as you, able to make your way within the Eye. In short, we need agents. We are going to send you back in.'

'No!' they both protested together. 'No! No!'

'The choice is yours, of course,' the officer said politely. 'But the question is more than one of trading in illicit goods. Anyone known to have had contact with... those of the Dark Powers is handed over to the Inquisition and put to death. It may not come to that. For refusing the wishes of the Emperor, as formulated by his loyal officers, one is put to death in a more unpleasant way.'

Rugolo groaned. And Calliden stared into space.

LORD MILITANT COMMANDER Drang was curious. A first officer had informed him that not only three individuals but a stock of Chaos artefacts had been recovered from the dissolving spacecraft.

He resolved to examine these artefacts for himself. The first officer led him to where the booty was stored, in a chamber that had only just been made airtight. Their boots clanged on the decks as they walked. All around them the structurally weakened ship creaked and groaned ominously as its unsteady engines pushed it through the warp.

On the way he peered briefly through his monocle. Strange. His impending second meeting with the Callidus assassin, which had beckoned him for so long, was no longer there. Instead there was something else, something glowing and inexplicable.

Could it really be that the assassination edict was to be rescinded, in view of his gallantry?

'Wait here,' he told the first officer outside the door to the chamber.

Drang went in. The chamber was dank and dimly lit. There were a number of open-topped bins and a line of crates. He went to one of the bins. It was filled with small, bulbous bottles of ribbed glass, containing liquids of various colours. He raised one, inspecting it. His monocle flared briefly, responding to the bottle, showing something swirling within in – a beverage of some kind. He put it back carefully.

He found a jemmy and levered open the first crate. It contained a jumble of objects. A tetrahedron which changed shape as he picked it up, and flew out of his hand to rattle on the floor on the other side of the chamber. A sparkling carousel which began to revolve as he lifted it, carrying unrecognisable figures and mounts which changed and mutated all the time; it filled him with distaste and he let the trinket drop.

Here was something which looked slightly familiar: a filigreed cylinder, a little like a telescope. He lifted it to his natural eye. A scene opened up before him. A vast nave, vaster than any he had ever seen, so vast it contained two immense Titans, full of bustle, and at the far end–

He snatched the instrument away, shock on his face.

No! It could not be!

For a moment he didn't realise that the 'telescope' had lifted itself out of his hand. Only then did it strike him how much it resembled a larger version of his monocle. And when the two merged he tried to pull both away, to wrench the monocle out of his eye socket if need be, but his hands seemed to encounter only a yielding liquid.

What he could see through the joint instruments now struck such terror into him as he had never felt before.

A caressing voice sounded in the depths of his being. *This is what it has all been leading to, commander. This was the real meaning of your lust for glory. Did your mother not tell you never to buy anything alien?*

How Lord Militant Commander Drang wished now that he could meet death at the hands of the kindly Callidus assassin. Alive and fully conscious, he was drawn kicking and screaming into the warp.

LORD MILITANT COMMANDER Invisticone was thinking of Drang as he lounged in his quarters in Base Pacificus. He was thinking that he never did get to have the pleasure of that final duel. Still, he was sure that Drang met his end as he would have wished, with a power sabre in his hand.

Battlefleet Pacificus had returned to dock several days before. He had submitted his report to the High Lords. Now he awaited their final message.

He reached out to refill his wine glass from a bottle he had been keeping for ten years. As he did so he noticed a flicker of movement from the other side of the room. A young man stood there, though he was not naked this time.

'So it is you,' Invisticone murmured. And he smiled.

THE CHI'KHAMI'TZANN TSUNOI, the Feathered Lord, ragged and tattered from his bloody fight with the Bloodthirster, sagged and lashed out in rage while his fellow Lords of Change whirled around him, mocking and jeering.

'The Great Inventor!'

'The Weaver of Stratagems that Fall Apart!'

'With a single Space Marine the Emperor has foiled all your plans!'

'Maker of matter!'

One stood before him. 'Did you think you were the first to make false matter? It cannot be made stable! The cosmic balance is not upset so easily!'

The Great Inventor, the Weaver of Stratagems that Fall Apart, was a young greater daemon of Tzeentch. He had committed the sin of over-confidence.

And for that he was to be punished.

'You have displeased the Great Conspirator! He has given us power over you. *He has revealed your secret name!*'

And as they mocked, as they intoned the unpronounceable syllables that robbed him of potency, the Feathered Lord wilted and fled into a wildernesses peopled only by gibbering, mindless daemons which bubbled in and out of existence moment by moment.

THERE WAS ONLY one end for a Dark Angel who had submitted to Chaos, that is to say, a Fallen Angel, once he fell into the hands of his chapter. Taken to the great fortress-monastery on the Rock, the only remaining fragment of the Dark Angels' home world of Caliban, Abdaziel Magron spent many months in a cold dungeon, interrogated by the great Chapter's chaplains and librarians. The interrogation was exhaustive. It used any available means where it was suspected that Magron might be holding back information or harbouring secret thoughts.

Magron made a complete confession and repented his loss of faith in the Emperor. The harsher methods used on him dragged no complaint from his lips. He said nothing in mitigation of his sin. But finally he was allowed extreme unction, offered the last blessings and given a quick death.

There are secrets known not even to the Inner Circle of the Fallen Angels, and one final secret is known only to the God-Emperor himself. Deep, deep within the Rock, at the centre of what was once the planet Caliban, lies a sealed, unreachable chamber. Here lies sleeping the Chapter Primarch, Lion El'Jonson, carried away by the Watchers in the Dark on that terrible day when the Dark Angels Chapter tore itself apart.

Only the God-Emperor, and possibly the unconscious mind of the Primarch through which the God-Emperor had acted, knew what had nudged and guided the frozen body of Sergeant Magron on his long journey into the Eye of Terror, a secret weapon aimed at the heart of Chaos.

Only them – and perhaps one other.

IN A LOFTY, secluded palace far off in the warp, a truly ancient Chi'khami'tzann Tsunoi nodded and blinked in admiration for the Emperor of mankind.

The Chi'khami'tzann Tsunoi was one of the first ever to be created by the great Lord of Change, and was reckoned by some to be almost as wise and cunning as Tzeentch himself. He it was who had manipulated the young, inexperienced Great Inventor – and then discarded him. He acknowledged that the Emperor was a god in his own right, worthy to be an ally of Tzeentch himself, so great was his foresight, so subtle his ability to pinpoint cusps which, with the slightest of nudges, could deflect events on to another course. He had even utilised the forces of Chaos, to manoeuvre his actors into position.

But the game was still afoot, and would be for millennia. The Emperor had manipulated Chaos but the greater daemon, in turn, had manipulated the Emperor. There were manipulations within manipulations, and only he who failed to see them all would lose.

The Emperor was a great lord, but he was shackled to the husk of his material form, kept alive by mortals who feared to lose their protector. Eventually their efforts would fail. The husk would die, and the Emperor would be released unfettered into the heavenly realms.

Then the true war would begin. The Emperor would exert himself to cancel out the four Chaos powers and integrate them into a sane and harmonious whole, thereby harmonising the psyche of mankind. But the heavenly masters did not want to be so absorbed. What was sanity compared with the glorious insanity of the separate Chaos Gods, forever at war with one another?

The ancient daemon was patient, as strategists must be. His ultimate aim was the death of the Emperor. To that end, he had set in train impulses which no one but he and blessed Tzeentch himself could see.

In his lofty, secluded palace, the Chi'khami'tzann Tsunoi watched, and waited.